CASSIDY

IN THE COMPANY OF SNIPERS
Book 10

IRISH WINTERS

COPYRIGHT

CASSIDY; In the Company of Snipers, 10

Cover design and author photo by Kelli Ann Morgan,
http://www.inspirecreativeservices.com

Interior book design by Bob Houston eBook Formatting

Editor: Lauren McKellar, McStellar editing,
http://mcstellarediting.blogspot.com

Editor: Katie Johnson, katiestefan333@gmail.com

ISBN Paperback: 978-1-942895-20-6
ISBN eBook: 978-1-942895-19-0
Library of Congress Control Number: 2016930784

Irish Winter's author websites are: http://www.irishwinters.com
and irishwinters.blogspot.com

In the Company of Snipers

You can find Irish Winters on Facebook:
https://www.facebook.com/author.irishwinters

On Twitter: https://twitter.com/irishwinters1

For news on upcoming releases, sign up for Irish Winters' Newsletter at IrishWinters.com.

For more information about all my books, visit IrishWinters.com.

IN THE COMPANY OF SNIPERS

This series revolves around ex-Marine scout sniper, Alex Stewart, and his covert surveillance company, The TEAM, home-based out of Alexandria, Virginia. An obsessive patriot and workaholic, he created the company to give ex-military snipers like him a chance at returning to civilian life with a decent job.

This is not a serial with each book ending at a cliffhanger. I wouldn't do that to you. *In the Company of Snipers* is a collection of passionate love stories involving women and men who are tough enough to take on the world alone. Each is a stand-alone read, where in the course of an active TEAM operation, one agent comes face to face with his or her demons. The men and women I write about are all patriots and warriors, dealing with what they've lived through or the mistakes they've made

Spoiler alert: Every novel contains adult scenes including sexual situations (some explicit), language, and violence. I don't write sweet romance, so be forewarned.

At the end of each story, it's my hope that you, along with my heroes, will come to realize...

Love changes everything.

Chapter One

She woke. Face down. Palms to the floor. Too weak to lift her head.

With one eye swollen shut and blood in her nose, Junior Agent Cassidy Dancer's blurry view was limited to a murky stretch of damp wooden planks. The vibrations beneath her aching body soothed as much as they worried her. Her last coherent memory consisted of—stars.

Where am I?

The floor moved; that was why the vibrations. It creaked. It rattled. Despite her poor bloody nose, it smelled. Really. Really. Bad.

I'm in the back of a... truck?

A glimmer of light reflected off the floor beneath her face, blinding her one good eye. Her brain struggled to explain, at last providing the disgusting answer. Her nose twitched to confirm.

Damn. I'm in a horse trailer behind a truck. In a puddle and it's not water. Ewww.

The well-muscled biceps that could pump quick sets of push-ups on a good day failed her. She willed her body to roll out of the mess. Not going to happen. The command center in her brain no longer controlled her limbs. Even her eyes felt crossed and unfocused—not the sharp vision of a highly-trained covert agent at all.

Never one to cry or whine, she cursed her agent-in-charge instead. "Damn you, Rourke."

Her scratchy voice sounded too weak for the tough woman she was. Her priorities changed. The filthy mess beneath her head galled her last nerve. Its sickening odor, mingled with the coppery smell of her own blood, roiled her stomach. The thought and feel of cow shit in her hair, on her cheek, and seeping up into her ear, and... *argh! Too much!*

She squeezed her eyes tight and promised, *I will not throw up. I will not—*

Wrong. She threw up. Not her finest moment. Summoning every shred of willpower, she borrowed Rourke's drill sergeant method of motivation. *Damn you, Dancer. Get your ass up and move. Don't just take it, you wuss. DO something about it.*

She couldn't—just plain, damned couldn't. Every muscle in her finely toned body had turned to lead. Still, she couldn't lie there in all that filth, either.

Where there was a will, there was a way, right?

And Cassidy Dancer was very willful, right?

And everyone on The TEAM knew that, right?

For some deep, dark reason she didn't understand, cussing helped during desperate times. "Son-of-a-bitch," she ground out, her teeth clenched, her very hardheaded spirit on task. At last, she—flopped over.

Damn. Never had doing so little reaped so much agony. Pain raced down her spine all the way to her toes. A whimper escaped. Tears filled her eyes and dripped down the sides of that hard head, but she was out of the puddle. Hers and Mister Ed's. Yeah. Damned good.

The truck changed directions. First, to the left, then, to the right. Not her. She had the mobility of concrete and intended to keep it that way.

Calming her wretched nausea took precedence until the trailer jerked to an abrupt stop. Its rear gate clanked, screeched, and fell to the ground, filling her box of a world with blinding sunlight. Someone climbed aboard. Heavy footsteps shuffled, stopping within inches of her nose. She kept her wits and feigned the smarts of a corpse.

"She alive?" a man asked.

Another male voice from the rear of the trailer grunted in reply.

Two guys. Easy. I can take 'em.

"Git her outta there," the shuffler ordered. Hands gripped her ankles, dragging her across the floor. Her resolved faltered at being so easily manhandled. *Damn. Maybe, I can't take 'em. Yet.*

"Git her in the barn 'fore Jerusha and the kids see her," Shuffler muttered.

One pair of hard hands under her armpits and another pair at her ankles made the transfer. They didn't lift her high enough, though. They dragged her, as if she were heavy or something. Either they were vertically challenged, or just plain rude. Her butt bumped along on the ground.

Like it or not, out of the light and into the dark she went. The barn door banged shut. She expected to be dropped, but Shuffler and Grunter took her farther into the building, away from the door. When they finally lowered her, they took extra care that her boots were next to each other, her arms at her side. Odd.

"Make 'em tight. He likes the belts extra snug," Shuffler ordered.

Her panic kicked into overdrive. *Belts?*

Cracking her one good eyelid, she spared a quick glance at her captors. Shuffler was the taller and thinner of the two. Receding hairline. Wispy goatee. Grunter owned no neck, just a sagging double chin. Both wore jeans and the standard gray shirt of the cult.

They crouched over her, fastening a series of belts around her ankles, thighs, hips, plain leather belts like the kind Dr. Frankenstein used when he created his monster. The kind with buckles. The kind a victim couldn't wiggle out of. Another scenario emerged in the recesses of this very dark place where no one could hear her.

Torture.

Thunder erupted in her chest.

"That oughta do it." Shuffler lifted to his feet. "She won't be going anywhere."

Grunter didn't reply.

The sound of their footsteps receding brought a small measure of relief. Cassidy blinked both eyes open, despite resistance from the swollen one. She needed all of her faculties, every last one of them, to get out of this latest predicament she had gotten herself into.

Lines of cheery sunshine streaked between the wooden planks of the barn walls. Dust hung in the air as if time stood still, but she knew better. Grunter and Shuffler would be back.

Get up. Move!

Her mental commands had no effect. She could wiggle her fingers, just not enough to reach the buckles and get the hell out of there. Butch Cassidy Dancer had done it this time. She was in deep with no one to blame but herself.

Resigned that she wasn't going anywhere very fast, she forced a deep breath to quiet her rattled nerves. The fragrance of freshly baled alfalfa settled over her as she revisited the morning's miscalculation. She'd thought she was so smart, even smarter than Senior Agent Rourke O'Neill. He'd told her to stay put, but had she? No, she'd seen an opportunity and she'd taken it. Her hard-charging mindset usually paid off in dividends. Covert surveillance rewarded risk-takers and fast-thinkers.

Not this time.

She'd not seen what smacked the back of her head, damn it, but whatever it was, it brought enlightenment she'd literally not seen coming, either. But really? How could she have known two Melissas belonged to this deranged cult? How bizarre that both were recently widowed *and* independently wealthy? How freaking coincidental was that?

Rourke's warning joined the noise in her pounding brain. *One of these days, your bullheaded ways are going to get you in trouble, Butch.* The smart ass. How many times had she heard that before? Like a gazillion, maybe? Butch Cassidy, his nickname for the outlaw he claimed she was, the rebel who thought she knew everything. He wasn't too far off base. Most times, she did.

Cassidy tried to recall her smart remark back at him, no doubt her usual, *'Yeah, yeah, yeah. Whatever.'* But damn. There she was, bloodied, strapped to a board, and lucky she could breath. Rourke might've been right. Today might be the day she'd gotten herself into more trouble than she could handle.

But then again...

Squeezing her eyes tightly shut, she sent a mental command to the only one in the world who could rescue her sorry butt. *Get me the hell outta here, Rourke!*

"If you're happy and you know it, clap your hands!" Jerusha clapped a happy pantomime to the five-year-olds at her feet.

Jude Cannon kept his eye on the stern woman dressed in a long gray dress and singing. The song sounded cheerful, but she didn't fool him. Jerusha Gordon might look like a saint to those adoring other parents' children in her care, but he knew better. Those children were only there because their parents had no choice in deciding who taught their kids. They were in the fields, forced to menial labor while their offspring were supposedly in gospel class. Yeah, right. The gospel Jerusha taught was as sick and twisted as she was. Everything brought forth from Lucien Cain, the self-proclaimed prophet of the Palma Christi Cult, was.

Jude had been sent back to the compound for a sharpening stone for his scythe when he'd caught sight of Hank Crews and Greg Gleason dragging the unconscious woman out of the horse trailer and into the barn. Whoever she was, she had no business being inside the cult compound, not the way she was dressed. Her tan and khaki camouflage pants looked more military than sisterly. Definitely, not cult issue. If she'd planned to blend in with that get-up, she'd blown it. Big time. She wouldn't last long, not once the prophet got hold of her.

Not my problem.

Jude forced his eyes away from the barn, more important things on his mind than some nosey woman who didn't know when to mind her business. Like Judith, his missing fourteen-year-old daughter, the real reason he was in this lousy excuse for a church. Named after him, she'd been unreachable for months, her whereabouts as much a mystery as her mother, Rachel's.

After prying into his ex-wife's life and questioning her neighbors, Jude finally got his only solid lead—the notorious Palma Christi Cult, known for its strict so-called religious values, if that was what you wanted to call depriving adults of their right to freedom of speech, their finances, and most importantly, their children.

Rachel's neighbor remembered two nice men pestering Rachel time and time again until she'd finally invited them in. But then she couldn't get rid of them. They kept coming back. They called themselves disciples of the Lord's prophet, and supposedly brought peace and understanding in the form of an alternate religion. A better lifestyle.

When they finally put the question of commitment to her, she'd sought her elderly neighbor's advice. For the first time in her life, Rachel had declared she felt spiritually awakened. She wanted to repent. Not only wanted to, but needed to. Her salvation depended on it. Judith's too.

But then she disappeared. Judith too.

Jude hadn't slept a decent night since. He'd already wasted enough time at the south compound of this demented cult. Neither Rachel nor Judith were there. Since the bean fields were close to harvest, Jude volunteered to come north.

He'd kept his eyes and ears open but had yet to locate his family.

The barn called to him, reminding him that the stranger had nothing but trouble in store for her, some of it painful. Still, *it's not my business.*

Yes, it is, his prickly conscience whispered.

"No, damn it," he growled under his breath. "I'm only here because of Judith. That woman's in here because she meant to be here. It's her fault. Her problem. Not mine."

Cowardice rankled thick at the back of his throat. He'd been in that woman's position not long ago. No one had helped him. Why should he risk his daughter's life to help a total stranger? *Besides, look at that gal's commando-style clothing. She's probably FBI or CIA. Someone's probably coming for her. She'll be out of here in no time.*

Jerusha's clap startled him. He dropped his gaze in case she'd seen him watching the barn.

But she's in trouble now, his internal Jiminy Cricket scolded.

For God's sake, I can't save everyone. But still...

He glanced back at the barn. She sure looked like she was alone. If her buddies were coming, they'd better step on it and get her out of there before Cain showed. The barn meant discipline, and not the good-stiff-talking-to kind.

She's helpless. Like I was. Damn it!

Exasperated, he brushed a hand through his hair. The one thing Jude knew for certain was that he was no hero. If anything, he was the exact opposite, and yet... the prophet hadn't returned. There was still time to act. He could be in and out of that barn before the prophet's butt-kissing henchmen returned.

There might be a way.

"There were three on the bed, and the little one said..." Jerusha prompted, her back to Jude while she and her class strolled toward the corncrib and silo at the opposite end of the barn.

A plan solidified. *I might be able help her. If I'm lucky. Maybe.*

"Roll over. Roll over," Seven children squealed with delight, trailing after their teacher.

Jude hesitated. The question in his mind had more to do with bravery than luck. His bravery. He was a man of numbers, prone to precise planning after careful deliberation. An accountant. A bean counter. Nothing more. His days had once revolved around cost of goods sold schedules and subsidiary ledgers. Reconciling debits and credits. Forecasting trends. Profits. Losses. Nothing remotely related to the high-value commodities of *risk* and *courage*.

Yet there he was. The only one around who could help that damned woman.

His heart raced at what he knew lay in store fore her.

The irony didn't escape him. With his real life safely stored behind him in Florida, he'd set out alone to find his missing wife and daughter. He'd traded in his clean-cut persona for that of a transient. Opted for anonymity. Changed his name from Cannon to Clark. He'd left his old self behind, and hidden behind a ragged shirt, threadbare denims, and mismatched hiking boots.

That was October. Seven months ago.

Only his wire-rimmed glasses reminded him whom he was, and even they were broken, taped at the bridge of his nose to hold the lenses in place. They gave him the nerdy look others mistook for weakness, and he was okay with that. He *was* weak. Didn't mind being perceived that way. He didn't want to be strong or cruel enough to be one of Cain's Elite, those few members of the prophet's inner circle, the ones everyone else was afraid of. Neither was he on anyone's radar. He intended to keep it that way.

The California spring sun was warm. Sweat stung his eyes. The barn loomed big and red—and damned scary.

Truth was, he'd already surprised himself plenty. It had taken nerve to track Rachel and Judith across the country to the compound, thirteen thousand acres locked behind an eight-foot high concrete fence in northern California. But he'd done it. Seeking permission to enter the cult's compound near Boggs Mountain turned out to be another scary thing, but a father's desperation turned Jude into someone else entirely. He used to be the quiet, meek face in the back of the crowd. He didn't know who the hell he was now.

Damn. That lady needs real help. My help. With a backward glance over his shoulder, he pushed his glasses up his nose and borrowed the line from a real hero. Todd Beamer's courage on 9-11 had always inspired him.

"Let's roll."

Summoning his nerve, Jude made certain Jerusha wasn't looking. Neither were the kids. Instead of marching right up to the barn like a real man, he turned away from it and slunk toward the long dormitory for married couples at the opposite end of the yard.

At the end of the dorm, he turned right, crossed over to the row of private homes and headed north. Jude crossed the yard between the single dwellings and ducked behind the granary where he turned east. It was the long way around, but it wouldn't raise suspicion.

At the granary, he picked up a couple of empty buckets to add credence to his subterfuge, his heart a banging drum in his chest. *Why the hell am I doing this?*

But he kept going. With the granary behind him, he headed along the far side of the garden, as if he'd been sent to collect the daily portion of carrots for the mass meal called supper. Only he didn't stop to load up, even though the women working in the garden looked expectantly at him. He didn't offer a single, "Good morning, sisters," like he should have. He just kept going, before he chickened out or someone caught him.

His very intelligent brain screamed, *You're no hero.*

Like he didn't know that?

But that Jiminy Cricket conscience of his kept squeaking, *But you can do something.*

God, I hope Hank and Greg take their time coming back.

Jude second-guessed himself every step of the way, wondering why he had to be the one. Hadn't that woman brought any help with her? Was she truly alone? Armed? Her uniform suggested some kind of organized help to take down the cult might finally be on its way. Was it? Should he just hang around, wait and see?

But Cain is coming now. Hurry!

I am hurrying! Hank and Greg hadn't left for no reason at all. They went for their master. Only then could the discipline begin. Jude rounded the stone silo on a dead run along the backside of the barn.

He used to like barns. Not anymore. Not this one. Dairy cattle were kept there once, but along came the cult's troublemakers and misfits, runaways, and rebels. The cattle were moved to the south compound. The barn had become a place where discipline was meted out. None of it pleasant.

In the mighty order of the prophet and world-class liar, Cain, there were four levels of chastisement: penance, punishment, branding, and censure. They all took place during secret meetings with the Elite, Cain's henchmen and henchwomen. Always in the dark of night.

First, *penance*, when a reluctant follower was assigned to work the fields. Fourteen-hour days of backbreaking work had a way of wearing stubborn members down, and tired people made compliant people.

Second, *punishment.* Work got harder. Days got longer. Cain didn't believe in common conveniences like electricity or tractors inside the cult. He encouraged hard, backbreaking work. Said the soul could only reach its highest glory when the body was broken.

Men were turned into beasts of burden, forced to pull either the carts that hauled crops in from the fields, or the plows that broke hard ground. A woman might be sentenced to the hot house where mighty kettles of water were heated for laundry, baths, and slaughter. There they also prepared animal skins for leather, or boiled slaughtered pigs and chickens for skinning.

Third, *branding.* Jude rubbed the scar on his palm. His throat closed remembering the gleam in Cain's eye when he'd declared Jude to be less than worthy. His sin? Showing up at the cult's gates in rags and begging to be allowed inside.

Hank and Greg let him inside the compound wall, all right. Dragged him in was more like it. They'd strapped him to the two-by-twelve, ten-foot-long plank in the barn. Made him prove his pure intent. Greg held his arm in the vice-like grip, but Hank did the actual branding. Both men seemed proud of themselves afterwards. Jude only recalled the smell of his burning flesh, throwing up not so much from the pain as the inhumanity of what those two bullies had done to him.

It was a hard price to pay at the hands of cruel men, but it served his purpose. The raised welt of a crescent moon burned on his palm declared he'd never be good enough for the prophet's inner-circle. It provided camouflage, and Jude was all about blending in. He was only there for Judith, and Rachel, if she'd let him be.

But there was another type of discipline, this one not meted out within the dusty walls of the barn. *Censure.* His wound had cracked and bled, but it had healed. People tolerated him. He still had a place to sleep and food to eat. Not the *Censured.*

Their humiliation was passed in full view of all members so all would know their crimes. So all would get that self-righteous opportunity to turn their backs on their brother or sister. Or their spouse. From the moment Cain declared a person a sinner, they were labeled invisible, like lepers of biblical times.

It was the duty of the *Censured* to maintain that separation between the so-called pure and the impure, to declare their unclean status so others steered clear. The Elite spat on them. Children were encouraged to throw stones. Jude never understood how a spouse could turn from their dearly beloved just because Cain told them to. Yet it happened.

Standing at the barn's side door, he summoned his last nerve, his mouth as dry as the warm Californian air.

Jude eased his muscular frame inside the barn, letting his eyes grow accustomed to the dim light. Just as he suspected, the woman was bound to the branding board. She'd been placed near the farthest wall from the door, her arms bound at the elbow, her forearms and hands free for whatever discipline Cain might decide.

Jude went purposefully to her side and placed a hand on her shoulder to announce his arrival. He startled her anyway.

She jumped, her petite frame jerking against the board. "Shit!"

"Sorry," he muttered, more sorry for her than he could tell. "I didn't mean to scare you. Let's get you out of here."

"Who the hell are you?"

Her demeanor surprised him. With her fists clenched and her jaw tight, she looked ready to fight and yet, her lower lip trembled. He smoothed the hair off her face to get a better look. She didn't look military. Didn't look tough enough to be there, either. Even with the damp manure clinging to her cheek, the soft brown eyes of a beautiful blonde blinked back at him.

"I'm Jude Clark, and I'm not here to hurt you. Who are you?" *Actually, Jude Cannon, but Clark will work for now. You don't need to know who I really am.*

She angled her head to peer up at him. "C-C-Cassidy. Cassidy Dancer."

Noticing the blood in her hair, he worked his fingers through the back of her head until he felt it. A large goose egg with a jagged cut rested beneath the dirty tangles in his hands. It had been years since he'd held a woman's head like this, and the smaller small size of Cassidy's skull reminded him how fragile her gender was. How lovely. She shouldn't have been struck, much less dragged in here like a side of beef to wait on the prophet. *What made some men so brutally cruel? So damned indecent?*

"Listen, I don't think you're hurt real bad," he whispered. "Can you walk?"

"Hell yes," she hissed. "Get me out of here."

He leaned over her waist to unbuckle her restraints. Damn. These belts weren't just buckled. They were locked. He should've brought that scythe with him.

The rumbling engine of the truck sounded outside the barn. Damn. He'd wasted his one opportunity to do some good.

"Listen to me, Cassidy Dancer. I don't know who you're working with, but things will go a lot easier if you fake it. Act like you've lost your memory or something. Faint. Can you do that?"

"You... you're leaving me?" she asked breathlessly. She was scared, and he was afraid for her. He already knew how bad it could get, but he couldn't stay.

He glanced worriedly at the door. In one second, all his hopes of finding Judith would be destroyed forever. "I've got to, but... but they won't hurt you if they think they can win you over."

"Win me... over?"

A tear glimmered in the corner of her eye, but he knew better. He was no hero. He was a coward who didn't know the first thing about fighting or rescuing people. Above all, he had to keep his cover. It meant everything. Hers was already blown, but he had to find Judith. Cassidy was just... was just...

Damn. He bowed his head, the clock ticking and his options gone. Cassidy was just a very frightened woman in the wrong place at the wrong time. She shouldn't have to endure what the prophet had in store for her. The anguish of his dilemma stabbed him.

I have to go! Now!

"Go," she said bravely, nodding toward the other door as if she'd heard his thoughts. "Take off. I understand. I'll be okay."

Jude felt the depth of sadness in her eyes, but he also saw something else. Cassidy might be afraid, but there was still fight left in her. Even tied to a board and in damned desperate straits, she was braver than he was. He made a vow right then and there. "Trust me," he whispered, his eyes on the door. "Play dead when they come in here. I'll come back for you. I'll find a way."

If she answered, he didn't hear it. Before the door opened to the prophet, Jude was hidden in the shadows once more, feeling more like the dog he was than the hero he wished he were. Very quietly, he closed the side barn door behind him. He'd gotten out just in time. He was safe.

The loud voice of the insidious self-proclaimed prophet Lucien Cain reverberated from inside the barn. "Well, well, well. Who do we have here?"

Chapter Two

"Damn it!" She might have been restrained, but Cassidy could still cuss. "Stop it! You're hurting me!"

The man she knew as Lucien Cain peered into her face. One of his goons braced the board she was strapped to on its end so she faced the prophet as if she were standing. Only, she wasn't. Her toes couldn't touch the floor, and the belts bit into her arms. Goon One had a handful of her hair, twisting her head to meet Cain's commanding stare.

She stifled the urge to spit in his face because she could also smell fire, and it wasn't the outdoorsy kind for roasting marshmallows. No. This fire smelled of iron and heat, of metal cooking, like a fry pan left too long on a stove burner. Or a cattle brand.

The prophet towered over her. She had no choice but to look up. He had to be more than six-foot-six. Maybe taller. He had thinning gray hair, oiled and combed back. Angular build. Thick lips. Gaunt cheeks. Kind of skeletal. His faded-blue eyes, the same color as the ocean on a sunless day, flat as if the light had been drained out of them, burrowed into hers.

Goon Two handed Cain a plastic zip-lock bag he'd taken from her pants pocket. She'd learned a few tricks from Rourke, and they were all in that bag: extra ammo, her handy-dandy Swiss army knife, lip balm, and Advil.

"She's not a Fed," Goon Two said calmly. "This stuff isn't government issue. None of it."

Cain scanned the bag full of evidence, then her. His expression changed the second he spied the gold logo on her black polo. The TEAM. An odd light flickered across his features. He reached for her.

She cringed, expecting a slap, but when his fingers brushed over her breast, she wanted to kick the crap out of him. He stared her down, his index finger traveling the centerline of her body, between her breasts to her belt. This creep was all about intimidation, and no one got away with that. Not with Cassidy Dancer. Every muscle strained to wreak havoc on this slimy man and his evil minions, but she couldn't budge.

Cain toyed with her belt buckle while he asked Goon Two, "What exactly is The TEAM?"

"A private company out of Virginia. They handle security for the Feds. Other stuff, too."

"Like?" Cain raised a brow, once again fingering the logo over her left breast, damn him. He rested the back of his fingers on her shirt, as if he had a right to touch her. She'd never been this helpless before. He had all the power.

Goon Two lifted a shoulder. "Like bodyguards and private investigating. I couldn't hack into their server. Had to Google them, so there's not much to tell. Looks like they're a big-time covert ops business, stateside and abroad. They work a lot of federal jobs, and partner with Special Forces. She's one of them."

"She's Special Forces?" Cain lifted a brow, sarcasm thick in his tone.

I wish! I'd show you!

"Must be. She's here, isn't she? You might want to go easy on her. We don't need anymore like her snooping around."

"Nothing is so big it can't be overcome, Greg," Cain purred. He removed his hand from Cassidy's shirt and handed the bag back to Goon Two, now known as Greg.

"She had this in her shoulder holster." Greg handed Cain her SIG.

She cringed to see it in this despicable man's hands. It was the nicest little gun she'd owned in a long time, and her fingers itched to use it now. Just three shots. That was all she needed. Maybe six if she took time for double taps. She'd show them who was powerless.

Finally, Goon One let loose of her hair. He still stood too close.

Cassidy leaned her head against the board. He was there to hurt her, to make her do what Cain wanted. Breaking into this looney bin was probably punishable by death and burial in an unmarked grave. Both of these men had reason enough to kill her on the spot.

She attempted to stare Cain down, but as dizzy as she still was, it took all she could muster to keep her head upright on her neck. Two of him danced in front of her, sometimes four. Maintaining a mean stare took effort.

Maybe that chicken-shit Jude was right. Maybe her best option was to play the part of a helpless woman. Not her forte, but she could do it. For now.

She closed her eyes and let her body go slack. With a stupid, ultra-feminine huff that in no way resembled the real Cassidy Dancer, she faked a faint and dropped her chin to her chest. She was, after all, a member of the inferior gender, according to Cain's self-proclaimed philosophy. Maybe these guys actually believed the poison they spewed.

"Shit." Goon One reclaimed his hold on her hair and tilted her head upward. "She's out."

The smell of his bad breath filled her face, but Cassidy stifled her response to cry out, curse like crazy, or hold her breath. They needed to believe she was out for the count. She remained as limp as a noodle. No problem.

"Hank, do you believe our little soldier girl really passed out?" Cain asked softly.

Cassidy felt a wimpy hand on her cheek and a thumb under her chin. It had to be Cain's. Her stomach lifted up the back of her throat. He was a suspected pedophile. A pervert. Some creep who assaulted innocent little girls and stupid women under the guise of prophetic revelations. And the bastard had his hands on her.

He lifted her head and blew a breath into her face. A distinct odor of cumin and chili filled her nose. He'd had tacos or burritos for lunch. Dis-gust-ing!

She refrained from reacting, though, as hard as it was. Didn't even breathe. When he blew another breath, she knew precisely why he did that. As much as the thought of his lips on hers repulsed her, Cassidy remained still. He had to believe.

"Discipline will answer all of your questions," Goon One, Hank, grumbled. "You want me to get started on her? I can have her talking like a magpie if you wait."

For too long, Cain's breath remained in her face. Small, smelly huffs wafted over her cheeks and into her nose. Again, intimidation. The jerk was a pro at it. He just wanted her to think he might kiss her. At least, she hoped that was all he wanted.

"This woman is a soldier. She came here looking for someone. Who's she after?" Cain asked. Slowly, he removed his hand from her chin and stepped back. "Do you know?"

Cassidy let her head drop forward. *I'm no soldier, you morons. I'm the woman who's going to kick your asses. A little later.*

"Not sure," Greg answered quietly. "None of the Gentiles could've gotten a word out. We took care of them as soon as you gave us the sign."

Gentiles? We took care of them? That didn't sound good.

Cain grunted. He walked a full circle around her, muttering all the way. She stilled her wild thoughts. They'd only get her blood pressure up and her mouth flapping. For once, she needed to play it smart. Maybe she could convince him that she was unconscious and nothing more than a weak-willed woman? Maybe they would just walk away and let her sleep it off?

"Say the word," Hank muttered. "Me and Greg can make this gal disappear, too. He needs the practice."

"Was she alone?" Cain asked.

Cassidy's ears pricked to hear that answer. Rourke might have followed her. He did crazy stuff like that—watched out for his guys and gals. Had he been caught, too? She hoped not. As much as these men despised women, they'd go harder on a strange man caught inside their perimeter.

"Sister Melissa didn't see anyone else," Greg replied.

"But this one got as far as the south compound." Irritation tightened Cain's tone.

Greg placed a hand on Cassidy's bicep, his fingers squeezing hard, feeling the muscles she commanded to remain flaccid. "I'm surprised Sister Melissa was able to subdue this one with just a shovel. This woman is no weakling."

"That old biddy must have surprised her," Hank said. "This chick had a Bluetooth earpiece on her. A cell phone. She's got company somewhere, and they're missing her by now. We need to make her disappear and plead ignorance when they come looking for her. No one knows she's here yet. We got a little time."

"Who are you?" Cassidy didn't understand which one of his goons Cain was talking to until his next question. He tapped at something and asked, "Can you hear me?"

Ha! He had to be talking into her earpiece. Cain was an idiot to taunt Rourke like he was, and she'd give ten-to-one odds that Rourke was on his way. As much as she probably needed Rourke to save her, she wanted to be the one who brought this phony prophet to his knees. She didn't want to be known as the feminine shadow to Rourke's very masculine hero. This was her chance to prove she was as good as every military-trained sniper on The TEAM, and she'd blown it.

"Now that I have your attention..." Cain's tone changed from inquisitive to hard, "hear this. Whoever you are, the second you breach my walls I will kill your little, blonde girlfriend. Yes. I have her, and I intend to keep her."

Great. Now you've really pissed him off. He's coming for you. Do it again.

"And I will do it," Cain hissed, "right out in the open where you can watch."

Cassidy had to hold her breath to keep from reacting. Her helpless situation fueled her rage. She might be a little tied up at the moment, but she was willing to join her senior agent in whatever payback he was planning.

Hank lowered the board to the floor and let it drop that last few inches with a thud. Judging by the diminishing sound of his voice and footsteps, Cain was leaving. But one of his goons had walked to the other side of the barn. Metal clanged against metal. Some kind of a door screeched open. "Which brand you want me to use?" Hank asked from the shadows, his voice filled with a creepy delight.

A full-blown shiver skated up Cassidy's bare neck. *B-b-brand?* Oh, damn. He did enjoy hurting others.

Cain hadn't left like she'd thought, either. He'd only walked to the rear of the barn with Hank.

Greg still stood at her side, and then she felt it. He pressed something small and circular into the palm of her hand. A ring? "It's okay," he whispered, still clutching her hand. "I know you're not unconscious. Trust me. I won't let them hurt you."

She faltered, not sure how to respond. Cain and Hank still conversed in low tones at the other side of the barn. They couldn't hear what Greg was telling her, but trust one of Cain's henchmen? *Do I dare?*

"Don't lose it," he whispered. Without another word, he removed the ring from her limp hand and tucked it into her front pants pocket. "This will be our little secret. It's a gift of my true feelings. Keep it safe for me, will you please?"

Another loud clang broke through the confusion in her head. She smelled heat again. Cain and Hank were suddenly too close, and the thing they had brought with them was searing, damned hot.

She forced her mind to a calm place, the way she'd been taught when she joined The TEAM and learned to be a real sniper. What was it Rourke had always told her? *Find your happy place. Plant your mind. Block the world. Focus.*

His words bounced off the rising panic skittering up her spine. Growing up in Utah, her happy place had always been Tony Grove up Logan Canyon—one of the prettiest places in her world. She summoned the essence of that singular place, focused on it like she'd never focused before. *Pristine mountain lake. Moose browsing in the willows. Mule deer sauntering through fragrant pines. Beavers slapping their tails on the water. Albino trout. Clear blue sky. The scent of sage. Take me away,* she prayed. *Please. Take me away.*

Someone lifted the brand to her face. Had to be Hank. She doubted the fake prophet would do his own dirty work, and Greg seemed—safe. Maybe.

Hank didn't have to touch her. The heat roiling off the metal was enough to singe her chin and make her want to scream. Her skin felt as if it were melting, dripping like tears down her neck.

Her panic tripped over itself. *Tony Grove. Hawks on the wind. Sheep on the hillside. Sage. I'd rather smell sage. Give me sage. Now, damn it!* The chant cranked up faster in her head. *Bluebirds. Midnight canoe rides. Bat cave. Skinny-dipping. Albino trout. Sage. Sage. Sage!*

The smell of scorching flesh tickled up her nostrils. *God, help me, damn it! I'm being barbequed!*

Hank's hard hand gripped her wrist. "You want me to burn the palm of her hand or her ass?"

Neither! God! Don't let them do this!

"Hmm-m-m." Cain sounded as close as Hank, but thoughtful. Watchful. Like a son-of-a-bitchin' snake stalking its warm-blooded prey. Waiting for the right opening to strike. "The crescent moon on her hand would show her sins to the world, but..." He paused.

Thank God! Her heart launched into the end of the *1812th Overture*, beating so strong and so hard they had to be fools not to detect the drumming pulse at her neck.

"But a brand on her ass would be so much more fun," he purred.

The roar of the cannons' volley blocked any happy thoughts. *No. No! Don't! Do not violate me, or I'll... I'll...*

Hank grabbed her belt buckle, and Cassidy's heart stopped. *Or I'll cry.*

Tony Grove slipped away. Panic ruled. She was alone in the middle of a barn where no one would hear her scream, held captive by psychotic men who had no trouble torturing women. Suppressing the cry at the back of her throat took all the willpower she had left, and there wasn't much.

Unbuckling her belt, Hank grunted in her face. "You ain't kidding no one. You're faking. I can tell."

She caught herself just before she would've rammed her head into his nose and given him some of his own medicine. But who held the brand if Hank had hold of her belt? Cain? Greg? Her spirit cringed, even as she steeled her body not to react.

The awful thing these men meant to do to her was going to happen.

Hank slid his hand inside her waistband. With his fingers against her bare skin, he gripped her pants like he intended to pull them off without bothering with the zipper. She prepared mentally to be stripped bare, trying desperately to control her breathing. This pig was going to lay his hands on her, and she would take it. She needed to keep her cover and not destroy the mission that she'd jeopardized. This was all her fault. She knew it. She deserved this, and she was going to take one for The TEAM, and for Melissa McCormack, and—

Damn you, Alex Stewart. Damn you, Rourke. The things I do for The TEAM.

The blistering brand came too near her face again. Why? Had she missed something? Had Cain changed his mind? Was she to be branded on the face instead of her backside? *God, please, don't let them blind me.*

"She really is unconscious," Greg offered quietly from the sidelines. "She would've screamed by now. No woman is that tough. Give her the benefit of the doubt."

Yes! Give me the benefit of the doubt.

"No." Hank jerked at the waist of her pants. "She ain't. I can tell." He stuck his nose in the side of her face. "I can smell her fear. She reeks of it."

"She reeks of cow shit," Greg muttered disgustedly. "You had to go and drop her in that crap."

"You got a problem with how I do my—"

Cain finally spoke. "That's enough, Hank."

Hank snorted, but he let go of Cassidy's pants and stepped back. It took more strength to not blow out a huge sigh of relief. Cassidy congratulated herself mentally even as she tried to calm the adrenaline rush hammering through her system like an out of control bull elk during fall rut.

See, Rourke? I really am tougher than you. Maybe. Sheesh.

"But she needs to be cleansed and taught the gospel if she's going to stay." Cain had turned away again. Once more he was headed away from her and hopefully toward the door.

"Let her go?" Hank didn't seem too happy. "Just like that, you want me to let her go? Without any punishment? At least, let me mark her. She's got that much coming. For God's sake, she's a trespasser, and one of her Special Forces buddies is probably on his way in to get her right now. They don't leave any of their guys behind, or have you two forgotten that?"

"I said no," Cain growled. "Greg will keep an eye on her. He'll make her his."

"Will do," Greg answered quickly, sounding more like a butt-kisser instead of a trusted savior.

"And then what?" Hank was definitely perturbed, his voice low and sharp.

"Penance for now," Cain replied.

"The garden?" Hank growled. "That's all? You're only gonna make her work in the garden and pull weeds after what she's done?"

"Punishment will come later, when and if I'm sure she deserves it."

"But she's a spy."

"She could be useful to us alive." Light flooded the barn as Cain opened the door. "Very useful."

Hank continued grumbling, but suck-up Greg spoke right up. "Very wise, Prophet Cain. Converting this woman will prove the power of your ways. Turning a professional soldier into a believer will fortify your teachings. More and more followers will come."

The creep just wouldn't quit.

Cassidy knew what Cain meant by her being useful, and it had nothing to do with religious conversion. S he'd be reduced to slave labor or a whore, or worse, a poster girl for the infamous Palma Christi Cult. One of those pioneer-dress-wearing women who looked like they needed a shot of B-12 and a night out on the town. Maybe a good stiff drink, too.

"Exactly." Cain was back to purring again, his self-satisfaction evident.

The heavy metal brand clanged, once more stored in its place and far from her. She hoped.

"Greg," Cain said. "Strip her down and put her in a dress. Secure her pistol and ammo in my home. Burn everything else. We don't want any sign of her previous life to interfere with our indoctrination. Be thorough."

"Will do, Prophet."

So, Greg is the yes man. Hank is the enforcer. Cain is still the ass. Good to know.

"Begin prayers immediately. The sooner she hears the words, the quicker she'll accept them and belong."

"Yes, Prophet."

Belong? That word caught her attention. Belong to who? Or What? This insane cult? To Greg? That wasn't going to happen. Cassidy allowed herself to relax when Hank left with Cain, still grumbling. She almost sighed out loud, but Greg was still there. At least he hadn't assisted with the branding. Maybe she could trust him. Prayers were just words, and words she could handle.

Being scarred for life? Not so much.

Chapter Three

Not good. Only Cain and Hank left the barn. Definitely, not good.

Greg was still in there. Jude brushed a quick hand over his head, knowing what he should do but scared to do it. He'd already acquired a sharp knife, but he cussed his weakness. If only Cassidy hadn't looked at him. If only he hadn't seen the fear in those damned brown eyes. But he had.

What have I gotten myself into? I'm already on a mission. This is about Judith. I can't waste time on anyone else. I can't. But... I could create a diversion.

He ducked inside the milk house, looking for anything to fit the bill. A fairly sanitary little building once used to cool and store milk, it stood whitewashed and empty at the moment. It held no secrets and less help. The dusty green pop bottle on the windowsill caught his eye. A plan evolved. *I know how to start fires. I was a Boy Scout.*

Grabbing the bottle, he stepped outside. The cows might not be there anymore, but their memory lingered. The huge mound of manure they'd left behind had been concealed with straw months ago, but what lay beneath still contained great potential. Jude broke the bottle against the stone foundation, finally ready and able.

Angling the thick glass to narrow the beam of sunlight, he tucked it in nice and tight, then retreated to watch. This little distraction might give him enough time. *Time for what?* The row of empty wheelbarrows lined against the back of the barn gave him another idea.

A wisp of smoke drifted up from the pile, then flash—an orange flame whooshed to life. Perfect. His heart pounded. He needed to hurry, but this next part of his impromptu plan had to be timed just right. Greg hadn't come out of the barn yet.

Whistling an approved hymn, Jude grabbed a wheelbarrow and pushed it alongside the barn and away from the fire, biding his time. There were two exits on the south-facing wall of the barn, one toward the west corner, the other at the east. As quickly as Greg came out to help fight the fire, Jude intended to go in. He'd have to be fast, but for now, he moved methodically slow, waiting for someone to raise the alarm.

For once, he approved of Cain's archaic commandment against modern conveniences, including rubber hoses. This fire should burn hot and quick. It should put the adjoining bean fields at risk. He hoped. Everyone needed to be too busy hauling water to notice him.

At last some guy bellowed, "Fire!"

Right on cue, Greg slammed open the west door. Jude kept his head down. Sure enough, every man and woman within distance of the dinner bell ran east. Greg too.

Jude ducked inside the barn and ran that wheelbarrow straight to Cassidy, his heart beating out of control. She lay still tied to the board. A large tub of water nearby. He screeched to a halt alongside the board. "What'd he do to you?"

She didn't answer. Unconscious and wet from her waist up, her hair laid sodden in a puddle beneath her. He dropped to his knees and cut the belts. Too late, he had her off the board and in his arms, but what had Greg done?

Jude pushed the wet hair off her face, the poor thing. Round blisters pocked the right of her chin, a very delicate chin. Frantically, he cupped her throat until he located a steady pulse. Thank God. Tucking her under his chin, he pushed off the floor. She whimpered, sounding more like a hurt little girl than a tough private eye. Dipping his chin to the top of her head, he said the only thing he could while he transferred her to his getaway vehicle. "You're safe now."

Grabbing a dusty pair of coveralls from a hook near the door, he draped them over the wheelbarrow to keep her hidden, needing to run before they were both caught. This next part to his hasty plan could end everything.

He swallowed hard and braced a palm to crack the door just enough to see what was going on. The east side of the yard came into view. Sure enough, a bright orange band of flames spread into the field. An enormous black cloud of smoke billowed overhead. People ran in all directions. Some barked orders while most followed.

Anxiety hurried him out the door and into sight. He had his few precious minutes. He hustled, damn it. Around the front of the barn. Past the silo. Through the deserted garden. Straight for the root cellar at the nearest end of the granary. He nearly stumbled over his own clumsy feet in his haste, damn it.

Cassidy hadn't made a sound, but this was the stupidest, bravest thing he'd ever done. Would she survive? He honestly didn't know, but dead or alive, she was out of the barn, and that was good enough.

He banked too sharply at the cellar, nearly losing his cargo. With a groan and a grunt, he righted the wheelbarrow and pulled up just short of the slanted, ground level door.

"We're here," he muttered more to himself than to her. Casting the coveralls aside, two brown eyes stared back at him, and his heart fell. A trembling girl with tears in her eyes had replaced the gutsy woman.

"I won't hurt you," he offered immediately, needing her not to scream and draw attention to him. Keeping his eye on the still empty yard, he asked, "Can you walk?"

She nodded, but when he lifted her to her feet, her knees buckled. He caught her easily. She was all of one hundred pounds of bone china delicate. His stupid heart stuttered, like he had time to think how delightful this woman's body felt. But he did. Jude noticed every last thing. The lift of her breasts when she sighed. The brush of her wet hair on his cheek. The fact that her soft, compact build fit snuggly into his taller, wider frame.

A quiet murmur breathed out between her lips and seeped straight into his soul like sugar water on a dying plant. Five warm, slender fingers splayed over his chest, as if she needed help balancing.

He ducked to peer into the sweet, pale face tucked against him. "I won't let them get you." He'd no sooner made another promise he might not be able to keep, when sheer panic threw his heart into cardiac arrest. *What am I thinking? The penalty for betrayal of the cult and its prophet might be death. Where would Judith be then?*

With Cassidy barely on her feet, he pulled the cellar door open and right away lost hold of the handle. The damned wooden door fell with a loud thud. So did his heart. He shot a worried look at the yard, but it was empty. So far so good, but *hurry, damn it!*

Well on his way to coming unraveled, he half-dragged, half-carried Cassidy down the stairs and into the depths of the dark, cool cellar, positive everyone had heard the racket.

"I have a fire to put out," he told her brusquely. *And I can't be seen with you. I didn't suffer what I've suffered to save you. Only Judith.*

Cassidy staggered and clutched his shirtsleeve, which was really not much help since it threw him off balance. The last thing he needed. He tripped off the last step with her still in his arms, crashing into several empty crates at the bottom of the steps. *Way to go, genius.*

In the tumble, Cassidy landed on top of him. She flattened her body to his chest and stomach, her cheek over his heart. Jude froze. She made that little sound again. This woman was scared.

He pressed a palm between her shoulder blades and gave her a moment to collect herself. She hadn't made any attempt to move once she'd landed, and honestly, what's a man to do? Push her away? Not him. He comforted her as best he knew how. "You'll be safe down here for a while, honest. They'll be too busy with the fire to come look for you."

She didn't speak, just kept her cheek to his chest, panting in what he hoped was relief. He wrapped his arms around her and held on tight, needing her to feel safe before he left her alone. It was the least he could do. This was his fault. She'd needed a hero before, but all she'd gotten was him. A worthless bean counter.

The potato, onion, and carrot bins stood empty at his left. The fruit bins were just empty. She could hide under the stairs where bundles of burlap bags had been tossed for the upcoming bean harvest. That gave her at most a month to recover, but Jude hoped she'd be gone long before then.

"Ready to move yet" he asked, his arms still around her.

"Yes," she answered hoarsely. Rolling to one side, she slid off of him.

He scrambled to his feet, fully aware the cellar door still laid wide open and visible to anyone who might be nearby. When she made no effort to stand, he scooped her gently off the floor and angled her beneath the stair joists. Lowering her onto the burlap beneath the steps, his anxiety spiked higher with each second he wasn't at the fire. The prophet and his Elite would definitely be watching. He had to be seen.

"Thanks," she whispered again, shivering as she pulled one bag to her chin.

"Yeah, well, I'm sorry these aren't better accommodations." Cupping her chin, he traced his thumb near the oblong, oozing sore. "They burned you?"

She blinked up at him, her brown eyes melting his resolve not to care for her. "Y-yes."

"I'll... I'll..." he stuttered like the class geek asking the most popular cheerleader to the prom. *I'll what? Return? Put myself at risk again? Lose Judith for good?* This quick rescue had turned into something he might not be man enough to finish, but damn it. Cassidy needed him. He made the promise anyway. "I'll bring something to put on that burn. I'll be back. I'll get you out of here."

"S'okay. You don't have to."

The need to offer encouragement prevailed. He smoothed his hand along her cheek, relishing the softness. *I never should've left you.* "I will help you. I will. Promise."

She looked up at him from her burlap-camouflage, tears brimming, but her lip tight as if she'd rather die than let them fall. This was another class of woman than what he was used to, and he was in awe.

"You're very brave," she said quietly.

He shook his head. "If I was brave, I wouldn't have left you."

"But you came back. That Greg guy can't drown me anymore." Her voice grew squeaky as she ended.

I suck, damn it. He ignored her kindness. "They'll be looking for you. Keep quiet and stay hidden. Can you do that?"

She bobbed her head.

Just as he lifted the heavy door to shut Cassidy in darkness, he couldn't help himself. She needed to know she wouldn't be alone for long if he could help it. "I promise I'll be back. You can trust me."

The quiet affirmation of a strong but fragile woman lifted up from the dark. "I do."

Jude made quick work of reacquiring the empty buckets, which he filled with water from the horse trough before he joined the ranks of the fire brigade. He scanned the mob of men and women, looking for the prophet and his goons. Both

Lucien and Hank were involved in shouting orders, both seemed to be vying for control instead of doing the dirty work. But Greg?

Jude couldn't see him anywhere, and that didn't set well. The man could be back with Cassidy, doing his worst to her and laying for Jude, too. Nervous anxiety skittered up the back of Jude's neck. He should have minded his own damned business.

The fire had spread greedily into the dry field, advancing quickly toward the neighboring bean field. Black and gray smoke billowed overhead, but it was impossible to get control over the rapidly racing flames using simply buckets of water. Even a damned garden hose would have made a difference.

Jude ran back to the garden and grabbed an armful of shovels from the tool shed. Shouting, he raced to the front of the fire line, knowing he had to be seen by everyone to support his alibi. If he still needed one. "Dig a trench," he bellowed, waving a shovel as he ran. "Now. Run. Get ahead of the fire. Quick. Before it takes everything!"

An army of men joined him, working frantically along the dirt road that separated the fields. He hated the fire as much as he appreciated it. It was no longer the friendly thing he'd started. Huge tongues of flames leapt skyward into the black and white smoke. It burned hot and fast and literally blocked the sun. Still, he didn't regret starting it. A man had to do what a man had to do, and this fire was another means to an end.

A frission of pride stoked his usually bland, hero-less persona. He'd saved a woman's life today. That ought to count for something.

Another one of the solitary souls in the cult, Tucker Chase, joined him, both men shoveling as fast as they could to create a fire line the flames couldn't jump. Like Jude, Tucker kept a low profile. He didn't speak as he applied muscle and brawn to the dirt flying over his shoulder and into the fire that flowed toward them like a scorched ocean of orange on black.

Tucker shoveled faster. Jude matched his efforts. He hadn't noticed before, but this guy was big-shouldered with muscular biceps. When his shovel bit the earth, it threw hefty mouthfuls aside. His shirt stretched its buttons, and didn't stay tucked into his pants. Sweat dripped off his face and neck from the steady exertion, but not once did he hesitate or slow down.

Jude kept watch on the running flames now licking at his boot heels. This fire couldn't get anymore out of control. He headed in one direction while Tucker battled in the opposite direction. Jude didn't look up again until his elbow collided with Greg's arm. At least, he wasn't in the cellar.

"Uh, sorry."

"No problem. Good job, Brother Clark," Greg muttered, his face smudged with sweat and soot as he worked. "Were you a fireman before you accepted the gospel?"

"No. Just don't like fire."

"Me neither."

Jude attacked another furrow. He dug faster and threw dirt farther, wishing this particular henchman would work someplace else. Having one of Cain's buddies out amongst the flock should have been a good thing. It wasn't. Not all snakes crawled on their bellies. Greg wasn't firefighting as much as he was chumming for clues that might indict a man.

That he could act like he cared enough to pitch in and help after what he'd just done to Cassidy, made Jude want to use his shovel for something besides fire control. A grave came to mind.

"I saw..." Greg paused to stomp his boot to his shovel, groaning loudly as if it were difficult.

Jude's heart thudded to a screeching halt. He gripped his shovel handle hard, willing to use it as a weapon if needed. *You saw what?*

"I saw..." Greg blew out a breath, "...an apartment fire once. Helped the firemen put it out."

Jude kept his mouth shut. He refused to banter with a man he didn't trust.

"Praise the Lord I just happened to be there at the right time," Greg exclaimed with his usual religious rhetoric, grunting as he dug another shovelful. "It was a lucky day for Jerusha. Don't know what the fire department would have done without me."

Curiosity spiked Jude's eyebrow, but he held his tongue. Luck nothing. Greg had probably started Jerusha's apartment fire in order to *convert* her. That was how the Elite worked. There was no sacrifice too small, as long as it came at another's expense. Jerusha must have had money back then. No doubt the prophet owned it all now.

Greg tossed several quick and light loads of dirt into the air, panting with each one. "Yes, that's when she finally knew she could trust me."

Jude surpassed Greg's slower pace, hoping to leave him behind.

Greg stuck to Jude's side, damn it. "She surely knew the Lord saved her that day. God bless her."

Jude grunted, feigning interest when his mind was back in the root cellar and the nearly drowned woman hiding beneath the burlap, the one with the third-degree burn on her chin because of a noble jerk like Greg. Already planning how to get water and food to Cassidy, he put his back into his work. Blisters on his palms, he was used to. The fire, he could deal with. He just couldn't take the chance of anyone finding or hurting Cassidy again.

Good men didn't bully women or children, damn it. It just wasn't done.

He paused to catch his breath and take stock of the near catastrophe he'd created. The burned field could've passed for Hades the way smoke hung over it and the ash-filled spirals curliqued heavenward. As many men as women helped at the trench line and the bucket brigade, and slowly but surely, the fire line held. No flames jumped the breach.

He leaned against his shovel handle and watched the final orange tongues lap against the fire line only to die. Thankfully, the blustery warm Santa Ana winds Southern California was known for didn't stray this far north, or this little fire could have been a real monster.

The last flame down the row finally succumbed beneath Tucker's hefty shovelful. Jude wiped the sweat and grime out of his eyes and off his brow, finally able to relax.

Everything would still hit the fan when Cassidy's escape was discovered. The prophet and his Elite would go after the traitor who'd cut her belts, but for this one golden moment, Jude felt like a man again. The damsel in distress was safe, and the fire was out. He lifted a thankful prayer up to the pale, northern California sky and praised the Lord indeed. The real Lord.

Under the drifting white smoke, the group of disheveled firefighters ambled passed the barn and into the yard. Greg hurried to the prophet's side. Good riddance.

Jude stuck his shovel blade in the ground as he walked, using it as a walking stick. A sudden breeze swirled up across the fields, wafting the dust and cinders into the sir with the smoke. Watching it swirl upward instead of watching where he was going, he stepped on Tucker Chase's boot.

"Sorry," Jude mumbled. "Didn't see you."

Tucker didn't answer, but Jude noticed he matched him step for step. Jude let the uncomfortable silence linger between them. The biggest disease in this so-called church was the distrust among its members. Too many turned on others to gain favor with their prophet, or worse, with Hank or Greg. No one was who he or she appeared to be. Jude surely wasn't.

They'd almost reached the yard when Tucker stumbled into his side. Jude looked up, not sure if the man was drunk, sick, or just plain stupid.

Intelligent blue eyes flickered over his face. "Watch your back," Tucker muttered under his breath. He took one more step alongside Jude before he turned and headed toward the horse trough where Cain stood gathering his flock.

Jude followed. *What was that supposed to mean?*

"Brothers and sisters, your attention." Cain held his soot-covered hands up for attention. "Please. Silence."

Everyone moved to their prophet's command. Jude stepped up front, needing to make certain that he was seen. That's all this was about. Alibi. Looking good. All that crap.

"We have a problem." Lucien extended his arms toward Jude, one imperious brow lifted. "Brother Clark. Please step forward. Come. Join me."

Damn. That's me. I'm Brother Clark. It was never a good thing to be singled out by the prophet, especially after that covert warning from Tucker. Jude's panic button flashed a bright red warning light in his head. With a quick glance, he scanned the end of the granary. The root cellar stood wide open. A man leaned over the edge, peering down the stairs. Someone had found Cassidy.

Jude sucked it up and stepped forward with his shovel, but then Cain made it worse. He grasped Jude by the hand and pulled him to stand at his side.

"Brother Clark. Would you care to tell us what you've done?" Cain asked confidentially.

Jude kept his eyes on the dirt at his feet, not willing to give anything away. Not yet. Not until he had to. He didn't regret saving Cassidy. He only wished he'd found his daughter before he'd risked his life—that he had the chance to tell Judith he loved her one last time. His lungs filled with regret.

Cain's grip turned into a stranglehold Jude couldn't escape. He took a deep breath and prepared for the worst. What else could they possibly do to him? *Censure* him? Who cared? He had a little girl to find and save. Let the world shun him. They could all go to hell.

The gathering quieted. All eyes were on him, and Jude wished the earth would swallow him up and spit him back out in Florida with Judith safely at his side. Only the meadowlark on the fence post interrupted the prolonged silence with a bright, cheery whistle, while all the members of the cult waited to hear Jude's latest sin. Waited to watch him receive his just due, and maybe die for helping another. He swallowed hard.

"Brother Clark," Cain said in a strong, clear voice, digging his fingernails into Jude's shoulder muscle as he paused for effect, "is too humble. I'm here to tell you that today, he saved our noble cult with his humble actions."

I what? Jude jerked his head up at Cain, shocked. His mouth dropped open, but Cain didn't see it. The man was on a roll. Jude was just a prop and Cain the ultimate actor.

"Brothers and sisters, we have in our midst a genuine hero." Cain raised his free hand in a mighty salute. "We shall convene to the chapel to absolve Brother Clark of his previous sin. From this day forth, you shall ignore the mark of the crescent moon. We welcome him as a full convert. Praise be to Brother Clark."

"Praise be to Brother Clark!" the congregation shouted.

Jude blew out a soft breath of relief. Maybe no one had discovered Cassidy was missing after all. Maybe he really was a hero? Okay, no. Not him. But at least, he wasn't the scum of the church at the moment at the moment. He had a little more breathing room to find Judith.

"Let us give thanks for the day Brother Clark joined our congregation. Praise be to the truth that reveals all," Cain declared, his palms lifted over the crowd.

"And to the prophet who sets us free," the congregation chanted automatically.

"Praise be to life."

"And praise to our almighty prophet, the giver of life."

Jude walked in step with Cain. If this wasn't a charade, and if he really was in the prophet's good graces, this was a most extraordinary day after all. Weird, but extraordinary.

Chapter Four

"There are spiders down there, Chloe."

"I like spiders."

"Well, I don't."

"Saffron, you're such a sissy."

"Am not," Saffron answered, her voice tight and squeaky. "I got bit by a big spider one time, and my whole arm swelled up. It hurt."

"Sister Jerusha says spiders are our friends," Chloe said. "She says God made them for a good purpose, just like he made us for the blessing."

Cassidy listened as only one set of feet tread lightly down the stairs.

"Hurry it up," a gruff man's voice called from above. "If the prophet sees you stealing a bag for your dolls, he'll whup your bottom."

For some reason, that only made Chloe giggle. "Then don't let him see me, Brother Derrick. Besides, he wouldn't hurt me. Prophet Cain likes us girls. I know he does. Sister Jerusha says so."

Cassidy couldn't help but roll her eyes at the girl's naïveté. *If you only knew.*

"We're missing his meeting, and..." Cassidy couldn't make out the rest of Brother Derrick's admonition. Just as well. She strained to quiet her breathing, hoping Chloe would grab the nearest bag and leave.

"Hurry it up, Chloe," Saffron whined. "You're gonna get us in trouble. We're supposed to be over with the prophet right now. Something important's going on. They're going into the chapel and we're missing it."

"I'm coming," Chloe muttered. "Just a sec."

Cassidy saw her then, a pretty teenage girl with strawberry blonde hair pulled back in a long ponytail and a sunbonnet perched on her head.

That silly head covering was another of the prophet's mandates. All women, young or old, had to keep their heads covered at all times, even indoors. The bonnets' wide brims kept the sun from damaging fair skin with freckles and sunburn. It also kept little girls' and older women's eyes focused on the task set before them instead of socializing. Cain didn't allow idle chatter, gossip, friendship, or camaraderie. A woman's place was to serve, work, and bear children. Nothing more.

Chloe stopped within inches of Cassidy. *Just get your bag and go. Please.*

"You got it yet?" Brother Derrick asked.

"Almost. I need to pick the perfect bag that's so, so—" Chloe gasped. She'd pulled the burlap from Cassidy's face, her gray eyes scanning the strange woman she'd just uncovered.

Cassidy put a finger to her lips, hoping Chloe wouldn't scream for help.

Oddly, she didn't. Instead, she took another step forward, her eyes bright and curious. "Who are you? Why are you hiding down here?"

"Don't tell anyone," Cassidy whispered.

"I won't," Chloe answered, quietly, glancing over her shoulder, "I promise."

This young woman had to be Jude's daughter. She had his gray eyes. The same gentle brows. The same elegant nose. "What's your name?"

"It used to be Judith, but I'm to be blessed on my next birthday, so the prophet has given me a new name. Now I'm called Chloe. Just Chloe."

"You're Judith Cannon?" Cassidy asked to be sure.

"Yes." Judith peered more intently at Cassidy. "Do I know you?"

Cassidy bit back the truth. She needed to be sure before she trusted this young woman. Judith didn't need false hope, and Jude didn't need incriminating evidence piled against him, not in this crazy cult where children were encouraged to turn on their parents. "You don't need to be blessed, Judith."

A frown furrowed those gentle brows. "But it's my right. Sister Jerusha said so."

Cassidy groaned. The blessing wasn't a right, it was a crime, but how to explain it to a child brought up inside this insane cult and indoctrinated day in and day out? For that matter, did Judith understand what really took place during the blessing?

"Chloe!" the man called sharply. "Move it!"

"I have to go." Judith pulled a cookie out of her dress pocket and set in within Cassidy's reach. "You must be hungry. Take this."

"What?" Saffron snapped from the stairs. "Are you talking to me? What'd you want now?"

"No, I'm talking to my pet spider. Want to see him? He's so cute."

"No!" Saffron shrieked. "Keep it away from me!"

"Aw, come on." Judith gathered her skirts, giggling while she climbed the stairs with a bag over her arm and one hand extended. "Look at him. He's just a hoppy spider with hairy legs. He won't—"

The door crashed into place, plunging Cassidy into darkness once more. She blew out a big sigh, relaxing into her scratchy mattress of bags and who knew what else was down there. Her fingertips fluttered over the burlap for the treat Judith had left behind. Hmmm. Oatmeal and raisin. Tasty. Jude's daughter seemed to be a lot like him. Kind to a stranger.

Cassidy savored every last morsel. Fingering the bump at the back of her head revealed a good-sized knot, but other than that, nothing else was too damaged. The burn Hank had left on her chin still oozed, but her vision was back to normal. If only she could wash the stink of the manure out of her clothes and off her body.

After Greg prevented the branding, she hadn't been sure what to expect. She'd almost trusted him. He'd helped her, but doubt had still whispered at the back of her mind, 'Not yet.' So she'd waited. It'd been a damned good thing, too.

When he'd lifted the board and settled her into his arms, foolishly, she'd hoped he might take pity on her, that maybe he wanted to wipe her bloodied face or something just as kind, like let her go. But then he'd whispered almost lover-like in her ear, "And now we shall pray, Sister Whoever-You-Really-Are."

The lying prophet's yes-man turned out to be a cold-blooded murderer, and prayers were another term for water boarding. Turning the board over landed Cassidy on some kind of a teeter-totter contraption that raised her feet off the ground while it lowered her head. With a grunt, Greg had placed one palm at the back of her head, then dunk, underwater she went. She hadn't been able to fight back, not tied to the board like she was.

"You must learn to pray," he'd hissed when he raised her face clear of the water the first time. "Repeat after me. The prophet is all wise."

"Bullshit!" She'd choked out, determined to get one word in. Big mistake. She never got a chance at another. Under she'd gone again. It felt like minutes before he'd pulled her up that time, choking for breath. She could barely remember what he'd wanted her to say.

"Believe in the prophet with all thy heart," the bastard preached. "Tell me why you're here, and this pain shall end. I'll let you leave."

Liar. Before she'd been able to inhale one complete breath, he'd shoved her so far down she'd scraped her forehead on the bottom of the tub. Her oxygen deprived lungs inhaled reflexively, drawing in water.

Once more Greg yanked her topside, dripping, gagging, and sure she'd die at his hand. "You must believe before the blessing, you wayward bitch. Say it! That's all you have to do. Say 'I believe.'"

She'd sputtered. *Air. Just let me breathe! I believe already.*

"I didn't think you would say it, but you will," he'd said, his lying face next to her dripping wet cheek. "You're a strong one, but you will beg to believe by the time I'm through with you. You'll beg for daily discipline at my hand, too. They all do." He'd twisted her hair into a knot, and shoved her underwater again.

The end of Butch Cassidy Dancer had finally come. There was no way out of this mess. The fight went out of her. Cassidy opened her eyes and prepared to embrace her watery death. It wouldn't take long.

But suddenly, the board lifted up and fell with a hard thump to its side. She'd never been so glad for the painful effort of coughing and choking. God, it hurt to breathe. It took every last ounce of her strength to retch the water up and out of her lungs and stomach. When she could finally focus enough to see, Greg was gone.

She fingered her wet hair now, thankful for that Jude guy. When she'd first seen him, she'd still been dazed, and only noticed those thick, Coke-bottle glasses at the end of his nose. The shock of dark, messy hair on his head only added to the unsure hero thing he had going for him. She thought an owl had saved her. Or Harry Potter.

Cassidy sighed. The odors of fruits, vegetables, and dirt in this dark place had a calming effect. She was safe for the time being, but tired beyond belief. And worried for Rourke.

"We'll wait until dark to go in," he'd told her only the night before. They were the only two agents assigned to this operation. After two weeks of gathering intel on the Palma Christi Cult, they knew they'd locate Ms. Melissa McCormack in the northern compound since the single women were housed there.

Cassidy knew Melissa's story well. The only daughter-in-law of Jed McCormack, a prestigious entrepreneur and close friend to Alex Stewart, the man who owned The TEAM, Melissa was a rock star in Cassidy's estimation. When Jed's son, Brady, came home a quadriplegic from Iraq, she'd put her life on hold to attend to him and all of his medical and personal needs.

She loved him, pure and simple. Through months of surgeries and physical therapies, she became a fixture and a godsend in the McCormack home. When Melissa arranged for his transfer to their specially designed residence in Maryland, specifically built to accommodate a man with no functioning limbs, Brady's heart was won over again. They married and fell into a daily life of struggles and discouragement, but also filled with love. Surgeries were a common occurrence, and Brady suffered multiple setbacks. Pneumonia finally won. Death took him at the age of thirty-one.

It wasn't the hard task of loving him that had claimed Melissa. It was losing him. Steadfast and strong during all his years of need, she'd fallen into a dark depression when she was finally free to live her life. His death might have been a relief for others, but Melissa had only lived for Brady. Surviving him proved the real challenge.

When she'd disappeared, Jed contacted Alex. Within days, The TEAM had located Melissa. By then her bank account had been emptied, and the home built by love was owned by an out-of-state entity, an obscure corporation from northern California called, you got it, the Church of the Palma Christi. The real problem began.

Neither Jed nor The TEAM had spoken to Melissa since she'd disappeared, nor could they get inside the front gate of the cult. For all intents and purposes, Melissa had dropped off the grid. So Alex sent Rourke and Cassidy to do the impossible.

Rourke had devised a plan to infiltrate with Cassidy taking the lead. He'd personally trained her in the art of deception and camouflage. She knew how to get in, get out, and never be seen. Actually, she thrived on the adrenaline of those risky adventures. It was amazing to know that she had the innate talent and skill to infiltrate an enemy's camp, to get close enough to her targets that she could smell them, and yet, they had never known she was within arm's reach.

This mission was no different than others she'd been on. It was her turn to shine, her chance to prove she belonged on this team of ex-military snipers. Only she couldn't wait, not when she thought Melissa McCormack was in danger. Cassidy had been listening on the parabolic ears.

Apparently Melissa wasn't willing to turn over one hundred percent of her assets and, judging by the conversation, Cain wanted it all. But Melissa proved more obstinate than he'd expected. That woman had to be Melissa McCormack. Everything Cain and Jerusha discussed had described the grieving widow perfectly. She'd just lost her husband to pneumonia, she had substantial family wealth, and she was sick with grief. Who else could it have been?

So, like the hardheaded renegade Rourke claimed she was, Cassidy jumped the gun and proved him absolutely right. She infiltrated the compound alone.

Imagine her surprise when that Melissa turned out to be an elderly, dyed-in-the-wool, no-kidding convert dedicated to the church, and who, by the way, could scream her guts out in a bizarre attack of self-righteous hysteria. She didn't need help, and didn't want to be rescued. Damn it to hell. Cain and

Jerusha might have been talking about the right Melissa, but Cassidy had zeroed in on the wrong one. It ended up being Cassidy who'd needed the help.

Argh. The blessing. The very name gave her the creeps. In no way, shape, or form was sexual intercourse with the older and creepier prophet a spiritual *gift*. The thought made her skin crawl. Cain was nothing more than a child molester and a pervert. With her whole heart and soul, she wanted to bring Cain and his minions down and send them all to hell, right before she saved the right Melissa.

With a tired sigh, she pushed her strong opinion aside and let the cool of the cellar lull her into a more relaxed state. If her instincts were right, Chloe wouldn't tell anyone. If her heart was right, Rourke was champing at the bit, already on his way to pull his dumb-ass agent's butt out of the fire.

The glimmer of respect in his sexy hazel eyes came to mind. Definitely one of the good guys, Rourke was a tall, handsome hunk with the same color hair as his eyes. He stood a good foot taller than Cassidy, and she liked the advantage it gave him. It made her feel feminine, and she wasn't often susceptible to that feeling.

Born a tomboy in a family of older brothers, she was given to outdoor sports. She'd rather work all day in a garden instead of wasting time dusting, vacuuming, or baking. The few times she'd had occasion to stand beside Rourke, she'd definitely appreciated the fact that she had to look up. All her female instincts kicked into high gear. She'd been glad she was a woman.

He had to have felt the same attraction, didn't he? Wasn't that why he always took a step into her personal space? True, he'd never taken any liberties, hadn't even laid a hand on her, but didn't he feel that same tingle she did? Just once, she wished he'd been a little inappropriate, made a move, or something. Anything. But Rourke was steady, dependable, and trustworthy to a fault.

Alex Stewart, their tough boss, relied on him as senior agent to the Seattle boss, Murphy Finnegan, who had come out of retirement when sitting around home drove him crazy. That was probably what kept Rourke at bay. As senior agent, he was management, and management didn't play with the women who worked for The TEAM, at least not in Alex's company.

A top gun in his own right, Rourke was next in line for Murphy's position. If the truth were known, most of the ex-military agents in the office were worthy of the senior agent title. They had all been to battle. In her estimation, Rourke was her equal. At least, he was pretty close.

The truth was, she was the odd duck in The TEAM, an ex-DEA agent who'd mutinied against her DEA superiors on a difficult operation that landed her inside Mexico. The TEAM had joined forces with the DEA on that op, something her DEA supervisor refused to accept. Things went from bad to worse to damned ugly. A couple agents died, but the senior agent-in-charge of The TEAM, Mark Houston, gave her a thumbs-up. Alex hired her after she'd assisted Mark inside Mexico instead of sitting on her ass with her DEA buddies in Utah. Alex respected her. Enough said. He should.

Then there was Rourke. Cassidy closed her eyes, imagining all the things she might like to do with him when she got out of this mess. *Maybe I'll invite him over for wine coolers and a deli tray. He lives in Olympia, just off I-5. I'm an hour north in Puyallup. That's not too far by interstate.*

But as quick as that pleasant thought came to her mind, reality struck. She'd screwed the pooch on this op. She could hear Alex the second he caught wind of this debacle. One of the toughest men she'd ever worked for, he could leave a wayward agent feeling like a mule deer that had been field dressed and skinned after a clean kill.

He hadn't chewed her out yet. If anything, she'd detected his respect after she'd told her DEA superior to go to hell, but she had a chewing out coming now. He might be as angry as Rourke. She pushed that unpleasant future event from her head. Cassidy saw right through it. Bellowing was how men vented. They cursed and sometimes broke things, but that was because they cared. They were passionate.

There was a time she thought Rourke hated her. He'd treated her like a low-life grunt when she'd first joined the Seattle team, made her feel inadequate and inferior. Plus, he'd acted as if she knew nothing about surveillance and weaponry, as if she wasn't already a highly-trained federal agent.

To make matters worse, she was the rogue agent who'd quit the DEA. That kind of insubordination didn't sit well with Rourke, even though she'd worked freelance for Alex the minute she'd left the DEA. She was no quitter, but Rourke didn't seem to see her as anything but. He just plain didn't respect her.

She hadn't liked him, either. He was full of himself and the rudest man alive—full of that Army be-all-you-can-be bullshit and always up in her face. One scorching look from him could wilt her then.

He'd bullied her every step of the way, and Cassidy understood why. She got it. She really did. He didn't want a quitter on his watch. She might have been right to leave the DEA like she did, but she'd come into The TEAM with an unforgivable blight on her record, at least, in his estimation. To win him over, she'd sucked up her pride and worked every piece-of-crap assignment he gave her.

When she wasn't kissing his ass, she lived at the range until she could hit any target at any distance. She could disassemble and reassemble every weapon she'd ever trained on in her sleep. Her sniper rifle became an extension of her hand and fingers. She lived, breathed, and ate target practice. She stayed low, and she stayed determined. Just because she'd quit once didn't make her a quitter. She needed to show him.

It was their chance meeting at the range one afternoon that had turned the tides. She hadn't known that he stood watching while she'd pounded target after target, one headshot after another. The only things different that day were the four words he'd said after she'd packed her gear and shouldered past him on the way to her car.

"Good shooting, Butch Cassidy."

She had to turn back to him to be certain he'd really spoken to her. "Excuse me?"

His upper lip had twitched, but no smile. No wink. No repeat of that once-in-a-lifetime compliment, either. He'd shown her his broad back and strode purposefully away from her to the range. But just like that, they were friends, and she'd earned a cool nickname. It wasn't the last time he called her Butch.

Exhaustion lulled her to sleep.

"Rourke," she whispered as the worries of the day drifted away. "I'm still waiting."

Chapter Five

Jude endured the humiliation of being held up to the congregation as one of Cain's heroes. The impromptu gathering offered a different perspective, though. Sitting on the stand with Lucien, Hank, and Greg, he faced everyone else for a change. He might not be enjoying his sixty seconds of fame, but there he was, up front and center, finally able to see everyone.

He stretched his neck and strained to see past the sea of sooty bonnets and sweaty heads to no avail. His heart sank. Where could Judith and Rachel be? His gaze zeroed all the way to the back of the chapel, all the way to Tucker Chase, one of those back-of-the-room benchwarmers. The rest of the congregation appeared to be listening to their prophet with zombie-like attention. Not Tucker. His head was down, his eyes fastened to the floor.

Jerusha sat in the first row with her class of other parents' perfect children. All beamed up at Cain as he elaborated the heroic actions of the man who was anything but a hero. That Hank and Greg were present and nodding in sync with each other told Jude that Cassidy was still safe.

"My brothers and sisters, today is a profoundly great day. As you all know, in the past I have allowed those who disagreed with the Lord's teachings to leave our fair valley. Many Gentiles left, but many have chosen to stay. It is with great honor that I present Brother Jude Cannon. He has not only chosen to struggle with us, but he put his life on the line and fought to protect each and every one of us. I recommend his status be changed from outcast to common member?" Cain asked proudly from the pulpit, gesturing toward Jude. "All in favor give the appropriate sign of approval."

Every last member raised their right hand. Jude couldn't remember a time anyone had disagreed. Didn't even know what the appropriate sign of disapproval might have been. *Good enough for me. Means I'm somebody who's still a nobody.*

"Would you like to say a few words?" Cain asked graciously.

No! Jude thought, but he shuffled to the podium anyway. Gripping the sides of the stand, he looked the audience over, searching all those bonnets for the bright smiling face of his daughter. He let the moment stretch until he knew for sure she wasn't there.

"I, umm…" He cleared his throat, still not sure he could choke through the lies he knew Cain expected him to spout. "I'm thankful to be here today." That much was true.

Jerusha nodded approvingly, as did a few others on the front rows. The pious looks on their faces dried every modicum of saliva in his mouth. *What a joke.* He straightened his taped up, nerdy glasses and started again. "And I'm, umm, thankful for the opportunity to serve."

Quietly, the back door of the chapel opened as two young girls sneaked in and made their way to the bench near Tucker. Jude's heart leapt to his throat, but both kept their heads and bonnets bowed, probably afraid to be noticed. *Look up,* Jude mentally commanded. *See me!*

"Anyway," he continued gruffly. And suddenly he had a reason to talk. "Ever since I been here, I been looking for a good woman."

Jerusha raised her brows in surprise, not the girls. They were too busy passing something back and forth, their heads down and whispering like normal youngsters stuck in boring church meetings.

Jude cleared his throat extra loudly. "Anyway I'd like to ask Prophet Cain's permission to marry."

Judith looked up. Straight at him, her mouth opened wide in surprise. The loveliest smile blossomed over her face as tears filled her eyes. The young lady at her side nudged her, but Judith blinked rapidly, her bottom lip caught in her teeth.

Please don't cry. Not yet. Not here. Everything's going to be okay, but we have to play this smart. Don't let anyone see. I promise I'll take you home. God, I promise with all my heart.

"I think we can take care of that." Cain interrupted Jude's impulse to run to his little girl. The prophet's long, bony hand landed on his shoulder again, but Jude only had eyes for his namesake. She'd pinched her lips. Even across the room, he saw her questions. Her loneliness. She needed him. Now, damn it.

"Let us sing the closing hymn." Cain rattled off a hymn number that Jude could no longer hear. Or sing. His heart and soul were at the rear of the chapel, dancing with his beautiful daughter on their way out of this hell.

The congregation stood, and Jude strained to keep Judith in sight over all the bobbing bonnets and heads. *Don't go, Judith. Please stay put. Let me talk to you.*

At last the song ended, Jude fled the stand, but wily Jerusha still caught him at the first row. "Very well done, Brother Clark." She nodded as if she approved. "It isn't often we get a marriage proposal from the stand. Do you have a certain young lady in mind?"

He shook his head, peering past Jerusha for another glimpse of Judith, and still looking for Rachel. "Just an honest woman will be good enough for me."

The prophet's good friend latched onto his arm. "My, aren't you the accommodating gentleman? Another good answer. Free choice isn't allowed in this church anyway."

"Works for me," he lied. He knew who he'd remarry, only it was Cassidy's face that flashed into his nervous head. *What? No! I'd marry Rachel, if she'd have me again.*

He had yet to see her though. A frission of fear blossomed in his heart. What could be so important that Rachel had left Judith to fend for herself?

"I'll speak with Prophet Cain this evening," Jerusha assured him. "We'll have you betrothed and married in no time. It will be good to hear the sacred vows of the marriage ceremony again, won't it?"

"Yes, ma'am. It will." *Damn. I'm going to hell for lying while I'm living in hell.*

"Looking for someone?" Jerusha asked slyly.

"Tucker," Jude lied again. His gut filled with acid as Cain stalked past him, Hank and Greg in close pursuit. Jerusha needed to buzz off, damn it.

"Brother Chase?" Her lips twisted with disgust. "What on earth for?" She turned to the back of the room, too.

For some reason, Judith and her girlfriend were now talking with the man in question. They kept a distance of two seats between them, which was proper etiquette in this crazy church for an unmarried man in the presence of women. The only ones exempt were the Elite. Of course. People like Cain, Hank, Greg, and Jerusha definitely needed to be able to reach out and touch.

"Why would a man of your noble position need the likes of Brother Chase?"

So now I'm noble? Alarm bells rang loud and clear in Jude's head for the first time. That was why Tucker kept a low profile. He was the leper, the guy no one in their right mind was supposed to see, much less stop and talk to. Much less seek out. He was one of the *Censured*.

Damn. Jude thought fast. "He, umm... he had a few ideas on fire prevention. We worked side by side putting that fire out, and—"

"You may speak with him," Jerusha interrupted him with a sideways glance at Tucker. She still watched Tucker and the girls. "Just keep it brief. He doesn't deserve your company."

What a farce. "Thank you, Sister Jerusha. I will."

Finally free of her clutches, he beelined to Judith. The minute Tucker lifted his head, Jude knew. The man wasn't who he pretended to be, either.

"Hey," Tucker said quietly. "I should've said something before. I'm supposed to warn you I'm—"

"I know. I know." Jude cut him off. "You're *Censured*. Got it. Consider me warned."

Tucker shrugged, the brim of his ball cap wrung tight in his hands. "Yeah. Whatever."

"We need to talk," Jude said, "but not now." He turned to Judith. Every ounce of his heart yearned to reach out and gather her into his arms. He read the same desire in hers, but her little friend stood watching, and he had to be careful. He had to stay focused, proper and distant, worthless traits for a father who had finally found his lost child. "May I escort you young sisters home?"

Judith nodded, her eyes aglow with little girl adoration. "Yes, please."

Her friend sniffed. "I guess. If you have to."

"Ladies." He bowed slightly and made a small flourish toward the door.

"Why are you crying?" the girl at Judith's side asked sharply.

He wiped his face, not even realizing his cheeks were wet with his joy.

"I... I..." There were simply no words. The tender expression of overwhelming love was not only forbidden, but also indescribable.

"I believe you're overcome with your new prospect of marriage," Judith spoke up, the knowing light on her face saving him from looking like a fool.

"Be careful," Tucker muttered under his breath, the brim of his cap pulled low as he stood to leave. "You're playing with fire again."

Jude glanced sharply at him, not sure he'd heard right. This guy acted as if he knew an awful lot about him. Why? Jude hesitated, but Tucker had already turned away, the proper cult etiquette for a Censured man. He had no business looking at Jude, much less talking face to face with anyone except the Elite.

"A war's coming. Grab your kid and go." With those few words, Tucker tipped the brim of his cap again, walked to the far side of the chapel and out the opposing exit.

"Brother Clark?" Judith waited. "Is everything okay?'

Jude couldn't answer. Tucker's words were not the desperate words of a *Censured*. He'd spoken with authority, like he really knew something. A thousand questions flooded Jude's mind, but now wasn't the time. He had his daughter within reach. *Finally. Judith came first. Tucker could wait. Cassidy, too.*

"Everything's fine," he lied again. "Let me walk you home."

"I would like that," Judith said shyly. And the sun came out. The minute she smiled, Jude remembered what it felt like to be a father, to be loved perfectly and unconditionally. There was no better gift in a lonely man's world than to see the adoration in his daughter's eyes.

He held the chapel door for the two young women and kept the appropriate distance from them while they walked. Across the yard, Greg marched briskly toward the barn. Jude pulled his gaze off Greg, stifled the nagging panic in his head, and glanced sideways at Judith.

"I assume I'm taking you to the family building?" he asked.

"No. Of course not." Judith's friend spoke up. "We live with Sister Jerusha, if it's any of your business."

"Why?" *God, why her? That made everything more complicated.*

"Because she's our mother," the girl snapped. "Why else?"

"But..." Jude stopped in his tracks. "Where are your real mothers?"

A shadow darkened Judith's face. Her lips pinched the way they used to when she was a little girl, right before she'd burst into tears.

"My mother was nothing but a dirty Gentile," Judith's friend announced tartly. "She had her chance at redemption, but she threw it away."

"Saffron." Judith scowled, swiping her eye. "You don't mean that. You miss your mother. I know you do."

"No, I don't," Saffron's haughty nose tilted a fraction higher. "Jerusha says I'm better off without her."

Judith shook her head. "No, you're not. You don't know what you're saying."

"Yes, I do, and you're better off without yours, too."

"Where is your mother, Sister Judith?" Jude had to know. A parent who didn't follow the teachings and commandments of the prophet was swiftly dealt with, maybe removed from the cult. Cain couldn't have non-believers polluting his congregation. Gentile was another dirty word, as bad as *Censured*. Both destroyed families. Both bred nothing but lies. But God, not Rachel.

"I am no longer called by my birth name," Judith said softly as she walked, not answering the real question and her eyes on the ground. "You must call me Chloe from now on."

Jude couldn't speak. His heart stopped beating as anger spiked hot and fast in his blood. *Not the blessing. Hell no!*

"It's okay." Judith must have seen the anguish he couldn't hide. "It's time. Most young women are blessed on their twelfth birthday. I'm ready."

He met her eyes, the same color as his, filled with the same strength and love. The same depth of foolish compassion for others. It was all he could do to not take hold of her and run. How did a father conceal his fury and fear in the face of such an awful pronouncement? Good God, she had no idea what she was talking about or had agreed to. Damn this wretched cult. Damn Lucien Cain!

"Where is your mother, Sister Judith?" he asked again, refusing to use the name the prophet had given her.

"She passed over," Judith whispered simply, swallowing a gulp that registered all the way down her slender neck. "Her grave is in the cemetery. I would love to show you sometime."

His heart sank. "When?"

"Before Christmas." Her eyes brimmed and he could've cried with her. Wanted to. The need to take hold of his flesh and blood and tell her that everything would be okay mounted an aching tsunami in his heart. *God! My poor baby's been at the mercy of these wolves for months.*

But there was nothing to be done, though, not without endangering Judith more. He clenched his fingers into fists, each wooden step forward another step farther away from the child his soul craved to protect.

"Come on, Chloe. Let's go." Saffron pulled Judith into step with her. "We're home. We gotta go in."

Jude looked up, surprised they already stood at the door to Jerusha's private dwelling. He had so much more to say, so much more to ask. "No. Wait. I... I..." No wise words came to him when he needed them most.

There was no reason for a strange man to linger at their doorstep once they'd arrived—*Home*. The insane notion that Jerusha's private quarters could ever be called a word that evoked love and shelter choked Jude. This was nothing but a spider's den, filled with a web of lies and false teachings. He couldn't leave Judith there one more night.

She reached for his hand, wrapping her fingers around his, tucking her palm to his, the same way she'd done since she was ever so tiny. Their pinkie fingers interlocked. Even this simple act of childish love put her at risk. According to this warped church, she'd just sinned. "I'll be okay. Honest I will."

"Chloe!" Saffron's disapproval snapped out of her, but Judith didn't release her father's finger and neither did he release hers. One little pinkie. He clung tight, their joints locked in love and despair.

Jude looked into the sweet gray depths that used to make him cry when they cried, that made him laugh when they laughed. How could he let her go? But the girl he once knew didn't look back at him. Instead, a very mature fourteen-year-old woman who had his eyes and Rachel's beautiful nose offered a grave smile.

A heavy door slammed behind him. He looked across the yard to see Greg marching from the barn. *They know.*

"How did your mother die?" Jude asked again, ignoring the adrenaline coursing through his head. Despite the commotion he knew was headed his way, he had to know what had happened to his ex-wife. Rachel might have hated him, but he still cared.

"Penance," Judith whispered sadly. "She had to atone for her sin of arguing with the prophet in front of the congregation. He sent her to the fields."

"To pull wagons?" Jude asked in disbelief. "In the winter?"

Judith squeezed her father's hand tightly and nodded. She wiped the tear out of her eye without Saffron noticing. "He made her carry rocks."

"What sin?" He heard the anger snap out of him. Rachel hadn't deserved to die. Yes, she made for a stubborn adversary, and yes, she had made poor choices, but to die in the service of this godless cult for rocks?

"Jerusha's coming." Saffron tugged at Judith's arm. "We have to go inside. Now. Come on, Chloe."

"She wanted to go home," Judith said sadly. She straightened her pinkie and let him go.

"And still you will be blessed?" he asked softly. "By him?"

A shadow flitted over Judith's lovely features. "I must. There is no other way."

He couldn't even blink. *This isn't right! I can't let it happen! No!*

"Thank you for your kindness, Brother Clark," she said, goodbye in her tone, the last thing he ever thought he'd hear from his one and only child. "Maybe I'll see you in the garden. I'm the keeper of the watermelon patch, you know."

He nodded like a big dumb dog, his heart in his throat as she climbed the three steps away from him to Jerusha's door. Watermelons were part of the summer crop and summer was months away. If Jerusha caught wind of his interest in Judith, she might send his daughter away. He couldn't take the hint and just leave, not if it meant losing her all over again.

"Thank you, Brother Clark," Saffron said, her dander up. "I'm the other keeper of the watermelon patch. Now, will you please leave so we can go inside?"

He looked at Saffron for the first time. Of slighter build than Judith, she had white-blonde hair and the same self-righteous tilt to her chin as Jerusha. He saw it in the depths of her sharp blue eyes. Too immature to realize what she was doing, Saffron was one of *those members,* the kind willing to spread half-truths and innuendo if it served their purpose. The way she'd just informed him that she'd be with Judith in the watermelon patch, proved it. She'd tell Jerusha everything that had just transpired. Maybe more if it sounded good.

Jude took a step back to protect what little was left of his cover and to safeguard his daughter. He broke eye contact and forced his gaze to the burned field and the yard. "Good afternoon, ladies."

"Peace be with you, Brother Clark," Saffron said quickly. "Now let's go."

"Peace be with you, Brother Clark," Judith repeated softly, holding her position. "It was good to meet you."

He couldn't speak the customary and prophet commanded response. He couldn't just say, *'And with you,'* and leave, not with his heart stuck in his throat. Not when every fatherly instinct screamed: *Protect her. Save her. Run like hell.*

Only when Saffron huffed and stomped inside did Jude turn to the child he adored. Judith stood there waiting for him, using the door as a shield between her and Saffron.

I love you, Daddy, she mouthed.

Tears flooded his vision. His fist went to his breaking heart. "I love you, baby girl," he whispered. *Forever,* he thought.

And then she was gone.

Chapter Six

"Damn it, Rourke." Cassidy woke up grumpy, not unusual for a woman with a splitting headache, who smelled like cow shit, and who now had a botched mission to live down. The guys back at the office would give her hell once she made it back. If she did.

After stretching her achy body all the way to her toes, she sat straight up, and right away knocked her forehead on the stair joists overhead. "Ouch! Damn it!" she muttered, angry that Rourke hadn't yet contacted her. She knew she was being unreasonable. There was no logical way he could contact her, but still. It was his job to come looking for her. Was he?

She was rested and ready for action, only there she was, trapped in a hole in the ground that really did have spiders in it, thank you very much, Miss Judith. Friendly, beneficial or not, Cassidy didn't like creepy little insects dropping into her hair while she napped.

It aggravated her that she didn't know what time it was, not that it mattered. She was ready to get out of this insane cult. Back at camp, she'd grab another pistol, maybe two; load up on ammo, and return to extract the real Melissa. Maybe that guy, Jude, and his daughter, too. Maybe a little payback while she was at it. Greg sure had one Cassidy-sized kick in the ass coming.

Keeping her head low, she crawled out from beneath the staircase on her hands and knees. Time to get back to being her over-confident self and investigate. By the time Jude returned, she intended to be the expert of this dark little kingdom.

Ten minutes later she plopped to the fourth step, still just as aggravated and smelly, but not a whole lot smarter. It didn't take long to become queen of a dirt room. The heavy door overhead was wide and slanted. Solid wood. No knob or latch. She'd pressed her weight against it. It didn't even creak. Damn. Locked on the outside.

The crates and bins offered a few shriveled fruits and vegetables, all inedible. The only thing odd about the place was the boarded section of wall under the steps where she'd been sleeping. Could it conceal another room? A tunnel? An oddly medicinal odor wafted between the cracks in the boards. It prickled her over-active curiosity. A tunnel might mean escape. Or more trouble.

Cassidy hated waiting. She opted for positivity. A little adventure wouldn't hurt, either. Leaving the stairs behind, she walked carefully with her hands forward, feeling through the darkness for the edge of the steps so she wouldn't hit her head again. Helen Keller jokes popped into her head.

What is Helen Keller's favorite color? Ha! She knew the answer to that one because right then her favorite color was—burlap. It didn't make sense. Didn't have to. The real answer to the silly question didn't make sense, either. Corduroy. As if a color was in any way tangible.

Another joke prodded. *How do you make Helen Keller mad?* Answer: Move her furniture. Honestly, how could people joke about a blind person's unfortunate situation? Not very funny, when you were the one who couldn't see. All this darkness sucked.

She knelt on her burlap bed beneath the steps and smoothed her fingers over the boarded-up wall, her next target. A definite draft flowed through the cracks between the boards from the space beyond. Nails edged the wooden perimeter, not the middle. "I can do this," she muttered out loud. "I can get in there. I know I can."

Bracing her boots against the sides of wood, she pried her fingertips in between the top two boards and pulled. Nothing happened. The boards weren't old enough to break, and apparently, the nails weren't old, either. Neither gave an inch.

"I can do this," she repeated, her jaw clenched in determination. Squeezing her fingers between the boards until her knuckles scraped, she tried again. Cassidy Dancer did not back down from a challenge. She'd lived by one rule her whole life. *Where there's a will, there's a way.* And Cassidy could be damned willful.

She braced her feet again, stabbed her fingernails into the board, and pulled. Still nothing. Damn it. Blowing her bangs out of her eyes, a waste of effort since it was too dark to see, she threw her weight into it. Gritted her teeth. Gave it her all, and—the sturdy board creaked.

Encouraging. I can do better.

Squeezing her eyes tight out of sheer bullheadedness, she jerked backward and pulled the board so hard that fluid dripped out of the burn on her chin. "I. Can. Do. This."

The board held. So did Cassidy. She only needed this one... board... to... budge. Damn it to—

OOMPH! It gave. She won! She also flew backwards and hit her head on the joists. Again!

"Ouch." She rubbed the growing goose egg beneath her scalp. Her poor head would never heal at this rate. But the wall had been breached. She was successful, just as she'd known she'd be. She dusted her scuffed up fingers over her pants and prepared for more success. The challenges life threw her way were simply about mind over matter, and she was all about winning.

When she'd dismantled the next three boards, she kicked off her boots, but kept her socks on. Into the tunnel she went on hands and knees. Brushing spider webs out of her face and off her hair, she ran her palms over the ceiling and walls for height and width. Darkness she could handle. Closed-in places, not so much.

Nothing but a smooth dirt surface met her touch. The ceiling was just as smooth and just as close. All she had to do was hunch her back to feel it. Overall, the tunnel was maybe three feet by three feet. Plenty of room. Maybe not for Rourke, but perfect for her.

After travelling several feet, she came to a two-by-four frame that seemed to support the ceiling and walls. A burlap bag had been hung over it like a curtain.

"Why would a psycho dig a secret tunnel in his root cellar?" she wondered out loud. "What do you have to hide, Lucien Cain, you big freak?"

No light showed through the burlap, so Cassidy pushed it aside and kept going. She sensed she'd entered a wider part of the tunnel. Maybe a room. Pushing up off the ground, she stood, her hands extended to make sure she didn't bump her poor head.

Again, that odd odor crinkled her nose. Sweet, but medicinal. Musty, but—medicinal. Kind of antiseptic. Kind of not. More—medicinal. The musty smell of decay wafted along a draft that seemed to come from above. She waved her arms to determine the width and breadth of this new space. When she couldn't feel anything above her, she stood taller, still feeling for a ceiling. Her fingertips touched nothing but air.

"I'm in a room," she announced to absolutely no one. "A big empty... ouch. What's this?"

Her foot had struck something solid. The discovery reduced her to her knees, waving her hands along the floor to determine exactly what she'd found. Crap. It felt round, like a—skull. A human skull with hair and leathery skin. Goosebumps skittered up her spine. She chucked the skull.

"Damn it!" She threw herself backwards from her awful discovery. Another rounded object met her left hand while her right crashed onto a definite ribcage. *Crunch. Snap.* Something broke. She jerked her hands to her chest. Skulls and bones. This place was full of *d-d-dead people.*

"No way!" Cassidy rolled to her hands and knees, her heart a runaway racehorse in her chest. *Oomph!* She ran headfirst into a wall. She'd misplaced the entrance. Exit. Whatever the hell it was.

This was not a good time to forget how she'd gotten in there. Panic kicked her into overdrive, but she was lost in a lightless room full of the creepy dead.

Her throat squeezed shut. She lifter to her feet, clinging to the wall, sure it would lead her back to the opening. It didn't. Not until she'd circled the entire room and ran into more bones and bodies, some stacked on each other. Ewww!

She cringed with every step in the dark. All those damned teenage scream flicks accompanied every step. *Freddie*

Krueger. Michael Myers. Jason. The evil dead breathed over her shoulder and down her neck and—

Ewww! Just ewww!

At last, her trembling outstretched fingertips touched burlap. Cassidy dropped to her knees and hightailed it out of the morgue. By then, she was in full panic and absolutely sure one of those gruesome dead guys would grab her ankle and drag her backwards to spend eternity with them. Her heart pounded to the tinkling bells theme song from the *Exorcist*. By the time she burst out of the tunnel, she needed a good stiff drink, and a—

"Where have you been?"

"ARGHHH!" She jumped so hard that her poor skull collided with the stair joists again. Her fight-or-flight instinct pinged on fight, damn it! She struck out just in case she'd been caught and all but screamed, "What the hell?"

"Shhhhh. Cassidy. Settle down. You're making too much noise."

Oh. It's him, that Jude guy. Her body turned to jelly. With a huge breath she collapsed onto her bed of burlap. It took a moment before she could speak over the roar of adrenaline in her head.

Jude reached for her, making contact with her ankle first, then feeling his way to her shin with one hand. She grabbed hold of him, needing something strong to hang on to after what she'd just *not* seen. And she was embarrassed. She smelled like manure. She needed clean clothes in the worst way. Oh, hell! Had the entire universe conspired to humble her?

"Are you okay?" he asked, gently pulling her into a sitting position where she couldn't hit her head. That was kind of thoughtful, but she was damned if she could catch her breath to answer.

"Never mind. I'll be right back." He dropped her hand. The cellar door squeaked open and closed.

Cassidy scrambled to her feet. No light entered her dark world when he'd left, so it had to be the nighttime of her day from hell that wouldn't end. She scrubbed the spooky chill from having just escaped the tunnel off her biceps, but damned if it didn't slither up the back of her neck. Goosebumps cascaded over her shoulders and down her arms. Crap. She needed to get a lot farther away from those dead bodies.

Cassidy settled her breathing. Maybe Jude had left the door open. Now would be a good time to sneak away, but no. He returned in too few seconds. She didn't have time to check, but man, was he a gentleman. He'd brought a bucket of water with him. It sloshed as he crept down the steps.

She swallowed the last of her fear. All the best scream-flick ghouls were not after her. They didn't scare her. Much. She was Butch Cassidy Dancer, remember?

"Hold your hands out."

She complied. They might have trembled a bit, but she was back in control.

Jude placed a very rough towel and a couple of articles of clothing in her hands. "I'm sorry. I should've come back sooner."

"It's okay. Thanks." She brushed her embarrassment aside and stripped down to her underwear while he stood there. It was dark enough. He couldn't see anything, and she'd already made the worst first impression a strong woman could make. Screaming like a little girl? Not her best moment.

"I'll be right back," he whispered politely. "Take your time cleaning up."

She didn't care if he stayed or left. "Just give me a couple minutes."

"No problem." He lifted the heavy door and was gone.

Jude had hidden a small, square piece of soap within the folded clothing, its lavender fragrance now one of her absolute favorites smells in the world of all those frilly, foo-foo handmade soaps. Cassidy couldn't help it. Her gaze strayed in the direction of the tunnel to hell. Shaking like a leaf, she dunked her head into the bucket of water and washed her hair. Within minutes, the odor of manure was gone. She was clean and her nerves calm.

A quick and chilly sponge bath followed. Fumbling for the towel, she made quick work of drying off. Interesting. The clothing he'd given her felt like some kind of shorts and a long dress, not her favorite thing to wear, but okay. Beggars couldn't be choosers. She slid the dress over her head and buttoned it. Ugh. She didn't own a dress, much less a floor-length number with long sleeves to boot. And all those buttons. *Oh, my hell. I'll look like one of the cult sisters.*

The other garment was smaller, like a pair of baggy shorts. Bloomers? Someone else's bloomers? *Ewww again.* What was he thinking? Clean or not, a woman just didn't use another woman's underwear. Ever. She kept her own boy shorts on her spanking clean bottom, but slid those bloomers on just in case she'd need them later. Double protection seemed like a good idea after the kind of day she'd had.

Cassidy rolled her soiled clothing into a manageable bundle, and stashed the smell of *Eau de Bovine* in a burlap bag.

"Damn you, Rourke. I wouldn't have to worry about my wardrobe if you'd hustle your butt and get here." Even she heard the petulant tone in her voice as she washed her hands one last time and prepared to greet her rescuer in a better frame of mind.

The cellar door opened. "Did you say something?" Jude asked quietly from overhead.

"No," Cassidy snapped, worried he might have heard her talking to herself. "It's just that... I mean..."

He closed the door behind him as he descended. "It's my fault. I shouldn't have stayed away so long."

Cassidy didn't answer. For the first time in a long time, she, the boldest, strongest, most determined gal on The TEAM, was coming undone. Her nerves were shot. She'd embarrassed herself by her cowardly retreat from the tunnel, and humiliated herself again by screeching at Jude like some hysterical woman. Absolutely nothing could top this day.

"What time is it?" She changed the subject, needing to get her bearings once and for all.

"'Round midnight. I brought you something to eat, too. Can you walk toward the sound of my voice?"

And just like that, she forgot her pride. "Yes."

Hunger made a person very compliant. *And I'm damn hungry.*

Holding her hands out in front of her, she edged closer, trying carefully to avoid falling up the steps. She had enough bumps on her head. Thankfully, Jude reached out for her, too. When her fingers brushed his, he grasped her hand and pulled her closer. Instantly, an electrical charge zipped up her arm and crackled in her chest. More like it exploded. She gasped, the current so strong it stopped her breath and her heart along with it. *Sheesh.* This guy had some serious animal magnetism, or she'd hit her head harder than she thought.

With her brain circuitry overloaded, her foot snagged on a loose burlap bag. She pitched forward, right into his arms. Could anything else go wrong?

"I'm sorry," she squeaked out a pathetic apology. With her palm flat in the middle of his chest, she tried to push away, but not until she got a good handful of muscle. Her breath caught again. Then again when he easily bested her and circled her with two very strong arms. Owl-guy pressed her under his chin like a little girl who needed comforting. "There now," he whispered. "It's going to be okay. I promise."

That simple act of kindness became her undoing. Tears sprang to her eyes, and if there was one thing Cassidy Dancer didn't do, it was cry like a baby, which was exactly what was happening now if she wanted it or not. She gulped back her silly, feminine emotions.

"It's just that..." She hiccupped, another very un-Cassidy-like reaction. For some reason, this man made her feel vulnerable and safe at the same time. He unbalanced her at the same time as he balanced her, and she hadn't a clue how he did it.

"It's just that you're hurt, hungry, and tired," he answered for her. "You'll feel better after you have something to eat."

"I suck!" She couldn't help it, she whined. "And I'm wearing a dress."

He suppressed a very small chuckle, and normally, she would've belted anyone who laughed at her, but she didn't belt Jude. He deserved more than a deranged woman.

"I'm sorry." He stroked a gentle hand over her head. "That dress was the only thing on the clothesline. I thought it would help you stay undercover better. I could check for a pair of men's jeans if you want me to."

"No." She repented instantly for her prima donna attitude. He'd only tried to help, but she'd returned his kindness by acting like a spoiled teenager in return. It was time to man up, so to speak, and stop with the poor-me attitude. "Thank you. You didn't have to help me escape. I really am grateful."

"S'okay. You hungry?"

She nodded, but didn't step away, content to feel his shirt against her cheek for as long as he'd let her. This was the first time she didn't feel the need to be stronger. The heartbeat beneath that shirt sounded strong enough for the two of them. He smelled good, too. Sweaty. Smoky. Manly.

Cassidy closed her eyes to her troubles and let this all-male body strengthen her. Today was just another setback to overcome. She could do it.

Chapter Seven

"You smell like flowers." With one last squeeze and that very gentlemanly comment, Jude tugged her to sit beside him on the steps. He pushed a cloth bundle onto her lap. "Here I brought food, but it isn't much."

"Thank you." Suddenly famished, Cassidy unwrapped two slices of hard bread and a greasy slice of some kind of meat.

Jude supplied the answer to the mystery meat. "I sneaked into the kitchen. It's just bread and cheese. Here's some water to wash it down."

The water bottle wasn't what she expected. It felt more like the kind dish detergent came in. She swallowed a big gulp. Plain old water never tasted so good.

"Sorry I couldn't get real food," he said, but by then, she was tearing the bread with her teeth and snarfing it down like a ravenous wolf. She couldn't respond with her mouth full, so she just patted where she thought his knee might be. She was right.

Immediately, he covered her hand with his. Normally she would've batted any guy's paw away, even Rourke's, but not this time. Jude's hand was her only lifeline in a very dark place. Just by squeezing her fingers, he seemed to pour strength into her, and she needed that more than the bread and cheese. She returned the squeeze and blinked another chorus of girly tears away, glad he couldn't see them, either. He'd seen enough.

"All hell broke loose when they discovered you were gone."

"I'll bet," she mumbled. "I didn't really think I'd see you this soon. Thought maybe you left me."

"Yeah, well…" He had a weary tone to his voice, but his rough hand felt warm and strong. "Who are you looking for?"

She wiggled her fingers until they interlocked with his. "Melissa McCormack," she blurted it right out, instantly regretting her big mouth.

"You're a private investigator or something?"

She hesitated telling him more.

"I don't blame you for not talking. It's hard to know who to trust topside, too."

"Who are you?" she asked when she finished swallowing and could finally talk. Every instinct told her to trust him. She just needed to know more.

"My real name's Jude Cannon, but everyone here knows me as Jude Clark. Guess you could say it's my cover."

"Nice to meet you, Jude Cannon. I'm Cassidy Dancer, junior agent for a covert surveillance company out of Seattle. Why are you here?"

He blew out a big sigh. "To get my daughter out of this freak show."

Cassidy nodded at his astute assessment. "It's unreal, huh?"

"It's wrong, is what it is. There ought to be laws against the crap these guys are pulling."

"There are. We just have to prove they're breaking them." Her confidence in Jude increased. She squeezed his hand. "I met your daughter."

"When?" He snapped to attention, breaking the physical connection.

"She and another little girl came down here looking for a burlap bag not too long after you left."

"Did she see you? Did Saffron?"

"Only Chloe, ah, Judith. She has your eyes."

"I have to get her out of here."

Breaking the next awful news was going to be hard, so Cassidy delayed it as long as possible. After she'd finished the last crust of bread and swallowed the last drop of water, she just spat the words out. "She's going to be blessed on the next—"

"No, she isn't!"

Cassidy held her breath. The blessing wasn't a stoppable event, and Judith had seemed willing. "She said it was her right."

"I don't care what she said," he growled. "I only just found her this afternoon. That bastard's not touching her. Besides, she's brainwashed. What fourteen-year-old can make a decision that big?"

This father was going against some powerful people if he thought he could simply waltz out of this compound with his little girl. There was no way Cain or his goons would let that happen.

"I've had four months to think of nothing but this day. Judith's probably been told it's some kind of a special ceremony, like a baptism or a confirmation. Jerusha's probably made it sound holy and reverent, the way a real blessing might be done in a proper church."

"You're right." Cassidy handed Jude the ring. "That Greg guy gave me this, just before he tried to drown me. He's an ass."

Jude's hands encompassed hers as he felt for the ring and took it. "Do you know what this ring means?"

"No. Course not."

"It's a claiming ring. He claimed you as lost property. Now you're his property. He'll consummate the claiming during the next full moon, if that's what you want to call rape."

"Get outta here," Cassidy muttered, her anger rising. "I'd like to see him try. That sleazebag's got another thing coming if he thinks he's going to climb all over me."

"Believe me, he won't ask. You'll be unconscious when he takes you. I shouldn't have left you alone with them," Jude groaned, pulling her against him in the dark. "I'm sorry, Cassidy. I truly am. God. What was I thinking?"

Once again Cassidy found herself in his arms, her face pressed against his shoulder. Jude seemed to have an instinctive need to hold her, probably because that was what good fathers and kind husbands did. They took care of the women in their lives. She didn't pull away.

"I kept thinking of what you told me. You know, when you told me I could trust you."

"Do you honestly think I'm one of them?" he asked sharply. "That I'm down here lying to you? That I'm anything like Greg?"

She paused, the answer to that question more difficult than she expected.

"Here. Maybe this will help you make up your mind." He pushed his hand beneath hers on his chest.

Her fingers outlined his knuckles and then shifted to the palm. There, in raised flesh, was a crescent-shaped scar. Her breath caught. Jude had endured precisely what he'd rescued her from. "They branded you? Why?"

"Because I showed up at their front gate four months ago with no assets to my name, and I dared seek membership in this circus."

She smoothed her fingertips gently over the welt. "I'm sorry."

"Why? You didn't do it."

"I know, but..." His story touched her. She knew what he'd gone through. *Almost.* "How'd your daughter get involved with this cult?"

"My ex-wife."

Cassidy heard the bitterness in his words, but she also heard a measure of grief. "What's her name?"

"Rachel. I just found out that she died last December. Judith's been alone since..." A shudder passed through him, and Cassidy was done guessing whether or not he was telling the truth. There was no way this man could be lying The look in Judith's innocent gray eyes earlier validated everything he'd just said.

Cassidy reached for his face.

He groaned softly, his breath hitching back in his throat as if she'd hurt him. He clasped her hand against his cheek. "What are you doing?' he asked, his voice full of torment.

"I need to know who I'm trusting," she said. Okay, so it sounded stupid. She wasn't Helen Keller or anyone smart like that. She didn't know the first thing about Braille, but she knew people. She needed to reinforce the mental image of him that she thought she remembered.

He released her hand and let her continue.

Cassidy traced his brows and forehead, trying to match the geography beneath her fingertips with the fuzzy memory in her head. When her hands brushed the stems of his glasses, he removed them. She let her fingers massage the edge of his scalp at his temples, just enough to determine the length of his hair. Scruffy, maybe three to four inches in length. A well-trimmed haircut would've grown an inch each month. His story fit.

Dropping her thumb down his forehead, she outlined a very straight nose before she ended at his chin. Scratchy stubble bristled against her palm. A handsome image materialized. Shaggy dark hair. Square jaw. Rugged chin, not too big. Not too wimpy. Just right. Perfect eyebrows that ended at the corners of his eyes near what might've been laugh lines once upon a time, only now they matched the *V* she felt above the bridge of his nose. Stress and worry etched his handsome face.

She pulled her hands back, but not far enough.

He quickly reclaimed them. "No," he whispered hoarsely. "Don't stop."

She obliged him, her palms flat to the side of his face, her thumbs caressing his cheeks. That simple contact elicited a pang of heat deep inside her body, a sensation she hadn't felt in years and had yet to accommodate. No man had ever felt this weak in her hands, or so strong. Jude was putty. Strong. Weak. Gray putty.

Anxiety radiated off of him, and she had to know. Something else was going on between them, so she persisted. "Are you okay? You can tell me. I'll understand."

"No..." He halted, and she thought he'd push her away. But he didn't. "It's just that... Cassidy, no woman has touched me in a very long time. Rachel quit... God, she quit everything long before she left. It almost hurts, it feels so good."

The sound of her name tripping off of his lips did something warm and wonderful to her heart. She cast her hesitation aside, but the moment she moved in to hug him, he bowed his face into her shoulder. She settled, her cheek against his ear. Now she was the comforter. "It's okay," she whispered, patting his very strong back like she would a little boy. "I promise. Everything will be okay."

He didn't answer, probably because men didn't like it when they had a meltdown around their woman. *Their woman.* That errant notion raised a little red caution sign for attention in her tomboy psyche, but she liked it. Holding this particular male body made the dark place seem bearable. He needed her. In order to do what had still to be done, they needed each other.

Her story poured out. She told Jude about The TEAM and her boss, Alex Stewart, her senior agent, Rourke O'Neill, and exactly who she was looking for, Melissa McCormack. And why. When she was through, Jude knew she was a very capable covert agent, a trained sniper, single, and that she lived alone in Puyallup, Washington. He knew her home state was Utah, her cat's name was Magic, and that Magic ate gourmet cat food from a footed, crystal dessert bowl. Like royalty, or something. Cassidy didn't leave a thing out.

He reciprocated with how he'd met his wife Rachel, and how she'd cheated on him long before she divorced him. Cassidy knew the color of Rachel's lying eyes, and that Jude had hoped against hope right up 'til the bitter end that he could salvage their marriage, but then she disappeared. He'd been searching for his ex-wife and daughter ever since.

He explained as much as he knew about the inner workings of the cult, the bizarre midnight ceremonies of the Elite, the four circles of hell, and the continual brainwashing carried on against the children. The Elite were always listening, always watching, but mostly always laying in wait. Cain had a list of commandments that he seemingly pulled out of his hat at his convenience. Members who stepped out of line ended up in the barn at one of those late-night meetings. All were to be taught the *excellent ways* of the prophet, and, of course, to turn over all financial assets. Nothing more. Nothing less.

Cassidy also knew how Judith was born one month premature without complications, that her favorite color was red, and that she loved to read. She adored the opera *Les Misérables* and knew every last line and song. The warmth in his voice said it all. Jude's only child was his favorite topic.

Miss Fluffy, Judith's cat, lounged her life away in a three-story high, pink-carpeted cathouse that looked more like a dollhouse. Judith had her own bedroom at Jude's place, even though Rachel had filed for and won sole custody. His world was about to implode when Rachel and Judith disappeared. Most importantly, Jude wouldn't leave the Palma Christi Cult without his daughter.

"The thing is, Judith's why I came here in the first place. I never thought Rachel would come back with me. I'm not sure Judith will, either. She seems to think the blessing is her right, and why not? Jerusha's had her in her clutches since December."

Sitting there in the dark, side by side with a man who had risked his personal mission to save her, Cassidy deliberated her next words. Accountant, nothing. This was no ordinary guy and infiltrating the cult was no small feat. Most parents would have called the police and sat back and waited. They'd have wrung their hands and prayed. Not Jude. There he was, branded and taking chances he shouldn't. He needed hope to hang onto, or they'd fail before they started.

"She loves you," she said quietly.

"Yeah. Thank God. She does."

"Then that's all we need."

"The old 'love is all you need' ploy, huh?"

That word. That one word. Despite his nonchalance, it sounded different out of Jude's mouth. Most guys used it to get what they wanted, but Jude wasn't most men. Love meant something to him. He would die trying to save his child.

Kiss him.

Thunder erupted in chest at that wild notion. It might be precisely what Jude needed. Cassidy lifted to one knee on the step beside Jude, her heart pounding. She'd been aggressive with men in plenty of sports competitions and certainly in her line of work, but this was her first in the intimacy arena. Very carefully, she closed the distance.

He stiffened when her fingers made contact with his chin. "What are you doing?"

"This," she whispered, for once not doubting a guy's intentions. Trembling at her audacity, Cassidy intended nothing more than that one foolish kiss. She'd never done anything so out of character. Cheerleaders blatantly used their femininity. Cassidy Dancer, never.

Palming his scruffy cheek, she zeroed in on his mouth. Jude was big enough. Man enough. He could always stop her.

He didn't.

Her lips touched his with a quiet groan from her savior, and Jude took over. With one gentle tug, she was on his lap and in his arms. Deliciously enfolded within muscle and man.

She laced her fingers around his neck, consumed with the taste of his mouth. Gently, his tongue ran the seam of her lips, asking, not demanding. Compliance blossomed deep within Cassidy. She let him in. Every nerve ending flared to life. *Oh, my hell. He tastes so good.*

Achingly slow, his fingertips trailed downward. Never big enough to attract attention, her breasts were small and solid from her physical activities and sports. No need for C-cups when a little padding and a decent B would do. Only now...

She arched into him, wanting his hands on her aching breasts. Willing to comply for her first time ever. The hopelessness of their predicament slipped away. The darkness faded. The only sound the thrumming beat of his heart in time with hers.

One kiss was not enough. The warmth of his body spiked crazy desire down to her core. No sooner did that delicious thought flit through her mind than he stilled. His hand retreated to her cheek, his tongue still making love with her mouth.

No. Don't stop.

But Jude wasn't a mind reader, or maybe he was. He pulled away from her demanding mouth, breathing heavily into her face. With his forehead against hers and her palms cupping his cheek, she felt the crinkle of a smile. "You're something else, Cassidy Dancer. You made me forget my problems for a moment there."

He was right to stop. She should have never taken the liberty of kissing this tormented man. He seemed to be as much a moth to a flame as she was, but this craziness had to cease. He needed help, not to get laid.

Cassidy extricated herself from his embrace. Swallowing past the dry knot in her throat, she sat a respectable distance from Jude, breathing hard and not exactly sure what she'd done. He seemed to understand, but she was pretty sure that huff of his was frustration. Smoothing her trembling fingers over her dress, she straightened her attitude along with it. "We need a plan," she said, hoping she sounded more in control than she felt.

"I plan to get Judith out of here." He made it sound doable and simple.

"But exactly how will you do that? It's taken months to find her."

"I'll find a way." Again with the bravado of a desperate father who hadn't a clue what it took to extricate a person from this volatile situation.

Butch, her alternate persona, kicked into gear, and she was back on track. "Listen up, Cannon. You're outnumbered and outgunned. So am I, but if I can get out of here tonight, I'll be back by morning. We can stop the blessing and get your daughter."

"What about your client?"

"She doesn't know I'm here. Besides, Melissa McCormack chose this lifestyle. Judith didn't. Let's focus on rescuing your endangered little girl first."

"You would do that?" God, this man was running on empty. The incredulity in his tone stabbed her common sense along with her heart, but wouldn't Rourke be thrilled to learn she'd just tripled the risk to their operation?

"Oh, hell yeah. I'm part of The TEAM," she stated boldly despite a frission of unease at making a promise for Rourke and ultimately her boss, too. "That's what we do. Find people. Save people. Kick ass when we have to. Are you with me or not?" *Right, Alex Stewart? Isn't that what you'd be saying if you were here?*

Jude reached through the dark until he clenched her hand between both of his. Cassidy honestly didn't know which of them trembled more. Maybe both. She swallowed hard and turned to face the man she couldn't see. She didn't need to. Sight seemed unnecessary after what they'd shared.

The fervent kiss to the back of her hand melted her resistance. With that simple touch, he'd gotten past Butch, her avatar, and straight into Cassidy. She meant to squelch her feelings for this guy before they got the best of her. Honest, she did. Someone should have told her tomboy's heart. All that came out of her mouth was a totally unexpected and a very breathy, "Who can you trust?"

"I trust you," he said without hesitation. But then he made it worse. "I'd rather you call me Jude, Cassidy. Cannon sounds too formal. When Judith is finally safe at home, I want you to visit me in Florida. I want to get to know you better. Would you consider it?"

She swallowed past the lump in her throat, the lump that felt like her impulsive, stubborn, hardheaded heart intended to get the last word in. Damned if it didn't speak right up.

"I'd like that very much. Jude."

Chapter Eight

"It's back here under the stairs."

Cassidy gathered her courage and led the way into the tunnel. She needed physical evidence. Not only would it serve to indict Lucien Cain and his Elite, but it might buy her some wiggle room with her uptight companion agent once she returned to camp. Knowing she wasn't alone anymore helped. Knowing Jude was behind her? Yeah. She couldn't focus for shit.

Her errant mind wandered to that handsome man following. She wished he wasn't half the gentleman she now knew he was. A heartfelt hand on her ass would certainly bring a lot of—comfort. At the burlap drape, she shook off the lust-filled thoughts and entered the den of horrors. Climbing to her feet, she stepped aside to make room for Jude.

"I believe this is directly under the silo," he said. "Watch out. Low ceiling."

She scoffed. "Like I could ever bump my head in here?"

His hand came to rest on top of her skull. Ruffling his fingers through her slightly damp hair, she sighed. He had yet to touch her in a way that didn't bring warmth to her belly. "Guess you are kind of short, aren't you? So where are they?"

She batted his fingers away. Keeping one hand on the wall to keep track of the exit, she turned to the opposite wall.

"The first one is on your right, about three feet from the entrance. The rest seem to be placed around the edge of the room. I think."

"You don't know for sure though, do you? You didn't make it to the center of the room, did you?"

He was right. The moment she freaked, she'd roared out of this creepy chamber in a silly, schoolgirl panic. It still kind of lingered, her scream lodged down deep in her throat. A damned light would've been nice. Why hadn't Jude thought to bring a lantern? Oh, wait. Prophet's rules. No modern conveniences, or something just as stupid.

She had a feeling Jude had no plan after he found his daughter, likely because it had taken months to accomplish that single goal. Not good. He'd been too careful, not that he had much choice. This cult ruled with fear and that damned discipline board, but too much caution could get a man killed. Maybe Judith too.

He grasped her hand and together, they edged forward. "Now, don't scream," he said firmly.

"I'm not going to scream," she retorted, but then chuckled. "I already did that."

"I found one," he said quietly.

At the same moment, her probing toes, which she'd safely secured inside her boots again, made contact with something solid. "Me, too," she said, cringing as she tapped the body with the tip of her boot. "Feels like an arm and, there it is. A skull. Wow. There are quite a few dead people down here."

"It could be an ancient Indian burial ground," he offered.

"Underneath Cain's silo? I don't hardly think so."

"You're right. If he's involved, these people were murdered."

"I don't think they've been dead that long. The bones I felt earlier weren't all dried up. Only the skulls were. I think." Not wanting to step too far from the safety of the tunnel exit, Cassidy turned toward the way they'd come. "This place gives me the creeps."

"Then let's go back."

"I can't. Not yet. I have to take something back with me."

"You what?" he asked sharply. "Like a souvenir?"

Cassidy wished she could see Jude's face. He sounded shocked.

"Sorry, but I need a small forensic sample," she explained. "It's evidence, and it'll help with body identification and a conviction."

"Index finger okay?" he asked from somewhere near her feet. How cavalier. He meant to get that sample for her.

"Yes. Perfect." She tore a piece from the hem of her dress in preparation for the finger, and waved it in the direction he was kneeling. "Here's something to wrap it in."

Snap. Jude grunted, then took the cloth. Another snap and the sound of sawing met her ears.

"Do you have a knife?" That would have been good to know earlier.

"Of course." At last, he stood. "You don't think I'd chew a finger off one of these bodies, do you?"

"Did you get one?"

"Got two, just in case. Is there anything else you need while I'm down here?"

"No, thanks. That's good."

"Go on then. I'll give them to you when we're out of here."

This time Cassidy knew exactly where the exit was. The stair joists, too. "That's a lot of dead people in there," she said, her butt back on the steps. "Did you notice they're not all decayed?"

"They smelled plenty decayed to me. When you're ready to leave, your evidence is right here. Top step," Jude tapped where he meant.

"Thanks again," she murmured. "It's a different dead smell. Think about it. The ones I touched were just lying there. Nobody was bloated, gooey or—"

"Okay. You can stop now. I get the picture."

"You understand what I'm asking though, right? Decaying bodies reek and fall apart. These don't smell, and they're not squishy."

"Maybe Cain's trying to make mummies."

"Embalming would keep the odor and decay down."

"It would also keep the bugs away. Nobody would ask questions."

She shivered at all that creepiness just down the tunnel from where she'd napped. "I really need my cell phone, but Greg has it."

"Well, then that's out, isn't it?" Jude asked. "They're looking for you. It's only a matter of time before they check down here."

She blew out a deep breath, rubbing the knot on the back of her head in reminder of her last encounter with Cain and his buddies. "If they're so smart, why don't they already know you're down here with me?"

"I guess they aren't watching me right now."

"Why not?"

"Because. I needed a distraction to get you out of the barn, so I started a fire. Long story short, when I went back to help put it out, Cain thought I was some kind of hero."

"He didn't know you started it?"

"Guess not. All of a sudden, I'm good enough for everyone to associate with. Crazy damned church."

She heard an undertone to his answer that she couldn't identify, but it had to wait. She had a plan, and it needed immediate execution. "You need to leave, Jude. Unlatch the door and go back to your dormitory, or wherever you sleep, while I—"

"No. I will not leave you again. No way. Whatever you've got planned, count me in."

She heard the steel in his voice. "Okay, then. We go together, but once I hit the compound wall, you need to get back here, find your daughter, and stay out of trouble until I get back."

"There's a trail behind the willows we can use. It runs along the wall. It's safe."

"Are you sure?" This wasn't a time for heroics. She had to know he wouldn't do anything foolish until she returned with reinforcements.

Out of the dark, his hands reached for her and she found herself tucked under his chin. His next words cut her to the quick. "I promise, Cassidy. I promise with all my heart."

"Ready?"

Cassidy's answer beside him was a quick and definite "yes."

Whoosh. The cool night dropped into the root cellar when he lifted the door, bringing silvery moonlight with it. But sunrise was close. Jude needed to get Cassidy to safety before she lost her only chance to bring help.

Standing beside him, she took a deep breath while he held the door above his head with one hand. He flinched when her palm skimmed his ribcage for support. A feminine touch wasn't what he needed on a daring night like this. As if his nerves weren't already strung tight—just the close proximity of this woman elicited immediate masculine reactions, some he wasn't exactly proud of.

This touch felt more intimate, as if she knew him and his body better than she did. It was done in innocence, but he liked it. A lot. He just couldn't concentrate. She hadn't even handled him like he wished she had, and he'd turned into a fifteen-year-old boy with raging hormones and a flag at half-staff. Make that full-staff.

He forced his mind to concentrate. With the limited viewing at ground level, the way appeared clear, but something felt amiss. Why weren't the prowling Elite making rounds like they usually did? Jude expected more surveillance now that Cassidy had escaped. Where was it?

"Anything?" she asked.

"No," Jude whispered back, fighting the acid unease in his gut. "Something's wrong. I don't like it. Maybe they're waiting us out."

"Let me see." She brushed against him, straining her neck to peer into the yard.

Looking down, he blinked twice. The sight of her so close to his side stopped his brain in its tracks. Moonlight turned her hair silver. Excitement danced in her sharp eyes as she scanned the yard while her hand rested comfortably on his left pectoral muscle. Tingling warmth radiated from those slender fingertips all the way to his groin.

She glanced up at him, a shy smile in her eyes. "It's nice to finally see you, Mr. Cannon."

"Yes, ma'am," he mumbled. "Good to, umm, see you, too." *Man, is it ever good to see you. You're beautiful.*

Cassidy scanned the yard again. "You're right, though. It's awful quiet. I wonder where that creep Greg is."

Jude was ready to tell her to stand back so he could think with his brain, when he thought of a diversion, this one not as dramatic as the inferno he'd started earlier. "Listen. I'll be right back. Step back inside so I can close the door."

He didn't wait for her concurrence as he lifted the door to clear the cellar. Closing her in ensured her safety but mostly, he needed her out of sight so he could concentrate. Strolling over to the trough at the corner of the garden, he cranked the pump handle just enough to cup a splash of water in his hands. Pushing the coolness of it over his face and into his hair helped clear his mind. He needed help again, this time from some of the livestock.

Jude glanced at the dormitories as he made his way past them, sure to keep to the shadows of the windbreak of poplars between the yard and the buildings. There were three, each nothing more than remodeled one-story barns. In the center stood the couples' dorm, where the obedient husbands and wives were allowed to live together. The one to the north housed single woman, single men resided in the dorm to the south. Jude lived there now, in a cell-like room with nothing more than a narrow bunk bed and a metal footlocker to his name. He'd worked long hours in the field to earn the right to sleep indoors.

Several dozen cabin-type homes lined the outer perimeter. Only the Elite and the wealthier converts lived there. All children were kept separate in the schoolhouse dorm where the teachers lived. That building lay a good distance to the south of the others close to the prophet's home. The predator.

Jude stared at Cain's home. Why were all the lower level lights on? Electrical lights, not the propane or kerosene lighting everyone else endured. What was so important that it kept Cain up until all hours?

Despite the commandment that unmarried men and women were not to mingle in private, Cain was seldom alone. Jude had taken enough rambling midnight walks in his quest to locate Judith to know that Jerusha visited Lucien regularly. Other women, too.

In the last month, an army of teenage boys had been tasked to clear the meadow east of the prophet's home for a temple. He'd already bequeathed the proposed monument with a pretentious name—*Sanctuary*. Another lie. The cult had nothing to do with worship or holiness. Certainly not refuge from any personal storm. If anything, the Church of the Palma Christi was the storm. Jude couldn't help but wonder if Cain's perversion had turned to young men. Or had they always been on his menu, and Jude had been so consumed with finding Judith that he'd not thought of the others in Cain's reach?

Only one place was worse. The place of the blessing, the cult's tent in the grove of scraggly pines and pinions where the so-called 'man of god' *blessed* young women. Jude tamped his father's rage down to manageable. There would be no such blessing for Judith.

Stopping in the garden, Jude pulled a few turnips for his next trick. Time for another show. Cain kept more than fifty pigs, all in ramshackle wooden pens known to buckle or break when one of the bigger boars used enough muscle. It didn't happen often, but it was going to happen tonight.

Soft grunts met his approach. Lobbing the turnips into the middle of the herd of bristling pork ribs on hooves caused the stir Jude wanted. Next he eased a loose upright support up and out of its hole enough that it sagged. He loosened two more uprights and the hungry pigs took over. Once they were happily rooting around in the garden, Jude high tailed it back to the cellar and slid down the stairs to Cassidy.

"Come on. Let's move." He pushed the cellar door open wider, still watching the living quarters for any sign of increased activity. A light flickered on in the closest private home. Jerusha was up. Time to hurry.

He blocked the view of Cassidy's departure with his body. Only after she was safely north of the granary and out of sight, did he lower the door into place. Time to run.

Grabbing her hand, he pulled her into a jog through the orchard. The pigs would find this wonderland of littered green apples soon enough. At the other side of the orchard, Jude paused to listen. Pigs squealed behind him. Men shouted. *Good job, Cannon.*

"I think we're safe," he muttered quietly.

"Which way?"

He pointed west. To the wall.

She turned without hesitation, and before he knew it, he was telling her which landmarks and trails to take while he stayed close behind. Until they'd stepped out of the root cellar, he hadn't realized how bossy she was. She actually led the way, and like a gentleman, he let her. He didn't mind. It gave him a pleasant view of her backside swaying beneath that ratty old dress. She wasn't a tall woman by any means, but she was athletic.

Neither said a word for several miles, but finally, he couldn't take it. "Hold up," he said, knowing she'd turn around. He got what he asked for. The minute she pivoted, he saw the spark of impatience in her eyes. It mellowed into something else he couldn't identify, or maybe, he didn't want to admit to. Or believe. Not yet.

He'd been so focused on his ruined marriage and then his missing child that he'd ignored women in general. Standing in the ambient light of the moon, her blonde hair tousled and framing her face, his heart stuttered to a thumping halt. There would be no ignoring this goddess at the edge of the trees.

"Your mouth is open," she said shyly.

He couldn't help it. His heart felt wide open, too, like a fool who should be kneeling, maybe even groveling to this petite woman who'd already changed his world. "Cassidy."

"Yes?" She took a step back toward him.

Recovering some semblance of brainpower, he could only nod in reply.

"We don't have a lot of time," she said. "What did you want?"

He knew exactly what he wanted. With two steps, he was at her side. Dark eyes smiled up at him. She reached one hand to brush her fingers through his sideburn while her other hand rested on his shoulder. "You okay?" she asked. "Am I going the right way?"

Oh, honey. Are you ever going the right way. He caressed her cheek, speechless on a night finally filled with hope.

"Remember your promise?" she asked, her fingers working magic through the scalp around his ear. It tickled in a most erotic way. She had him in the palm of her hand.

"Uh-huh."

"You and me are going to get to know each other?" she prompted.

"Right. I knew that," he said quickly. Really. He did.

She stepped into his arms and waited, her eyes bright with promise. Hesitantly, he lowered his head to hers, searching for any hint of rejection. Their kiss in the cellar had been a delightful surprise he hadn't seen coming. This one, he wanted to watch unfold.

She lifted her chin with her tongue skating over her lower lip, and that was his undoing. Dipping lower, he saw the moment she closed her eyes and lifted her mouth. When his lips touched hers, she sighed a breathy, feminine sigh. Framed in a tangle of curls, he watched the sigh blossom on her face. The delicate arches of her brows lifted. Every muscle on her face seemed to follow suit.

It might have only been a trick of the moon's lighting, but a more radiant being he'd never held before. Her eyelashes settled like tiny angel wings over her cheeks, the crinkles at the corners of her eyes turned up. Soft lips melted against his. The ache in his heart exploded. He didn't even know this woman, yet she'd reached a place deep inside of him that hadn't been alive in years, a place where he wasn't a failure or a coward, a place where he was very much still a man to be reckoned with. She pulled him closer, and he wanted every last piece of her.

Unfortunately, logic re-engaged. *Stick to your promise, Cannon.*

He eased back, breaking the luscious contact between heaven and earth. This wasn't about him. Only Judith. With another sigh, Cassidy nestled under his chin, and he held her to him, kissing the top of her head.

"I want to stay with you," she whispered as she pushed away from him, "but I have to leave."

He nodded quickly, summoning courage he didn't feel. With the proverbial stiff upper lip, he could only say, "Right. Let's do this."

They made it to the wall in record time. They had to, or he would've changed his mind. His protective instincts had risen to the surface the closer it came to her leaving. There'd be no way to help Cassidy once she left his side, and it galled him that she'd soon leave him behind. How could he let her go and keep her safe at the same time?

"We're here. Boost me up," she commanded, her eyes aglitter in the darkness.

He went to one knee, interlocked his fingers, and made a step for her to slide her boot into.

"Wait." She stopped short. With a determined gleam in her eye, she pulled the dress up to her knee, and his heart stopped. His mouth dropped open again. Damn. He had little restraint left.

One look at her naked body under the moonlight, and they wouldn't accomplish what they'd set out to do. Thank heavens. She'd only ripped the lower part of her long dress and transformed it into a really mini, umm, thing. She had long legs. Strong calves, too. He took a half-step back to take in the luscious view. This woman was an athlete from head to toe. A sexy athlete.

"Oh, hell," she muttered, as she looked up at him, a crooked smile on her lips. "I ripped it too short, huh?"

He tilted backward to admire the shorter-than-short minidress, her black bra beneath it and white cotton bloomers showing at her new hemline. Her tangled bangs hung into her eyes. What little blood might have been in his brain migrated lower. "Cassidy," he growled. "Not now."

She grinned and threw herself in his arms, damned near bowling him. Ahh! This woman drove him crazy. Him—a boring, mild-mannered accountant. He couldn't remember being this desired or overheated before. This virile. The blood in his veins burned in a really good way. He wanted her, every last tantalizing part of her. Now. Of all times.

Cassidy pushed herself into his face again. Jude couldn't stop the kisses raining over his mouth, cheeks, and chin. Didn't want to. Her mouth on his sparked playful desires. Holding her was like holding a puppy and a little girl at the same time, all wiggles and kisses, filled with a contagious zest for life. Every atom in his body ached to lay her on the ground and make love to her.

But he couldn't. Jude set Cassidy's feet to earth. The moment she stepped out of his arms, she took her energy with her. His heart dropped. An odd ache sprang up within; a nagging hunger mixed with the fear he could lose her before he ever had her.

"Okay now," she whispered softly, "when I come back tomorrow, be ready. I'll be bringing some heavy firepower with me."

He stood there, dazed. She'd turned from a tempting vixen into his warrior goddess in the blink of an eye. "Tomorrow? You mean today, right?"

"Yes. Sorry. It's already tomorrow." She glanced over her shoulder at the eight-foot high concrete block wall. "Get Judith to a safe place. Don't worry about me. I'll find you."

Jude brushed an anxious hand through his hair. This seemed backwards. He should be the one saving her, not the other way around. He should be the knight in shining armor wielding all that firepower, not her, a diminutive lady with grit in her eye. In a way, this whole mixed up thing made him the princess, and it galled him. He might not be the bravest guy on the planet, but he was damned sure not a princess.

"Jude." She latched onto the side of his head and pulled his face to her level. "Stop thinking so hard. I will find you."

All he saw were sparkling brown eyes, an upturned nose, and the most gorgeous woman in the world. He forgot his stupid, egotistical rant. "Where should we wait?"

A crooked smile tweaked her sassy lips. "How about in the barn? They'll never look for you and Judith there."

"Okay," he whispered, as he kissed her mouth, wanting with all his heart to savor the taste of this gentle creature for more than just seconds at a time. Eternity wouldn't be enough for the famished man he'd become over the years. Breathing hard, he disengaged. "We'll be waiting for you."

He crouched and clasped his hands, forming a launch pad for her boot. With hardly any effort at all, he boosted her high enough that she could grip the edge of the wall. Even with her so far above, all he noticed was her backside. His index finger automatically stabbed his glasses up high on his nose for a better view. With her hiking boots kicking for contact while she climbed the wall, and her white bloomers waving goodbye, it was a sweet sight on such a tenuous night. It dawned on him then. She was ten times the athlete he was. Doubt assailed him. *What in God's name does she see in me?*

"Tomorrow," she whispered from her perch high above him. "I *will* be back."

"Tomorrow," he echoed, hopeful yet achingly depressed at the same time. "I'll be waiting."

Cassidy dropped out of sight, just as gone as Judith.

Chapter Nine

Cassidy made quick time. Once she had her bearings, she bee-lined for the camp she and Rourke had established days earlier. Jude's kiss burned pleasantly into her lips as well as her mind. She rubbed her chin where his stubble had left a tingle. *Ah, the feel of a good man.*

Early morning light glimmered faintly on the horizon. With every step she took, her determination increased. Even knowing she still had to face Rourke's ire didn't flag her resolve. Jude needed help, and he was going to get it.

Mentally calculating how many magazines she could carry, which automatic rifle she should pack, and how many hand grenades she could stuff into the pockets of a clean pair of cargo pants, she prepared for a frontal assault on the cult. Before the day was through, Cain and his despot buddies would lay in smoking ruins. This wasn't the first fight she'd been in, and it wouldn't be the last, but it would be memorable.

Alex Stewart's ice blue eyes flashed to her mind in the middle of her mental rant. Training caught up with her out of control need for revenge. Her plan evaporated. It lacked finesse and strategy. A frontal assault was foolish. Not only would it be costly in lives and firepower, but it was wrong. Illegal. Immoral. She sighed. *Damn it.*

It was hard not to get carried away in the face of Cain's depravity, but she worked for Alex. Revenge might be sweet, but this operation had to be handled correctly and with honor. She couldn't impugn his name anymore than the agents she worked with.

No allegations must linger when this operation was done. No doubt. The sterling reputation of The TEAM couldn't be dragged through the mud for her self-serving vendetta. Not only would Alex not approve of revenge tactics, but that wasn't why he'd hired her in the first place. She wasn't a bounty hunter or a mercenary. She was better than that. Most of the time. But sometimes she just wanted to kick ass and get the job done.

Unwilling to let the image of Cain's smoking carcass go, Cassidy kicked at a rock. The feel of Jude's strong arms around her evoked an image of his grumpy face, and *poof!* Cain was gone. Jude won the contest, hands down.

The man didn't smile, even after she'd kissed him back there at the wall, and she knew why. He was focused on his daughter, and because he was, Cassidy was, too.

Not one to wallow in self-pity or worry about bumps and bruises, she lengthened her stride. She'd promised she would be packing some serious firepower when she returned, and she'd meant it. She might not go in hot, but she was definitely going back, and she would take Rourke with her. Speaking of which, where was he?

The prickly sensation that she was being watched dropped to one knee behind the scrub oak at the edge of camp. Cautiously, she peered through the leafy branches. Nothing seemed to be out of place. Both black TEAM vans were still parked where she'd left them. The utility trailer that stored the generator and supplies as well as weaponry and ammo was still attached to the one van.

Her sixth sense pinged on higher alert. The hair on the back of her neck stood up. Someone had her in their scope, and—

A gun barrel pressed hard into the back of her skull.

Shit. They followed me. Cassidy sucked in a deep breath and lifted her hands, prepared to kick the legs out from under whoever stood behind her if she got the chance.

"Where the hell have you been?"

She dropped her hands and whirled on her agent-in-charge instead. "Rourke?"

Oh, great. He'd ambushed her with nothing more than the end of his scope, his rifle still strapped over his shoulder. She huffed a sigh of relief, never so happy to see the big guy who had her back when the smoke cleared.

"Hey," she offered meekly as she jumped to her feet.

No smile welcomed her return. His brows furrowed into a dark *V*. Those twinkling hazel brown lasers skated down her scantily clothed body and up again. He never cracked the briefest hint of relief. Not good. "Answer me. Where the hell have you been, Butch?"

For one brief nano-second, embarrassment at her flimsy attire flooded her mind. Her insubordination, too, but mostly her flimsy get up. Rourke had never seen so much of her as he was seeing then. "I've been inside the—"

"You did exactly what I told you not to do, didn't you?"

She cringed, hating the ice in his tone. Still, she wasn't going to take it. She'd done what was right, like it or not. "Yes, I did. I—"

"And how'd that work out for you?" He reached two fingers to the scrape on her forehead, the one she'd received when Greg had rammed her face under water. But instead of smoothing over the wound like she'd expected, he snapped his fingernail into it, like it was a marble he meant to shoot to the moon. It stung, damn it.

"Ouch! Knock it off!" Now her dander was up, and Rourke could take a flying leap. "I got inside, which is more than you did," she countered, taking a step back and out of his reach. "Plus I got good intel. Now I know exactly—"

"You don't know shit. You disobeyed a direct order!"

She blinked and took another step backward, but only because he'd taken a threatening step closer. He was fast reaching the end of her good humor.

"We're a team!" He stowed the scope in the gear bag on his belt. "Team members don't take off on a wild goose chase. They don't move out until everyone's geared up and ready to march. They sure as hell don't leave their partner behind. Damn it, Dancer, I'm senior agent and you ain't squat, you got that?"

Cassidy squared her shoulders. Right now he wanted to hear 'Yes, sir,' like she was a meek little lamb or something. *Well, how's it feel to want?*

"I made two contacts," she spat back at him, even as a quiver of regret shivered over her shoulders for betraying his trust. "Not all of Cain's followers are—"

"What? You march down there in the middle of the night, and the first person you run into tells you exactly what you want to hear? You ever think maybe that person is as big a fool as you are? Maybe he's lying so he can get something from you? What'd you tell 'em, anyway?"

She rubbed the knot on the back of her head and gulped. How could she admit that she'd told Jude everything?

Rourke's eyes zeroed in on the burn on her chin. "Are you hurt?"

"No," she answered quickly.

"Yes. She is."

Alex? Cassidy whirled again, embarrassed she hadn't heard his approach any better than Rourke's. Two fatal errors in less than a few minutes, and one of them was the man she respected a whole lot more than Agent O'Neill. She was a dead man; make that a dead woman, standing.

"I'm not hurt," she insisted.

Alex walked straight to her side. "Yes, you are."

"I knew you were in deep the minute I heard Cain in my earpiece." Rourke's tone had softened.

Oh, hell. Not that. Cassidy couldn't deal with him using that tender touch on her. "I overreacted. I made a mistake. I heard Cain and his whore discussing Melissa." She stuck her palms to her hips, determined not to apologize anymore than she had to. "Did you know there are two Melissas in that stupid cult? They're both widows, and they're both blonde? Cain and Jerusha were planning to do something to one of them. She refused to turn over all of her assets. I thought she was Melissa McCormack. You tell me. What was I to do?"

He nodded as if he agreed and understood, damn him. Rourke could play her like a harp with those gentling skills he had. Angry one minute, kind the next. His eyes turned liquid, and Cassidy felt her leg bones melting. If he said anything nice, anything at all, she'd turn into a puddle at his feet.

"I get it. You mistook the wrong Melissa for Jed's daughter-in-law. Easy mistake for a novice operator. Go on."

She really wanted to argue with that novice operator crack, but she simply could. Not. Think. Not stuck there between two alpha males with eyes like eagles.

"You're right." *Damn. Did I just say that?* Must have. The confession just kept rolling over her tongue and off her lips. "I should've coordinated with you before I made my move. I'm sorry. It won't happen again."

Rourke winked as if he knew precisely how to coax compliance out of her. Sheesh. Maybe he did.

"You've got blood in your hair," Alex informed her like she didn't already know that. "And your forehead's black and blue."

Rourke took another appraising gander over her skimpy get-up. There she stood, dressed in nothing more than a thigh-high piece of see-through nothing, someone else's bloomers and hiking boots, and two handsome men were checking her out. Could a tough gal be more humiliated?

Alex cupped her shoulder. That gesture of camaraderie was bad enough, but his next words pushed her over the edge. "Did Cain hurt you?"

She stared at him, blinking like a bunny rabbit with its head in a wire loop. The thing about Alex was he could spot a lie in a heartbeat, and her heart was beating plenty. But this wasn't the way she'd planned on returning to camp—not as a weak female who couldn't handle herself under pressure. Unfortunately, someone forgot to tell her big mouth that.

"Yes," she answered quietly.

"What'd he do to you?" Alex's voice hardened.

"Nothing," Cassidy looked away, blinking tears she wouldn't let fall. Staring into the scrub oak gave her the reprieve she needed.

Alex didn't press. Instead, his hand stayed where it was while he spoke to Rourke. He only said one word. "Tonight."

"Yes, Boss," Rourke affirmed.

But Cassidy wasn't smart enough to know when to keep her big mouth shut. "Tonight's too late."

"No," Alex said sternly. "Tonight is soon enough. It gives us time to prepare."

"No, Boss." She held her ground. "It isn't. We've got to move now. I've got two contacts inside who—"

"Whom you put in danger because you acted without backup or forethought," Rourke bellowed. His gaze hardened. "Isn't that right, *junior agent?*"

Damn. Why'd he pull that condescending *junior agent* card? It made her sound like a wannabe. "They both helped me," she growled back at him. "I won't let them risk their lives just because I—"

"You'll do what you're told." Rourke's retort cut her off quick and neat at the knees. His order had the desired effect, and she hated it because he was right. Alex owned the ammo and weaponry she needed to rescue Jude. She couldn't go in alone—not this time. She needed to be well armed. A couple ex-military snipers at her back would be nice, and, oh, by the way, she had yet to come up with a good plan. Everything hung in the balance.

The enormity of all she stood to lose sneaked up on her. She'd left Jude behind. Judith was going to be blessed. And Cain had her SIG. She still had to confess that major blunder. Good operators didn't lose their weapons. Her fists clenched and unclenched at her side. Quitting wasn't an option. Anger or tears? Wait or charge straight into danger?

Alex diffused the standoff. "Go take a shower, Cassidy."

She glanced at him, not willing to back down.

"Clean clothes wouldn't hurt." He pulled her gently in step beside him, forcing compliance. "Where'd you get that get-up?"

"From the man who helped me escape."

"What's his name?"

"Jude Cannon. He finally found his daughter, Judith. She's supposed to be blessed and—" The thought of sweet Judith forced to submit to a pig like Cain took the compliance right out of Cassidy. Her backbone stiffened. She stopped walking like a docile lamb to the shower and twisted out of Alex's grip. "I can't."

Marching to the nearest van, she flung the rear door open. She had a job to do and she'd made a promise. End of story. Her gear bag was right where she'd left it, complete with several changes of clothing, her spare pistol, and a few loaded magazines. Grabbing her towel, shower kit, and a clean bundle of clothes, she slammed the door and faced her very worthy adversaries.

"After I shower, I'm going back to Jude like I promised," she announced with all the willfulness she could muster. "I've got a fourteen-year-old girl to save from rape, and there isn't a damn thing either of you can do to stop me. Sit here in camp and do nothing. Play it safe. I don't care, but I'm going. Get out of my way."

The déjà vu of the moment didn't escape her. The words she'd just uttered sounded exactly like what she'd told her DEA superior the day he'd refused to step up and assist innocent people at risk from the infamous Sonoran drug cartel in Utah. That was why she'd quit in the middle of what had turned out to be a damned bloody op that took her into

Sonora Mexico, and almost got Mark Houston and junior agent Rory Dennison killed. The DEA's failure to act created the mess Alex had assumed responsibility for. Why couldn't he see that this was the exact same thing?

Rourke stood with his arms locked over his chest, his lips pursed and a closed-minded set to his jaw. Alex, on the other hand, had a scant smile on his smug face. "You're right, junior agent. You got a plan?"

She faltered. When he said junior agent, it held no sting or rebuke. It meant something. He trusted her. But she had no plan other than to blow Cain off the face of the earth, his Elite along with him. Greg and Hank for sure. She bit her lip in remorse for not being as good as her boss thought she was. *Damn it, Alex. How do you do this to me?*

He must've read her mind. "While you're showering, Rourke and I will start breakfast. Then we'll bring you up to speed."

"Up to speed?"

"Go." Alex shooed her off toward the makeshift canvas shower stall that Rourke had rigged up beside one of the vans. "Shower first. Then eat. Collaborate later."

Cassidy nodded obediently. Alex wasn't anything like her old supervisor. He wasn't the DEA. He might be a gruff cuss, but he cared.

Chapter Ten

"Well. Well. Well."

Cain stalked at the gaping mouth of the open root cellar. He'd called an early meeting, and all in the north compound were commanded to attend. Everyone stood, wondering what their prophet wanted. The chickens hadn't been fed. The pigs were hungry, despite the fact that they'd had a midnight snack. Not even morning prayers had been offered yet, which the congregation did en masse before breakfast, want to or not.

"It seems we've had an intruder," Cain announced. "A spy and an interloper—one who would tear this noble congregation apart from within."

Jude kept his head down, fearful Cain might be able to read minds like he claimed. Jude had made it back to the compound without notice, but he had yet to sleep. Once he helped round up the last of the squealing pigs, he'd offered to repair the fence. After all, he was the golden boy at the moment. Besides, he needed something to keep his mind off Cassidy. With no way to contact her, he had only faith and her promise to count on.

In the light of day, trusting a woman he didn't really know seemed like one of his dumber decisions. He'd heard promises before, but the cold, hard truth was that he'd saved her life instead of Judith's and wasted valuable time in the process. What if he never saw Cassidy again? What if she didn't come back? Desperate people lied. He wouldn't blame her, but what if he'd risked everything for nothing?

"There stands in the heart of this humble flock, a liar, a person who is not who we thought he or she was."

A murmur rolled through the gathering. Sunbonnets bobbed. Men and women clucked to each other as that news settled. Jude shifted his weight from one foot to the other, anxious to see how this meeting would evolve. He'd witnessed Cain's gatherings before. This was retribution time. Anyone who could offer evidence of another's guilt would be rewarded. The guilty would be punished swiftly, thoroughly, and without due process.

Hysteria ruled, and mob opinion was the wildfire that fed it. Anything could happen. Like all those bones lying in the tunnel below the silo. Maybe there was one more degree of hell in this sickening cult. *Death*. It made sense. The Elite were capable. Even now Hank and Greg stood beside Cain, waiting for someone to crack.

"It's time to step forward. Come. Confess your sins." Cain's sharp eyes surveyed his followers. A few members nearest to him shuffled uncomfortably. Others glanced at their neighbors. The woman behind Jude began whispering the Lord's Prayer. She got as far as, *'hallowed be thy name,'* when Cain got to the point.

"I want to know who aided and abetted the escape of the woman in the barn yesterday," he bellowed, pointing to his left as if nobody knew where the barn was. "She didn't get out of there on her own two feet!"

People gasped. Hank and Greg snapped to stiffer attention. Cain's sharp eyes coursed over the flock before him, glaring at some, sneering at others. But no one stepped forward to confess.

Jude held his breath and watched the drama unfold.

"I know what I'm asking is a hard thing. Only a true believer would have the courage of true faith to admit his weakness for the flesh." Cain's voice turned to conniving silk. "But if no one will confess, justice must still be served." With his long, steepled fingers to his lips, he closed his eyes and turned to Hank. "How hot is it supposed to be today?"

"Hot, Prophet Cain. Maybe one hundred degrees." Hank sneered at the congregation, his eyes full of contempt. "Maybe hotter than hell."

Cain nodded, his eyes still closed. A man could almost believe he was in communication with the powers of heaven, if not for the arrogant tilt of his head and the twitch of his nose. When he lifted his head and opened his eyes, Jude saw the wolf in sheep's clothing. There was no other way to describe him. Cain's gray-blue eyes darkened. His brows spiked. The so-called loving prophet had turned into an alpha predator with no need for the flock at his feet other than to eat them alive.

"The Lord hates a liar and a coward," he declared in the singsong voice he utilized best when preaching.

"Yes, Prophet Cain," the nervous congregation chanted. "The Lord hates a liar and a coward."

God. Make him stop. In a moment, Cain would single out one of the innocents for abuse until the guilty caved in and confessed.

"And what is the punishment for a liar and a coward?" Cain railed.

"Liars and cowards must burn in hellfire," the people chanted woodenly, their focus on the ground, the same as Jude's. No one dared look at their fierce leader, not now when he could strike them dead.

Jude gritted his teeth. This was his fault. Cassidy needed to escape, and he'd needed to make sure she was safe. But now...

"A liar is not a friend of the church!" Cain roared.

"A liar is not a friend of the church," the crowd repeated mechanically.

Jude bit the inside of his lip. Cain used psychological warfare to its fullest. Pretty soon, his tactics would work. Someone would bolt from the pressure. A woman might cry. Or faint.

Jude weighed his options. Step forward or wait. Confess or procrastinate. Hope against hope.

"No one shall be allowed to live who seeks to destroy this church," Cain shouted, the veins on his neck visible in his self-righteous rage.

"No one shall be allowed to live who seeks to destroy this church," the flock echoed.

Jude peered through his brows at the monster posed in front of these weak-kneed souls. Cain stood enraged before them, his finger pointed heavenward as if commanding the universe. *God, how pathetic.*

"Jerusha!"

Like a trained dog, she elbowed her way through the crowd, her chin stuck forward with the same self-righteous tilt as his.

He prowled in front of his masses. "From this day forward, one willing soul will be confined to the pig trough each day the liar does not come forth."

Willing soul? Pig trough? Jude groaned. No, no, no.

Jerusha took her place at Cain's side, scanning the cowering crowd through hooded eyes, her lips pinched tight and thin, as if determined to detect the liar for her prophet. Her gaze skated over Jude. Probably out of habit.

"But I will yet be lenient." Cain's finger again pointed heavenward. "After all, I am the father of this wayward church. I understand the difficult thing I have set before you. Because my heart has been sorely tried with this outrageous lie, there shall be no blood sacrifice. The trough will be moved to the middle of the yard."

The pretense at leniency galled Jude. Moving the trough might keep that poor soul from being mauled to death by hungry pigs with razor-sharp teeth, but they'd still bake in the sun while everyone else was forced to stand and watch.

Cain turned to Jerusha. He snapped his fingers and pointed to a spot on the ground next to him. "Kneel."

She dropped to his feet, her hands clasped as if in prayer and her face turned upward, still waiting on her lord and master.

"A name!" he demanded.

"Sister Priscilla!" she exclaimed with fervor.

"No!" a woman cried from the back of the congregation. "God! No! Not my Priscilla."

"Yes, God, yes," Cain hissed. With another snap of his fingers, he pointed to the ground at his other side. "Sister Priscilla. Come to me. Now."

Hank and Greg barged through the congregation and dragged an ashen-faced teenager with streaming black hair forward. She might as well have been Judith. Poor Priscilla stood trembling as she faced Cain, her body shaking hard enough that the entire congregation could see.

"Kneel!"

Priscilla dropped to her knees, her face as white as a ghost. "Y-y-yes, P-prophet Cain."

"You shall be the first," he declared, his eyes skimming back and forth across the crowd. "Do you understand how great an honor this is?"

"N-n-no," she cried, her eyes squeezed tight, and tears coursing down her cheeks.

No, Jude's heart cried. *Don't do this.*

"But it is," Cain rattled on. "You do believe in your holy prophet, don't you?"

"Y-y-yes, Prophet Cain," she sobbed, her hands gripping her skirt at her side.

Leave her alone!

"Do you know the reward of a liar?" Cain bellowed.

She sank face first into the dirt, her bonnet pushed back and her poor body quaking.

"No!" her poor mother screamed again. Greg and Hank had hold of her, barring her from reaching her daughter.

Cain's evil eye coursed the congregation again, cowing some, weakening others, but enraging Jude. He'd never owned a gun. Never needed one. But he wished for one now. Somebody needed to do something.

"Now that we have our willing sacrifice, maybe we'll get to the truth. I offer the liar amongst us one last chance. Who made it possible for the spy to escape? Whoever you are, I command you. Sinner. Come forth. Do what the Lord wants you to do and confess."

Jude's heart pounded in his chest with what he was about to do. He couldn't take it. Too many innocents had suffered. He looked at Judith. She stood looking at him from the edge of the crowd, tears streaming down her face, shaking her head, her lips forming, *No*. It was as if she'd read his mind.

He offered her one short nod. *Yes. I must.* The fear that she might beat him to it propelled his feet. With a sideways glance at his namesake, his baby, and his reason for living, Jude sucked up a deep breath, stiffened his spine, and lifted his hand. "I—"

"I did it!" Tucker yelled as he elbowed Jude out of his way. "I rescued the woman you guys hid in the barn. I saved her so you wouldn't hurt her, and I can prove it."

Jude gasped, his eyes riveted to the back of Tucker's head. *What? No. I did it.*

"I cut her off the board you guys strapped her to," Tucker declared. "I set her free, and I hid her in the root cellar, right under your noses. I started the fire, too, you dumbasses."

No, Jude groaned. *Don't do this.*

Tucker stopped at the front of the crowd, the brim of his ball cap squeezed tight in his hand, and his face blanched white. "And I'd do it again rather than let you guys burn her, bleed her, or brand her. The Lord doesn't want his children hurting each other like that. Y'all oughta be ashamed of yourselves, damn you."

Hank and Greg freed Priscilla's mother and jumped on Tucker. With his arms twisted behind his back, they dragged him forward. Hank landed a kidney punch, forcing Tucker to his hands and knees. The wily prophet's lip curled as he leaned over, his hand on Tucker's heaving shoulder, almost a paternal thump of approval. Almost.

But Jude caught the nearly imperceptible nod from Tucker to Priscilla and her tearful blink of thanks. Miracles did happen. While the noble Elite did nothing, one of the lowly *Censured* had just offered the noblest act any person could do for another. Tucker had laid down his life.

"Brother Tucker Chase," wily Cain purred. "One of my very best converts. I'm not surprised that it was you."

Jude's ears perked up. Cain sounded sincere, except for the ice in his gaze. Darkness shadowed his countenance. Jude shuddered, sure he'd witness Tucker's assassination on the spot.

Priscilla ran into her mother's open arms, disobeying the cult-mandated separation between parent and child. "Mama," she choked, and Jude had to look away. She was just a baby girl. Like Judith.

Cain faced the congregation again, his face relaxed, and a smile spread cheerfully across his face as if he'd never been upset. "Thank you, brothers and sisters. That will be all."

"No!" Jude heard his hoarse voice shout.

Cain stared at him, his brows lifted, shock replacing the smirk of his shallow victory. "Brother Clark?"

"I did it." Jude trembled at his own words. He might not be able to save his child, but he sure wasn't going to slink into history as a coward while another man died for his sin. Even with Tucker glaring at him like he was, Jude knew better. He would die a man. He owed Judith that much.

Cain offered a sickening, twisted smile. "Two is just as good as—"

"No! I am the one."

Jude's heart stopped. He recognized that third voice. He turned in panic. This wasn't what he'd intended. *God, no!*

But there she was. That defiant tilt to her head that he knew too well. The baby girl he'd chased through the green plastic alligator sprinkler in his backyard when she was afraid to get water in her eyes. The darling daughter he'd rocked for hours on end the time she caught the flu and cried all night with an earache. The child he loved with every last beat of his worthless soul. There she was, walking daintily and slowly into the lion's den.

Judith.

"I did it," she proudly announced. She didn't need to be dragged forward. Instead, she held her head high, the edge of her skirt lifted as if she were a queen instead of a fourteen-year-old in a peasant's frock. Never once did she take her eyes off the prophet.

Cain gasped. "You?"

A wave rippled through the crowd. One minute they were sheep; the next they were mothers and fathers, grandparents exclaiming, "She didn't do it! It was me! I did it!" An older man followed in Judith's path. "And I can prove it, too! Git outta my way, young one!"

"No! I did!" A middle-aged woman with long braids joined the parade, hurrying forward as if late. "I helped that poor woman escape. I saw what you guys did to her, and I'm glad I did it, and I'd do it again."

"It was us!" A man and woman stepped forward together, their hands linked. "If you need someone to blame, Prophet Cain, blame us. We'll take the punishment."

Others followed. More and more voices rang out until Cain paled. At last it was the wolf that stepped back from the flock. "No!" he roared, but by then, more than a dozen men and women stood in front of him, all claiming to have aided and abetted Cassidy's escape.

"But Prophet Cain." Judith's voice rang out like a breath from heaven. The crowd settled, and Jude was never more proud of her or more afraid for her. "I know your love for all members of your congregation is great," she said clearly and loudly, "but especially for those of us who have transgressed."

Don't do this, baby girl. You haven't transgressed. You're pure. Don't do this!

Cain stared at her as she twisted his words back on him, and Jude's heart sank.

"I stand ready, dear prophet." She glanced toward Tucker, and Jude saw the tremble of her fingers. She was scared to death, but she kept walking. "If you require a sacrifice, let it be me."

Cain mouthed a definitive *no*, but he didn't take his eyes off her.

"What say you, Prophet Cain?" Judith didn't falter. She challenged him and she did it with such poise and grace. Such finesse. Where had this courageous young woman come from? Jude was no longer sure. Was this noble creature truly his child?

The stare-down lasted a full minute. No one in the congregation breathed.

"Then come." Cain held out his hand for Judith. At the same time, he turned with an icy glare to Jerusha. "Leave my side and never return, woman," he snarled. He shot a look to Greg, and Jude caught the slight nod from Greg, the sneer from Hank. The wolf had set his jackals loose.

Frazzled, Jerusha grabbed up her skirt and made a hasty exit, glancing back at Greg while she elbowed her way into the anonymity of the crowd. Greg released Tucker to follow Jerusha.

Cain took the tips of Judith's fingers in his palm and drew her to his side as if she were his queen and he her humble servant. The prophet brought her hand to his lips. Jude shuddered when the despicable man's filthy lips kissed his daughter's clean, pure knuckles.

After the display of affection, Cain turned Judith to face the congregation, his dirty hands on her delicate shoulders. "I am pleased. This sacrifice is enough. I will make this woman my wife tonight."

You will not! Not my daughter!

Fury engulfed Jude, but Judith caught his eye. She shook her head ever so slightly, and he saw it then. She'd done this to save Priscilla, Tucker, and him. To do anything would diminish her heroic act and further endanger her life. Once again, he was the princess.

He turned from the scene, his fists clenched and his heart heavy. He couldn't bear it. Cassidy had to come back. Right damned now.

Chapter Eleven

Cassidy took one extra minute in the shower. A simple contraption, it utilized gravity along with a solar generator, a barrel of water Rourke had mounted on a wooden stand, a hose with a showerhead, and an off/on toggle switch. Canvas walls allowed for privacy, but not much more.

The cleansing process was just as simple. Turn the spigot on. Get wet. Turn the spigot off. Suds up. On. Off. On. Off.

The life of a covert operator didn't get any better. She bounced between boring time in her Seattle office to boring time in the field, interspersed with a few heart-pounding adventures.

Not one to fuss over her looks, she paid a little more attention to her reflection in the shower's mirror than she usually did. Jude's hands had been in her hair. The memory of his warm touch on her scalp still tingled. Cocking her head from one side to the other, she wondered what he'd seen that she didn't. The same plain Cassidy gazed back at her beneath spiraled, wet bangs, the kind that didn't require curling irons, blow driers or a dozen foo-foo products. Only fingers.

Her teeth were fairy straight. Her brown eyes bright at the moment, but that was because of Jude. She might not be a glam-doll, but neither was she drab like all those women in the cult with their long, lifeless ponytails hanging down their backs.

And yeah, she wasn't one of those long-legged, sleek runway-model types, either. If anything, she was the exact opposite, muscular, sturdy, maybe a little boxy. Her squared-off shoulders might not help her look feminine, but she was proud of them. Rourke had designed a decent routine for her at The TEAM's in-house gym. She liked the free-weights and she liked a good workout. Most of all, she liked kicking Rourke's butt when they wrestled and boxed together.

The canopy of pine overhead and the sounds of two men a few yards away making breakfast imbued her with a sense of peace, if only because she made a difference in this tough man's world. She'd saved people in the course of her duty, oftentimes standing between real evil and true innocence. That was why she loved her job.

Her nose twitched at the scent of bacon and eggs, but what she really wanted was coffee. By the time she was clean, dressed, and her damp hair fluffed into submission, she felt human again, a definite plus in the hardscrabble world she called the best job ever. Rounding the van, appreciation swelled for her senior agent. A tall cup of light roast rested at the end of Rourke's extended arm.

"Truce?" he asked, with an apologetic glint in his eye.

"Truce," she quickly agreed, taking a hit off the hot, black drink. "Thanks."

"Knew you'd need it, Butch. Take a load off." He nodded at the nearest campstool.

Rourke made her smile. He seemed to care about her, but looking at him now, she wondered if that moment was past. Had he missed his chance? Had she missed hers? Recalling the taste of Jude's lips in the moonlight, the answer to that rhetorical question was one huge YES.

Poor Rourke, she thought, taking her seat. *You'll never know what you missed.*

"Bacon and eggs are done." Alex slid the breakfast fare out of the cast-iron frying pan and onto a platter in the middle of the collapsible table. Rourke followed with toast he'd lightly burned over the camp stove. An open can of peaches completed the fare.

Both fit and trim, definite hunks in their own right, the sight of her boss and her senior agent waiting on her made Cassidy smile. All they needed now was a puppy or a baby in their arms, and they'd be irresistible. Almost. A certain owlish face still beckoned at the back of her mind. She needed to get moving.

"Hey." Alex intruded on her daydream. "Are you with us, Cassidy?"

"Ah, yeah." She placed her empty coffee on the edge of the table, caught red-handed.

"As I was saying…" He offered her a full plate and leveled a stern eye in her direction. "We've lost the element of surprise, but that does not equate with failure."

"I still think nighttime is preferable," Rourke said evenly. "Given the new surveillance photos—"

"Wait a minute," Cassidy cut him off as she skewered another slice of bacon. "What photos?"

Alex lifted a leather-bound folder to his knee. "Why the hell do you think you're here, Cassidy?"

She caught the sharp tone to his question. Alex might have been easy on her before, but he was not a boss to be taken lightly. And she still had a butt-chewing coming. She answered evenly. "I'm a woman, and it only makes sense that—"

"Wrong. You're here because you are the best damned ghost I've got on both seaboards. At least, I thought you were."

That sounded like praise. Almost.

"But you're too full of yourself, Dancer. You blew it because you're over-confident. You think you're always right and everyone else is always wrong." He let her have it. Over-confidence was her strong and weak point rolled into one. "You should've secured the package and retreated without detection. You're that good, and you know it. What went wrong?"

Cassidy agreed. Whether it was her size, her light touch, or some unseen quality that few others had, infiltration was her strong point. "I jumped the gun. I didn't follow orders. I..." *Damn. Eating crows sucks.* "I should've coordinated with Rourke and—"

"And it won't happen again. Understood?" The way Alex growled out that last word told her plenty. She'd better suck it up and find a way to be a team member instead of a lone wolf. Too bad obedience wasn't her strong point, either.

Cassidy girded her loins and faced her boss. "My contacts don't have the luxury of waiting."

Annoyance flickered deep in Alex's eye. Rourke huffed. Cassidy persisted. "They put their lives at risk for me, and I won't let them down. Neither would you if you were in my shoes."

Alex turned away. Great. He must've decided to ignore her. It had certainly been tried enough with her DEA supervisor. Something wordless passed between the two men before Cassidy's boss tossed the folder into her lap. "Then tell me where the hell Melissa McCormack is right damned now."

What he meant was *if you're so smart*. She met the challenge head-on and opened the folder, her nerves rattled. None of the several satellite images within showed much of anything she didn't already know. One private home on the far end of the row of singles cabins next to the orchard had been highlighted with a yellow circle and a question mark in the center of the circle.

Cassidy knew from her own surveillance that no sign of activity had been spotted at that house. It appeared vacant, even though she and Rourke had agreed that made no sense. Cain didn't have room in his compound to leave any of his private homes vacant. Everything else in the folder looked similar to the recon photos she'd already seen.

Alex pushed back in his chair, his elbows on the armrests and his fingers interlocked while he stared. "You haven't even sighted the real Melissa yet, have you?" he asked acidly.

"No." *Damn, I'm going down in flames.* "I don't know where she is." The truth was out. All hope for a quick turnaround faded. She'd never get back inside that compound now.

"Neither have we," he said quietly, "and we've been watching very closely."

Cassidy met his eyes. Alex wasn't angry anymore. He'd transformed into the master strategist he was. "And that's why we know she's there."

"Huh?" *Okay, what*? She couldn't miss Rourke's smirk or the twitch at the corners of Alex's mouth, but neither could she understand how the absence of a missing woman proved her presence. "What do you mean?"

"Think better, Cassidy," Alex prompted. "You know as well as I do that Melissa McCormack is in that compound. All the evidence confirms it."

Evidence? Enlightenment came slowly. She stared at Alex's blue eyes while she re-evaluated what she thought she knew. Melissa had contributed enormous amounts of her inheritance as well as McCormack family money to this cult. She was definitely one of Cain's favored, and only the favored lived in private dwellings. Plus, she was clinically depressed when she'd disappeared from the real world. A depressed person dealing with overwhelming grief wasn't inclined toward a normal daily routine, much less outdoor activity where an orbiting DoD satellite skimming high above the earth's atmosphere could detect her. Oh. *Oh!* Melissa was in that house circled with yellow.

"So…" Cassidy couldn't help it. She actually wiggled in her chair at this new development. "When do we leave?"

Alex smirked. "First, tell me what Cain did to you. I want to know it all. And tell me about these two contacts you've made. Don't leave anything out."

Cassidy relaxed. This kind of butt-chewing she could deal with. It didn't take long to relate what had happened in the course of her harrowing adventure inside the compound. She described all Jude had done to help, and how she'd met his daughter, Judith.

Alex maintained his cool until she mentioned the water boarding, the near branding, and exactly what Judith's upcoming blessing meant. The light in his eyes changed to dark and lethal. His lips thinned. It was good to see, because his feelings matched hers. She might be an impulsive agent he had to put up with, but he disliked Cain as strongly as she did.

"Almost forgot." She jumped up and ran to her bundle of soiled clothing in the van. There, inside the dress pocket, rested the evidence. She tossed it to Rourke. "Cain's got a morgue beneath the silo. This ought to put him away for a while."

Rourke opened the cloth napkin carefully. "Fingers? Whew! No wonder you smelled when you showed up." He went to the van and returned with a plastic evidence bag. In went the fingers. "Good heck. Go wash."

Cassidy did what she was told, but she'd seen Alex's nod of approval. Smugly, she rejoined her fellow operators once her hands were clean. "How can we get that evidence to Mother?"

"Don't need to," Alex replied. "The FBI has a mobile lab set up down the road. They're on their way."

"How long will it take before we know who those fingers belonged to?"

"Soon." Alex arched a brow in her direction.

"Assuming Melissa is in that home, I can get to her," Cassidy stated. "You know I can."

"I never doubted that."

"The orchard behind her place will cover me all the way to her door." Cassidy's confidence increased. "The only trouble I'll have is if she refuses to leave."

Alex reached for the folder and pulled out a manila envelope. "Give her this."

When Cassidy opened it, a glossy photograph fell out—a military shot of Brady McCormack in his USMC blues, the red, white, and blue unfurled behind him. The guy was damned handsome. Cocky. Sure of himself and his dream. A diehard patriot. Like her.

But coming up with the words to persuade a grieving widow to leave the cult was something else. "What do I say to her, Boss?"

Alex met her head on. "Simple. Tell her Brady might be gone, but he still loves her. That will never change. Tell her it's time to go home."

Chapter Twelve

"Dumb ass!"

Jude picked himself up off the ground, mad as hell, and his lip bloodied. He and Tucker Chase were battling behind the barn, both ready to knock the other's head off, only this guy was a much better fighter. Tucker was a scrapper. Jude was an accountant. He hadn't landed a punch yet.

Tucker sure had. He charged again, his chin tucked to his chest and his fist swinging. "I had it handled!"

Jude faked to the left, thinking he could dodge Tucker's hard right. No such luck. Tucker's meaty fist hit Jude's chin solid, knocking his head back and his glasses off. Down he went.

"It wasn't your place," Jude mumbled even as he knelt, spitting blood into the dirt. "It was my fault! My place to make everything right, and—"

"You're a moron, you know that, Cannon?" Tucker pulled him to his feet only to punch him in the face and knock him down again.

Jude took the hit as more blood and spit flew. Yeah. He'd been told he was stupid before, most recently by Rachel but now he felt more like the hog carcass hanging by its rear legs inside the smokehouse. His gut hurt, his nose was bleeding, and his face wasn't doing much better. Staggering to his feet, he wasn't about to let Tucker get the best of him. "B-b-but..."

"But nothing! Shit! I told you to get her the hell out of here, but no. You gotta play hero, and now your daughter's stuck in the middle of a war zone." Tucker kicked Jude's feet out from under him, and this time when Jude fell, he decided to stay down. He was no match for Tucker. The man knew how to fight. Jude didn't. If he could only see.

Tucker wouldn't let up. Grabbing Jude's shirt collar, he jerked him out of the dirt. Nose to nose, he bellowed, "I'm not a freaking bum and neither are you. You've screwed every shitting thing up."

"I... I…"

"Shut up!" Tucker shoved Jude back to his ass, his elbows behind him.

"What do you want? What? Just to beat the crap out of me?"

"Yes," Tucker growled. "No. Hell. What difference does it make now?" He stilled, his index finger to his ear.

"God, you think I don't feel like shit already?" Jude cringed, fully anticipating a kick to the head or something equally as painful. But Tucker had pressed his palm to his ear. "Say again?"

"I said—"

"Damn it, Cannon. Shut the hell up." Tucker turned his back. Tucker seemed to be talking to someone else, someone inside his ear. "Say again. I've got some idiot here who can't shut his friggin' trap."

Jude spat the accumulating blood from his mouth and blew more of it out of his poor nose. Neither action alleviated the red stream running from his nostrils, so he leaned back and let it run down his throat.

"Copy that," Tucker said to whoever. "What are you doing now, dumbass?"

"Who? Me? I'm trying to stop bleeding." Jude closed his eyes at Tucker's stupid question. Everything out of his mouth was just plain mean. *Leave me alone.*

Still, the man crouched beside him. Tucker jerked Jude forward and squeezed the bridge of his nose with his index finger and thumb without asking. "Lean forward, idiot. Keep your head down. Spit. Pinch here. Shit. What the hell were you growing up, a mama's boy? Don't you know anything?"

"What were you? A bully?" But Jude did as he was told and rattled off a few things he knew as once more, he faced a puddle of his blood. "I know debits. Credits. Account payables. Depreciation. Amortization schedules.

"No kidding? You're a shithead tax man?" Tucker asked, his hand still clamped onto Jude's shoulder.

"Accountant," Jude mumbled, sounding like a total nerd with his nose plugged up like it was. "Did you break it?"

"Hope so."

"You're an ass, Chase."

"Yeah. Pretty much. You ever serve?"

"Serve what?"

"In the military, moron."

"Uh-uh." Jude wiped his bloody chin on his sleeve. The bleeding had slowed. Maybe Tucker knew something after all.

"That explains why you're such a wuss. I'm gonna start calling you Sally."

Jude pushed Tucker's hand off his shoulder, not willing to engage in childish name-calling. "Who are you really? Army? Air Force? Marines?"

"Hell, no. I'm Navy property—least I was." Tucker pushed to his feet and stomped away, and for a second, Jude thought maybe he'd made him mad. *Good riddance.*

But Tucker returned. Dropping to one knee, he stuck something in Jude's face. "Here."

Oh. My glasses. "Thanks," Jude muttered as he fingered his mangled spectacles. The wire rims were bent and both lenses were shattered but still in place. He held them up to his eyes, squinting in the hope he could see through the cracks. Not so much. He hated being blind, and that was pretty much what he was—a wuss according to Tucker, in danger of losing his daughter, and blind as a bat now, too. "Damn it. You broke 'em."

Tucker slapped one hand to his muscled thigh and growled. In between name-calling and cursing, the man did a lot of growling. "You got another pair?"

"No. I don't *got another pair.*" Jude mimicked the dumb question, letting his sarcasm speak for itself.

"How bad is your vision anyway?" Tucker's voice softened.

"Bad enough that I can't see anything, thanks to you." Jude turned his shoulder, shrugging off Tucker's misplaced concern. He didn't need anything except distance from this muscle-bound Neanderthal and a way to help Judith. "Who are you, anyway?"

"You've never been in a fight before, have you?" Damn it. The man wouldn't answer a direct question, either.

"No," Jude admitted. "Never needed to."

Tucker's hand was on his shoulder again, and one more time, Jude brushed the unwelcomed attempt at camaraderie off. It was too late for friendship.

Tucker blew out a big sigh. "You're in for one helluva fight now. This is gonna get ugly before it's over. Sure wish you'd listened to what I told you before."

"Stop already!" Jude snapped, sick to death of the drama. "You think I don't know that my only daughter's marrying a child molester from hell? It freaking sucks! What the hell else do you know? And who were you talking to before?"

"Look around, Jude," Tucker said steadily, his hand returned to Jude's shoulder. "You want to know why no one was watching the compound last night when you and your girlfriend hightailed it out of here? You want to know why Cain's good ol' boys aren't trying to stop this little meeting we're having right now? You ever think about any of that? Hell, do you think at all?"

Jude clenched his fist, wishing he were equal in physical strength to this rough-spirited jerk so he could return as good as he got. Those were both good questions, but he was tired of playing Tucker's game. Besides, it only confirmed what he suspected. Tucker *had* been watching him for some time now. "Would you just answer a question for once? Do you know how to do that?"

Tucker's voice dropped a few decibels. "I was talking to my superiors in D.C. just now. Yeah, I saw you and that blonde troublemaker sneak out of here last night. The reason no one's running security around this place is because Cain and his henchmen are too busy preparing for blessing, only this one is going to be the mother of all blessings."

"What's that supposed to mean?"

"They've got a boat-load of valium." Tucker gripped Jude's shoulder hard before he let his hand drop. "And cyanide. You know what that means?"

"No." Jude's heart fell. "I mean, yes. I know what that means." *I think.*

Tucker nodded. "You saw what happened with the congregation. These folks are discontent, and discontent people breed rebellion. I was surprised they stood up to Cain the way they did back there. There are a lot of brave people in this northern group, but that's the last thing Cain wants. He plans to eliminate every last one of them tonight. He only wants true followers. This stupid charade ends in..." Tucker looked up at the sun, "six hours or so. Maybe less."

"My daughter," Jude groaned.

"Yep." Tucker pursed his lips and sighed. "She's in a bad way. If he can keep his hands off her until the blessing, she's still going to wind up Mrs. Lucien Cain before the night's over."

"And then what?" Jude cringed at the thought of Cain's hands on Judith, but he needed to know the whole wicked plan.

"Before the so-called marriage ceremony, they'll force everyone to celebrate with a toast out of the old man's private wine cellar, only it will be laced with poison. By then, your daughter will be incapacitated. She won't have to drink. You do know that, don't you?"

"Yes," Jude answered, his heart pounding at what lay ahead for his pure baby girl.

Tucker nodded. "I'm sorry, but we're all invited to witness Cain's marriage. He's supposed to announce the second coming or something just as full of shit. He'll have his dogs there to make sure we drink. You can count on it. Everyone who drinks will die." He clapped a hand to Jude's back before he pushed up off the ground. Don't worry. I'll stay close by."

Jude tucked his broken glass frames into his shirt pocket, and wished Cassidy were with him instead of Tucker. "How do you know so much?"

Tucker tapped his ear. "I'm FBI, Jude. We know everything."

"But I don't see an earpiece or a wire or—"

"Cochlear implant. I'm hardwired. Part of the damned job."

Jude let that unexpected news sink in for about two seconds. "You've got Cain's place bugged, don't you?"

"Let's just say that I've been in here longer than you or your little girlfriend." Tucker turned toward the empty yard where a half hour earlier they'd been part of the rebellious congregation.

"Is Judith in Cain's place?"

"To be honest?" Tucker sighed. "I don't know. We're hearing a lot of chatter about tonight, so my guess is no. They wouldn't allow your daughter near them while they were planning mass suicide."

"Then where is she?"

"Maybe stashed with Jerusha."

"No," Jude muttered. "Cain's done with Jerusha. That's why she took off like her dress was on fire."

"Now you're thinking. You're right. Cain's never mentioned marriage before today, either. He must want your daughter to authenticate his role as the loving father of this messed up congregation," Tucker admitted. "Damn. I can't imagine she'd be with Greg or Hank, either."

Jude's heart all but stopped at that awful possibility. "Why? What are they doing?"

Tucker lifted one shoulder. "My guess is nothing to do with religion if they've got Jerusha. You do know who your girlfriend is, don't you?"

"You mean Cassidy?"

"Yeah. Cassidy Dancer. As in, Junior Agent Dancer." Tucker caught his eye. "That gal's part of an elite group operating out of either their Virginia office or Seattle. They call themselves The TEAM. They're damn good, but I sure as hell wasn't expecting to see one of them in here, especially not with you."

"Give it a rest, Tucker. I know who she is. We talked."

Tucker chuckled softly. "Get used to it. You're stuck with me, and your girlfriend needs to mind her own damned business. She's trouble. You'd do good to stay away from her. The FBI's handling this cult's take down. We're not going to make the mistakes we made last time."

"Last time?"

"The name David Koresh ring a bell?"

Oh, hell. That last time. When members of the Branch Davidian cult in Texas burned to death in a standoff with the FBI. Jude's heart plummeted. "What are you guys going to do?" he asked warily, no longer sure he wanted to be a part of Tucker's plan. Between Jonestown and the Branch Davidians, cults were an ugly phenomenon, but the FBI's blunders in confronting them were nothing to brag about, either.

"What do you mean *us guys*? You're in this, too, Cannon. Shit. My guys were set to intercept Cain, but now that you got all self-righteous and heroic on me..."

Jude held his breath. Tucker was right. If Jude had kept his pride in check earlier, not only would Judith not be trapped inside Cain's web, but Tucker might be where he was meant to be for this FBI operation to be successful. Maybe that was why he'd confessed as quickly as he had.

But just as that assumption registered, Jude knew better. It didn't matter what he or Tucker did. It didn't matter what the FBI planned, either. He'd seen the look in Judith's eye. *That* look. She'd intended to offer herself as a scapegoat the moment Jerusha named Priscilla. That was how Judith was made. She couldn't bear to watch another suffer.

In a way, she shared a common trait with Tucker. Both were hardwired, Tucker with an ear implant and Judith with compassion. Since the day she'd stood up to a bully who'd thought torturing a kitten was fun, Jude had been proud of her. Yeah, he'd also inherited Miss Fluffy in the process, but that straggly cat was the only thing he had left of his daughter at the moment. Even now, the shaggy beast resided in a neighbor's home until he returned to Florida.

"Hey." Tucker's voice snapped Jude out of his melancholy thoughts. "You listening, fathead?"

"What?" Jude asked tiredly.

"I need you to focus. If you're gonna help get your daughter back, you've got to man up and do it now." Tucker stilled, an index finger to his ear again.

This time, Jude knew to keep his mouth shut.

"Copy that," Tucker muttered. "Shit."

"What now?"

"We've got trouble. Damn that know-it-all to hell. I'll bust his ass this time. I swear I will."

"What's going on?"

Tucker glared. "Your girlfriend's on her way back and she's bringing her boss. That's what's wrong."

"Alex Stewart? Isn't that good?" Jude didn't need glasses to catch Tucker's annoyed look.

"Shit, you know about him, too? No, it's not good. And what's this crap about bodies hidden in a tunnel? Your girlfriend's got forensic evidence to bring Cain down for good. You want to tell me about that?"

"Sure," Jude answered, surprised Tucker didn't already know about the bodies. He acted like he knew everything else. "Cassidy found a tunnel under the root cellar stairs. She kicked out a few boards to get to it. It leads to a bigger room under the silo. We found quite a few corpses."

"No shit?"

"Umm, yeah," Jude amended the vulgarity to, "No kidding."

Tucker held to no such verbal restraint. "Show me, asshole."

Chapter Thirteen

"I've got a message for you direct from FBI Director Zachary Strong. Stand down. Pack up and clear out."

Cassidy lifted a brow at this FBI agent's tone. Obviously, he hadn't worked with The TEAM before. Dressed in the official black jacket and work pants of the Bureau, the idiot kept his hand on his holstered pistol when he approached, like he'd walked into danger. Hell, maybe he had. He'd come for the evidence bag, but the guy's condescending attitude and swagger had to go.

She'd reconvened along with Alex and Rourke to their portable breakfast table. A map of the north compound of the cult lay ready and waiting. She was just about to argue her case when Mr. FBI showed up in his dusty van and his dark glasses.

"I don't stand down," Alex growled.

Rourke's lips twisted with amusement. He folded his arms over his chest and tipped back on his chair. Cassidy did, too. Alex's brand of diplomacy was always entertaining to watch—from a distance.

"Yes, sir, you do," the Bureau's finest and obviously the dumbest had the nerve to declare. "I expect you to pack up and—"

"Unless you've got a warrant for my arrest, you can take that order and—"

"Mr. Stewart!" the poor dumb guy snapped. "I can and I will charge you with interference with a federal officer in the performance of his—"

"Then do it!" Alex lifted to his feet, his fists curled. "But you'd better be brave enough to call Jed McCormack then and tell him you had the balls to fire me. Are you?"

The powerful name hung in the air. Most of the civilized world knew of Jed McCormack, the entrepreneur and self-made billionaire who'd fought relentlessly in support of men and women in the military. He'd never been elected to public office. Didn't need to be. Jed had the kind of power most senators wished for, prayed for, and dreamed of. A friend to many, he'd befriended every president in the last twenty years, their political affiliation not withstanding. The man was the living epitome of compromise. And he wanted his daughter-in-law back.

"Strong knows I'm here, damn it," Alex growled. "You want to try that line of bullshit on me again?"

Mr. FBI's mouth snapped shut as if it were spring-loaded. His nostrils flared. Cassidy really wanted to smile, but she didn't dare, not until her boss did. She had yet to see the person who could back Alex into a corner and not come out bloody.

Rourke stabbed his finger to the printed form on the table in front of the chastised agent. "Need you to sign for those fingers. Trail of evidence, you understand."

With pursed lips, the agent stepped up to the table and signed on the dotted line. Rourke offered him the bag, but didn't release it when the agent took hold of it. Instead, he taunted. "You'll take good care of this, won't you, Agent..." His eyes scrolled over the unfortunate man's jacket. "I'm not seeing a federal ID. Who exactly are you? Where's your badge?"

Mr. FBI huffed, but he did produce his credentials and his badge. "Agent Latham. Will that be all?"

"No. It won't. I expect a complete report by the end of the day," Alex snapped.

Agent Latham tugged the evidence from Rourke's fingers, pivoted on his heel, and left in a cloud of dust and gravel.

"Bastard," Alex hissed. "Lie to me like I'm supposed to kiss his ass. That'll be the son-of-a-bitchin' day."

Rourke winked at Cassidy. She lowered her head and grinned at the table, positive she had the best job on the planet. Working with these tougher-than-tough, decorated veterans made every day an adventure.

"Speak up if I'm missing anything." Alex turned to her with a quick command. "You've been inside. You're the expert here."

She nodded as he stood over the map. "At seventeen hundred hours, we infiltrate here." His fingernail hit the wall directly opposite Melissa's location. "Chatter indicates this will be the final blessing."

Cassidy met his gaze. "What do you mean? What are you hearing?"

"Mother called while you were showering. She picked up FBI chatter about a mass suicide within the compound. Tonight." Alex glared at the road Agent Latham had roared off on. "Sure would have been nice if he'd shared that intel instead of playing god."

Cassidy's heart dropped. She jumped to her feet. "We've got to go now."

Alex captured her wrist before she could step away from the table. The authority in his blue eyes reached all the way to her gut. "No, you stay. If we do this right, we'll save more than just three people."

Anxiety rippled up every muscle in her legs and back. By the time it reached her neck, standing still wasn't an option. This whole simple operation of rescuing three people had just escalated into a disaster similar to the Jonestown massacre in Guyana. Nine hundred people had died there. Woman and children, too. That Jude and Judith were now in the middle of the same sort of nightmare rattled her to her core. Adrenaline flooded every vein and artery with the need to move.

"But I can't let him and his daughter down," she said, her heart already flying over the wall and on its way to Jude. Want to or not, a single tear dropped from her eyelid like the weakling she was not.

"You won't." Alex hadn't taken his gaze off of her.

A light flashed on inside his blue eyes. She held her breath.

"You will lead this maneuver," he told her firmly. "Once we reach the wall, you'll go over first, but you will hold that position until Rourke and I are boots on the ground."

Her eyes shifted to the map. The sight of Alex made her feel incredibly weak. He was the strong one. With her heart in her throat like it had been since she'd been strapped to that damned board, she was everything but.

"You will cover us while we clear the wall, is that understood?"

"Yes, Boss," she replied quickly, trying to focus on the map, but only seeing Jude's gray eyes. The man had trusted her with his daughter's life. Cassidy couldn't swallow.

"From there we proceed to the home we believe Melissa McCormack to be in, and we acquire our first target."

First target. It dawned on her then. Someone had to facilitate Melissa's prompt extraction, and that same someone should probably be a woman, especially if Melissa was found to be in a fragile state. And that person was—Cassidy.

Alex couldn't fool her. Melissa was their prime objective. Not Jude.

"Boss, I can't leave with just Mel—"

Alex glared at her. "You will retrieve the package, no ifs, ands, or buts."

If ever there was a time to cower, it was now. Alex brooked no dissension in his ranks. Cassidy took a deep breath and prepared to go toe-to-toe with her boss.

"Calm down. No one said you have to stay with her once we locate her." Rourke's hazel eyes met hers across the table, saving the day with his gentle intervention. "It depends on what shape she's in. Besides, someone's already inside the cult with her."

"Who?" Cassidy licked her lower lip, not having considered that possibility.

"We have confirmation from Director Strong. He has a man inside, and no, it's not your buddy, Jude," Rourke replied. "This guy's a real agent."

"He's been passing intel to the Bureau for weeks," Alex confirmed. "The FBI's prepared to blow the front gate of this cult open tonight, which is why we need to get Melissa and your friends out first. We must ensure we aren't seen. We cannot compromise the FBI's effort."

"I'm surprised they agreed to let you go in first."

"They didn't get a choice," Alex replied stiffly.

"You still don't trust them." Cassidy stated the obvious. Alex's long-running feud with the Bureau stemmed from too many federal operations with The TEAM gone wrong.

"Now you've got the picture." Rourke shot her one of his lopsided smirks. "We want our client out of their way long before they show. Man, you're slow."

She took a breath. Insults from Rourke she could take—they actually diffused some of the tension—but Jude's implicit trust in her lingered. All he wanted was to save his daughter, and that had to happen sooner than later. Cassidy struggled to hold still and listen.

Alex ignored the banter. "The real problem begins after we acquire our first target. Do you have any idea where Jude will be?"

"The barn."

Rourke eyed her with blatant mischief written all over his handsome face, probably trying to distract her. It wasn't working. Her heart pounded harder for Jude and Judith with every second she wasn't headed their way. "One of us needs to go undercover once we get inside the compound, as in, dress the part and act the part."

Cassidy nodded. "Okay. That makes sense." She caught the sneaky look between her fellow agents. "Wait. You want me to wear one of those stupid dresses and—"

"Of course. We don't want anyone recognizing you."

She would've punched him if Alex hadn't been there. "Boss. You don't really need me to..." She stopped mid-sentence. That Alex hadn't come to her defense said volumes. From the shifty looks on these guys' faces, they already had her camouflaged in the cult's drab get-up.

"Where am I supposed to conceal my SIG? And how about spare mags? You don't expect me to go in unarmed, do you?"

"Oughta fit in your underwear." Rourke smirked. "Those bloomers looked plenty baggy to me."

She closed her eyes and counted to ten. *I don't have time for this.*

"Suck it up," Alex ordered calmly. "You're the only one who knows her way around inside the compound."

"I hate you guys," she muttered, "but I'll do it. Then what?"

"Maintain contact at all times. Once you locate Jude and his daughter, retreat to Melissa's home where Rourke and I will be waiting. If you encounter any trouble, you damned well better notify me instead of handling it yourself."

"I will, Boss. I won't take any chances. Promise. You're taking Melissa out first?" she asked, needing to be sure she understood.

"No. We're taking them all out together," Rourke replied. "One trip. One chance. We run less risk if we move as a unit. If push comes to shove, we'll have three guns. Sound good?"

"Sounds better." It made sense. The only ones she expected serious trouble from were the Elite, who would definitely be armed. She welcomed the idea of engaging them. She owed Greg—big time. Hank, too.

Chapter Fourteen

"Your girlfriend is an annoying pain in the ass, you know that? So's the bastard she works for."

Jude didn't care what Tucker thought, so he didn't answer. His only option at the moment was sticking close to the guy whom he wasn't so sure could save his daughter. But Tucker could see, and Jude couldn't, unless shadows counted as vision. Crossing behind the barn to the root cellar wasn't the problem. Being able to distinguish a person standing in the shadows of the nearest tree trunk was.

"FBI and Stewart are like oil and water. The man's a flaming asshole. Most arrogant son-of-a-bitch I've ever met. Hope I never work with him again."

Jude kept walking. This Stewart guy hadn't sounded so bad when Cassidy talked about him. She made it sound more like he walked on water.

"Worked an op with him in Wisconsin a few years back. Bastard stormed in and took over our operation. Really pissed the old FBI director off."

Jude bit his lip. Sounded more like the old director didn't know much if a civilian contractor could make him look bad. He didn't say that, though.

"Stewart only hires ex-military snipers." Tucker was a wealth of trivia Jude didn't care about. "'Cept your girlfriend. I think she was ATF or something."

"DEA." Jude finally had something to say.

"Whatever." Tucker grunted. "She's as bad as Stewart. Cocky. Smart-mouthed. Probably keeps a pair of brass balls in her pants, too."

Jude let it go. Tucker was one of those guys who had to keep running his mouth. At least he scanned the yard with some degree of caution before they ducked inside the root cellar, relaying what he saw to Jude. A few *lame-brained* brothers were securing the pigpen while a handful of *brain-dead* sisters hung laundry on the clotheslines between the dorms. Other zombies worked the gardens. Tucker had an interesting view on the world and everyone in it.

"You see Greg or Hank anywhere?" Jude whispered.

"Not yet. Let's make this quick. Wait!"

Jude's blood froze at Tucker's command. The FBI agent stilled, his head cocked, the cords in his neck tight. His head swiveled slowly toward Jude. "Did you hear that?"

"What?"

Tucker looked toward the barn. "Not sure. A scream maybe?"

"I didn't hear anything." The icy fingertips of anxiety tap-danced up Jude's spine. How could he have heard anything over Tucker's incessant chitchat?

Shaken, he dropped into the cellar, while Tucker eased the slanted door closed. He flicked a flashlight seemingly from thin air, and clicked it on. "Where's this damned tunnel?"

"Where'd you get a light?" Jude countered.

"In my boot, right next to my KA-BAR and my pistol. Where do you keep yours?"

"Damn, I don't have a flashlight. You've got a knife and a pistol in your boot?" Jude still wasn't sure he could believe Tucker. The man seemed bigger than life. His head seemed that way, too.

"A smart man doesn't leave home without plenty of weapons. Now move it. Show me the bodies."

"Here." With help from Tucker's light, Jude maneuvered behind the stairs and into the narrow tunnel. Before long, he and Tucker stood in the larger room. It was a whole different place with a flashlight to brighten the scene. Even a guy with bad vision could see enough to know how truly evil Cain and the Elite were.

Ghastly corpses littered the floor, a couple dozen or so stacked like cord wood in the center. Others were laid flat, their arms wrapped to their sides and their feet bound with bands of gray cloth. Still clothed, the male corpses wore work trousers and long-sleeved shirts, the women in the traditional long-sleeved dresses.

Jude squinted down at the body whose finger he'd removed. She was a woman with white-blonde hair wrapped up in a bun on top of her head, her face turned sideways as if she were simply asleep. He couldn't tell how long she'd been dead. Her skin looked smooth, except for the sagging of the muscles around her mouth and eyes. He knelt at her side. "I'm so sorry."

Tucker wandered around the room with the light. "How'd you get your evidence? You know, how'd you cut the fingers off that old bag for your girlfriend?"

"Pocket knife," Jude answered solemnly, his heart heavy now that he could see the human being he'd personally defiled. That she was a defenseless woman made his crime seem more abhorrent. A black man lay flat on his back beside her, his eyes also closed as if in peaceful slumber, his hands crossed over his stomach. Other bodies rested nearby. They all looked peacefully—staged.

"You? A knife?" Tucker mocked. "Wow. That's a shocker. What kind?"

Jude paused to scratch between his eyebrows with his index finger, sure Tucker would only humiliate him further.

"Come on, bro. Tell me." Tucker nudged Jude's foot with his boot. "What? It come in a box of Cracker Jacks? You flip coins at a circus for it? The county fair? Tell me. How'd a pipsqueak like you come to own a decent knife?"

"Boy Scouts," Jude muttered wearily, fully expecting another insult.

It never came.

"Shit. Will you look at this?" Tucker's light flickered across white lettering scrawled on the far wall. The bright red words: *CRYPT of the GENTILES* lit up under the narrow beam.

Squinting to make out the words, it dawned on Jude who these dead people were. "Cain lied," he said, still not wanting to believe what his eyes were telling him. "He never let the Gentiles leave. They're still here."

He took a second look at the faces of some of those bodies. Sure enough, old man Michaels and his wife were there. So was Hinton Sweeney, the old codger who had challenged Cain's right to lead the cult. And that younger woman with the white-blonde hair? *My heck. Saffron's mother.*

Jude dropped to his knees beside the body. While Judith's self-righteous little friend clung to Jerusha's lies, even to the point of defending her, the mighty prophet she followed had had her mother killed. *Poor, poor Saffron.*

Tucker moved closer to the stacked bodies in the corner. "Did you notice none of these folks are wearing shoes. They're all barefoot. Wonder what that's about?"

A grating sound overhead pulled Jude's attention from that interesting observation and up to the ceiling. "I estimated we're right beneath the silo," he said quietly.

Tucker flicked the beam of the flashlight upward while trickles of dust and gravel rained down. "It's a hatch," he muttered. "Shit. Someone's opening it. Hide."

Both men scrambled into the cover of the tunnel, Tucker in the lead. Jude had barely pulled the burlap flap behind him when bright sunlight filled the crypt. Twisting around, he held his position on his hands and knees, determined to find out what else Cain had done. *If this next body was Judith's, so help me God...* He gritted his teeth and planned like never before. His worthless knife might not kill a man, but Cain would pay.

The shadowy shape of a ladder dropped to the floor, then a man climbed down. Another long shape fell through the ceiling and landed with a thud, barely missing the ladder.

"Take it easy," Hank complained. "That bitch almost hit me."

It had to be Greg climbing down next. "Cry-baby."

"Easy for you to say. You've never had her stab you in the back like I did."

"That's because she liked me better."

Damn. That dead body had to be Jerusha.

Jude's mouth went dry when Cain's assassins lifted Jerusha to her final resting place—right next to Saffron's mother. The poor gal still had her hand extended, two fingers missing, just the way he'd left her. If these guys decided to revisit their previous handiwork…

"It's kinda fitting, her being down here with all the folks she lied about, don't ya think?"

"Yeah." Greg stood over Jerusha. "I knew damn well old man Jenkins didn't touch those little girls like she said he did."

"Me, too." Hank nudged her head with his boot. "But what were we going to do? Once she started spinning her web of lies, it was just a matter of time 'fore Cain agreed with her and started preaching and condemning. If you ask me, he figured Jenkins was moving in on his territory, them both liking little girls and all."

"But Jenkins didn't like little girls."

"I know, but once Jerusha said he did, he was done for."

"She doesn't look half bad now that we've got her big mouth glued shut," Greg muttered thoughtfully. "You think anyone heard the ruckus she made?"

"In the silo?" Hank asked. "Fat chance. Them walls are solid granite. Can't hear a thing in there. Stand outside next time we put someone down. You'll see."

"There isn't going to be a next time."

"Yeah. Right." Hank didn't sound convinced. "Look around. Seems to me we heard that crap before."

"You don't believe the prophet?"

"Just saying I'll believe it when I see it. You and me both know Cain and his brother got bigger plans than this cult. This stupid church is just a means to an end."

"You may be right." Greg turned around, as if reviewing the entire room. "I like this place. I feel like I'm in a museum."

"You're a sick bastard, you know that?"

"Whether you believe it or not, embalming the dead is an art form." Greg peered at the bodies stacked in the corner. "Morticians are like any other artist. We're proud of our work. These pieces should be displayed, not treated like junk in an attic. It's not right."

"Humph," Hank growled. "You're making me wanna cry. Boohoo."

Tucker crawled up alongside Jude. "What's going on?"

"Shhhhh," Jude ordered softly. Now wasn't the time for chitchat.

"We need more room." Greg sighed. "If we're not going to display these corpses properly, we might as well bury them."

"I been saying that all along, but no. You pump 'em so full of that toxic crap—"

"It's embalming fluid, Hank. Simple formaldehyde, methanol, disinfectants, anti-edemic chemicals, and—"

"I don't care what it is. It keeps 'em from stinking and rotting. That's the only reason you get to play with 'em once they're dead. I'm outta here." Greg was already halfway up the ladder. Hank followed. Within seconds, it was lifted out of sight and the trapdoor shut.

"Shit, those guys are sickos." Tucker all but pushed Jude back into the crypt. "That was close."

He flicked his light over the room, but Jude was already standing over the body Hank and Greg had left behind. "Bring your light over here. Now."

The second Tucker's light hit the corpse's face, Jude breathed a sigh of relief. Despite what Hank and Greg had said he needed to be sure. Thank God. It *was* Jerusha.

"Shit! Will you look at that? He killed his old lady," Tucker exclaimed.

"No, he didn't. Greg and Hank did. That's why they followed Jerusha after the meeting," Jude said sadly. "They were killing her while the rest of the congregation did chores."

Jude's anxiety meter peaked. Only this morning Jerusha had been one of the prophet's favored. How long before he tired of Judith?

"So Greg embalmed all these folks, huh?" Tucker knelt next to the body. "Look at the hole in her neck. Some asshole stitched her carotid."

"Why?" Jude heard the anguish in his own voice.

Tucker's gentle grip on his shoulder surprised him. "You've got to remember that we're not dealing with normal guys here, Jude. Men like Hank and Greg zero in on each other's perversions and band together. It happens all the time. Remember Hitler? Idi Amin in Uganda? Pol Pot in Cambodia? It's a sick and twisted world, in case you haven't noticed."

"Let's get out of here," Jude said. "I've got to find my—"

"Freeze!"

A blinding spotlight hit Jude full in the face. Greg and Hank had come through the tunnel. "Why Brother Chase," Greg said with certain satisfaction. "Figured you might be the one snooping around."

"Told you it had to be Brother Clark," Hank said from behind the light, his voice twisted with sarcasm, "seeing as how his little girl's gonna get fucked by the prophet tonight."

Rage ignited deep within at that despicable word, flooding Jude's cautious nature into submission. With a crash, he charged the cowards. Greg's flashlight flew to the ground and rolled, sending weird shadows dancing across the ceiling and walls. Jude's fist connected with a cheekbone, and instinctively, he ducked as someone else's fist in flight brushed his forehead.

He'd already spent too many years living with limited vision to let it work against him now. Darkness was familiar territory and fighting for his daughter was something he damned well knew how to do. Every fierce, fatherly instinct surged forward, finally at his command. He charged again, ready to receive, but damned well ready to give.

His fist connected over and over again. He kicked out at the slightest hint of shadows. He rolled. He spun around. *Crunch.* Someone dropped to the ground at his feet, and he honestly didn't know who it was, Greg or Hank. He just kept kicking out at the unlucky bastard.

"Son-of-a-bitch," Hank cursed weakly from the floor nearby. Good to know. One down.

Jude didn't have to worry where know-it-all Tucker was, but he knew exactly where Hank crouched. With his fists clasped together like a hammer, he dropped to his knees and blasted Hank's chops with every ounce of strength he had. "Not my daughter, damn you," he bellowed as he hit the cruel man again and again. "Not. My. Judith!"

Hank had to be badly hurt. He offered little resistance.

A sixth sense warned Jude he still had an enemy at his rear. Spinning around, his fist struck who he hoped was Greg sneaking up behind him. Instead, a sliver of light flew high above his head. He paused, not believing what he saw. Greg's spotlight still bathed half of the room in brightness, but the penlight flipped end over end until a hand reached up from the dark side and caught it.

"Shit," Tucker groaned, the penlight in his grip. "Why didn't you tell me you were a black belt?"

Jude shook that ridiculous notion away. It took a second to understand that he was the only man standing in the disgusting room full of corpses. Sucking in a ragged breath, he dragged the back of his bloody hand over his mouth, and took stock of the situation. Pulling Hank's spotlight off the floor, he cast the beam around the room. Hank lay very still and bloodied where Jude had left him. Tucker was sprawled against a corpse with Greg crumpled face down at his side.

"What... what just happened?"

"You don't know?" Tucker asked weakly, shoving away from Greg with a grimace. "Hey, can you give me a hand up? Please?"

Please? That was different.

"Sure." Jude extended a hand until the spotlight caught a glint of silver protruding just below Tucker's left collarbone. "You're hurt."

Tucker staggered to his feet. "Shithead stabbed me."

"You need a doctor." Jude propped the spotlight on the ground so he could wrap Tucker's arm over his shoulder for support. "Shouldn't we remove that knife?"

"Hell no. That'll just make me bleed to death."

Jude looked at the widening red stain seeping through Tucker's shirt. How could it possibly bleed more? "You sure? I could rig a bandage with my shirt."

"I'm fine," Tucker mutter, but he couldn't seem to catch his breath. He was far from fine.

Jude found it unbelievable that Hank and Greg were unconscious while he and Tucker were alive. But he couldn't take chances. Those men might be unconscious now, but he needed them incapacitated until help arrived.

"Wait here." He leaned Tucker against the wall by the tunnel entrance. Marching back to Hank, he stripped the man's shirt off, and used it to tie his hands behind his back, then his legs together. He did the same with Greg. By the time he finished, Greg and Hank resembled the corpses they lay next to, only not so peaceful.

"I'm sure glad you got Greg. I had my hands full with—"

"I didn't *get Greg*, you moron." Tucker gasped, his voice edgy with pain and sarcasm.

Jude turned in annoyance. Now wasn't the time for one of Tucker's annoying mind games. There was still a lot of work to be done. Cain would miss Greg and Hank before long, and someone would be looking for them. Besides, Tucker wasn't too cocky anymore. He might be hurt worse than he let on. Selfishly, Jude worried he might loose his only ally—and his eyes.

This next part was going to be hard. Tucker would have to be extra careful not to dislodge or bump the knife while he crawled through the tunnel to safety.

"You really don't know, do you?"

"Know what?" Jude steadied Tucker as he lifted the burlap curtain out of the way.

"You did all this."

"I did what?"

Tucker waved his penlight toward Hank and Greg's prone bodies. "I've never seen a guy move so fast." His voice filled with something akin to awe. "Greg stuck me the minute I kicked the light out of his hands. All I saw was this shadow come to life. Man, you were everywhere at once. The next thing I know, Greg drops like a bag of bricks, and you're turning Hank's face into hamburger."

Jude blinked at Tucker's incorrect assessment. "No. Not me. I—"

"Yes, dumb shit, you. Do I look like I could've fought them off with a knife sticking in me?"

Jude really looked at Tucker, and then he was scared. They'd never make it through the tunnel. It didn't matter who'd knocked Greg and Hank down. Maybe it was just the brightness of the spotlight, but even Tucker's lips looked gray. He was bleeding to death. Gently, Jude dropped the burlap and used both hands to force Tucker back to the ground.

"No, I..." Tucker winced, even though he complied with the assist. "We gotta go."

"We need to pull that knife out first."

"No, I—"

"Shut up. There's no way I can get you through that narrow tunnel with a knife in your chest."

"But I—"

"But nothing." Jude secured the light so the beam remained stationary on Tucker's chest. He reached over his shoulder and pulled his shirt off. He still wore a dingy white T-shirt, which would also make decent packing to stop the bleeding if needed. Quickly, he ripped two long lengths from the bottom edge of his shirt, folded the rest of it into one thick pad, and positioned a palm against the hole where the knife protruded. "Hold your breath or something. This is going to hurt."

"You think?" Jude gave him no time to argue. Pushing with one hand, he pulled the knife straight up and out with his other hand while Tucker hissed one long, "Son... of... a... bitch!"

Jude ignored him, more concerned with the flow spilling out of the FBI agent's body than his curse words. Tucker was right. He was bleeding a lot more now. Working quickly, Jude pressed the packing into the wound and applied two-handed pressure. Doubt created panic. What had he just done? He wasn't a medic. Why did he think he knew anything about first aid for this magnitude of a chest wound?

Tucker glared up at him, clearly in pain. "Told you so."

Jude focused on the bandage instead of the hateful glare, convinced he had done the right thing given the circumstances. Pushing harder into the wound, he applied more pressure. Then more. Tucker moaned and groaned, but at last the blood loss slowed.

Jude swallowed a shaky gulp and deftly wrapped the longer lengths of cloth around Tucker's torso to hold the packing in place. "Hold this," he ordered his bossy companion to keep pressure on the packing while he tied the strips off.

"Got it." Tucker meekly complied; two fingers on the first knot while Jude tied another.

Once he was sure the simple bandages would hold, he sat back, shaking like a leaf and sure Tucker would toss out another biting comment because of it. Jude tilted the spotlight away. No sense drawing attention to the weakling in the room.

Tucker glanced at his chest. "Will ya look at that. The son-of-a-bitch stabbed my wife."

"Your what?"

"My heart tattoo with my wife's name in the middle of it. He stabbed her."

"You're a married man?" That surprised Jude.

"Nah," Tucker said weakly. "She said I was an ass. Took the boy and left."

Jude rolled his eyes. Wow. Tucker an ass? Who would've thought? He had no comment to Tucker's ex-wife's assessment other than *she must be a very smart woman*. But the insight made Jude think. Despite Tucker's crude language and high opinion of himself, they had something in common. They were fathers.

Jude grabbed Greg's spotlight and changed the subject. "Do you think you can crawl through the tunnel now?"

"Yeah." Tucker rolled to his side and proved he was superior to Jude all over again. They were under the stair joists when Tucker asked, "So, how'd you do all that back there?"

Jude glanced back to where Hank and Greg lay in the dark, half-naked and hopefully still out cold. He couldn't see them, and he didn't remember most of it, just going berserk. "I didn't like what they said about Judith. I got mad."

Tucker gave him a weak smile. "Man, I gotta piss you off more often."

Chapter Fifteen

She wanted to run. Better yet, she wanted to drive one of the vans so they wouldn't have to waste time walking, but no. Both guys insisted on maintaining the current location of their camp in the interest of safety and cover. Alex and Rourke wanted solid walls to retreat to. A van near the cult wall would raise suspicion. They geared up, locked up, and left both vans behind.

With every step, her gut twisted at what might be happening inside the compound. The phone call Alex received before they left made everything worse.

"Stewart." He'd stilled as he listened. "And you verified this how?" A frown deepened over his brows as the one-sided conversation continued. He'd hung up without another word and turned on Cassidy and Rourke. "Pack up, damn it. We're going in now."

"What's up?" Rourke asked.

"FBI's got a man down. Bastards want us to retrieve him. We leave in five."

"Where is he? Has he seen Jude?" Cassidy needed to know.

Alex nodded. "Agent Tucker Chase. He's in the root cellar, but no, Jude Cannon isn't with him."

"Why not? Where'd he go?"

"To find his daughter, what else?"

"Don't worry," Rourke offered. "You told him to meet you at the barn. He'll be there."

Cassidy wasn't so sure. "How'd Agent Chase get hurt?"

Alex pursed his lips before he answered. "He and Cannon tangled with two of Cain's Elite. Chase caught a knife in his chest. He needs an assist."

"Is Jude okay?"

"According to Chase, he's out looking for his daughter, now move."

She bit her lip. Alex tended to believe his agents did what they were told when they were told to. No questions asked. But damn it to hell. Removing three people would've been difficult enough, but four? Insane, especially if this FBI guy was badly injured and couldn't walk on his own two feet.

And yet... The schedule change suited Cassidy, so she didn't ask for more intel. Antsy and edgy, it was all she could do to keep a civil tongue in her head when Rourke started interrogating her on the trail. "What's this Jude guy do for a living?"

"Accountant," she answered quickly.

"You like him?"

"He's a good man in a tight spot."

"That's not what I asked."

Cassidy glanced sideways at her senior agent. Rourke had a right to ask anything he wanted. Everything impacted the mission, no matter how trivial. She just wasn't sure how much she wanted to divulge. After all, she'd only met Jude the day before and under the worst circumstances. What did she really know? "Yeah. I like him. I guess."

"What's he look like? You know, so I'll recognize him when I see him."

She smiled, remembering her first impression of Owl-man. "Your height. Brown hair with sun bleached streaks. Needs a shave. He wears glasses."

"Glasses?" For some reason, that shortcoming was all that caught Rourke's attention.

"Yes." She focused on the forced march. "Gray eyes like Judith's. She's a pretty strawberry blonde. Fourteen years old, but mature for her age."

Rourke was quiet for a few minutes before he spoke again, his words somber. "Sounds like you like him a lot the way you're talking about his kid."

Cassidy shrugged. She just wanted to get into the compound and do what she'd promised.

He persisted. "You do, don't you?"

Well, wasn't that a bunch of interesting? It sounded like Mr. Hands-Off was suddenly jealous of a guy he hadn't met. Why now? Rourke had had plenty of time to make a move before, but he hadn't, and that was where Cassidy reached her limit. Confidence sharing time ended. "You got any extra mags on you?"

He tossed her two, one after the other. As she caught them, Cassidy slipped them into the last empty pocket of her cargo pants, the best invention on earth for a covert agent. The wall had just come into view, stretched along the western cult property like a concrete snake basking in the sun, its venom all stored on the opposite side.

"Be careful, Butch," Rourke said quietly. "You just met this guy, this Cannon dude. Take it slow. Don't do anything stupid."

That raised Cassidy's hackles. "What do you care?" she asked, suddenly angry. Her nerves were tight. The last thing she needed was unwarranted advice from someone who had yet to make a move on her, who should've done it a long time ago *if* he'd ever wanted to, and who'd certainly had plenty of opportunity. But Rourke hadn't, had he? Not once. So what if she liked Jude? Why should she hang around and wait for hell to freeze over?

Her spike of blistering anger met the kind warmth of Rourke's hazel eyes. The smile that curled his lips was small, almost sad. "Believe it or not, I do care. I don't want to see you hurt."

"I'm fine," she huffed. *Fine time to tell me that worthless piece of yesterday's news, O'Neill.*

Alex shot her a quick and questioning look when she tossed her pack to the ground.

"You guys want to hoist me up or should I use the hook?" she asked, her eyes upward, mentally calculating the jump she needed to make, and done worrying about Rourke and his feelings. A toss up would be quicker, but the climbing rope would work just as well, and she was done wondering and waiting on a guy who was obviously more worried about his career than her. Sheesh!

"On three." Alex knelt, his gloved fingers interlocked as he transformed into her catapult.

She took a deep breath and stepped into his grasp, one hand on his shoulder, the other on the wall. On the count of three, he tossed her high enough that she should've been able to grab hold of the ledge with no trouble. She was lithe and agile, an easy toss. It was just a concrete wall. No concertina wire. No alarms. No armed guards blocking her path. She'd done it just hours ago, but, damn it. She missed.

With a very un-agent-like *'oomph,'* she hit the wall hard and knew she had no chance of getting anymore height. Only her fingertips gripped the ragged edge. With a grunt, she dug in, determined not to fail. But she was heavier since Jude had hefted her over this very same wall. Now she wore a bulletproof vest and carried ammo. Cassidy slid to earth at Alex's feet angry she couldn't get her mind off Rourke. Or Jude.

Alex didn't say a word, just gave her that searching look of his, the look that said he didn't understand how she could've missed. She didn't, either. Once again he knelt.

"Come on," Rourke encouraged. "This is nothing. You can fly. Go for it."

She clenched her teeth and nodded. *Yes, I can fly, damn it. Now stop talking to me.*

Shaking her anxiety off, she focused on the ledge overhead, placed the toe of her boot into her boss's capable hands, and prepared for another take-off.

Blue sky beyond. Then Jude. Not Rourke. I can do this. I can fly.

"On three," Alex repeated patiently. "One. Two. Three."

Up she went. Touchdown.

Cassidy scrambled topside and waved for Rourke to toss her gear bag up. Once he did, she unzipped it and lifted the rope out for Alex and Rourke. They weren't so good at flying. After clamping the anchor securely over the opposing edge of the wall, she tossed the rope down to them.

Alex came first. While he scaled the wall, she took in the view and made certain she hadn't been seen. Apple orchards and willows stretched below. If she didn't know better, she wouldn't know the compound lay so close. Only the top peak of the barn and the rounded rock wall of the silo showed above the tree line.

When Alex drew close to the top, she dropped off the other side, leaving her camouflaged ammo bag behind. The stash of bullets would serve as their last resort should all else fail. A well-armed sniper on a wall made for a daunting enemy, and she intended to be that person if push came to shove.

Once on the ground, she unholstered her pistol, ready for trouble. Alex and Rourke were on the wall. She heard the rope hit her side of the concrete barrier. Like her ammo bag, the rope would be left behind after Alex and Rourke touched down. If the worst possible scenario unfolded, a rope at the ready could mean the difference between death and life during retreat.

Rourke was right. Taking all targets out at the same time was the only way, but retreating over any wall in the middle of a firefight would prove a formidable task.

Alex dropped beside her, crouching immediately as he took in the terrain from one knee. Rourke dropped a second later.

"We'll only have cover in the willows. Once we reach the orchard, we'll use the trees."

Alex nodded.

Cassidy took lead. At the edge of the willows, her senses heightened. One child playing hooky or one adult cult member out of their appointed place could end the extraction. She surveyed the way forward one last time before she signaled Rourke to advance first, Alex second. Bringing up the rear, Cassidy maintained close cover over her guys, her pistol's scope panning back and forth. Both Alex and Rourke had their ARs tucked in tight against their chest, up and ready. So far, so good.

At the edge of the orchard, Rourke halted. When Alex reached him, he tapped Rourke once on the shoulder to indicate all accounted for. Rourke ran to the target. At the corner of the cabin, he turned and waved Alex on.

A prickle of unease slid over Cassidy's neck and down her spine. Women usually worked in the garden. One of the Elite was always on guard. Teachers were always out and about with a class of children. Where was everyone?

Cassidy covered Alex, but lost sight of Rourke the minute he dodged to the side of the target house. When Alex hit the corner of the same home, her gut clenched. This was it. Showdown. The right Melissa better be in that damned house.

Her turn. Alex signaled for her to advance. Rourke was still out of sight, safe she hoped.

She allowed a short breath before she took off. Running through open spaces worked her last nerve. Once she reached Alex, she nodded once for go. He nodded back. Message received, and rounded the corner to follow Rourke, hopefully inside the home. Acid poured into her stomach. Her companion agents were out of sight. So much could go wrong.

Pausing at the corner of the home, she surveyed the orchard and willows behind her one last time. Everything was too quiet. Not good. Something had happened, and she wished she knew what. Sucking up a quick breath, she followed her boss.

She could've kissed the smirk off his smug face when she caught up with him. Thank God. There was no way the satellite surveillance footage could've shown the lattice wall separating each private home from the next.

Alex stood at the open door and waved her inside. "Good job, junior agent," he said softly as she passed him. "You were right. Melissa's here."

Cassidy stepped inside. A thin woman with straggly, chestnut brown hair and sad eyes stood in the center of the only room of the very small cabin, welcoming her visitors as if this kind of thing happened everyday. Melissa gave Alex an extra long hug. "It is so good to see you again. How's Jed?"

"He'll be fine once you're home safe," Alex replied, nodding to his agents. "Rourke and Cassidy are here to make sure that happens. You're coming with us. Now."

Cassidy had to give it to Alex. He hadn't asked Melissa if she wanted to leave. His mission was to retrieve her, and that was all there was to it.

The light on Melissa's face at his firmly spoken command was answer enough. "I made an awful mistake. I'm sorry you had to come get me."

"No problem, ma'am." Rourke spoke up. "Our pleasure."

Cassidy smirked. *Rourke, you big suck-up.*

"But first..." Alex looked to Cassidy, "we a dress and a bonnet."

"Why?" Melissa asked. "It's not safe here. Surely you're not thinking of going out among the congregation. Not tonight."

"Yes," Cassidy answered. "I've been here before. I can do it again."

"But why?"

"We have two other contacts to retrieve. Jude Cannon and his daughter, Judith. You might know him as Jude Clark and her as Chloe."

Melissa's breath hitched. "The prophet's Chloe? But she's to be married during the blessing. Tonight."

"To that perv, Cain?" Cassidy asked.

"Yes," Melissa whispered, her fingers to her throat. "He's such an evil man, Cassidy. You three don't stand a chance against his Elite."

Melissa's words only added more fuel to Cassidy's hatred for the man. She'd known about the blessing, but marriage? "When did that happen?"

"This morning." Melissa looked to Alex. "There was quite a stir when—Oh, my. *You're* the spy he was looking for. It all makes sense. For the first time since I've been here, the entire congregation stood up to Cain. It was incredible. I thought his men would start shooting, but in the middle of all the commotion, Judith bested Lucien. She offered herself as his betrothed."

"Why'd she do that?" Alex asked.

"Because Cain wanted someone to pay for helping the spy escape." Melissa nodded to Cassidy. "Your spy, Alex. He wanted a confession, but when no one came forward, he asked Jerusha to name a blood sacrifice, someone else to suffer until the evildoer confessed. Jerusha fingered Priscilla. The poor girl and her mother barely left my home before you got here. They're frightened to death, Alex. They want to go home."

Cassidy glared at Alex. "He's mine, Boss. Before we leave here, he's mine."

Alex didn't offer any comment, but turned to Melissa. "Where is Jude's daughter now?"

"She's with the sisters of the Elite just six doors away from here. They're preparing her dress for the marriage ceremony."

Cassidy blew out a huge sigh of frustration. "She's freaking fourteen years old."

"Why poison a young woman you just married? It doesn't make sense," Alex muttered.

"Poison?" Melissa asked, her eyes widened in surprise.

"Yes. The FBI's got solid intel that Cain means to end the cult tonight. No one else knows, only..." Alex drew in a deep breath. "I don't know. Something's still not right with that intel."

"Nothing makes sense," Melissa whispered. "I shouldn't have come here. I don't know what I was thinking or... why... or..." The seemingly strong woman melted into Alex's arms. "I miss Brady so much. God, I don't know how you lived through this awful, awful thing."

Alex stroked a hand over her hair. "I'd lie and tell you it gets easier, but it doesn't, honey. You just learn to live around it. You adjust. You'll see."

Cassidy turned away, her eyes watering at the tenderness of her tough boss. Melissa was hurting for the man she loved, and for the first time in her life, Cassidy knew the feeling. Alex seemed to understand, too.

"Is there any way you could get Chloe to come here?" Rourke asked.

"I could do that." Melissa's eyes brightened. Pulling away from Alex, she smoothed one hand over her bed. "I'll go get Chloe. I'll tell them I made a wedding present for her. I made this quilt while I've been here. It's... It's..." She froze as she fingered the masterpiece. A patchwork of muted greens, tans, and denims, some cammies, it seemed to hold a spell over her. "I made it out of his clothes." Her words faded as she lifted the quilt to her nose. "It still smells like... my Brady."

"Melissa," Alex said gently. "If this is too hard for you—"

"No." She snapped out of her trance. "I need to help. Yes. I'll go ask if I can borrow Chloe for a moment. The sisters of the Elite will believe me. I won't let on that I know about the poison. I'll tell them I just want to give the prophet's bride-to-be a wedding present. In the meantime," she turned to Cassidy. "I have the perfect dress for you."

"And bloomers," Rourke reminded her with a cheeky smirk.

Melissa retrieved a full-length, gray, go-to-meeting dress from a small trunk at the foot of her bed. "You're shorter than me. This might be a little large. I do have a pair of new undergarments if you want those, too."

"She does, thanks," Rourke pitched in before Cassidy could speak up. "Go get Judith while Cassidy changes, Melissa."

"I'll be watching," Alex said, already peering out the door. "If you run into trouble, scream."

Melissa shook her head, tsking as she passed him at the threshold. "You know me better than that, Alex. A lady never screams. She calls out. Trust me. I'll be fine."

Alex offered a curt nod, his gaze on the path. "If you're not back in five, I'm coming to get you."

The relationship between Alex and Melissa caught Cassidy by surprise. It wasn't often he exposed his tender side, but undressing in a one-room cabin while her boss and senior agent stood only feet away? Weird, really weird.

She turned her back and examined those damned bloomers. Why should she wear them? No one needed to know what she had on beneath her clothes. But the dress? Sheesh. A guy had to have designed this ridiculous style. A sick, twisted guy who liked scratchy fabric and tiny little buttons. No wonder the sisters in this cult were pasty white and lifeless. They never got enough vitamin D.

Rourke must've been watching. "Aw, go on. Put 'em on."

Cassidy shot him a not-too-ladylike hand signal, turned her back, and dropped her cargoes, well on her way to feeling like the low man on the totem pole. Slipping out of her shirt, she fumbled into the dress. But the look in Rourke's eyes when she pivoted to show off her ugly apparel, the damned bloomers undercover where they belonged? Enlightening to say the least.

"What are you looking at?" she challenged, checking her cleavage in case she'd missed one of the gazillion buttons keeping every last inch of her covered.

Rourke let out a quiet wolf whistle. "Nothing. Absolutely nothing."

"Damn right." She did what any other covert agent would've done. She flipped him off again and picked up her pistol, ready to get this op finished.

"Where do you think you're going to put that?" Alex asked.

She looked down at her dress, hoping for a pocket hidden in all that fabric. Nothing.

"How about this?" Rourke retrieved a small woven basket with a checkered cloth from the counter. "If anyone asks, you're collecting eggs." A crooked smile tweaked his lips. "Damn. You look like you're off to see the wizard."

"Shut up," she hissed one last time. With her pistol concealed in that stupid egg basket, Cassidy left the relative safety of Melissa's cabin behind and headed out to locate Jude. If all went as planned, he'd be in the barn and everyone could be out of this looney bin before a single moonbeam lit the eastern horizon.

Yeah, right. Cassidy knew better.

Something always went wrong.

Chapter Sixteen

Tucker was in bad shape. He'd collapsed on the burlap bags just outside the tunnel opening, but the cellar wasn't safe. No place was, not with Greg and Hank missing.

"We should keep moving," Jude suggested, "or I could go for water and first-aid."

Tucker rolled with a groan onto his side. "Shut up. I'm talking."

Well, excuse me all to hell. Jude positioned the spotlight on the middle step and faced it toward the ceiling to diffuse the blinding beam while Tucker mumbled. Jude tried not to listen. "Damn it, not him. She's with him, isn't she?" A pause, then, "Shit. Is that the best you guys can do?"

The conversation didn't seem to end the way Tucker wanted. "Shit."

"What's up?"

"Nothing. HQ wants me to stay put and wait for rescue. Who do they think I am, some pansy-assed civilian?" He closed his eyes and gritted his teeth, a good enough answer for Jude. He had no problem leaving Tucker behind. He stood to do just that.

"Where you going?"

"My plans haven't changed. I need to be at the barn with Judith before Cassidy gets back."

"I thought you didn't know where your kid is?"

"I don't, but if she's marrying Cain tonight, she's probably in one of the Elite's homes. Cain would trust them. I'll check there first."

"But you can't see."

"I'll be fine," Jude insisted. "I can make my way around. It's daytime. I can do it."

Tucker dropped his head in his hands, staring at his boots.

Jude took another step up the cellar stairs. "Take care of yourself."

"Shit." Tucker kicked against the dirt floor, then let out a rumbling groan because that simple action must've hurt.

"What is wrong with you?" When he got no answer, Jude placed one palm to the cellar door. He had better things to do than wait on this obnoxious FBI agent with a big opinion of himself.

"Stay!" Tucker barked.

"No, *you* stay," Jude barked back. "I've got better things to do than listen to you whine and denigrate everything and everyone. Judith needs me. Wait here like you were told and—"

"Shit! Will you give me a second, damn it?" Tucker roared. "I'm thinking!"

Jude clenched his fist and held while Tucker growled, like all that growling did any good. The guy was half animal and most of it big-mouthed and cantankerous. At the moment, Tucker sat beyond the slats of the stairs. It looked like he was behind bars, right where animals like him belonged.

At last, Tucker reached inside his boot and retrieved a small gun. "Never thought I'd be saying this, but you'll need a way to protect yourself. That little knife of yours won't hurt a flea. Here. Take this."

Jude turned up his nose at the gun Tucker extended, his palm still on the door and ready to leave. "No thanks. If I was going to use a weapon, it'd be a lot bigger than that."

"Take it," Tucker growled. "It ain't no toy. It's a P232. A pocket pistol. Packs a helluva—"

"No." The silver-barreled pistol looked like a water gun. Who'd be scared of that? "Like I said—"

"Take it!"

Jude rounded the steps and took the damned pistol, but only to shut Tucker up. The weight in his palm confirmed this was no toy. Okay, so Tucker's generosity was unexpected. Jude tucked the weapon into his belt and bloused his shirt to conceal it.

Tucker tossed him an extra magazine, grimacing in obvious pain at the effort. "Take this, too. The pistol holds seven rounds. It's loaded so be careful. The mag gives you seven more. Don't waste 'em. God, do you even know how to shoot?"

"I do," Jude retorted. *Maybe.*

Tucker pulled a knife out of his boot. "I'd send this KA-BAR with you, but you've got no place to hide it, and I need some way to defend myself in case Cain's goons come calling." He leaned back onto the burlap. "It would've been nice if your girlfriend really meant what she said, huh? Would've helped if she'd come back."

"She did and she will." Jude came swiftly to Cassidy's defense. He'd seen the light in her eyes. Tucker hadn't.

"Ha. That's what they all say. How long's it take to grab some gear and bust ass back here?"

Jude had no answer. He didn't know precisely where Cassidy had gone once she'd left him at the wall. She could be in the next town for all he knew, but she'd promised she'd return for Judith, and he trusted her.

Tucker wiped the blade down his pant leg. "I got news for you, Poindexter. If that gal really intended on saving your dumb ass, she would've been here by now. Would've brought the rest of her team with her, too."

"She'll be here," Jude said more firmly.

"How many guys you think she's bringing back with her? If she comes, that is? One? Ten? A hundred?"

Jude didn't answer. She'd never mentioned numbers, only that she'd be bringing some serious firepower.

"The agents on The TEAM travel in pairs, moron," Tucker explained. "Always. Think about it. Her partner's probably some big, beefy, black ops guy, and if he's anything like the rest of Stewart's guys, he's ex-military and all muscle. He's covered with tats and he probably smokes, drinks, and carouses. Where do you suppose she and that guy-friend snooze when they're not getting water-boarded by the cult, huh? You think they don't horse around when they're on remote ops like this one? Give me a break. Everyone does."

Jude quit listening. Back on the steps, he on his way out. "You're an ass, Tucker, you know that? Have a great life."

Tucker groaned, and Jude took that for goodbye. He pressed one hand against the cellar door and pushed upwards.

"Bye, moron."

Jude didn't answer, just shut Tucker in and walked away from the most annoying, helpful man he'd ever had the misfortune to meet.

He scanned the garden where he could just barely make out three sisters on their knees. They faced away from him, so he turned toward the orchard. If his previous assumptions were right, Judith was in one of the homes reserved for the Elite. He intended to find her.

A shadowy sister passed by him with a laundry basket on her hip, headed toward the clotheslines behind the dorms. Maintaining a respectable distance, he followed. Turning the corner of the final private home, the young woman began humming a melody that stopped Jude cold.

"I Dreamed a Dream" from *Les Misérables*. Judith's favorite song. It was as if she were suddenly with him, singing of days when men were kind, of dreams where love would never die. She'd lived, breathed, and slept the movie score for so many days after he'd taken her to see it. Judith had danced through the halls of his home in Florida, a silken scarf tossed over her head and shoulders, as she'd transformed herself into poor Fantine.

Jude knew the words by heart, if not by choice, only they weren't just the score to a tragic play. They were the epitome of his daughter and her love for the downtrodden. They were her toes on the hardwood floor. Her gentle murmurs as she lost herself in the music and filled his house with light. They were pieces of her soul, the tendrils of her heart, they were— everything he loved.

A thousand doubts assailed him. What if she wasn't in any of those private homes? What if he searched in vain? Where else did he need to look? The barn? The milk house? The damned silo? Where might Cain have imprisoned her if she'd changed her mind and refused to go through with the wedding?

His heart throbbed as the list of possibilities morphed into an impossible task. He was just one man. One. Desperate. Inept. Father. And Judith was everything.

Only the woman with the clothesbasket stood nearby, still humming the song that had bludgeoned Jude's determination into shards of doubt and hopelessness. The blurry, gray scene reflected the despair of the day. The woman looked up from her basket of clothes and offered him a shy wave. Jude waved back, hoping she was waving at him and not someone behind him. She seemed as lost as everyone else in this godforsaken cult.

Cassidy's promise came to him on the wind. *I will find you.*

He looked around, sure he'd heard her. Goosebumps shivered across his arms and shoulders, as if she'd reached across the miles to him. *Then find me now. Come to me. I need your over-confidence. I crave the stars in your eyes, and the shy smile on your lips. I need you, Cassidy Dancer. Come to me right damned now.*

Jude bowed his head. His doubt fled. She was on her way.

With dusk just hours away, he continued to the first private home at the northern edge of the compound. He knew most of the brothers and sisters who lived there, all except this one. Hunkering down as if pulling weeds at the foundation, he strained to listen to any noises from inside. Nothing.

Anxiety stole the saliva in his mouth. It was now or never. Jude stepped around the house to knock or peer through the window, but the crunch of boots on gravel stopped him cold. Jude pulled back and broke out in a cold sweat. The moment the door squeaked open, a man bellowed, "Where is she?"

Jude strained to hear the woman's quiet steady reply. "She isn't here, Prophet Cain."

"I can see that. Answer me. Where'd she go? What's going on around here? First Hank and Greg run off, now my bride!"

"Oh, no," the woman answered sweetly. "Tsk, tsk. Sister Chloe didn't run off. She wouldn't do that to you. I'm surprised you'd suspect such disloyalty from a beautiful spirit as her."

Jude clenched his fist. *Judith. Her name is Judith.*

The tone of reproach in this woman's voice caught him by surprise. She had a lot of nerve to talk back to Cain the way she had. She didn't sound like one of the obedient flock, either. Jude couldn't put his finger on it, but this woman was different. Her calm seemed to have an immediate effect on Cain, too.

"Then where is she, Sister Melissa?" Cain's voice mellowed. "Sister Butler said she came to see you, that you had a special wedding gift for us."

Jude cocked his head. Melissa? Could this be Cassidy's Melissa?

"I do," she exclaimed, and Jude heard the door squeak open wider. "I'm afraid I made a quilt too beautiful for me to keep. When you announced your plan to marry this morning, I knew it was made for you and Sister Chloe. She was only here for a minute. After she saw it, I could tell she wasn't in the best frame of mind for such an important day."

"Oh?" Cain sounded taken aback.

"Yes. She seemed quite troubled," Melissa said. "I offered her a cup of chamomile tea to settle her nerves. Most new brides are overwhelmed on the day of their wedding, but she is marrying the most important man in the country, and she is so young. Of course she's stressed."

"I suppose she might be a little nervous," he admitted.

"Oh, she is, but do you know else what she told me?" Melissa asked.

"Ma'am?" For the first time since entering the cult, Jude detected a note of respect in the prophet's tone.

"Your new bride is happy for this day," Melissa gushed, "but she also wanted to surprise you. Please don't tell her that you heard it from me, but she has gone to the place of the blessing ahead of you."

"She has?" Cain sounded truly dumbfounded.

Jude's jaw dropped. Why on earth would Judith run off to such an awful place? That alone proved she didn't have a clue what happened during the blessing.

"Why yes." This Melissa gal was really starting to bug Jude. She oozed honey and syrup all over the pig on her porch. It was all Jude could do to not reach out and choke the living crap out of the both of them. *You're talking about my daughter!*

"She knew the tent would already be in place. Is that okay with you?" Melissa asked, her voice full of innocence. "She told me that she needed a reverent and quiet place to meditate. Chloe wants to be in the right mental state when she is joined to her dearly beloved. She didn't want to be a bundle of nerves. That's how she put it. Isn't that sweet? She wanted to be calm and beautiful so you wouldn't feel as if you'd made a mistake in marrying a giddy child instead of a mature woman."

"She did?" By now the prophet sounded like a love-struck teenager listening to Melissa tell him secrets about his girlfriend.

"Prophet Cain," Melissa said, with a clear note of scolding. "Sister Chloe idolizes you. Surely you didn't for one moment believe she would leave, did you?"

"Ah n-no," Cain stuttered. "Why no, of course not. She offered herself to me at a time when everyone else deserted me. I have no doubt she's the one."

Jude heard an odd bump from inside Melissa's house, which she promptly dismissed. "Oh, my," she told Cain. "What a silly goose I am. I didn't set my cup of tea all the way on my nightstand when you knocked. It fell. Oh, my."

"Excuse me, Sister Melissa." Cain bowed as he stepped off her porch. "I have taken too much of your time. Thank you for your wedding gift and your very kind words. I will—"

"Oh, don't leave," Melissa said. "Don't you want to see the quilt? It's right here."

With all his heart, Jude wanted her to shut the hell up. This woman was the reason the cult prospered. She was a fool through and through, someone who blindly followed and foolishly funded the evil that Lucien Cain professed as truth.

"I must," Cain answered politely. "This is a great day of reckoning for the church. There is much to be done, the wedding notwithstanding."

"Well, okay then. If you must," Melissa demurred. "But it's bad luck for the groom to see his bride before the wedding ceremony. Don't spoil the surprise your sweet Chloe has in store for you. Promise?"

Gag me with a spoon. I have got to get to that damned tent before Cain does.

"I promise, Sister Melissa. My Chloe will be a beautiful bride," Cain replied with an odd strain in his voice.

Jude's fists clenched as Melissa rattled on. "And the next time you stop by, I'll make us a cup of chamomile tea, and maybe we can discuss a class on self-sacrifice and obedience I'd like to begin teaching the girls."

Jude gritted his teeth. The gun felt hard and solid at his belt. *Yeah, well I want to teach them gun safety, self-defense, and how to kick butt.*

"Peace be with you, Sister Melissa," the prophet said respectfully as he turned and left.

"And with you, Prophet Cain," she answered happily from her door, waving. "Goodbye! I'll see you tonight at the blessing!"

Jude waited while the prophet retreated and Melissa Jabber Jaws shut her damned door. Aggravated that he'd lost precious time listening to so much baloney, Jude had still gotten exactly what he came for. He knew where Judith was, and she was close.

His feet flew. The place of the blessing resided within a grove of trees less than a mile away, south of the compound. Jude had only visited it once. Even now, goose flesh crept up his neck at the awful sensation that permeated the unholy ground. It felt haunted, as if the spirits of all the poor women and children Cain had robbed of their virtue still lingered.

He had to hurry. The white four-cornered tent would have been erected by now, and Judith was there. Relief washed over Jude. He was finally on his way out of this zoo, and Judith with him. Doubt fled. She loved him, and somehow, she would be miles away from here before Tucker's FBI friends ever knocked at the compound gate. Nearly giddy with relief, he failed to slow his pace at the corner of the granary. He should've.

Blam. Oomph. *Damn.* He ran into someone. Someone who towered over him.

Cain sounded surprised, too. "Brother Clark? Just the man I've been looking for."

Chapter Seventeen

Where is he?

Cassidy headed straight to the barn. The damned board that Hank and Greg had her strapped to only yesterday morning rested against the wall by the door, probably until they needed to torture someone else. The empty washtub leaned beside it. Greg's sinister, lying eyes came to mind. *I'm so gonna make you pay.*

But no Jude.

Treading quietly, she ventured farther into the dimly lit building. "Jude?" she called softly. "Are you in here?"

No answer, damn it. He wasn't there.

At the sound of pigeons cooing and fluttering overhead, she glanced up to the rafters, expecting to see hay bales. Instead, wooden crates lined the edge of the open loft, something she'd been in no condition to notice the last time.

"What the heck?" Climbing the rung ladder proved difficult with an egg basket, but not impossible. Within minutes, she had caught Cain red-handed. Several crate tops were already pried open. The tire iron someone had neglected to put away made opening a few more easy. Cain had guns. Lots of them.

"Hey Boss," she whispered. The sunbonnet had finally proven useful. It hid her earpiece. "Just located a huge stash of weaponry. Hundreds of AKs, AR-15s, Uzi's, and a boatload of ammo."

"Copy that," Alex replied from the relative safety of Melissa's cabin. "FBI didn't have confirmation that Cain was running guns until now. Good job."

"Wait." She grunted as she pried another lid up and off. "Lots of C4 in here, too."

"Blasting caps? Det cord?"

"No." She glanced around to see if she'd missed anything. "Is this why the FBI's involved?"

"Partially, but it's not why—"

"Hold on," she whispered. "Oh, hell. The prophet's here. He's holding a meeting with his Elite."

"In the barn?" Alex asked sharply.

"Copy that." She flattened to the floor and listened as several men in black robes gathered around Cain.

"In less than two hours the purge will commence." He gestured to three men standing together. "Brothers Alan, Mickey, and Clyde, leave now. You know what you to do."

The three bowed and answered as one, "We will not fail." Then they turned and left through the front door of the barn. Cassidy strained to listen as the one and only vehicle allowed on the compound started up and drove away.

"The rest of you will do what you've always done," Cain continued. "Keep the peace. Make sure no one panics. Most sinners will be in bed by the time the cyanide starts working."

Cassidy increased the volume to her earpiece. "Boss? Are you getting this?"

"Cyanide. Copy that."

"Tomorrow our message goes forth into the world," Cain proclaimed.

She rolled her eyes. This freak really thought he was something.

"We begin with the New York subway."

Wait a minute. What? The New York subway?

The Elite answered as one again. "We will not fail."

"The D.C. Metro, the Chicago L, Boston, and the BART will be next." Cain's voice increased in volume and excitement. "Once the weapons of confusion are placed, the second coming will commence."

"We will not fail."

"Those are the largest mass-transit systems in the country," Alex commented.

"We expect resistance, but we will continue to strike back during the second coming." Cain's voice boomed. "Now go to your assigned places. Await my signal."

While watching the spectacle below, Cassidy caught sight of a stack of grain bags against the lowest eaves of the barn roof where the loft floor met the ceiling. "Wait a minute, Boss. There's something else up here."

Quietly, she scurried over to the bags. Pulling her knife from her boot, she sliced a small hole in one of them, just small enough to pull out a small sample of whatever Cain had stashed. She crinkled her nose. "Never mind. Nothing but beans."

"Beans? What kind?"

"I don't know. Dried beans. They're just—"

"What color are they?"

"Tan and black."

"Castor oil beans," Alex hissed. "That son-of-a-bitch is making ricin."

With her mouth dry and her heart pounding, it was hard to spit out the words. "B-b-boss. The mass suicide. It's just a distraction. His real plan is to bring the country to its knees."

"Then he's a bigger fool than I thought. Ricin's not effective for large-scale chemical warfare. It's been tried. Get back here. Now."

"No." The word of defiance slipped so quickly from her lips, she scarcely knew she'd uttered it.

But Alex did. "Now, Dancer," he ground out.

"No. I have to find Jude." There was no sense arguing, so Cassidy did the only thing she could. She turned her earpiece off. Cain seemed to be wrapping the meeting up below anyway. She couldn't listen with Alex barking in her ear.

"I have located Brother Cannon or Brother Clark or whatever you want to call him," Cain bragged. "He thinks he's fooled us, but he'll soon understand how powerful I am. His daughter *will* be my wife. By the time I consummate my marriage with her, he'll be dead. Brother Victor will make certain he witnesses the entire blessing and drinks. Nothing will interfere with the second coming. Remember, brothers. You go forth to do the will of your prophet."

"We will not fail."

"Look to the day this nation is brought to its knees."

"We will not fail."

"From the spires of our noble temple, the second coming will go forth!" Cain's fervor peaked.

The Elite answered with a final shout of, "We will not fail!"

Oh, bullshit. You're all going to fail, and I'm just the one to make sure you do.

Cassidy couldn't get out of the loft fast enough after Cain and his goons left. Sliding down the ladder fireman-style with her dress hiked up to her thighs, her boots hit the ground in record time. She just didn't expect to run into a brick wall when she spun around. An angry brick wall named Alex.

Shit. "How'd you get here so f—" She looked into smoking blue eyes intended to wilt her. They did.

"You turn your earpiece off again, Dancer, and so help me, I'll break you down so low you'll need a ladder to tie your boots," he hissed into her face.

"But they're going to kill him." Her fear squeaked out. "I just heard them. He has to drink the poison. He'll be one of the—"

"He won't, but I'll personally kick your ass at the next hint of insubordination!"

Humiliated, a quick, small "Yes, sir," was all she could muster. Cassidy bowed her head in rare submission to a man whose fierce anger had just stopped her cold. The fear she'd been fighting stormed over her confidence and mashed it into the ground at her feet. Alex had won.

Tears welled up. Blinking furiously didn't do a thing to stop them from running down her face and dripping onto her boots, which just happened to be showing out from under the hem of her ugly, long dress. Ah! She wanted to scream defiance, but her heart was no longer in it. She needed Alex's help.

Alex lifted her chin with one finger, raising her teary eyes to his level. "You're one of my best," he said hoarsely. "I'm not going to lose you just because you're as hot-headed as me."

She blinked big, wide alligator-tear-filled eyes. *Shoot me now. I'm crying in front of my boss, and he's looking right at me. I'm freaking mush!*

"Where haven't you looked yet?"

"Umm, the root cellar and granary," she whispered, fidgeting with that darned egg basket that made her feel like some little red-necked hick instead of a very capable agent. "I was going to check when..." She couldn't say it. *When you caught me.*

"Stick to your plan. Root cellar first. Granary second. What about the silo?"

"But I really thought he'd be here," she offered.

Alex turned his back on her and strode to the side door of the barn. "You going to stand there all day?" He waved her to go ahead of him as they headed to the cellar. "Judith is already with Rourke and Melissa. Once we find Jude, we'll retreat back to camp and come back for Agent Chase."

"The Elite aren't looking for her?"

"Cain is, but Melissa told him Judith had already gone to the place of the blessing."

"He bought that?"

"She handled him like a pro."

Knowing Judith was safe took a load off Cassidy's heart. Jude would be happy, but she wanted him as safe as his daughter. Cassidy led the way behind the barn until they came to the opposite corner. Being careful to keep her egg basket out of sight, she peered around the silo to make sure the coast was clear.

"Don't worry. Most people have already gone to the blessing," Alex answered her unspoken question.

Cassidy was once again amazed at the nerve of her boss when he stepped out from cover and all but strolled through the garden to the cellar. Embarrassed that she'd dishonored his faith in her, she meekly followed. He eased the metal rod out of the hasp that secured the door.

She cringed. It was now or never. Jude had to be down there.

Alex dropped to the floor and crouched, his pistol drawn. "Who's there? Show yourself."

Cassidy hadn't taken the first step yet when her boss secured his weapon and disappeared from view. She tossed the basket aside and pulled her pistol. Cautiously, she joined Alex behind the steps. There on the mattress of burlap bags lay a guy with a bloody bandage on his chest. The light of a big spotlight gleamed off his sweaty face. "You," he said accusingly. "You must be Cassidy Dancer."

Despite his disdainful tone, she nodded as she lowered her gun. "Do I know you?"

"Hell, no, But I know you, and you are one hard-headed woman, aren't you?"

"If you only knew," Alex grumbled, and with that disparaging remark, Cassidy relaxed.

"Special Agent Tucker Chase at your service, Mr. Stewart. Good to see you again."

Alex shook Tucker's hand cautiously. "Again?"

"Spencer, Wisconsin, ring a bell?"

Alex stiffened. "You were there?"

"Yes, sir. I was one of the agents at the safe house that didn't get blown up."

Cassidy felt the shift in Alex and decided she needed to find out more about that Wisconsin op. Whatever happened there, it must have something to do with Alex's intense dislike for the Bureau.

"Can you walk?" Alex asked, his tone decidedly cooler.

Tucker blew out a big breath. "You bet, but you'll want to see what Jude left for you in the crypt before you head out."

Alex nodded to Cassidy while he checked Tucker's wound. "Take the light. Go see what he's talking about."

Cassidy dropped to her knees and obeyed, crawling through the tunnel with the light in one hand and her pistol in the other. The second she pushed through the last burlap curtain at the other end of the tunnel, she heard whimpering and groaning. The reflection of two pairs of eyes glittered back at her briefly, just before she saw the gagged faces of Greg and Hank.

"Well, hello boys." She scanned the room for more surprises other than the corpses. It was a whole different place with the spotlight, but it still gave her the creeps. She strutted over to where Greg lay, and blinded him in the eyeballs intentionally. "Remember me? Your future unwilling bride?"

He growled something, but the gag prevented serious conversation, not that she would have entertained it. She finally had him where she wanted him—at boot level. The memory of him preaching at her and holding her head underwater while she fought to breathe resurfaced.

"Wow. This is so much better than I imagined." She waved her pistol with malicious joy and serious consideration of how much she wanted to return the pain they had inflicted. "Here you are tied up like pigs. All I need is two apples, a freaking long stick and a bed of red-hot coals. I could roast you alive and no one would know. Should we have *prayers* now, Greg?"

Flashing the light beyond the nervous looking goon, she noticed the lettering on the wall. If what Tucker had just said was true, Jude had done this. He'd intentionally left Greg gagged and tied beneath the words *Crypt of the Gentiles*. Her heart did a silly flip-flop. *Oh, Jude. You got the guys who hurt me. You are so my hero.*

Alex climbed through the tunnel. As he stood and dusted his hands on his pants, his eyes travelled over the abundance of corpses before they settled on the two bound and gagged trolls.

"Hey, Boss. I'd like you to meet Greg Gleason and, I'm sorry Hank. I don't even know your last name."

Hank muttered something unintelligible, but Alex went straightway to Greg. Cassidy had told him everything. With one knee on the ground, he grabbed Greg's collar, pulling his face close. "You hurt my agent."

Cassidy stared, not sure what her boss had in mind. Silver flashed in his free hand. Greg twisted to get free. For a split second, Cassidy thought Alex had knifed him, but then she saw it. Alex's blade protruded from the ground between Greg's legs, damned close to the guy's crotch. *Good thing you didn't have your legs crossed, Greg ol' buddy, ol' pal. You'd be singing soprano.*

"Let's see how tough you really are," Alex hissed, his fist clenched tight. "I'll make you a one-time good deal. Reach that knife first, and I won't cut your throat."

Cassidy had never seen anyone move faster. The second Greg rolled his eyes Alex had the blade at his throat. "Look at me. I said, look at me!"

Blinking through sweat and tears, Greg obeyed. Moaning through his gag like he was, he might've convinced some stupid person he was sorry. Not Alex. He leaned in, nose to nose with the quivering man. "Remember my face, you son-of-a-bitch. You ever touch one of my people again, and I'll be the last thing you see."

Alex shoved Greg away from him and stood. He didn't waste a second on Hank, just turned to Cassidy with, "Let's move."

Chapter Eighteen

Tucker's right. I am a moron.

Once again, Jude's hopes of finding Judith were obliterated by his own idiocy. Instead of coming up with a brilliant reason why he couldn't accompany Cain, he'd complied in hopes of a quick meeting followed by a quicker getaway. Damned wrong strategy. His good intentions went sideways when Brother Victor came out of nowhere and strong-armed him. Jude found himself hurried along toward the silo by a man twice his size. Into the circular dungeon he went, shoved through the heavy door when he balked at the smells and sights within.

He peered at the disgusting place where Jerusha had to have screamed her last breath. In falling, he'd landed on the trap door to the crypt below. A large plastic barrel stood against the far wall. Black drips striped the sides of it. Probably blood. A stainless steel autopsy table stood next to it.

He'd pushed quickly to his feet only to get knocked back down by the ham-sized fist of Brother Victor. The man looked the part of a medieval village blacksmith. Everything about him was thick, from his neck and arms to the bushy black unibrow over his squinty black eyes.

"You'll stay down if you know what's good for you," he threatened Jude with a fat finger in his face. "You hear?"

Jude had no choice, not until he caught his second wind. For a man who didn't know how to fight, he'd already gone too many rounds with Tucker, then Hank and Greg. He'd never survive a physical confrontation against a guy built like an ox.

Pushing his back against the stone silo wall, Jude wiped the blood off his lip, and faced the saddest truth. He *was* pitiful. He *had* failed. Judith was the only good thing he'd accomplished in his life, the only reason anything else mattered, but he'd failed her, too.

Brother Victor had taken up residence near the door, dwarfing the three-legged stool while he eyed Jude. The long black robe of the Elite added to his sinister countenance.

Anxiety crept up the back of Jude's neck, whispering it was time to do something before it got any later. But logic stared through the cold, hard eyes stuck in an ugly man's hairy face. Brother Victor ducked when he lumbered through the silo door. Not Jude. His arms hadn't even brushed the sides of the doorframe. He'd just flown in like a ragdoll, kicked around to the bitter end. Damn. Why wasn't he more like Tucker and less like—him?

Jude buried his face in his crossed arms on his knees. Even Judith was made of tougher stuff. He couldn't understand how his lovely little girl would have gone to the place of the blessing as joyfully as that Melissa person said she did.

The puzzle of Cassidy's Melissa plagued him. She'd sounded so kind to Cain. Too kind. Her very maternal manner of dealing with such an evil man offended Jude. At first. But now that he had time to think... what was it she'd said? That her teacup fell off the counter? Really?

Jude straightened his spine as he replayed what he'd heard. No glass breaking, and he'd been close enough he should have. The sound from inside Melissa's tiny cabin was more like a bump, like an elbow hitting a wall, or a boot against a baseboard, or—Cassidy!

An inkling of hope reached out and slapped the *poor-me-bullshit* right out of Jude's hard head. Cassidy was back. She'd made that noise. She was inside Melissa's cabin the whole time the prophet had stood at the front door. No wonder Melissa had spoken right up. No coffee cup broke. If Cassidy was back, Judith had hope, and if Judith had hope...

"You're here," he whispered to the woman he cared about. "I know you are. I feel your smile. Please, Cassidy. Get to Judith before he does. Save Judith."

"Who you talking to?" Brother Victor demanded.

"Just saying my prayers," Jude muttered without looking up.

Like the coward he knew he was, he let his tears fall. He might no longer be a player in Cain's evil scheme, but Cassidy was, and she was ten times the hero he would ever be. Yes, he'd felt the softness of her body when they'd hugged, and yes, he'd held her when she was weak, but he knew deep down that Cassidy was made of steel. Real, tempered steel, forged in the heat of battle. That was why she'd been inside the cult to begin with. Any woman crazy enough to attempt what she'd done was one tough gal.

His mild-mannered heart soared knowing the world had tilted a fraction to the side of good and—Cassidy. *God, be with her,* he thought, but then Jude winced. His prayer sounded exactly like the dribble spoken by Cain's chanting congregation. He'd heard those insincere words spouted more times than he cared to count. *But there is a God and He knows me.* Jude lowered his forehead to his clenched fingers. He bared his heart to the real Lord and master.

Please be with Cassidy. Help her. Bless her with your amazing grace and power to save my baby girl. Don't worry 'bout me. Only Judith. Please, God. Please.

"You're awful quiet," Brother Victor prodded.

"That's when prayers are best." Jude raised his gaze to the ugly face of his executioner. Brother Victor looked away. Okay, that was odd. Jude had never intimidated anyone before. Or maybe Brother Victor felt something more inside that stuffy silo with no air circulation. Jude certainly did. "Do you always follow the prophet even when you know he's wrong?"

"He's never wrong," Brother Victor shot back without a moment's hesitation, still not meeting Jude's gaze. "That's why he's the prophet."

"How do you think you'll feel come judgment day when you have to face the real God?"

Brother Victor glared. "Shut up 'fore I come over there and give you a good kick in your lying mouth."

Jude didn't need to speak anymore. He had what he wanted—the belief that Cassidy would not fail. That Judith would live. He leaned his head back and closed his eyes. Resting his open palms to the silo floor, he took a deep breath. This day wasn't over yet.

Jude damned near smiled. His elbow had just bumped something solid. *I have Tucker's gun.* In all his worrying and running around like a chicken with his head cut off, he'd forgotten he was armed. He looked up at Brother Victor through different eyes. "Do you have family in here? A wife? Children?"

Brother Victor shook his head deliberately from side to side. "You just don't know how to shut it, do you?" Heaving up from the stool, he grabbed the wooden bat next to the door, already splashed with what was probably Jerusha's blood. "Damn it. The prophet wanted you to watch what he does to your kid." He took a menacing step toward Jude. "Looks like you won't make it to the blessing after all."

He stood less than five feet away, and Jude knew he'd better calculate his next move perfectly. He might have a gun, but he was no sharpshooter. It might take all six of those rounds to knock Brother Victor down, and honestly, Jude had no idea how to reload a magazine.

Of all things, the Pythagorean theorem flashed to his mind, the geometric theory put forth by a Greek mathematician, eons ago. It did nothing more than define the precise relationship between the hypotenuse of a right triangle to its two opposing sides. Most people could've cared less about it and probably never studied it, but Jude had. What he did next had to be accomplished with the same degree of perfection as that age-old mathematical proof.

There was beauty in mathematical logic. It powered Jude's very analytically centric mind and made him a darned good accountant. Make that damned good. His spine stiffened as a sudden awareness of his place in the universe enhanced his reality. He might not be an undercover agent or a sniper, but neither was he a moron.

All the stupid things he'd done over the last few days, and that included helping a strange woman get out of Cain's clutches, had led him to this singular moment in time and space. All his weaknesses, missteps, and fears had brought him there. He was the human equivalent of that hypotenuse. He was equal to the challenge of the opposing sides, regardless of their size or might. By the grace of God, he *was* equal to the evil that stood before him now.

Brother Victor cocked his hairy arm over his head and grunted, ready to bash Jude's head in.

Jude never blinked as he lifted his hand.

Brother Victor's eye's widened. His bushy brows peaked. *Surprise!*

Jude squeezed the trigger and the gun in his palm spit one shiny round. So. Damned. Fast.

He didn't hear the blast when the round erupted from the barrel of Tucker's weapon. Neither did he feel the repercussion from that incredibly deadly discharge ripple up his forearm to lose itself in his bicep and shoulder muscles. It all happened in a slow-motion heartbeat, and when it was done, Brother Victor had gone to meet his maker, to finally answer for the crimes he'd knowingly committed in the name of a false prophet.

Jude scrambled to stand over the brute, shaken at what he'd just done. Brother Victor had fallen face first. His bulky body rested on the bat. His face looked just as ugly as it had before, only now his mouth was open and his jaw had gone slack. Two black eyes stared at nothing. His robe pooled around him, absorbing the deep crimson splash from what had to be a damned large exit wound at his back.

This was Jude's first kill, and he wasn't proud of it. His logical brain argued with his nauseous stomach. The reality of taking a life sucked away any bravado. This was the most repugnant thing he'd ever done. He shook his head, summoning the light of his daughter's eyes to his weary mind. He felt bad. Heck, he felt awful—just not bad enough to trade Judith's life for Brother Victor's.

The universe righted. His little girl was safe. There was still time.

Jude stepped away from the grisly scene with his back straight and his eyes clear. He secured the safety switch on the gun and stuck it into his belt. Jude Cannon was back in the house, umm, silo.

He jerked the door open without cowering. Not this time. Not anymore. Let Lucien come. Let them all come. Nothing could stop Jude now. *Get the hell out of my way.*

Chapter Nineteen

"Easy now." Cassidy helped Alex tip Tucker backward onto Melissa's bed. Knowing they were bringing an injured man with them had energized Melissa. She'd prepared all the supplies needed to clean and re-bandage the stranger. The minute Cassidy and Alex stepped away, she moved in and went to work. The FBI agent groaned, but damned if the guy's face didn't light up with a smile while a real angel of mercy peeled the blood-soaked bandage off his chest. Priceless. Just damned priceless was what it was.

But it had taken longer than expected to get Tucker to safety, and Cassidy was anxious to leave. She had somewhere else to be. Before she could voice her opinion, a timid voice behind her asked, "Sister Cassidy?"

When Cassidy turned to face Jude's daughter, she flung herself into Cassidy's arms in a burst of tears. "You're that woman in the root cellar. Agent Rourke says you're here to help my dad."

Cassidy glanced over Judith's head at Rourke, but he was busy assisting Melissa. "Your father's my next target. Don't worry. I'll bring him back to you."

The poor little thing shuddered. "Please don't let them hurt him. He's not like them. They're cruel and hard, but he's... he's..." She hiccupped. "He's my dad."

Alex rested a hand on Judith's shoulder. "No one's going to get hurt. We're here to help him."

"But he doesn't know I'm safe yet, does he?" Judith's chin quivered at that sad question. "He's still out there looking for me. He's in trouble; I know he is. And they'll hurt him if they find him."

"Don't you worry—Agent Dancer is right," Alex assured her. "He's the only one we're looking for right now, and there are two of us. We'll find him."

Cassidy looked to Alex. He sounded so sure of himself. He nodded toward the door, so she untangled herself from Judith's embrace. "We need to go. You stay here and help Melissa, okay?"

Gray eyes welled with tears and blinked back at her. "Okay," Judith said sadly.

"Rourke. Get everyone to safety as soon as you can." Alex loosened his pistol from his thigh holster and set it on the nightstand. "Melissa, take this. Most of the cult members are at the blessing, but just in case."

His cell phone vibrated at this hip. "Stewart." Alex listened and hung up without a word. "FBI has the name to match that female you found in the crypt. Veronica Schwartz; missing for—"

"Saffron's mother?" Judith gasped. "B-but the prophet said she couldn't stay. He said she had to leave. He said—" She froze, her mouth still trying to form the words but with no sound. Suddenly she was back in Cassidy's arms, crying, "He lied."

All Cassidy could do was hold her. Cain's despicable crimes angered her all over again. There simply was no hole deep enough on earth to put him into. He needed to go back to hell where he belonged, and she wanted to be the one who sent him there.

Rourke wrapped a sling around Tucker's arm. "You think you can walk another few miles to our camp?"

Tucker pushed up on one elbow, brushing Melissa's last minute ministrations aside. "I'm a SEAL. What do you think?"

"I think Rangers make squids look like sissies," Rourke countered without batting an eye, "every last damned one of them."

Tucker's boots hit the floor. He was once more sitting. Sweating. Gritting his teeth. But ramrod straight. "Try and keep up, girly boy."

Rourke growled at Alex. "We'll be fine unless we've got to carry this guy."

Cassidy had to smile. Leave it to Rourke to know how to incentivize a Navy SEAL.

"Get moving. You're liable to get caught in a showdown if you're still here when the FBI shows," Alex warned as he glanced outside. "Melissa, will you be okay?"

She nodded, her arms around Judith. Now for Jude.

Rourke mustered his troops. Melissa and Judith supported Tucker under each arm, but he seemed able to travel. Rourke stalked out the door behind them, actively surveying their path to the wall, his rifle ready. He turned at the edge of the orchard and flashed a grin at Cassidy. Then a quick salute.

Warmth flooded her chest. He might not have crossed that line between management and employee like she wished he had, but he'd always been there for her. Handsome. Big brotherly. She needed to hug him whether he liked it or not. *Wait!* she thought, wanting to tell him she cared before the moment got away from her. But she held her ground and said nothing. Did nothing.

"You ready?" Alex interrupted.

She pulled her gaze from the group blending into the fruit trees, the first of many refugees fleeing the cult if she had her way. Cassidy eyed her boss, not sure he'd go along with this next idea. "Sorry, but you can't go out there looking like Special Forces."

"What do you have in mind?"

She stabbed her index finger at him, signaling him to stay where he was while she hurried to the community clothesline behind Melissa's cabin and grabbed a pair of men's pants and a shirt. It'd be nice not to be the only agent looking like a pioneer. Only Alex didn't. Once changed, he achieved a debonair James Bond effect while Cassidy still looked like Dorothy from *The Wizard of Oz*. All she needed was Toto to make her ensemble complete.

Alex didn't seem to notice. He placed a quick call to the FBI to advise that their man was on his way out, for them to watch for him at The TEAM camp. He followed that up with the intel Cassidy had overheard on Cain's ricin attack and about the weapons and explosives cache she'd found. Pocketing his cell, Alex opened Melissa's door and nodded for Cassidy to lead.

Her aggravation peaked. She dropped the brim of her bonnet, and growled back at him. "I can't lead. You're a man. That makes you superior to me, according to Cain's commandments. I have to follow five steps behind you. We aren't supposed to talk to each other, either."

He stepped out of the house and into view. "I don't give a rat's ass about Cain's bullshit commandments. Lead, damn it."

"But Boss—"

His chin lift dared her to argue.

She huffed. "You're going to get us into trouble."

"Trouble is why we're here," he quipped. "Did you forget who you work for?"

Cassidy couldn't help it. She smiled. Yeah, trouble was her middle name, and she intended to bring plenty of it to Lucien Cain before the day was done. "To the silo then?" she asked when they reached the open yard.

"Where are they going?" Alex asked, his gaze on the few cult members scurrying past them on the dirt path led up the hill and into the trees south of the barn, a two-mile walk behind Cain's home.

"To the place of the blessing up in that grove of trees," Cassidy answered, watching those people hurry with furtive glances over their shoulders. None of them seemed happy. "Jude will be there. Come on. Let's go."

Alex followed, his head down and avoiding eye contact. Cassidy made sure the brim of her bonnet shielded her face. Neither spoke as they hurried—not that the other cult members chattered. The mood was somber and shadows were long. At last the place of the blessing came into view.

Holy shit didn't begin to describe it. The group of stragglers filtered into a large clearing where a four-cornered tent had been erected, its back wall tucked into the brush, a red carpet at the front entry and a torch beside the draped entrance. A deep red pennant with a full moon decorated the peak.

Wooden benches faced the tent. A raised platform with a lectern stood to one side, a portable sound system at the other side. Standing torches circled the clearing. Since the benches were already filled, the latecomers settled onto blankets they'd brought with them. Couples sat together, but peered toward the path, obviously watching for someone. Overall, there had to be around three hundred members in attendance, with maybe ten percent of them dressed in the garb of the Elite.

Cassidy accompanied Alex to the edge of the clearing where they took up positions in the shadows, watching. Night fell. Her gut clenched tight when it became obvious why the anxious looks from the parents. She leaned into Alex. "The children aren't here."

"Shit. Where would he be keeping them?"

"I don't know. The barn maybe? I hope." She couldn't bring herself to think the worst, that all those children weren't coming. That they might already be dead.

"I'll contact the Bureau to step on it, to secure the kids first. Keep your head on a swivel." Alex nudged her elbow, nodding toward the path they had just travelled.

The crowd hushed as all eyes turned to the procession entering the clearing. Cain led, the hood of his black robe thrown back, the tips of his steepled fingers at his lips. His proud band of Elite marched under the same cover of darkness, their palms together as if in prayer, their hoods drawn over their heads.

The Elite with Cain circled the assembly. They dropped out of rank by twos at each torch. Cassidy looked to Alex. He seemed to be staring across the gathering. Her eyes followed his gaze, but there were so many people. She couldn't pick out a recognizable face in the crowd, not even Jude's.

The final Elite reached the tent entrance as Cain took the podium. Cassidy expected him to look a little frazzled or worried since his two favorite goons were missing, but he didn't. With his chin tilted up, Cain looked serene. Pompous. Arrogant as hell.

Her trigger finger itched. *Let me wipe that self-righteous smirk off your face, you pig.*

Did he know where Greg and Hank were? Did he suspect that the FBI even now was breaching the walls of the cult? At least, that's what they were supposed to be doing. They'd been awful damned quiet for an operation this size. Maybe that's what Alex was looking for, some sign that he and she weren't in this mess alone.

Cain adjusted the long sleeves of his robe and faced his congregation. "Brothers and sisters, honored Elite, we are gathered on this momentous evening to pay homage to our mother the moon. Arise. Behold the light of the blessing."

The Elite extinguished the torches, and the audience climbed to their feet. The muted moonlight turned everything the color of pewter as the white globe in the east inched over the horizon. Cassidy shivered at the knowledge of all those guns in the hands of these black-robed bullies. Did these foolish followers have any clue how much danger they were in? *God, they looked stupid.*

Alex stiffened even as her own sixth sense pinged on alert in the darkness. He'd sensed trouble, too. She pulled her pistol and let the egg basket drop. Now wasn't the time for Dorothy from Kansas. She needed to be Butch Cassidy. Brave. Daring. Damned sure of herself.

Cain stretched forth both arms. "Earlier today, I chose Sister Charlotte to prepare my bride. Fortunately, Sister Chloe is a pure and trusting lamb. To honor me, she decided to embrace the blessing early. She's been here with Sister Charlotte for hours preparing to be my most worthy companion. See how the mighty hand of God works his wonders to perform?" His tone had risen to a fervent pitch by the time he'd finished.

"The mighty hand of God," his followers chanted.

Guess again, dumbass. Judith is on her way out of this nightmare. "I have to get inside that tent," Cassidy whispered to Alex.

"Agreed. Stay in touch." He tapped his hidden Bluetooth earpiece.

"Copy that." Cassidy stepped away. The moon's light enhanced the clearing, but it offered enough of what Cassidy needed. Shadows. She took several more quick steps to the rear of the tent. *Please let there be a flap.* There was. As quietly as possible, she racked her pistol and eased within the darkness.

Someone in a black robe spun to face her. Had to be Cain's buddy, Sister Charlotte. The older woman looked up for one surprised moment, her palms opened wide and foolishly believing that Cassidy had come to help. "The prophet's betrothed never came," she whispered. "How can I tell him there will be no wedding?"

"Simple. You don't," Cassidy whispered and—BAM! She let Sister Charlotte have it with the butt of her pistol right between her lying eyes. Down the woman went. With bizarre delight, Cassidy laid her first Elite trophy on the wooden bench meant for Judith. At first she thought it was simply a bed without a mattress, but most box springs didn't come with handcuffs at all four corners. Within seconds, Sister Charlotte was spread-eagled, gagged and cuffed.

Cassidy took stock of the dimly lighted tent. A white robe hung off a post in the center, no doubt also for Judith. The moment Cassidy fingered the silky material it slipped to the floor. *What have we here?*

The post seemed oddly placed. She'd thought it held the center of the tent up, but no. It didn't reach high enough. Cassidy ran her fingers up the post's smooth surface, then jerked her hand back. *Shit.* The last time she'd seen a device like this was deep inside a South American prison. She'd been part of the team sent by Alex to rescue three American priests. Holes had been drilled through the post at twelve-inch intervals. The holes were meant for a steel dowel, but no position of that dowel was meant for good. Not higher. Not lower.

It turned the post into a crucifix of sorts, where a person could be hung, stripped, flogged, or raped. Sure enough, the missing dowel hung like an ordinary tent peg off the back of a nearby wooden chair. No one could understand how evil this simple contraption was unless they'd seen it in action.

Her heart pounded, a racehorse come to life in her chest. Those priests had all been brutalized, but Father Damien, the youngest, had amazed her. The poor man had lifted his right hand, and blessed her with the sign of the cross. He'd whispered, "His peace I give to you. Go now. Before they return."

Cassidy sucked in a deep breath through her nostrils at the memory of that stinking cell. Father Damien had no way to know that the bastard rebels who'd tortured him couldn't return. They'd been reduced to ash and blood at the combined hands of the state militia and The TEAM.

Cain was just as depraved. How many young girls had he robbed of their innocence in this place of so-called blessings? How many women? Or young boys?

She wrapped herself in the silken robe. There would be no innocent little girl bride for Lucien Cain tonight. Only hell and vengeance in the guise of one pissed-off Butch Cassidy Dancer.

Chapter Twenty

I stink. Jude kept his head low inside the hooded robe he'd removed from Brother Victor. Thankful for the dark that hid the bloody bullet holes, he wished for a gasmask. One thing was certain—Brother Victor hadn't spent much time with soap during his life. The robe reeked of sweat and body odor, but it kept everyone at a healthy distance. His eyes watered while he studied the crowd gathered in the clearing. Anymore he detested these cult members. There were all as guilty as Lucien Cain. He just wished he had his glasses , so he could see them better.

Cassidy's friend, Melissa, had told the prophet that Judith would be there, but was she really? Jude didn't think so, but Cain seemed certain. Fear that he'd come too late propelled Jude through the shadows. Cain kept rambling, but when a gentle moan came from within the tent, Jude's heart sank. He cast caution aside. With a quick flick of his wrist, he took his gun off safety and parted the back flap, prepared to take on Sister Charlotte. He didn't have much of a plan after that, other than to grab his daughter and start shooting if he needed to.

"Not so fast," a woman growled very quietly. "One more step and I'll end you."

Jude stopped cold. A circle of steel pressed hard and deadly into his forehead. His arrival had been anticipated. He thrust his own pistol forward, just as determined. "You first."

"Don't think I won't kill you, asshole."

He cocked his head. The audacity in that voice. Could it be? "Cassidy?"

"Jude?" She pulled her hood off at the same time that he lowered his. As dark as it was, it was still possible to make out her blond hair. She took firm hold of his wrists. "It's me. I'm in the bride's robe. Judith is safe. We got her out of the cult. Tucker Chase, too."

His brain couldn't process what he thought he'd just heard fast enough. "You've got my daughter? And Tucker? You've got them both? Judith's safe?"

Cassidy's head bobbed as she confirmed again. "Of course. I told you I'd be back."

The weight of the world lifted at that very confidently spoken promise made and now fulfilled. He set his gun to safety, stuck it back in his belt, and pulled her into his arms, his hands searching over her face in the dark. Feeling his way to her smiling lips, he crushed his mouth to hers. "I knew you'd come."

She allowed one split second of pure bliss before she pushed away. "We're not out of this yet."

It might have been the endorphins released by his body at the knowledge of his daughter's safety, but Jude wasn't worried. He felt unstoppable. With Cassidy at his side, he could take on the world—and win by hell. He pulled her back again.

"Down boy," came her terse reply. "Cain will shut up pretty soon and he'll be in here."

He ran his fingers over her head, feeling for the golden locks of his warrior goddess.

"Jude," she murmured hoarsely. "We don't have time for this. You've got to help me bring this son-of-a-bitch down. Tonight we end Lucien Cain."

Reality got through to him. He stepped away. "Where's Sister Charlotte?"

"Over there. On the workbench. Old broad didn't know what hit her. Watch out for the post in the middle of the tent though. It's not a nice piece of equipment. Don't touch it. It's got to be full of evidence."

Jude grinned. Leave it to Cassidy to make his troubles disappear. Judith was safe, and everything else he'd ever wanted in life stood just inches away. He stilled his wayward hand even as it reached for Cassidy of its own accord. Gosh, he wanted to hug her in the worst way. Kiss her. Make crazy, passionate love to her.

The torches flickered to life in the clearing, lighting the exterior tent walls. Cain was coming, but Jude had to say one thing first. "I trusted you. I never doubted you," he declared as Cassidy came dimly into view.

"Of course." She smiled like he'd just said the most obvious thing in the world. "I told you I'd be back."

His heart stuttered to a screeching halt, stealing his breath along with it. There stood Cassidy in the pure white robes of the bride, the tent aglow around her. A more stunning sight Jude had never seen. The double meaning of the moment didn't escape his analytical mind. The innocence of this particular woman in such an evil place overwhelmed him. That was why she was able to do what she did. Cassidy was pure of heart. She'd overcome her own fate-worse-than-death. She'd persevered. And she looked like she enjoyed it.

"Brothers and sisters." The prophet's loud voice interrupted Jude's wandering thoughts, jerking him rudely away from the light in his life, and back to the ugly task at hand. "Tonight marks the beginning of the second coming. A new ritual of purification and a rebirth of loyalty will begin. In a few moments, the sisters of the Elite will serve wine from my private stock. It is my humble wish that you join me in a toast of celebration to honor my beloved Chloe, who even now awaits my blessing."

Jude's fist clenched. Cain was about to get Jude Cannon's version of a blessing.

"But I must warn you. To join me in such a tribute will also mean that you have chosen to put the old ways aside—that you desire to step into the inner circle. When you drink tonight, you too will become one of my Elite. What say you?" Cain cast a black shadow on the tent wall as he raised a goblet overhead.

The congregation chanted, "Yes, almighty prophet," to the sound of clinking glasses.

"Gosh, I hate him," Cassidy muttered out of the side of her mouth.

"I can't let this happen." Jude brushed Cassidy aside, his finger already on the safety of his pistol. "They have to be stopped before they drink."

"Jude!"

But he was out the front flap before she could stop him. Jude burst onto Cain's stage with his gun pointed skyward. "It's poison. Don't drink it. The wine's laced with cyanide."

Cain whirled on Jude, pointing a long bony finger. "He's the one. He helped the spy escape. Seize him."

"The wine's full of cyanide and valium!" Jude tried again, surprised not a single goblet had lowered. The congregation still stood with their glasses held high. How could this be? Where were all those discontented people who'd only this morning stood up to Cain?

The Elite charged. The pistol flew out of Jude's hand and he found himself face down. The knowledge of his foolish action overwhelmed him. He'd just traded a lifetime of loving Judith to save these very stupid people. Worse, where was Cassidy?

"People, please. Listen to reason. If what Brother Cannon said is true," Cain wheedled, "anyone who drinks the wine will drop dead. Let's put his brave words to the test, shall we? Would one of my most faithful converts join me?"

A chorus of hands shot into the air for that dubious distinction.

"Sister Elaine." Cain beckoned an elderly sister to his side with the kindest intonation while one of his Elite placed another goblet in his hand. "Please come to my rescue."

Sister Elaine had to be older than dirt, but up she came from the congregation, stabbing her cane into the red carpet with determination while she glared at Jude the entire time. Once at the forefront, Cain turned her to face the crowd. "Would you help me prove the error of this lost soul's ways?"

Sister Elaine nodded.

Cain placed a goblet into her frail, wrinkled hand. Without another word, she tilted the goblet to her lips and drained the glass dry, ending with a resounding smack of her lips.

The audience clapped.

Sister Elaine turned with contempt to Jude, shaking the empty goblet. "That'll teach you to blaspheme my prophet, you darned liar. I'm right as rain. Spry as a fiddle and ready to dance naked under the full moon."

A hard hand clamped over Jude's mouth, silencing him. Another arm snaked around his throat, squeezing him in a suffocating hold. Two dark-robed Elite pulled his hood over his head as they lifted him to his feet. "Now you will drink," one of them hissed into his ear, "and then you will watch while your prophet fucks your pretty little daughter."

Unable to speak, Jude writhed against the strong arms that held him tight. The hood slipped back, but not far enough. He caught a fuzzy glimpse of the audience at his peripheral. They'd lowered their goblets, but stood watching in silence, not one of them venturing forward to his aid. They hadn't believed him. He saw it clearly now. They were exactly where they had chosen to be.

Led.

"And now..." Cain stepped alongside Jude, his voice loud and gracious, but his grip as tight as a vise, "before we drink, I offer my forgiveness to this sinful man, this Brother Cannon upon which so many undeserved blessings have been bestowed. The time has come for you to confess aiding a spy. What say you?"

It was impossible to speak with his throat being crushed, but speak he did—through one of the liars choking him. "Yes, Prophet. I confess. I, Brother Cannon, am the guilty one."

Like hell I am!

Jude's body was turned, his back to the crowd. Someone handed Cain another goblet. "Will you join us in salvation, Brother Cannon?"

The man restraining Jude lied again. "Gladly."

No, I won't!

Cain tipped the goblet to Jude's lips as he courted the crowd again. "See how quickly the evildoer repents when faced with the truth? Let us all drink with Brother Cannon."

Jude writhed, his lips sealed tight. The Elite monster squeezing his throat clenched tighter and Jude had no choice. His lips parted. Cain smiled and—

"Stop!" The most glorious angel in white stepped through the tent flaps, her pistol on Cain. "Lucien Cain, you are under arrest for being the biggest asshole this side of hell. Please make another move," she coaxed, a hard edge to her voice. "Trust me. I can drop your ass faster than that cyanide you're peddling."

Cain lowered the goblet, but didn't drop it. "If you think killing me will stop the second coming, you're wrong. Murdering me will only give this cult its first martyr's blood."

Cassidy thrust her pistol into his robes. "I'm good with that. Just exactly what is this second coming?"

Jude flinched, wanting her to back off. God, she had a lot of nerve.

A shadow shifted across Cain's features. His chin lifted in arrogance and pride, as if his life didn't rest in the hands of a diminutive warrior goddess who even now made Jude's heart swell with pride. "It's the day when the whole world will know the power of my name."

"You're already famous, dirtbag. Hell. You're the biggest joke in the country."

Cain lashed out in an attempt to knock the gun from her hand. It didn't happen. She'd anticipated his move. They faced each other again, the Elite gathered around them while the drama between Cassidy and Cain played out center stage. It made for an interesting sight, a short, athletic woman facing off with a tall, gray-haired balding man who towered over her by more than a foot.

"They are but two," he hissed to his Elite. "Finish them now. Hurry."

Jude saw the flash out of the corner of his eye. The man who held him by the throat now brandished a knife as well. With a flying elbow, Jude jabbed him square in the gut. The knife clattered across the stage. Jude followed through with a fist and a sideways kick that sent the guy sprawling.

Jude rallied to Cassidy's side. The silly woman tried to push him behind her like he was the one who needed protection. He pushed back. A fleeting glitter danced in her eyes.

And there they stood, two against a small army, their backs against the wall, and nowhere to go but forward. Jude balanced his weight evenly and aimed, prepared for a frontal assault that would most likely leave him and Cassidy dead. He spared her a quick sideways glance. Now that Judith was safe, Jude was exactly where he needed to be. With Cassidy. Right to the bitter end.

She still had the drop on Cain. The Elite had yet to make a move. The congregation stood like sheep watching their favorite reality program. It was the proverbial standoff, but not for long.

He heard them first, and felt them all too soon. Several of the Elite had come through the tent behind him. The tables changed, and Jude's heart sank. Forced to his knees with Cassidy at his side was not how he wanted to die, but they were quickly subdued and made to kneel.

One of the Elite mumbled something into Cain's ear, and Jude allowed the briefest feeling of satisfaction. The veins in the proud man's neck enlarged and throbbed. He looked desperate. Vengeful. With a whirl of his robe, he turned to the congregation again, his voice pitched high in anger. "First blood! These sinners stole my bride!"

"Took you long enough to figure that out," Cassidy taunted.

A murmur stirred through the crowd.

"Drink up," Cain commanded, another cup of wine lifted high "Tonight we sacrifice two destroyers. Two!"

Being held face down to the carpet didn't prevent Jude from stealing a sideways glance at Cassidy. She winked back at him from the same awkward position, a playful light in her eye. Would he ever understand this beautiful woman who was part warrior, part girl, and very much a woman?

One of the Elite sliced Brother Victor's smelly robe into two pieces, and pulled it off, taking Jude's T-shirt with it. They must've tried the same thing with Cassidy, but he couldn't see her Someone's boot forced his face to the side, away from her. All he could do was listen to the scuffling.

"The knife," Cain commanded, and Jude's heart sank again. *Thank God Judith isn't here. I'm going to die like the fatted calf, bled out in front of an audience of fools.*

"Then give it to me!" Cain roared. "I'll do it myself."

Jude's ears perked up at the frustration in Cain's command. The prophet meant to do his own dirty work? More scuffling as Cain came forward. It was hard to decide who Cain meant to dispatch first.

"You're a pig, you know that, Cain?" Cassidy muttered. Ah, so she would die first, if only because she refused to go down without a fight. Jude smiled sadly. *That's my girl.*

His head was rudely jerked to the side. There she was, a half-naked woman, her clothes cast aside and a whole different distraction. The sight fueled his anger. Pain he could handle. He just couldn't stand it if they hurt her. "Leave her alone!"

No one heard him. Only Cassidy. She smiled across the short distance between them, her hands twisted behind her bare back. Even as blurry as things were, he could see the same spunk in her eyes, the fire that Cain hadn't extinguished, and Jude was awed. Here she knelt at death's door, her lovely breasts pressed into the carpet, all hope lost, but still she smiled.

He knew it then. If he died tonight, somehow in the great beyond, he would find this woman named Cassidy Dancer, and he would spend all eternity getting to know her better. If it was in any way possible in heaven, he'd romance her, and he'd love her, because he already did.

"Hey, Jude," she quipped. "Heck of a first date, huh?"

He returned her cavalier wink, cleared his throat and bellowed, "FBI!"

As if on cue, a single shot rang out. A body crashed to the ground. The boot that had held him prisoner relinquished its hold. Holy shit! Cain. The false prophet lay sprawled on his back, his head in a pool of blood, his arms opened wide. He was—dead.

Cassidy's eyes widened in awe of him for a change. Jude blinked, not sure. Could it be? With just one shot, could this evil menace really be dead? The Elite, who only seconds before seemed so fierce, now stood in shock over their fallen leader.

"Who's next?" A powerful voice rang out strong and clear from beyond the congregation.

Jude scrambled to his feet, reaching for Cassidy just as she reached for him. Pulling her close against his chest, he shielded her nakedness, his arms around her in a tight embrace.

"Drop the guns," the man in the dark commanded, "or we start picking you off, one by one."

The hooded Elite backed away from their dead leader. Some dropped their weapons.

"Alex is here," Cassidy whispered up at Jude, mischief in her eyes.

He pulled her out of the line of fire. The luscious swell of her soft breasts pressing against his chest beckoned. His body sprang to life. Warmth tingled between her bare body and his. Her dark eyes seemed to drink him in with nothing but delight. She didn't act worried. Instead, she looked happy. Willing. Sassy as hell.

The gleam of a blade flashed amongst the black robes of the Elite. Without thinking, Jude turned away, shielding Cassidy under his chin. He cringed, sure the knife would enter his ribs. It didn't. Another shot rang out and the would-be assassin dropped to the red carpet.

"We can do this all night. Look around," Alex commanded from the dark. "There will be no second coming tonight, but we *will* send then next person who moves straight to hell."

The nervous congregation milled around and Jude was glad. It was time they woke up. At last a man spoke up from the crowd. "Who are you guys?"

Alex didn't get the chance to answer. A crowd of federal officers flooded the clearing. "FBI! On your knees! Everyone!"

A lone man emerged from the trees, strolling straight for Jude and Cassidy like he had all the time in the world. His ramrod posture gave him away. The glimmer of gun metal in his hand told the rest of the story. Had to be Alex.

Chapter Twenty-One

Cassidy watched Alex make his way through the congregation. She saw the crooked smirk on his face when he waved the FBI agents out of his way, and she knew exactly what he was thinking. No doubt something along the lines of, *When is this girl ever going to learn?*

She scrunched her shoulders, her ear over Jude's heart. He snuggled her close, and she let him. Despite the fact that she was very nearly naked, this was the perfect way to end a tough operation. Let Alex scold her or chew her butt. The world had never felt more perfect. Of all the places to find the only man in the world who made her shiver all the way to her toes…

"See you finally got rid of that dress." Alex teased, his eyes skimming over her bare back before he stripped his cult shirt off and draped her shoulders.

"A girl's got to do what a girl's got to do," she teased, while she shrugged into the shirt. Jude seemed to have no intentions of letting her leave his side, though. After she did up the buttons, he secured her under his arm like this was their normal, every day position.

"Good to finally meet you, Jude Cannon. You've got a terrific daughter," Alex said as he grasped Jude's hand.

Jude returned the handshake. "Yes, sir, I do. You must be Cassidy's boss."

"Alex Stewart. Well done, Dancer. Interesting way to force Cain's hand."

"Did they bring enough antidote?" she asked.

"That's why the FBI was late. They couldn't breach the walls until their medical staff arrived. Anyone who drank is in for a hard time. Cyanide can be a slow killer. Diazepam, too."

"I don't think many of them did drink," Jude murmured.

"Do we know about the children yet?" Cassidy asked.

That spurred Alex into action. "Wait here. I'll find out."

For once, she was content to wait and watch. FBI agents handcuffed the Elite while more spotlights lit the clearing. None in the congregation tried to flee. They just stood in place until they were cuffed and told what to do, just like they'd been doing for months, maybe years. When the FBI stripped the tent and revealed a very unhappy Sister Charlotte and the insidious torture pole, some in the congregation looked away. Others seemed downright shocked.

Yeah, right, Cassidy thought. *You're all to blame. You let Lucien do all your thinking for you. Stupid, stupid people.*

The FBI had the entire clearing roped off with crime tape by then. Too soon, she'd be answering FBI questions for hours, but for now, standing inside the circle of Jude's arms, life was pretty darn good.

Jude moved his hand from her shoulder to cup her face. The tenderest emotions stared out from his smoldering, gray eyes. Finally able to see him without the discordant emotions of pain, fear, or worry clouding the view, Cassidy's heart failed. At least as tall as Alex, the sight of Jude's bare chest spiked her adrenaline-overloaded libido. A head full of dark, messy hair straggled over his forehead, adding a boyish charm to his gentle features. With his thumbs gently stroking her cheekbones, she could've stood there forever.

The most handsome man in the world smiled down at her in a heated combination of lust and adoration, and she knew he wasn't seeing her clearly at all. He couldn't be. His glasses were missing. She didn't deserve the blatant declaration of love in his eyes.

"You're my warrior princess," he whispered ardently.

She demurred. "Seems to me you had everything under control by the time I got here."

"You saved me."

She shook her head. "No. You saved me. Remember the—"

He placed a thumb over her lips. "Shut up and kiss me, Cassidy."

No sooner said than done. As his hands sunk over her ribcage to purchase the curves of her hips, she shivered. Every rib and every nerve responded to his touch, singing for more.

Stretching up on tiptoes, she wrapped her arms around his neck. He dipped his head, and *flash*, the heat of a thousand fireworks surged up from the earth below. The gentle question posed by his mouth turned urgent. His tongue caressed the daylights out of hers, and her knees turned to jelly.

With one sweep of his arms, he scooped her off the ground as if she, one of the toughest women on The TEAM, was no more than a little girl to be picked up, carried away and—

Oh, hell. I'm good with that. Yeah. I'm so good with that. Carry me away.

She gave in to the passion of his touch. For a moment she lost track of the sights and sounds of the very serious FBI agents bustling around her.

Jude eased away from her for a fraction, nipping her lower lip as he caught her eye. "I think maybe we ought to remember where we left off," he murmured hoarsely.

She nodded, totally content to go with the flow. It was kind of nice letting someone else be in charge for a change, especially this particular someone else. He eased her feet back to earth, his arms still around her ribs. "Let's go find your boss."

"Uh-huh," she acquiesced quickly, glancing shyly through the crowd to see if her boss had seen her latest indiscretion. Oh well, if he had.

Before they made it to Alex though, several FBI agents intercepted them. "Are you Cassidy Dancer?" the first body-armor-clad agent asked, his hand already wrapped around Jude's wrist.

"Yes, and this is Jude Cannon. He's—"

The agent grabbed both of Jude's hands behind his back, and proceeded to cuff him while the other launched into the Miranda rights. "Mr. Cannon, you have the right to remain silent and refuse to answer questions. Do you understand? Anything you do or say may be used against you in a court of law. Do you understand? You—"

"Wait a minute!" Cassidy interrupted. "Why are you doing this? He hasn't done anything wrong."

The agent ignored her. "You have the right to consult an attorney before speaking to the FBI and to have an attorney present during questioning now or in the future. Do you understand?"

"You guys can't do this," Cassidy argued. "You can't arrest a man simply for searching for his underage daughter."

"If you can't afford an attorney, one will be appointed for you before any questioning, if you wish. Do you understand?"

"We understand already! God, will you guys listen to me?" Cassidy yelled.

Jude shrugged. "It's okay. It looks like they're arresting everyone. Not just me. Don't worry. I'll be okay."

"No," she growled, clinging to his elbow. "It's not right."

One of the agents glowered at her. "You need to step back and let us do our job."

She ignored him, her eyes only for Jude. "You wait here. I'll get Alex." Brushing past the FBI agent, she planted a quick kiss on Jude's lips. "I'll be right back."

He beamed. "I know."

By the time she located Alex, the agents had hustled Jude off and half the congregation with him. She couldn't see him anywhere in the clearing.

"Where is he?" Cassidy confronted Agent Fitzgerald, the guy in charge. "Where are you taking everyone?"

"Local jails for tonight," he replied.

"Why?" Alex asked curtly. "Jude Cannon proved instrumental in taking down Cain. Without him—"

"Without him, we might have apprehended Lucien Cain alive. We might have been able to hold him accountable for his crimes," Agent Fitzgerald cut Alex off. "If I understand correctly, your legal obligation to Mr. McCormack was only to retrieve his daughter-in-law from this cult. Is that right?"

"Which Jude Cannon assisted with," Alex retorted. "Check the trap door in the silo. You'll find two of Cain's hit men tied up and waiting for you, courtesy of Mr. Cannon. You wouldn't know about any of the murders Cain committed either, if my agent and Mr. Cannon hadn't located Cain's crypt full of corpses. He provided nothing but engaged and helpful assistance during this entire operation."

"Listen. Unlike you, the FBI follows strict protocol," Agent Fitzgerald countered icily. "Take it up with Director Stone if you're not happy."

Alex flipped his cell phone open, his chin jutted forward. She waited anxiously while he placed a direct call to the national FBI Director in Washington D.C.

"Zach." Alex launched into the problem of the hour without any introduction. "Need your intercession with your Agent Fitzgerald out of the San Francisco field office, currently on site of the Church of the Palma Christi Cult near Boggs Mountain, California."

Cassidy watched her boss chat with one of the most powerful men in the country as if they were good friends. When he stowed his cell after a brief conversation, her heart sank.

"Sorry. They need to debrief everyone. Jude won't be allowed to speak with his daughter until they're through with him."

Cassidy glanced over her shoulder at Agent Fitzgerald. This operation was nothing but a boatload of admin work for him now, processing each member of the cult thoroughly and accurately. She and Jude had done the dangerous work, not the Bureau. Not fair!

"Let's head back to camp," Alex said. "At least you can tell Judith we found her dad and he's safe."

Cassidy didn't answer. She'd held Jude for such a short time, and now he was gone. Her eyes caught sight of three FBI buses parked down the hill at the compound, again with an accompanying orchestra of spotlights, agents, and police tape. Another bus had just pulled in. There was nothing to say. She wanted to punch something. Fitzgerald with his smirky, smart-ass attitude would do.

"Come on, Cassidy," Alex said gently. "Let's go home."

Chapter Twenty-Two

Jude watched Cassidy walk away, her eyes searching the compound for him as she left with her boss. Apparently she and Alex had an agreement with the FBI. After a very brief interrogation, both were released without having to go through what cult members, even phony ones like him, had to endure.

He'd been marched back to the compound once he'd been cuffed, and except for the fact he had to let Cassidy go and couldn't yet visit with his daughter, he was okay with it. He understood. Really, he did.

The FBI needed to know what had transpired within the Palma Christi Cult since Lucien Cain had established it nearly five years before. Jude just wished he could've seen Judith first, and hugged Cassidy one last time, maybe kissed her lips and breathed in the fragrance in her hair. She had beautiful hair. Heck. She had beautiful everything.

The FBI had a fairly smooth process for handling a large group of people, though. It was clear they'd done this before. Jude stood in one line for pictures, another for fingerprinting, and yet another to receive a clean set of gray coveralls. By the time he was done being processed, he'd had a hot shower and his first decent meal in weeks.

He'd also met Agent Floyd Stuckey. The taciturn guy ushered Jude into one of closet-sized interview rooms inside a long RV. An old-fashioned cassette-style tape recorder lay in the middle of the table and metal rings stuck up from the carpet. Probably for chains. Maybe shackles. Oh, well. *This is their show. I might as well go along with it.*

"Please state your name, address and phone number," Agent Stuckey requested in a monotone voice.

"Again?"

Stuckey nodded, so Jude answered all the questions, respectfully providing every last detail he could think of while the agent listened, questioned, and scribbled on his paper tablet. When he started asking the same questions over again, Jude knew he had a problem.

"I already told you what I know about Hank and Greg. I've told you everything. Twice. What's up?"

"Just answer the question."

Jude took a deep breath and played ball. It was very possible he'd missed something, so he gathered his patience, and once again went over the reason he'd joined the cult, why he'd been branded, and how he'd rescued Cassidy. As before, Stuckey seemed to be listening.

Finally, Jude stopped with a question of his own. "What's going to happen to me now?"

"You are a professed member of an illegal organization, Mr. Cannon. You established a viable alias, and you attempted to hide your fiscal assets. What do you think should happen?"

"But I only joined to save my daughter, and I had to hide my financial history or risk losing it to Cain." Jude studied this man's facial expression. Even without glasses, it was easy to see the indifference plastered on Stuckey's face. He was just a civil servant doing a distasteful job. There had to be some way to establish a rapport with this guy. "What would you have done if your daughter had been taken away like mine was? What would you have done if your ex-wife was murdered and your only child left alone in this insane cult?"

Stuckey finally looked at Jude instead of through him. He pushed back in his chair with a big sigh. "I guess I'd have done exactly what you did, Mr. Cannon."

Jude breathed a sigh of relief. At last. This guy appreciated his predicament.

"Listen." Agent Stuckey sighed. "Personally, I don't doubt you're telling the truth. We did locate Greg Gleason and Hank Crews precisely where you said they'd be, and we've corroborated your version of what happened in the silo. The evidence fits. We found the body of Victor Gonzales in the silo where you'd said you'd left him. Right now, an FBI forensic team is in the crypt. I've personally spoken with Agent Chase. Tucker's a good man. He's confirmed everything you've told us so far."

Floyd seemed intelligent. They were around the same age, and judging by the wrinkles on his brow and at the corners of his eyes, he'd seen the hard side of life, probably more than Jude had. Still, he seemed to be holding back.

"The thing is..." he scrubbed a hand over his face, "we've also discovered Cain's plan to sabotage the metro systems in five of the largest cities."

"He *what*?" That was news to Jude. "How?"

"You tell me." Once again, Agent Stuckey's eyes turned emotionless and distant. The indifferent G-man had returned.

"How would I know?" Jude shrugged. "What's Tucker think?"

"I'm not asking Agent Chase. I'm asking you. How did Lucien Cain plan to begin his second coming?"

Baffled, Jude could only shake his head. "But I thought the second coming was about poisoning everyone at the blessing tonight. That's what Tucker said."

"No. That wasn't the exact plan. Cain only intended to poison specific people who stood in his way. He concocted a dose of cyanide that would've taken hours to work, but he never intended it for everyone."

"Then what was he doing? I thought he wanted another Jonestown." Jude re-thought everything Tucker had told him. "Didn't he?"

"He was culling his flock," Agent Stuckey answered. "Only the most faithful could continue with him. He needed absolute allegiance. Did you realize that most of his acreage was devoted to the harvest of castor beans?"

Jude analyzed what he thought he knew. "Come to think of it, Cain did say something about a ritual of purification and a rebirth of loyalty. He wanted people who would never question him, didn't he?"

"Exactly."

Jude studied Agent Stuckey with renewed interest. Something was still unsaid. "Hey, umm, do you mind if I call you Floyd?" Jude reached his hand in friendship across the table. Under arrest or not, he was still damn glad to be safely in the FBI's possession instead of Cain's.

Floyd responded in kind. He gripped Jude in a solid hold. "Nice to meet you, Jude. You seem like a decent guy. I'm sorry you're caught up in this mess."

Jude relaxed. This guy he could work with. "I don't suppose you guys have any extra reading glasses around here? I kinda broke mine."

"You can't see?" Floyd leaned forward, his brows pinched to peer at Jude, as if that answered one of his questions.

"Not too well," Jude admitted with a small chuckle. "I had a pair, but they were cracked, and anyway, I lost them."

Floyd pushed away from the table and left the room. Within seconds, he was back with a couple of pairs of glasses. Jude was never so glad to be able to see. He took better stock of the room and his new friend. The carpet was a soft rose tone, not beige. A framed picture of the American flag was nailed to the wall behind him, and Floyd's eyes were hazel with flecks of black and gold radiating out from the pupils like bicycle spokes.

Jude extended his hand again. "Now I can honestly say I'm glad to see you."

A smile flashed over Floyd's face as he joined hands again. "That explains a lot."

"Like what?"

"Like why you've been acting suspicious since we cuffed you. You've been gawking around like you were looking for someone or something. We had you tagged as one of Cain's guys."

"Me?" Jude couldn't suppress his surprise. He borrowed one of Tucker's euphemisms. "Hell no. I just couldn't see shit."

Floyd chuckled, and Jude chuckled with him. The simple camaraderie in the tiny room flooded him with a sense of wellbeing. He leaned back in his chair, comfortable for the first time in months. "So what now? Can I leave?"

"Not yet." Floyd shook his head. "We still need to know more about Cain's second coming."

"But I already told you—"

"I know. I know." Floyd stopped further rebuttal with a palm to Jude's face. "It's just that you're the only man we've got who's been on the inside of this cult. You're the only one we can trust."

Oh, oh. A creepy awareness shivered up Jude's neck. He didn't like the direction this conversation had turned. "What about Tucker? Can't he tell you what you need to know?"

"Sure," Floyd agreed, "and he's told us plenty, but the problem is..." He paused, his eyes suddenly turned into lasers that seemed to penetrate all the way into Jude's overly rationale brain.

The light came on. Jude knew exactly what Floyd was going to ask next. "It's because Tucker's injured, isn't it? He can't go undercover anymore, can he?"

Jude wanted to bite his tongue as the truth spilled over it. If what he suspected was right, Floyd needed someone else entirely. He needed the GI Joes or Superman. Ironman. Anyone else—just not a mild-mannered accountant who wanted to go home and live happily ever after with his daughter and Miss Fluffy and maybe, a blonde warrior goddess.

"I'm an accountant." Jude offered the first dumb excuse his brain could come up with. It was a damned good one.

Floyd smiled. "You'll be wired, and FBI back-up will be close enough to pull you out at the first hint of trouble."

Reason number two showed up just in the nick of time. "But I'm a father," he whispered. "I have a daughter, and I haven't even had a chance to see her yet. She needs me. I'm all she's got."

"I'm a father, too. Five kids." Floyd nodded as he clinched the deal with his next words. "Our children are the reason your country needs your help, Jude. You know these people. You know how they think."

Jude searched his brain for reason number three, but Floyd seemed to be winning the debate.

"Do you know why Cain called his cult the Church of the Palma Christi?" Floyd changed the subject. He should've been a used car salesman, trying different tactics like he was.

"I don't know. I guess because Cain thought he was the hand of God?"

"No." Floyd's laser eyes somehow made Jude's mouth go dry. "It's named after a plant that's been used for medicinal purposes for centuries. The ancient Romans called it Palma Christi, the palm of Christ, because of its reputed healing power."

Jude waited. Floyd had gotten way too serious.

"It's what Cain's been growing inside this compound the last five years. They weren't just beans, they were castor beans. You know what that means?"

Floyd said that like Jude knew, but honest to God, he didn't. This whole conversation had taken a weird turn, and he wasn't a farmer or a gardener. "Just spit it out, Floyd. What are you trying to tell me?"

"Ricin is made from castor oil beans."

"Ricin? The deadly poison?" Now Jude was listening.

"Yes. Ricin. Cain sent three men to begin the next step in his plan for a second coming. He planned to use aerosolized ricin at five major US mass-transit systems."

Jude gulped as the new information filtered into his brain. Ricin. Holy cow.

"We just don't have anyone else who can get close enough to these guys." Floyd cinched the deal with his next words. "We know everything except where the aerosolized ricin canisters are being stored. We need you."

Jude coughed. The FBI wanted him to go undercover, like he was in any way trained, capable, or brave enough? Oh, hell no. The glasses he'd just been thankful for betrayed him now. If he hadn't asked for them, he'd still be under suspicion and not a candidate for a very risky operation. But still...

Cassidy's beautiful brown eyes sparkled up at him as if he still held her in his arms. She'd believed in him. The vision of her lovely nakedness teased him into thinking he could do it, that he could possibly be a James Bond kind of guy. For her.

Screech! No. Back that notion up. He jolted his dumb accountant's ass back to the real world. James Bond? Never. He was Jude Cannon and only Jude Cannon, a nerdy guy who'd tackled enormous obstacles only because he had to save his daughter.

Floyd sat waiting.

"I'm just an accountant," Jude offered one last time.

"That's not what Agent Chase said," Floyd answered with a glimmer of encouragement in his eyes. "He said he'd be proud to work beside you any day of the week. He said you were one of the best he's ever seen. Tucker believes in you, Mr. Cannon. So do I."

Jude didn't really care what Tucker or Floyd thought. He took a deep breath. He was tired and he wanted to go home, but Floyd's words had reached all the way into his father's heart.

Floyd hadn't said another word, which only made Jude more certain. In a false display of bravado, he used Tucker's words one last time.

"Shit. Why not?"

Chapter Twenty-Three

"What the hell?"

Cassidy ran the distance to their camp where a black FBI helicopter sat, its rotor spinning. With Alex on a dead run beside her, she couldn't process the scene fast enough. Melissa knelt on the ground performing chest compressions furiously on Tucker while a uniformed medic held an IV line in his bloodied hands.

How could this have happened? Where the hell is Rourke?

The real scene materialized. Melissa wasn't working on Tucker. He sat sprawled nearby, comforting a distraught Judith in his arms as he stared bleak, sad eyes at Cassidy. How could he be in two places at once? Who the hell was bleeding?

She didn't get it until she finally stood over Melissa. She wasn't working on Tucker. God no. It was Rourke.

Alex fell to his knees beside her. "What happened?"

"One of Cain's men came out of nowhere. Shot at us. He returned fire," Tucker offered weakly. "We cleared the wall fine. All of us. Almost made it back to your camp before he went down."

"He's dying," Judith whimpered.

"I doused him with all the blood stopper I had on me, but I had no idea he'd been hit until it was too late. Dumb shit should've told me. I couldn't,,, I couldn't help him."

"Son-of-a-bitch," Alex cursed, jerking his blowout kit off his belt. All tough guys carried a compact trauma kit for desperate times like this. Blood stopper. Compression bandages. Elastic wrap dressing. Stuff to save a guy's life. He went to work on his fallen agent.

Cassidy couldn't speak. Rourke lay with his head to one side. So damned pale. His eyes too dark, but not seeing her. A trickle of blood eked out of his mouth, dripping to the dirt. She dropped to her place at Rourke's side. "Hey, buddy," she whispered into his ear, her hand to his cheek. "I'm here."

His eyelids flickered. He blinked, struggling to focus. "Butch?"

"Yes, it's me," she cried. "I'm right here, Rourke. I've got your six."

"They... safe?"

Tears flooded her vision. "We're all safe. Now buck up. Let's get out of here and go home."

"G-g-good." He licked his lips, but forgot to close his mouth.

Cassidy glanced angrily at the medic who seemed to be helping Alex. "Do something!"

The young man shook his head without saying a word.

"Cassidy, leave him alone," Melissa ordered sternly. "Help me."

Cassidy did. She combined her hands with Melissa's, already covered in slippery, warm blood, but there was no chest wound. She cringed at the awful truth. The blood flow came from inside Rourke's thigh, from his femoral artery. He was bleeding out. His system didn't have enough blood supply left for his heart to pump. It couldn't work. That's why Melissa worked so feverishly on his heart. He was dying…

No!

Cassidy threw her whole self into chest compressions. Together, she and Melissa kept Rourke's heart beating while the medic hooked IV lines for an emergency transfusion. The metallic scent of blood mingled with sweat rose into Cassidy's nose. Until now, she had never known a tattoo of the American flag flew over Rourke's heart. There was so much to learn from him. This couldn't happen. Not to Rourke.

"One. Two," Melissa counted as they established a regular rhythm, "three. Four."

"Come on, O'Neill," Cassidy whimpered, her tears falling in perfect round splats onto his bare chest. Like raindrops. They looked like damned raindrops! On this, what had become the worst day of her life. "You've survived worse hits, damn you. You can do it. Like me. You can fly."

"One. Two. Three. Four."

"We need to roll," the medic said somberly. "Hospital's on standby."

Cassidy searched his eyes for the truth she didn't want to see, but the medic avoided her gaze. Even Alex looked away. She threw everything into stronger and better compressions, not allowing Melissa to stop, not for one damned second. "This is *not* going to happen. I won't let it."

Melissa endured with her. "One. Two. Three. Four."

"Try, Rourke," Cassidy commanded. "For God's sake, just try."

Alex tapped her gently on her wrist.

"Leave me alone," she snarled as tears dripped down her cheeks and neck. "He can do this."

Instead of arguing, Alex stepped back and let her work.

Melissa never faltered. "One. Two. Three. Four."

Rourke's eyelids blinked fast, his fingers rising to grasp nothing but air. Cassidy grabbed onto his hand, ready to hold his soul to earth if that was what it took.

"Butch," he groaned. "Always meant to tell... I... love you. Give 'em hell... for me." His hand went slack with the rest of his body.

"No!" she shrieked, clutching his bloody fingers to her cheek. This was *not* their last operation together.

Only when Alex and the medic lifted the gurney beneath Rourke did she realize they meant to take him. She rose alongside the senior agent she'd grown to—love. Yes, love. Rourke, her nemesis, her mentor, her worst nightmare, and sometimes her best friend.

The chopper's rotors picked up speed. Dirt and dust whirled, catching her in a stinging frenzy she barely felt. It was nothing compared to the pain ripping her heart apart. She had no choice. She let him go.

She let the wind hurl itself at her. *Not Rourke.*

She hurled her angst back at the goddamned wind. *Not Rourke!*

Alex stepped away from the chopper doors, his face set in stone. Judith whimpered in the background somewhere while the world Cassidy knew and loved fell apart. She stood too long, watching a dark sky that seemed to have swallowed the chopper alive. One minute, flashing orange and green lights glittered in the night; the next, gone.

Still, she watched. Voices buzzed behind and around her. Tucker explained to Alex how it had all gone down, how some kid had popped up from nowhere and fired. Rourke returned fire, but no one realized he'd been hit. It wasn't until they were back to camp that he dropped to one knee. As soon as he knew Rourke had been hit, Tucker had requested a medic from his FBI cohorts. The medic came right away. Within seconds, but the wound was—fatal.

Melissa comforted a sobbing Judith while Alex offered stiff-lipped answers that offered no solace. He'd already contacted the hospital. A trauma team waited on standby.

Cassidy stared into the dark where her buddy had gone. She heard it all, but the numbness of the sad night engulfed her. Crickets and frogs chirped from the creek that fed the willows on the other side of the wall—the wall that Rourke had so easily scaled earlier. The busybody who'd told her to take it slow with Jude; that he didn't want to see her get hurt. The man who'd drilled her over and over again at the shooting range until she was as good as him. The guy whose eyes twinkled when she'd least expected. Those willows. That wall. That Rourke.

She had nothing left to give. Her normally overflowing cup now stood not only drained dry as a bone, but run over and crushed to dust. Soldiers don't cry. She knew that. It was her motto, her mantra during tough ops, and her prayer in the worst of times. She'd seen carnage. Hell. She'd been on that awful Mexican op. She'd seen damned good men get shot and die. But—not Rourke.

The clouds let go of a flash of lightning and then a drop of rain. Thunder rumbled. Still, she stood and stared, her heart locked up tight and hard. At last a gentle hand jolted her from the edge of hopelessness. How long he'd stood beside her before he'd touched her, she didn't know. "The hospital will call," Alex said quietly.

She nodded. *And then what? Shouldn't we be there right now? Shouldn't we at least be on our way to be with Rourke? Aren't we even going to try? Is it already too late?*

The questions came without answers. She wouldn't have accepted them anyway. Not yet.

Alex pulled her into his side, his arm holding her together when she crumbled to her knees, taking him to the ground with her. The storm unleashed. Want to or not, she did what grieving women all over the world did when their hearts were broken. With her palms to the earth, she wailed, her keening a shrill angry hurt tossed into the universe.

There were no words strong enough, tough enough, or powerful enough to quench the pain inside. Cassidy Dancer forced her face into the dirt after a godawful day and hurled the only thing she had left back at God—all the hurt in her heart.

Not. Rourke.

Jude stood at the open door of the FBI RV with Agent Stuckey. Once he stepped onboard their waiting helicopter, his life would never be the same, and he knew it. Agent Stuckey said he'd have a team watching over Judith while Jude was gone. She'd be fine. Jude argued to at least speak with her before he left, but Stuckey flat-out refused. Said the mission would be compromised. It was too risky.

The knowledge that Judith and Cassidy were safe should've been all Jude needed to feel good, but still he stalled. So much of what lay ahead frightened the hell out of him.

He wasn't Tucker, and for sure, he wasn't Cassidy. They were precision-made patriots born in the refining fires of warfare, battle, and hardcore discipline. He was an accountant who calculated out of balances in his head and could tell anyone the amount in his checking account, right down to the penny.

Columnar spreadsheets littered his life, not brass shells, and certainly not the electronic listening device taped to the middle of his back right now, between his shoulder blades like an itch he couldn't reach. Somehow the FBI could turn it on and off so he could avoid detection should anyone scan him with a bug detector. An earpiece so small fit snuggly inside his ear canal. It was designed to escape notice, but it would also relay every single word he uttered for the next twenty-four hours. Longer, if needed.

In the blink of an eye, he'd become someone else. So he hesitated, like most sane men would on the edge of insanity, and he asked himself, *why am I doing this?*

Floyd stood with him. Waiting. This federal agent wasn't what Jude expected. Instead of badgering, he'd appealed to Jude's truest weakness—his instincts as a father. Belligerence and threats would've never won him over, only honesty. Jude respected Floyd. If nothing else, he was a pretty perceptive man, too. He seemed to return the respect. Darn it, anyway. Saying no to a jerk like Tucker Chase would have been easier.

The yard of the now-defunct cult compound looked more like a parking place for black SUVs, RVs and buses, all marked with the unmistakable seal of the federal government. Jude took it in with a quick glance. The flight back to D.C. would take several hours. From there, he'd catch a connecting flight and travel onto New York City to intercept Cain's three assassins, code-named the Brothers Grimm, also known as Alan Campbell, Mickey Perez and Clyde Fonda.

Jude barely knew them. The FBI knew exactly where they were, but locating them was never the reason they'd needed Jude in the first place. His assignment was to locate the primary supply of aerosolized ricin. The storehouse of death.

The FBI suspected the Brothers Grimm would utilize an HVAC to distribute the aerosolized poison more effectively at the targeted metro stations across the country. No one would know for sure until Jude intercepted and convinced the Brothers that Cain had sent him to assist. If asked why, he was supposed to give them further instructions to proceed to the next phase, whatever that was, insisting that Cain wanted all phases completed within weeks.

The only solid part of the plan was that Cain decried modern technology. The FBI was fairly certain none of the Brother's Grimm carried a cell phone. It made sense. There were no cell towers in that remote part of California near Boggs Mountain. Jude had already found out the hard way, the day he'd gotten branded.

His showing up out of the blue in New York, had to sound authentic, and that was where Jude knew he might fail. He could detect a lie easily since he'd endured years of Rachel's close-up-and-personal, hands-on training, but he couldn't for the life of him tell one. Neither could he tell a decent joke. She'd always complained he was too serious, that he didn't have a funny bone in his body. She might have been right. This next day or two might not prove too funny. He'd have to find a way to become a good enough liar to fool three truly evil men.

Floyd shuffled his feet, still waiting for Jude to commit once and for all. Other men might be excited at the adventure. Jude was not. Terrified butterflies churned like rabid bats in the pit of his stomach.

"You do remember I'm going with you?" Floyd offered.

Jude nodded without taking that final step.

"And we'll have plenty of back-up."

Jude blew out a big sigh, dropped to the ground, and wondered what on earth he was thinking. "Then let's do this."

Floyd nodded approvingly. Together they ran to the waiting helicopter. After it deposited them at the San Francisco airport, they'd catch a private jet to the East Coast. After a quick de-briefing in Washington D.C., Jude would be on the first flight out of New York City in twenty-four hours. In the meantime, FBI, local authorities, and Homeland Security had every metro station in the nation under high alert and swarming with undercover agents.

Knowing he was doing something for his country didn't ease Jude's misgivings. Just thinking about facing these specific cult members made his heart pound. His last encounter with evil rankled at the back of his mind, only this time he wouldn't be armed like he had been with Brother Victor. Not to mention that everything was unscripted. He'd have to play this entire charade by ear instead of a carefully thought out and prearranged plan. He wasn't a spontaneous man—another of his faults according to Rachel.

Wait. Why am I doing this?

Judith's pretty face came to mind as the helicopter lifted off. He stared out at the rapidly diminishing compound below. The last time he'd seen her was the morning Cain had demanded a sacrifice. If ever there was a hero in his family, it was her. Not him. Anything he did now was just icing on the family cake.

Then there was Cassidy. He had a long way to go to ever top that woman's bravery and audacity. They lived in different worlds, but somehow they had intersected, even if for just a little while. She was part of him, and that part came with him now into this crazy unknown adventure. He hoped to find a way to maintain that connection.

A trail of moisture condensing on the outside window caught his attention. It was raining. How fitting. Even the sky cried. Two different streams of rainwater trickled down the concave glass dome, suddenly driven together by the oncoming wind. They joined. *That's Cassidy and me,* he thought. *No matter what happens now, she'll always be with me.*

Looking up, he caught Floyd's thumbs-up signal from the next seat over. The agent looked optimistic. Jude returned the gesture without thought.

Yeah. Whatever.

Chapter Twenty-Four

Alex stayed on at the Seattle office after the cult operation. Cassidy didn't know why. She'd had the heart stomped out of her at Rourke's funeral, and lost track of time. Before she new it, a week had passed by.

Overall, the mission had been hailed a huge success. The missing children of the cult members were located in Cain's basement. Brother Roscoe had a hard time spitting it out when the FBI came calling, but apparently, Lucien had other plans for anyone under the age of twelve. Not anymore...

The FBI did a bang-up job reuniting long-lost children with parents, grandparents, and other family members. They processed all cult members in a timely manner, holding some for further investigation, but for the most part, releasing them to their semi-normal lives.

Most cult members recovered from their poisoning all except Sister Elaine. Cassidy found it interesting that Cain had meant to kill her, not once but twice despite her adamant support of him. But that was what happened. She'd dropped dead the same night from a double dose and an already compromised heart, and Cassidy honestly didn't care.

For now, the FBI maintained a strong-arm on the media. A court-ordered blackout precluded release of the cult's demise until the ricin threat was dogged and hopefully put to rest. But nothing could stop the constant reminder of

Rourke's death. Cassidy completed her written reports by herself. She'd suffered through the FBI debriefing like she'd been the only one on the operation. With Jude under the watchful eye of the FBI somewhere in New York, she just wanted to be left alone to lick her wounds, to try to remember why she did this godawful job.

Melissa McCormack was safely on the East Coast. Jed McCormack was happy. Tucker had already been released from the hospital, though Cassidy didn't know where he'd gone after he'd been discharged. The only one left with nowhere to go was Judith.

Some FBI agent called Alex. Said he'd made arrangements for her care, but Alex contacted Cassidy to accompany Judith to her father's place outside of Saint Augustine, Florida. The girl needed stability. Cassidy needed a new life. It seemed a good match.

Alex reached into his top desk drawer and pulled out two airline tickets. "I want you to take some time off. They're open-ended. Don't come back until you're ready."

She nodded, afraid to meet his eyes, her tears too close to the surface these days. He'd been there. He'd seen her meltdown. He didn't need to see more. "I'll be back in a week."

"No, you won't," he said softly. "This is a TEAM assignment. Stay with Judith until her father comes home. Longer if necessary. You decide."

She gulped and nodded again. She nodded a lot these days because words failed. She couldn't let them come out of her mouth. They wouldn't be intelligent anyway, and worse, sometimes they dissolved into tears.

In truth, she'd already taken Judith into her apartment. Alex knew that. After turning into a crazy woman back at camp, she'd run face first into Tucker, who'd still needed emergency treatment; Melissa, who was plenty distraught herself; but it was poor Judith who seemed to need Cassidy the most. The fourteen-year-old child had been turned into an orphan all over again, and her pain seemed to match Cassidy's.

So Cassidy bucked up. Manned up. Gave in. What else could she do? Judith was part of Jude. She had no mother, no other family, and, at least momentarily, no father. The stark fear in her gray eyes motivated Cassidy to keep on functioning. She did what she'd always done. She stepped in to help an innocent caught up in a blistering nightmare. And she wasn't able to stop.

"Thanks, Boss." She turned away, hoping to get away before Alex did anything else kind.

"I'm keeping track of him, too."

She froze, afraid to ask. *Who?*

"You need to know. Mother's been tracking him since he landed in D.C. She knows where he is in New York now, too. He's been in FBI custody, but he'll make initial contact with the Brothers Grimm in the next twenty-four hours. He'll be okay."

That helped. Jude must have willingly gone undercover since he hadn't even called. Hadn't even said goodbye, but Cassidy knew better. The FBI used bully tactics. He was a means to an end to them, but to her and Judith? He was everything.

"I have to go," she whispered, her eyes on the floor and her hand on the doorknob. Alex didn't speak again, so she hurried out of his office and walked straight to the elevator. It would've been a clean getaway if Murphy Finnegan hadn't intercepted her.

"Young lady," he called as she rang the elevator. "Wait up. I need to talk with you before you leave."

She hoped to make this short and sweet. No such luck. Murphy was the kindest, most grandfatherly man she'd ever known. The minute he was close enough, he grabbed her into a hug. "You take care," he muttered against her cheek. "We're all worried about you."

"I will," she squeaked out her promise. And the floodgates opened. She couldn't see the buttons on the elevator, much less anything else.

Murphy directed her into his office and shut the door. Without a word, he sat her down in the nearest chair, and gave her a handful of tissues. She was embarrassed, mad at herself, and too sad for words. There was nothing to say. Swearing didn't help. Neither did prayer. All the eulogies and all the tears in the world couldn't bring Rourke back.

Murphy pulled up a chair next to hers while she dabbed her eyes and blew her already sore nose. "You know this isn't your fault, don't you?"

"I know," Cassidy choked out. "I just wish I'd been there. He needed my gun. I could have helped."

"Now, now, that's what we all say, honey." He tapped her knee. "We all wish we were superhuman, able to be in two places at one time, able to leap tall buildings and save everyone, don't we?"

"But it was just a kid who did it?" she asked again, still finding it hard to believe that Rourke had been murdered by an over-zealous teenage cult member with a cheap .22 rifle.

Not a .50 cal, not a .9mm, not even a 30-06, and certainly not any kind of Lapua sniper round. Just a .22. Just a damned lucky shot that had hit Rourke's femoral artery while he was heroically covering Melissa, Judith, and Tucker's retreat to safety. Just doing what he'd always done. Serving others. Saving others. Thinking of everyone but himself. *Damn him.*

"Yes, a kid," Murphy agreed. "He's a real believer of all the Cain bullshit, this one. Only fifteen, and he's ready to avenge his prophet like one of those mid-eastern terrorist yahoos. The FBI has him under top-level security. He'll never see the light of day."

The inequity of the loss cut Cassidy to the bone. A dumb kid had murdered a highly-trained sniper who'd survived multiple overseas tours without serious injury. A boy had killed one of the nation's unsung heroes, and done it in cold blood. Nothing made sense. Nothing seemed fair.

She stuck two wads of tissues to her eyes, striving to get a grip on her emotions. "It's just that, Rourke was always so good to me. He was always there. He was... my friend."

"He's going to be hard to replace," Murphy muttered. "There's no doubt about that."

Cassidy couldn't speak. There was no way to replace Rourke. She wished she hadn't been so hardheaded and caused him all that trouble by getting caught by the cult. She wished she'd run to him at that last moment. Told him what he meant to her. Hugged him like her heart had urged her to. She wished... oh, hell, she wished she'd taken the hit instead of her dearest mentor. A thousand ways, her heart still cried, *not Rourke!*

"We lose good people in this line of business, honey. It's just the way it is."

She looked up from her grief at Murphy's gentle blue eyes. "Why do we do this, Murphy?" she asked tearfully. "Why do we walk into harm's way like we're invincible? Do we have something to prove? Are we all stupid?" She shook her head even as she asked. She already knew the answers. She just needed to hear the words.

"I guess it's the same reason you're going to Florida with Judith Cannon," he replied, his hand now moved to a gentle squeeze at her shoulder. "There's givers and there's takers in this world, kiddo. Guess we're just a bunch of crazy givers. I don't guess you'd want to be any other way, would you? I know I wouldn't."

She blew out a deep sigh, no longer sure what she wanted. "I'm tired, Murph. I'm really tired."

"You've got a right to be. Wish I could talk Alex into taking off for Florida with you and Judith. He's taking this pretty hard, too."

"He is?" That raised her eyes. Alex never seemed like an emotional man, except when he was angry. "Why doesn't he take some time off then? He owns this place. If anyone could, he could."

"That's not his way." Murphy's eyes twinkled with mischief. "You oughta know that by now. Besides, this whole thing made him mad, and you know how Alex is when he gets his dander up."

Cassidy wiped her eyes and took a deep breath. She definitely knew how Alex could be. "Well, tell him he's welcome to come for a visit. I hear Jude's home over looks the Saint John River."

"Sounds like a good place for a couple days of R&R."

"Hope so." Cassidy tucked her hair behind her ears. Even it felt dull and listless. Sad.

"Before you go..." Murphy went to his desk and pulled a small, brown-paper package out of his drawer. "Here's something I think Rourke intended you to have. Take it with you. Open it when you're ready."

She clasped the package against her chest and got to her shaky feet. "Thanks for the tissues."

He walked her to his office door. "I'll be waiting to hear from you."

With a final hug, she slipped away from the privacy of Murphy's office and bolted for the elevator. Finally in the TEAM garage, she placed Rourke's package on the passenger seat of her Subaru Forester and leaned her forehead to the steering wheel. Unbearable grief wrenched out of her. She couldn't stop sobbing. Her buddy and mentor was gone, she had yet to hear from Jude, and her heart was left with one big, gaping hole. The only thing remotely good was Judith waiting at home for her.

The storm passed. Cassidy gunned her trusty vehicle out The TEAM's parking garage and away from downtown Seattle, hooked into I-5, and headed south to Puyallup. She needed time away from the dream job that had become a nightmare.

The sight that met her eyes when she got home was just what she needed. Judith had traded her dingy cult apparel for a tiny pink T-shirt and a pair of acid-washed jeans that fit her slender figure perfectly. She sat curled and sound asleep in Cassidy's big wooden rocking chair on the wrap-around porch overlooking the gentle Puyallup River. Snuggled in one of Cassidy's over-sized sweaters, she held onto Magic like a little girl with a teddy bear. The sleek black feline didn't move off her new friend's warm lap.

"You look happy," Cassidy whispered.

Magic blinked as if to say, *I am now.*

Cassidy took a moment to drink in the peace of the backyard. The apartment she lived in was part of a remodeled Victorian-styled home with all the gingerbread cutouts at the eaves and dark-shingled siding instead of the more modern aluminum. She'd fallen in love with the restored home at first sight, but signed the lease mostly because of the porch. Each of the three tenants who shared the home with her had a river view. Here she sat with a cup of coffee on her few days off with the peaceful verdant splendor of the Pacific Northwest spread before her like a veritable paradise.

When she'd first moved from Utah, the sight of Mount Rainier used to tantalize her. She loved all the splendid vistas the Northwest offered, but this porch was where she re-energized her soul. Even now a hummingbird zipped up to the hanging baskets of pink and purple fuchsias, its quiet chirps and buzzing just another musical instrument against the backdrop of the murmuring river. The planters of purple and white pansies she'd scattered along the railing didn't hurt, either.

She breathed in a lungful of the cool, moist air, forgetting for a moment. The tranquility of her home surrounded her, and Cassidy knew she would live through this tragedy. Just like that, Rourke's eyes came to mind. He'd always had a way of seeing right through her. Regret slithered in where she'd just felt peace. *I should've invited him over for cheese and wine.*

It hurt knowing she'd missed her chances with him, especially with his dying words. Of all the times to finally tell her that he'd always loved her. She wished she'd known sooner. Maybe things would've turned out differently.

Magic's soft mew pulled Cassidy from her brooding. She looked at the childlike young woman in her charge. There was nothing she could do to change the past, but she could help Judith in the present.

With a resolute sigh, Cassidy packed and loaded their two bags of luggage into her Subaru, including the package Murphy had given her. When she returned for the cat carrier to transport Magic to a nearby friend's home, Judith was awake. "It's too bad we can't take her with us. Magic would have fun playing with Miss Fluffy."

"Or they'd fight tooth and nail and make us both miserable," Cassidy said. "You know how cats are."

"I think they'd get along." Judith eased up onto her feet, the cat still in her arms. "Cats are smarter than people."

Cassidy smiled as she ushered Judith and Magic to her vehicle.

Truer words were never spoken.

Chapter Twenty-Five

It's now or never, moron. Move your dumb ass.

Tucker's insults should have inspired more confidence. They didn't. Jude stood frozen at the orange-painted door to a cheap motel room outside New York City, his knuckles ready to rap, and his heart in his throat.

Floyd had made certain he got a decent hotel room before the job began. That first hot shower in months went a long ways to scrubbing the filth of the prophet away. The prime rib dinner filled a hole in his stomach Jude hadn't realized he had. But then all progress ground to a stop.

During the past few days, he'd been briefed and debriefed at FBI Headquarters in Washington D.C., then briefed and debriefed again at the New York field office. Jude set the record straight where he could, but the overall redundant bureaucracy of this federal agency had slowed the urgency of this undercover operation into a bad slow motion nightmare, one from which Jude wanted desperately to wake up from.

But now that the day for action had arrived, he was the one holding up the show. Only television noise came from within. Jude hesitated, his heart a jackhammer in his chest that wouldn't back off. If this charade worked, it would be the biggest miracle of the century.

"You're not alone." Floyd's calm voice deep inside his ear was no damned help now that Jude was about to come face to face with the Brothers Grimm. By themselves, Alan Campbell, Mickey Perez, and Clyde Fonda were no more offensive than Tucker Chase. But all together?

Jude had seen them around the cult, running to do Cain's bidding. He knew as much about them as he knew about other Elite, mostly to stay away from them.

He swallowed without any saliva in his mouth to actually make that bodily function work. Resolutely, he removed his new pair of glasses, FBI issue and supposedly unbreakable, and tucked them in his shirt pocket. He couldn't take the chance of being blind with these three, but damn.

This whole operation hinged on one big unknown. Cell phones. The FBI refused Jude telephone access in case he'd contact his daughter or Cassidy, but Cain was no dummy. Despite his *no modern conveniences* mandate inside the cult, he'd sold guns and he'd raised castor beans, two definite commodities that required communication with a seller or a buyer. He had to have a way to communicate with whomever that entity was. But the FBI had yet to find anything or anyone. The only electrical line ended at Cain's home. He had no computer, cell phone, or LAN line. If he'd ever contacted an outside source, it had to have happened during one of his few excursions into the nearby town.

The FBI assured Jude that the Brothers Grimm had no burner phones in their possession, that they hadn't placed a call since they'd stepped off the Jetway at La Guardia, either. Jude found that as hard to believe as Cain's no modern conveniences baloney. Yet, there he was, on the verge of doing something scary brave. Dressed in the same clothes he'd worn most days in the cult. Scroungy. Smelly. Yeah, exactly like the Brothers Grimm. He hoped.

He knocked at the door harder than he'd intended. Heavy footsteps responded.

"Here we go," Floyd murmured.

The door jerked open to a flabby man with hard eyes that skewered Jude straight to his accountant's soul. "You?" Alan Campbell sneered. "What you doing here?"

"The prophet sent me," Jude replied, surprised his voice sounded as strong as it did.

Alan's curled lip belied his disbelief. He jerked Jude through the door, spinning him into the room where Mickey and Clyde sprawled across the disheveled bed watching television.

"Cannon?" Mickey roared to his feet. "What do you want?"

Oh, great. These guys knew his given name, not his cult name. That could spell trouble. Before Jude answered, Alan had his arm around Jude's neck, and Mickey's fist rammed into his gut. Jude doubled over gasping for air, but Alan didn't release him, just jerked him upright for more of the same. Two more punches landed before Alan shoved him onto the motel's pressed wood coffee table. The flimsy furniture shattered under his weight.

By then, Clyde had rolled off the bed to watch. The shortest and roundest of the three brothers, he'd grabbed a donut box from the nightstand. He stood there stuffing one powdery confection after another into his face, crumbs falling over his big belly to the dirty beige carpet while Mickey and Alan pummeled Jude's back, head, and face. He ducked, trying to protect his eyes and nose while he was down.

At last Mickey jerked him back to his feet and pushed him up against the wall, his arm hard to Jude's throat. "What are you doing here, faggot?"

Jude dug deep into his jean's pocket and pulled out Cain's gold nugget ring, the one token he had to convince the Brothers. "This," he muttered hoarsely, Mickey's stranglehold difficult to talk past. "I got… orders from the… prophet. Here… Take it. Honest. I'm legit."

"You ain't nothin' but a lying snitch." Alan grabbed the ring and held it up to his eyeball, scrutinizing it. "Let him go, Mick. Why'd he give it to you, huh? Answer me and it better be good."

"Proof…" Jude wheezed, wishing he'd stayed in California. "He… he wanted you to know… for sure… that he… sent me."

Alan stared hard and long at Jude, then the ring, his lips pressed into a hard line, his jaw clenched.

Mickey still had his arm pressed to Jude's throat, making it damned hard to breathe. "He right? Is that really Cain's ring?"

Alan glanced around the room at his buddies. "Sure looks like it. It's got the sign inscribed inside it."

The sign—a five-leafed symbol of the castor bean plant, the hand of Christ. He and Floyd knew they'd need a way to convince these three Elite. The prophet's ring was the only thing that made sense.

"It is. Trust me." Jude hoped he sounded more convincing than he felt. "Look, he told me right where to find you three or I wouldn't be here, would I?"

Mickey seemed to believe. His hold loosened enough that Jude caught a full breath.

"But why you?" Clyde stood staring, the twisted snarl to his powdered-sugared lips evidence he wasn't persuaded. "You're Chloe's father. You're supposed to be dead. Has there been a change to that, too?"

Jude nodded quickly. "Yeah. I finally saw the light. Brother Victor converted me. He did." His stomach clenched at what he was about to say. "A guy can't fight the truth forever. Chloe belongs with the prophet. I know that now."

Alan still sneered. "Brother Victor converted you? The butcher? The only light he would've shown you was after he hit you between the eyes with his hammer."

Jude gulped. He hadn't known Brother Victor's assigned duty until then, but it made sense. The guy was solid muscle from head to toe. Handling a side of beef or a dead body would've been easy for him.

Clyde cocked his head as if to hear better, but Mickey only growled deeper in his throat. Jude panicked. These guys meant to kill him before he got started.

"Besides, Chloe's not just my daughter," Jude rasped, grasping at straws. "I mean, don't we all belong to the prophet?"

"Prophet said not to trust no one," Clyde grumbled.

Jude nodded again. "That's right. The prophet said you might not believe me. That's why the ring. By the way, he wants it back so keep it safe. Even if you don't believe me, at least put it where you won't lose it."

Alan's nose wrinkled. He peered closer at the ring and squinted, as if that helped him make up his mind, then glared at Mickey. "Let him go. I guess. Least 'til we got us a minute to discuss this supposed change in plans."

Jude slouched to the nearest chair while Alan, Mickey, and Clyde huddled by the motel door. Instead of listening, he shook his head, trying to clear the pounding inside his skull. Like it or not, he'd become everyone's whipping boy. "Hey, ah, mind if I use the bathroom? I need to clean up."

Alan shot him a dark look, which Jude interpreted to mean *if you have to*.

He ducked inside the bathroom, leaving the door wide open so the brothers could watch if it made them feel better. Jude put Tucker's lesson on how to stop a bleeding nose to practical application. A few cold handfuls of water in his face helped. The man staring back from the mirror still looked like hell, and the nose Tucker had mashed just days before looked worse. Might be broken. And now a black eye.

Jude groaned inwardly, trying hard to remember he was doing this for Judith. Only for her.

"Sorry about that." Floyd's voice filtered through the haze in Jude's brain. "You should've known they weren't going to be happy to see you."

"Shut up," Jude muttered quietly as he finished wiping his nose. Of course he knew that.

The bleeding stopped, but he wadded several tissues against it just in case. Sucking up a deep breath of *I-can-do-this*, he tossed the tissues and went back to wait out the Brothers' decision. Alan, Mickey, and Clyde each offered angry glances in his direction, and Jude prepared for another beat-down.

Damn, it had been a tough couple of days. He hadn't slept on the cross-country flight or any night since he'd left California. More like he couldn't, not after he'd left without a word to Cassidy or Judith. His heart hurt for the women he'd left behind. They deserved better, damn it. Floyd should've let him have that one last word.

Clyde raised his head from the huddle. "What's Cain want us to do now?"

"Not much," Jude answered. "He just wants the second coming completed. Fast."

"Why?" Alan still glared plenty, but Jude saw hopeful signs. Clyde, the stress eater, had stopped stuffing donuts into his mouth. Mickey's dark brows weren't furrowed as deeply.

Jude waved them off, feigning indifference. "Listen, you guys don't need me hanging around. I'm just the prophet's messenger. I promised I'd come, and I did. Keep the prophet's ring safe. I'm outta here." He lifted his butt from the chair, his heart doing Olympic-style cartwheels in his chest. Damn, where had all this bravado come from?

Mickey straightened. "Just hold on a minute. We ain't done decidin'. Shut up."

Jude shrugged and settled back to the chair, staring at his shoes instead of risking eye contact. Every time he turned around these days it seemed someone beat the heck out of him. This time he had no weapon, only a wire taped to his back and an earpiece, both which would get him killed by a savvy covert operator like Tucker or Cassidy maybe. He shot the Brothers Grimm a quick glance. They didn't look savvy. Just mean.

Alan and Mickey were both dark-haired and unshaven. Clyde, on the other hand, was clown-sized, as wide as he was tall. Clean-shaven, but triple-chinned. Bald. Squinty-eyed. The obvious weak link. Why he'd been given this dangerous assignment escaped Jude. But then, much of Cain's decisions made no sense.

By the sounds of their guarded conversation, Alan was against the idea of Jude staying. Mickey and Clyde seemed more amenable. Jude wiped his nose, wishing Alan would win the debate. Then Floyd would have to come up with a different plan, and Jude could go home.

Finally, the discussion ended. All three men faced Jude.

"Okay," Alan spoke up. "Message received. Now how's the prophet gonna know you talked with us? We can't get hold of him. Can you?"

Jude met his steely-eyed stare, relieved that FBI intel was accurate. "Easy. We don't. What you guys don't know is the FBI raided the compound right after you left. Only a few of us escaped. The prophet's gone into hiding, along with Greg and Hank. I don't even know where they are—that's how important I am. But Cain did give me orders before we split up. I'm to return to the compound if you can't complete your mission. Some of the Elite will be watching for me there. Is there a problem?"

Confronting Alan seemed to do the trick. The Elite weren't known for defying their prophet. "Ain't no problem. It's just strange is all. He wanted you dead last time I talked with him. Gave Brother Victor the job."

Jude nodded. "Yes. He was unhappy with me, and I did meet with Brother Victor. But here I am, still alive, and you know damned well I wouldn't be if Brother Victor had his way, would I?"

"Bet Cain's busy playing with that little girl of yours right now." Clyde stabbed an index finger into Jude's chest. He couldn't seem to shut up. "He always liked 'em young."

It took all Jude's willpower not to bend that powdered-sugar-coated finger back and break it off. *Don't let him get to you. Judith is safe. Cain is dead.*

Clyde snickered. "You gotta admit, he's a twisted old fart. He likes to tie 'em up sometimes and—"

"Shut up!" Alan roared. "We don't talk about the prophet that way. He can do what he wants with 'em. With all of 'em!"

When Clyde cowered, Jude knew for certain who was boss in this threesome. He directed his next question to Alan. "Am I staying or leaving?"

"Stay," Alan snapped back at him. "I don't much like it, but Mickey's got a point. We need someone to handle the ricin. Might as well be you instead of us."

Jude sighed. *Great. Like I don't have enough problems.* "What's the plan?"

"You tell me, smart guy. If you're so close to the prophet all of a sudden, you oughta know the plan."

"Yeah," Mickey joined in. "What's the plan, Cannon?"

Jude pulled a map of the New York subway out of his back pocket. He went over to the smashed desk and dragged the now mobile desktop over to the bed. In a second, he had Alan, Mickey, and Clyde peering over his shoulder. "It doesn't matter what the old plan was because the prophet changed it. Initially, he meant you guys to hit the Chambers Street Subway transfer station, right?"

Clyde and Mickey nodded.

"Now he wants you to plant another canister at Times Square."

"I still think you're lying," Alan argued. "That ain't going to effect enough people."

"Yeah, but it affects the World Trade Center," Jude replied. "Think about the panic that will cause, especially since 9-11."

"I like it," Mickey said thoughtfully. "It gives us four subway lines at Times Square, and you gotta admit, anything that hits near the World Trade Center will create a stink. Cops'll be all over the place. Firemen, too."

"If we time it right," Alan muttered, his lips in a permanent scowl.

"Makes sense," Clyde mumbled around another mouthful of cinnamon crumb. "I say go with it."

"It's what the prophet wanted. Two strikes instead of one. Twice the mayhem." Jude watched for any indication this conversation might lead to the whereabouts of the ricin stash. "Listen guys, this will be the prophet's declaration of war. It's got to be bigger than all the others. You might have to get more canisters."

Alan's mouth hardened into a thin line. "No one calls for the ricin but me."

"Whatever." Jude lifted one shoulder, hoping he looked more indifferent than he felt. "Just make sure you've got enough, and whatever you do, don't lose that ring."

"I said I'd take care of it!" Alan jabbed Cain's ring inside his front pants pocket, his teeth bared. "It ain't going nowhere else until I put it in Lucien's hand myself. That safe enough for you, Bozo?"

"Works for me. I'm going to get some shut-eye." Jude left the map for the three geniuses to argue over and slumped onto the couch. Turning his back to them, he breathed a quick sigh of relief, thankful they couldn't see the trembling fingers he clenched to his chest. He'd made some leeway, but Alan's distrust would be tough to overcome. At least, they hadn't searched him and found the wire.

"Good thinking, buddy," Floyd whispered deep inside his ear. "I like the 9-11 spin. I might make an FBI agent out of you yet."

The only answer Jude could afford was a groan and an unspoken *go to hell.*

Chapter Twenty-Six

"Where's my dad?"

Cassidy offered a small smile as she patiently answered for the umpteenth time, "He's still helping the FBI, Judith. Right now your father's on his way to San Francisco. Alex will call when he has more news, remember?"

Judith's gray eyes searched Cassidy's face for minutes before she looked away. It had been days, and Alex had called faithfully every morning with the current status of Jude's whereabouts. The once-confident girl Cassidy had met in the root cellar had transformed into an insecure teenager who startled easily and cried most of the time. Judith displayed all the symptoms of a trauma victim. She didn't have a clue who to trust. Not really. Not yet. She woke up screaming every night, and even Miss Fluffy couldn't keep the nightmares away.

Cassidy knew exactly how she felt.

Not one to resort to sedatives or anti-depressants, Cassidy wondered if that might be the only way to bring a measure of peace into Judith's life. Still—she waited. Jude should make that kind of a decision.

She uncurled her legs from the wicker bench on Jude's front porch. "I'm going out to the boat dock for a while. Join me? We might see those turtles again."

"Okay," Judith whispered. She placed Miss Fluffy inside, locked the door behind her, and pocketed her cell phone. Cassidy smiled sadly. Misplacing a cell phone these days could send Judith into a panic attack. She was convinced her father would call the first chance he got. The problem was, he hadn't.

"Here." Cassidy retrieved a small department store bag from her swimsuit cover-up pocket. "I got this for you at the airport the day we left Washington."

As Judith peered inside the bag, big alligator tears spilled down her face. "Oh, thank you. Thank you so, so much."

Everything was an occasion to hug, and Cassidy endured yet another soggy embrace. When it was over, Judith secured the gift, a cell phone holder, around her neck. She offered a weak smile. "It's red, my favorite color."

"I knew that." Parting her cover-up, Cassidy revealed the exact same contraption hanging around her neck. "I like blue. Now there's no way we'll miss your dad's call."

"Blue's my dad's favorite color, too." Judith's voice caught, and Cassidy held her breath. This was going to be another long day.

Together they walked the short distance to Jude's private dock where a pontoon boat bobbed under an aluminum canopy. The morning sun was high in the sky, but the breeze off the water had cooled everything down. Two eucalyptus-wood chaise lounges faced the peaceful Saint John's River, but Cassidy and Judith both preferred the edge of the dock. And another day of grief therapy got under way.

The longer she stayed with Judith, the more details Cassidy picked up about Jude and the daughter he adored. Not only was his favorite color blue, but he played the baby grand piano in his sitting room, and according to Judith, he enjoyed opera and theater as much as she did.

He'd chosen an exquisite site for his Spanish-style home with its white stucco walls and red-tiled roof, due west of Saint Augustine, Florida. Located on a private wooded acre, his plot included a thickly overgrown wooded area to one side, and a private boat dock at the other.

Other homes along the river were just as elegant. It seemed Jude wasn't just a lowly accountant working a nine-to-five kind of a job. The finely manicured lawn and the wrap-around porch that encircled the home declared a man of means lived there

Everything inside and out was neat, tidy, and fastidiously maintained, but it was the bedroom he kept for Judith that convinced Cassidy of Jude's heart. If the crazy pink and purple shag carpet wasn't a sure giveaway of a father's love and patience, the posters of the *Phantom of the Opera* and *Les Misérables* splashed across Judith's mauve walls were. Miss Fluffy's elegant pink and purple kitty house stood in the corner, and by the looks of it, nothing was denied the frail young woman wiggling her toes in the water like a little girl.

The ancient, loblolly pine sheltering Jude's home was another sure indicator of what kind of man he was. The construction company had to have taken great care not to damage the giant tree when they built the house. The old fellow lent a steady guard over Jude's home, sheltering it with needles and shade, along with the silvery-gray strands of Spanish moss dangling from every branch. It made for a timelessly beautiful setting. It reminded Cassidy of Jude with the way it stood steadfast over his family. The same way he'd tried to protect her.

"We had an alligator under our back porch one time," Judith said quietly.

"You did?" Cassidy lifted her bare feet from the river and glanced toward the house, checking for reptiles lurking in the shadows.

"It's okay. It's gone. Dad called an alligator wrestler, and he hauled it away in his truck."

"Did he really wrestle it?" Cassidy had to know.

"Oh, yes. He pulled it out from under the porch with this big long stick with a wire loop on the end. Once he wrapped duct tape around its snout, he had to wrestle it to get it up in his truck. Dad helped. It was so, so scary."

Cassidy smiled at the thought of Jude wrestling an alligator. That would've been a sight to see. "Where were you while all this was going on?"

"Dad made me stay inside and watch out the window." Judith's voice faded away. Just then, Miss Fluffy strolled along the dock and climbed up to join Judith. The Maine Coon padded Judith's lap for a moment before she settled down with a satisfied purr as if she had every right to be there.

"So tell me about Miss Fluffy. Like how did she just get out of the house?" Cassidy ruffled the silver tabby's long, thick fur.

"Hmm. I might have left the deck door open. Sorry. What else do you want to know?"

"Oh, nothing. Cats just seem to have their own stories. Like I found Magic under my car one morning when I was going to work. She was barely old enough to be away from her mom. Her eyes were infected and her ears were full of mites. All I could think was that maybe her mother was moving her litter and lost one of her kittens along the way."

"Aw, poor baby. She's lucky you found her."

"Or she knew exactly which house to show up at. Honestly, I think mine has a flashing neon sign over it that only animals can see that says, *'A sucker lives here!'*"

"I'd be okay with that," Judith murmured. "I like animals. All of them."

"So spill. Miss Fluffy is gorgeous. Where'd your dad buy her?"

"Nah-ah. He didn't." Judith drew in a deep breath. "She's a stray, too. I was coming home late from school one day after flute lessons, and some boys from my class were in a circle hollering. I thought maybe they were fighting or something." She gave Cassidy a tearful look. "But they weren't. One of them had a cigarette lighter. He held this little gray kitten by her tail while he burned her whiskers."

Cassidy cringed at the thought. "What'd you do?"

"I got so, so mad." Judith's eyes sparked. "I pushed that stupid boy, and I grabbed that poor little kitty. She scratched me, but I didn't care. She was going home with me."

"Did he let you just walk off with her?"

"No." Judith rubbed her cheek. "He punched me and screamed that she was his cat and he could do what he wanted with her. Poor Miss Fluffy fell when he hit me, so he grabbed her again. He swung her around like she was a toy or something. And she was crying. And I thought he might throw her and so I... and I..."

Cassidy waited.

Judith's fingers clenched into fists. "I don't really remember what happened next, but all of a sudden, I was on top of that stupid boy, and I hit him and his nose was bleeding and... and then I stopped. Everyone was watching, and I got embarrassed. He was crying that I'd hurt him, but I didn't care. I took Miss Fluffy, and I told him the next time he hurt anything, I was gonna beat him up again. And I meant it."

Judith stroked the silky motorboat on her lap. "I brought Miss Fluffy home and I asked Dad if I could keep her."

Cassidy grinned. "He said *you bet,* huh?"

"Yes, he did, and then he bundled her into a nice warm towel and we took her to our vet."

That sounded exactly like Jude.

Cassidy let the silence of the river work its magic, hoping it reached Judith, too. The opportunity to swim at any hour of the day went a long way toward restoring Judith's peace of mind. After everything that had gone down in California, she needed the therapy of swimming, snorkeling, and just lying around under a layer of suntan lotion and a wide-brimmed hat. Cassidy needed it, too.

She'd never been a late sleeper, but she'd become one now, mostly because she hadn't gotten a full night's worth of uninterrupted sleep since Rourke died.

"I'm so, so sorry about your friend," Judith whispered. "I can't stop thinking about him. Rourke seemed like a really good guy."

Cassidy instantly cast her gaze across the river. Judith loved the word '*so*' and '*so*' she over-used it. It typified teenage drama, but it was still just a word, and neither words nor the sparkling blue water could erase the fact that Rourke was gone.

Judith's continual apologizing for something no one had any control over didn't make it any better. Cassidy couldn't help Judith recover from her trauma anymore than she could help herself. Her heart hurt twenty-four-seven for Rourke, and most days her head hurt, too. The only thing she knew for sure was that hearts healed too damned slow.

She drew in a deep breath and slowly exhaled before she could answer. "I think the first year after you lose someone is the hardest. Least that's what I've read. You've had the mother of hard years. It's going to take a little longer. Be good to yourself. Be patient."

"Every day sucks," Judith answered quietly. "Every single one of them."

"You miss your mom, too." Cassidy hurt for the tender young woman next to her. She'd lost so much.

"Yes," Judith admitted, her one-word answer tight. The tears were sure to follow.

"So how do we help ourselves get through tough times, Judith?"

"I don't know. I thought I did, but now I'm not sure. Maybe one day I'll just walk out into the middle of the river until I can't walk anymore. Maybe once I get far enough, everything will stop hurting."

Cassidy listened and waited. She didn't respond. This wasn't the first time Judith had hinted at suicide, but Cassidy also knew this was a common reaction to loss. Hell, she had the same dark thoughts, which was why her pistol was unloaded and locked safely in the lockbox beneath her bed in the guest room instead of in her holster on her nightstand.

She didn't need it easily accessible right now. In fact, she wasn't sure she needed it at all. The TEAM could certainly get along without her. She contemplated making another career choice. Anything to help her move on.

What had Alex been thinking when he'd encouraged her to come to Florida with Judith? If he knew what a mess Cassidy was, he would've sent someone else. He should have. Anyone else. Two suicidal women together couldn't be smart, could it? She watched her young friend closely. Judith mirrored her. Yeah. Not good.

Cassidy took a deep breath and slowly exhaled. "I know you better than that, Judith. When your dad comes home, the first thing he'll do is come looking for you. You don't want him to find you floating in the river."

She let that thought linger between them. Judith was simply grasping for straws in the emotional hurricane her life had become. If Jude would just call, she'd be grounded again. Hearing his voice wouldn't hurt Cassidy, either.

The young woman's nightmares weren't the only ones Cassidy dealt with. Not knowing where Jude was or what he was doing made every night a little harder. It didn't help that he'd gone deep undercover on FBI business, or that Alex hated the FBI for good reason. Cassidy now knew about that bungled operation in Wisconsin where one of Mark Houston's sister-in-laws had died due to FBI negligence.

Jude wouldn't be safe until he was home. She could lose him the same way she'd lost Rourke. The thought always came like a sucker punch to her gut, leaving her breathless and sweaty, hyperventilating and scared out of her wits for the man whose strong arms she craved.

Rourke's cruel death had ripped the rug from beneath her and sent her flying. It left her floundering in a new and harsh reality, suspended like a kite in a vicious windstorm, never strong enough to touch down again, always fighting to hold on. If anything happened to Jude, she was afraid she'd fly off the edge of the world and never be seen again. Lost in space became a fearfully real possibility.

Placing a sweaty palm over Judith's hand, Cassidy nodded toward the pontoon boat bobbing placidly by the dock. "How about another day in the sun? You could teach me to drive that thing. We could fish a little."

"No," Judith said quietly. "I'm tired of sunshine and waves. I'm going inside."

"Well, then it's time to bring out the big guns."

"The what?" Judith looked sideways at her.

"I hate to do this," Cassidy muttered playfully, "I mean I *really* hate to do this. I'm not good at it, but I hear it helps."

Judith bit her lip, unshed tears glistening.

"Let's go shopping."

Judith didn't even smile. "Uh-uh. I think I'll just go feed my cat if it's okay with you."

"And let me go to the grocery store by myself?" Cassidy raised an evil brow, hoping to breach the storm of depression building behind Judith's gray eyes. "You now how I am. I get near all that fruit and—"

Judith offered a thin smile. "We could use something besides pineapple and dragon fruit."

"I never heard of dragon fruit before I came here," Cassidy muttered. "They're addictive. I'm hooked."

"And guava?"

"And watermelon." Cassidy pushed herself up from the chaise lounge and pulled Judith along with her. "See what I'm saying? I might need professional help."

The gentle banter did the trick. Judith agreed to help shop for dinner. That was all Cassidy wanted. Turning back to the house, she noticed a familiar face headed her way. She didn't want to admit it, but damn he looked good.

Judith squealed, "Tucker!"

Chapter Twenty-Seven

"Ladies and gentlemen, please fasten your seatbelts and prepare for take-off from O'Hare. The pilot will be pushing away from the gate in just a few minutes. Once again, thank you for choosing Delta for your travel to San Francisco, or as we call it, the City by the Bay. If there's anything we can do to make your flight more enjoyable, please don't hesitate to ask."

Jude froze. Another take-off meant another landing, and he didn't know which he hated worse, the heart stopping sensation of G-forces pushing him into his seat at lift-off or the irrational fear of crash landing. One was as bad as the other.

Now a trusted member of the Brothers Grimm, he had one more drop to make, and who knew how many more lies to tell. The annoying agent in the earpiece in his head advised him daily how successful he'd been, but this whole undercover thing had been more difficult than he'd expected. He still didn't know the location of the ricin, or who the mystery man was who appeared every morning with that special delivery—an unmarked canister.

The metro in Washington D.C. lay five days behind, New York City, another six. The last stop, San Francisco lay ahead. Boston and Chicago somewhere in between. By now he'd placed five of the deadly ricin-filled canisters, all set to go off at the same day and time according to Lucien Cain's devious, but recently FBI approved, plan. At every stop and treacherous drop site, the Bureau waited behind the scenes, invisible but prepared to secure the deadly poison.

"You ever consider working for the government?" Floyd's disembodied voice asked again.

"Never." Jude's quiet answer was swift and sure. The twenty-four-hour operation he'd signed up for had turned into too many risks and far too much worry. Not allowed to contact Judith or Cassidy yet, he wanted out of the Bureau's business in the worst way.

"What you saying?" Mickey asked from the aisle seat at Jude's left. "You talking to me?"

Jude shook his head, surprised Mickey had heard him over the engine noise. "Nothing. Just hate flying."

"You'd make a good agent. You ought to think about it." Floyd didn't know when to quit.

"Never," Jude muttered again, more quietly. *Not only no, but hell no.*

Trapped between Mickey Perez on the aisle and Alan Campbell at the window seat on a noisy Boeing 747 hurtling westward, did nothing to alleviate Jude's stress level. Every bump of air turbulence increased the roaring case of stomach distress he'd had since he'd agreed to this insane operation. And Mickey was a big man. He didn't appreciate having to move every time Jude needed to use the facilities at the back of the plane. Jude hated asking.

He was as tired of the three foul-mouthed degenerates he had to hang around with as he was of the FBI agent in his ear. Floyd was nice enough, but he'd become nothing more than an eavesdropping voyeur. The agent listened in on every conversation and offered plenty of free advice, but it wasn't his life on the line, was it?

But worst of all, Jude was afraid of what was happening inside his head. Inside his soul. He'd changed with every canister of death he'd placed. Every lie he told battled with the good man he used to be.

To make matters worse, Clyde had blessed him with a disgusting nickname, the Cannonball Express. Clyde thought he was clever, but little did he know. Although Jude walked through crowds and past security guards seemingly as fearless as his nickname declared, in reality, he only did what he did because the minute he turned his back, an FBI agent was there to save the day. That's who the real hero was. That nameless FBI agent and his Hazmat team. Not him.

Posing as an ex-HVAC repairman, he bragged it was the easiest part of the job. Because of his seemingly cold-blooded attitude, the Brothers Grimm claimed him their own, a damned dubious distinction. In truth, Jude was scared to death each time he ventured deeper into the intrigue of their warped thinking. He just never let it show because, well, he was scared of that, too. Showing fear with these animals would only mean another beating. Or death.

And therein lay the rub. The deceitful, hard man he'd been forced to become ate away at the person he really was. He missed Judith. He craved Cassidy. And he wanted to go home to his hide-away on the Saint John's.

Today's job entailed the final drop in San Francisco. Squelching his fear of flying down deep in his gut, Jude stared at the aircraft ceiling, if only because staring forced the visible signs of emotion from his face. Let the Brothers Grimm think he was scared of flying. He was, damn it. Man,

Tucker would have had a field day if he'd been onboard. Jude could almost hear the insults.

Jude tapped his buddy's forearm anyway.

"The crapper? Again?" Mickey glowered in disgust. "What's the matter with you, Cannonball?"

Jude shrugged as Mickey stepped out into the aisle and allowed him to pass. Between the fast food these guys consumed and the anxiety eating him from the inside out, Jude relished his alone time in the narrow, crowded place called the aircraft restroom. It seemed the only time he could relax. Plus, it was the only time he could speak to Floyd without being overheard.

The FBI agent had to be seated nearby. Floyd's calm voice entered Jude's ear the moment he stepped past Mickey toward the rear of the plane. "You need to up your dose of extra-strength Imodium."

"Yeah," Jude acknowledged, without explaining he'd already upped it four times over the recommended dosage. Nothing helped, least of all free advice.

"You do know I'm on the same flight, don't you? I've got your back."

Jude glanced around at his fellow passengers at the rear of the aircraft. No Floyd in sight. "Where? First class?"

"Second row from the bulkhead."

Figured. Might as well be on the moon. Jude was back of the bus. Way back. In the cheap seats.

"Next time you get up, leave your ear bud behind."

Jude entered the restroom accommodations and made himself comfortable before he answered. By now, Floyd had heard everything. One more ungracious noise wouldn't matter.

"Are you trying to get me caught?"

"You're smarter than that," Floyd muttered. "Don't be obvious, and they won't find it. We need to know what they're saying while you're gone. It's a solid plan. Give it a shot."

"Like where the rest of the ricin is?"

"Possibly. Intel can't place a fifth person, but someone's facilitating the transportation of the canisters besides that delivery guy. He doesn't know anything. We need a name instead of a delivery order placed from a public phone booth by an anonymous mastermind."

That was the understatement of the day. The ricin canisters were heavy, bulky, and looked like oxygen tanks. A cover over the top of the tanks hid the aerosol nozzle as well as the timer, already pre-set and ready to go. Every morning before show time, a canister was mysteriously delivered to their hotel room, no matter which city they were in. Jude had yet to intercept or connect with that supplier.

When he'd asked where the canisters came from, Mickey'd said it was none of his business, and Alan told him to shut up. Typical. The first phase of the prophet's second coming would be complete once they'd placed this final canister in the San Francisco Bay Area transit system, the BART. Jude didn't want to be anywhere near the Brothers Grimm for the second phase whatever it was, and smart-assed Floyd damned well knew it.

Jude was prepared nonetheless. He'd studied the online schematics of the Balboa Park BART transfer station at a local cyber café while Alan hunkered over his shoulder and literally breathed down his neck. Because of a recent environmental impact study, the ventilation system had been renovated. Additional HVACs had been added to the existing intake ducts.

Fortunately, the industrial-sized air-conditioning systems were installed between the air-filtration cleaners and the vents, which worked to the cult's advantage. Once Jude deposited the ricin canister inside that hard-to-reach free space, nothing would stand between the aerosolized mists and the unsuspecting crowds of mass-transit users. The odd thing was that no one at any of the metro or subway stations had yet questioned Jude as to why an HVAC repairman needed a full tank of oxygen to inspect an air conditioner. It seemed the FBI had a long reach.

"Tucker says to tell you he's on his way to visit your girlfriend," Floyd said. "She's still in Florida with your daughter, you know."

Great. While I'm stuck in limbo, Tucker's making moves on Cassidy. My life sucks. Jude finished what he'd started, washed and dried his hands, then flipped the occupied sign to unoccupied. "How are they?"

"Agent Dancer sticks pretty close to your daughter these days. Last status report says they're both doing fine."

Jude grunted. Knowing everything these two very important women in his life had to deal with right now didn't sound like they were doing fine, not by a long shot.

"Who's watching them?" Jude needed to know. *Please, not Tucker. He's such an ass.*

"If you must know, Alex Stewart has a man on sight. Senior Agent Mark Houston. You know him?"

"Sure don't. Is he decent?"

"If you mean can he take care of your daughter, all Stewart's men are ex-military snipers and extremely capable bodyguards. Trust me. She'll be safe."

Knowing that Alex Stewart had a guy on sight soothed Jude's nerves. He liked Stewart. If Mark Houston was anything like Alex, he had nothing to worry about.

"This is my last drop," he reminded Floyd as he exited the bathroom. "No more."

"Possibly," Floyd hedged.

"No possibly about it." Jude sidestepped a free-roaming toddler in the aisle on the way back to his seat. "Once I place this final can, I'm done. I'm going home. Plan on it."

"We'll see."

"Don't push me, Stuckey." Jude heard the harshness hidden in his whisper. Yeah. It was time to quit this job and return to who he used to be. Mickey, Alan, and Clyde were rubbing off on him, and he was seriously beginning to detest good ol' Floyd, too. "Get me the hell out of here."

Just then a man stood up at the front of the cabin. Second row from the bulkhead. Just where he said he was. Jude slowed his pace while FBI Agent Floyd Stuckey made his way down the aisle, damn it. Two seats behind Mickey and Alan, Floyd pressed what felt like a coin into Jude's palm and kept on going.

A bronze coin. One side proudly declared *Rangers Lead the Way*. The flip side showed the Army eagle, *United States Army* stamped at the edge. Great. Floyd had just reminded Jude big time who had paid the ultimate price in this war against evil. Rourke. Not Jude.

Shit.

Cassidy didn't expect Tucker's arrival to mean so much to Judith, but the moment the young woman spotted him, she barreled into his arms.

"You came!" she murmured as he hugged her tightly. "I'm so, so happy to see you."

The moment seemed to catch him off-guard, too. He winced when she hit his chest, but that didn't stop him from giving her a big hug. They stood for a long moment before Judith leaned back in his arms. Even then, she clutched his forearms as if she couldn't bear to let go. "I didn't think I'd ever, ever see you again."

"Now why would you think that, darlin'?" He brushed a tear off her cheek. "I'm a SEAL, and us SEALs never leave friends behind. I told you I'd come see you, and here I am."

Cassidy rolled her eyes at that big statement. It was just like Tucker to brag. "I'm surprised you're up and around already, but it is good to see you."

"Course." He shot her a dazzling smile. "Nothing keeps—"

"A frog down. Yeah, yeah, yeah." Cassidy interrupted another self-aggrandizing remark from the cocky guy. Despite his bravado, she couldn't help but like Tucker Chase. He seemed to be just what Judith needed. "We were just headed to the market. Do you have plans for lunch?"

"You cook?" he asked in mock surprise, his brows lifted and all those pearly whites on display. "This I've got to see."

"I've been known to," Cassidy answered. Under other circumstances, she might have encouraged his mild flirtation. Not today.

"Don't let her kid you. She's a great cook," Judith added, with genuine enthusiasm. "She grilled prawns last night. They were perfect."

"Are you holding out on me?" Tucker winked at Cassidy like she was as gullible as Judith.

"Always." He stood as much chance of landing her as the moon.

"How about if I take my best girls out to eat instead?"

"Oh! That would be so, so nice!" Judith exclaimed before Cassidy could get a word out.

What a smooth talker. Cassidy had to give him credit. Tucker's unexpected visit did have a good effect on Judith. She'd latched onto his arm like a young girl on a date, and his big hand over hers didn't help the situation. Tucker was obviously sweeping her off her feet, and why not? What was not to like about the guy? Besides his ego, that is. He had charm to spare in an abrasive sort of way.

Dressed in navy blue boat shorts and a white polo trimmed with navy pinstripes, he made for an easy sight on any woman's eyes. The closely cut dark hair against his dark tan didn't hurt, either.

"Hmm. Nice digs," he commented, as they climbed the three steps to the porch.

Cassidy caught the tone of surprise in his voice. "We make do," she countered airily, as if she actually owned the life of southern high society that Jude's home represented. "Let me grab my wallet and—"

"Nope," he interrupted. "I'm driving and I'm treating. You ladies don't need to bring anything but your appetites and your delightful conversation."

Cassidy cocked a crooked brow. "You're sure full of it, Tucker. What's really going on?"

He feigned amazement. "Can't a man take two good-looking women out to eat around here without making you suspicious?"

"Yeah, right. You came all the way to Florida to take us to lunch." She let that sarcastic statement hang.

"Nope. I came to see my best girl, if you want to know the truth." The dimple in his right cheek deepened right on cue, and the gleam in those blue eyes enticed. Yeah. This guy was handsome, and he probably knew it, too.

"I know a good place to eat," Judith said excitedly. "Lucky Lu Lu's has the biggest prawns around."

That put an end to the banter, but Cassidy still had a feeling there was more to Tucker's visit. In no time at all, he'd followed Judith's very precise directions to a little hole-in-the-wall joint overlooking the Saint John's. An open porch ran around the entire rickety establishment, but the smell of seafood on the grill made Cassidy's stomach growl. She hadn't eaten breakfast.

Judith ordered a basket of clam strips and calamari while Cassidy ordered her old standby of giant prawns. Grilled, boiled, sautéed—it didn't matter. She liked them every way and any way. Tucker, on the other hand, ordered a T-bone steak, rare, much to Judith's surprise. "You're eating red meat at a seafood place?"

"What can I say? I'm a meat-and-potatoes kind a guy. You want some?" He grinned devilishly and offered her the plastic-covered menu. "I'll order you so much steak you'll have to take a doggie bag home with you."

Judith scrunched her shoulders and giggled. Once again Cassidy was thankful he'd taken the time to show his ugly mug in Florida. The change in Judith's attitude made putting up with his bravado worthwhile. Before long the food arrived and they'd chatted like long lost friends.

Tucker regaled them with a few of his cleaner war stories. The best was the tale of the time his chair broke in the middle of a disciplinary meeting with two wayward sailors who'd decided to borrow his private vehicle for a joyride.

"So here I'm trying to impress them with how ornery I am. I mean, I'm glaring, and they're convinced I'm tough enough to eat them for breakfast and spit 'em back out again for lunch."

Judith rested her chin on her folded hands, her gray eyes filled with sparkles for a change.

"And they're shaking in their boots. I gave 'em one last dirty look before I sat down in my leather chair, and..." He paused and took a deep breath to draw Judith in. Cassidy lounged back in her seat and let him work his charm on the girl. He did know how to impress a fourteen-year-old.

Judith leaned forward. "What did you do next?" she asked breathlessly.

He grinned. "Hell, no. I fell on my son-of-a-bitchin' ass is what I did. The goddamned spindle on the chair broke. All those two jokers saw was my rear end flying over backwards."

Judith laughed while Cassidy shot him a warning look over his language, which he promptly ignored.

"Yeah," he continued, dabbing his napkin to his big mouth. "It's real hard disciplining a couple stupid kids when they're busting a gut and trying not to laugh."

"Language," Cassidy hinted again.

He waved her off. The napkin hit his plate. "Hell. I was laughing my guts out, too, but I was still so damned mad and, you know, I was embarrassed, and I don't get embarrassed much. But there I was looking like a fool. I had to do something so I picked up that damned chair and tossed it out my door just to prove I was still tougher than those two punks."

"Oh, my gosh. What did you do then?" Judith laughed, her eyes full of delight and maybe a touch of a schoolgirl crush, too. By the pink glow on her face, Tucker couldn't do a thing wrong.

He slapped his knee. "I told those kids to get the shit out of my office, and they'd better not let me catch them joyriding again. They were just a couple knuckleheads having some stupid fun. I wasn't really mad until that goddamned chair broke."

"That's so, so funny." Judith smiled, her basket of deep-fried food long forgotten.

"So how about you, little darlin'?" He pushed his empty plate away and leaned back in his chair. "How are you really doing?"

Her countenance fell. She looked down at her hands. "I'm okay."

"But you're still wondering what happened to your nice little world, aren't you?" he asked as the waitress came over to see if anyone wanted dessert. Cassidy meant to decline, but Tucker ordered three slices of chocolate cheesecake all around. "With raspberry drizzle and a dollop of real whipped cream, none of that fake spray-on shit out of a can, either," he proclaimed, loud enough for everyone to hear.

As soon as the waitress left, Tucker turned his full attention to Judith. He leaned toward her. "That's how it feels, doesn't it? Like nothing will ever be good again? Like life's not worth a shit?"

Her eyes brimmed. She nodded without answering, suddenly transformed into the frightened little girl without a mother and a father again. Tucker laid his hand over hers, and Cassidy wished he would shut up and knock it off. Judith didn't need some charming, big-talking jerk giving her the wrong impression that he cared for her on top of everything else she had to deal with.

"Let me tell you something, darlin'." Tucker's tone softened. "Your dad's one of the bravest men I've ever had the privilege to work with. He's serving his country right now. That's something to be damned proud of. You need to keep the porch light on and keep strong. Trust him, kiddo. He can't do what he needs to do if you're falling apart back here."

Cassidy's jaw dropped.

"I've worked with the FBI for seven years now—eleven with the SEALs. I'm here to tell you, young lady, your father is the only reason I'm alive today. God's honest truth."

Judith's eyes teared up. "He... he is?"

"You bet." Tucker tapped his index finger to the tip of her nose. "I know things are kind of hard for you right now. You're scared, and you've seen some shit you shouldn't have, but it's okay to be sad. It's okay to be scared, too. Life is hard sometimes, and you're going to lose people you love, but you know what?"

"What?" Judith's lower lip quivered.

Cassidy leaned forward, not sure exactly who Tucker was talking to right now, Judith or her. *Yeah, what, you big oaf?*

"The only reason it hurts losing anyone is because you loved them with all your heart to begin with. Don't matter if they're your mother, your father or some guy beside you in a firefight. You give a piece of your heart away every time you do that, Judith, and well, it hurts like a mother. It just plain sucks. I've only met a couple people like you in my whole life. Heck, I can count them on one hand and still have fingers left over. You love your dad and good on you."

Cassidy blinked her tears away, thankful Tucker was focused on Judith. It gave Cassidy time to wipe her face without drawing attention. The big jerk's words were getting to her.

"You're stronger than you realize, darlin'. Always remember, the only thing that makes us strong is the love we give away. Besides, look at your old man. You're his daughter, aren't you?"

Judith's eyes glistened as she nodded. "Uh-huh."

"Well, there you have it," Tucker announced, like that took care of all Judith's problems. He picked up his napkin and wiped Judith's tears. "Any kid of Jude Cannon's is gonna be just fine. You'll see, baby girl. He'll come home and you'll have that happily-ever-after you need. Trust me. He won't let you down, so don't you let him down."

"B-b-but... I want my dad now," Judith burst into tears.

Damned if that smug, know-it-all FBI agent didn't pull her chair next to his and wrap his arm around her. He pressed his lips to her forehead while he patted her trembling shoulder. "I know you do, baby girl, but you've got to know deep down in that sad little heart of yours that he's coming home. Believe in him. Pray for him. Never give up on him. Never. Ever. You hear me? That's what he needs most of all. You keeping strong makes him strong, too."

She sucked up a wet sniffle, but nodded. "'Kay."

Cassidy coughed politely over the lump in her throat. *Damn it, Tucker. You're not so bad after all.*

Chapter Twenty-Eight

"Time to celebrate!"

Mickey insisted they stop at a little sports bar off Mission Street after Jude placed the final ricin canister deep within the maintenance shaft at the Balboa Park transfer station. With beers and pizza ordered all around, Jude stifled a groan. This was the last place he wanted to be. He'd hoped for a quick trip back to Florida, not partying with the Brothers Grimm.

The bright idea Floyd had to use his earpiece as a listening device on the aircraft had failed miserably. The first time Jude left it behind during one of his frequent trips to the restroom, Floyd was rewarded with nothing but static. The next time, the only intel it revealed ended up being a sparring match between Mickey and Clyde over who could tell the worst lewd joke. Clyde won. Go figure.

The chubby guy slapped Jude's back as they bellied up to the bar. "Man, Cannonball, you've got balls of steel. Might hafta come up with another nickname for you. Steelballs instead of Cannonball. How's that grab ya?"

Jude shrugged, but Clyde's comment seemed to trigger something in Alan. "How is it that a simple accountant like you can be so calm when he's playing with something as deadly as ricin? You ever done this kinda work before?" Alan's dark eyes kept track of the waitress while he talked.

"I've been wondering that myself," nosey Floyd added his two cents' worth. "Sounds like you're perfect FBI material if you ask me."

"Guess I'm a changed man now that I've seen the light," Jude said indifferently. *But it will be a cold day in hell that I turn FBI.*

Alan looked around the place again before he lowered his voice still further. "I gotta admit. I wasn't inclined to let you work with us, but now I'm glad we did. You make it look easy."

"Why's that?" Jude acted like he was bored with the whole conversation. The waitress brought their first round of beers, and Clyde promptly ordered a pitcher and garlic breadsticks for the next.

"'Cause it's your fingerprints all over them cans, not ours," Alan gloated. "You never even used gloves handling that crap. You're going to be a wanted man for sure once the cops find 'em. You ever think of that?"

"Let them come. I'm only here to serve the prophet," Jude said easily. He'd gotten good at this lying business.

Mickey leaned forward on his elbows. "You think it's time to let old Cannonball here in on the next phase?"

"Yeah." Clyde nodded as he sucked his beer through a straw, while Jude waited.

"You think he's ready?" Alan asked. "I mean, you think Brother Aloysius would go along with it?"

That perked Jude's ears up. Floyd's, too. "Aloysius who?"

"Sure," Mickey answered. "If Lucien thinks he's safe, his brother should."

"His brother?" Floyd asked, and Jude wished he'd shut the hell up and butt out.

Alan emptied his schooner. He slapped Jude a hard one on the back and wiped his mouth with his other hand. "Let's find out. I'll call him soon as we spot a pay phone."

Mickey's eyes gleamed. "Now you're really gonna be one of us, Cannonball. Ha, I mean Mr. Balls-o-steel."

"Steelballs," Clyde corrected. "Don't go changing his new name the minute I come up with it."

"Whatcha gonna do, cry in your beer?" Mickey taunted.

Jude kept his focus on the last swallow of the amber drink in the bottom of his glass while the idiocy of idiots whirled around him. "What does Cain's brother do? Is he another deliveryman? Another convert?" *Another idiot like me?*

"Not exactly," Alan muttered. "He's smarter than all of us put together, maybe even smarted than the prophet. We grow the beans. He makes the poison. It's easy in California. That's why the prophet chose that scab of land near Boggs Mountain. Perfect climate. Perfect location. Perfect everything."

Jude let that interesting tidbit of *perfect* information settle into Floyd's big head. Asking questions usually created more problems, and this late in the game, he didn't need any. But what made Boggs Mountain so damned perfect? Surely Cain's crop of castor beans could be grown in other places.

The waitress brought three extra-large pizzas to the table, the bread sticks, and another pitcher of beer. "Anything more I can get for you boys?" she asked sweetly.

Clyde lifted one bushy brow and gave her a suggestive leer all the way down to her toes, then burped. "When do you get off?"

Jude wanted to belt him. The man was a pig from the ground up, but she handled him well. "Sorry. I own the place. I work twenty-four-seven. You gonna hang around that long just to wait for me?"

He grunted. "Maybe."

She winked over a sweet smile. "Well good, big guy, 'cause I promise I'll wait until the day after never for you."

Mickey nearly spit his beer, but if Clyde got the hint to drop dead, he didn't show it. Just grinned like he really did have a chance at dating that savvy woman. The one walking away from him.

"See what you can find out about this Aloysius guy," Floyd urged. "Go on. Get 'em to talk. They're warming up to you. Now's your chance."

Instead, Jude tapped his earpiece just to annoy his friendly FBI agent. He knew Floyd was probably sitting close by with a headset on, all safe and comfortable in his air-conditioned vehicle while Jude sat with three cold-blooded murderers in a greasy diner. Making outrageous demands was easy for a man who had nothing to lose.

"Lucien's brother must be damned smart," Jude offered somberly as he grabbed a slice of pepperoni pizza. "I imagine it takes a pretty expensive lab to make that ricin stuff."

Alan shrugged. "Hell, I dunno how he makes it. We send him the beans. The rest of it's his problem."

"Yeah, but ricin is damn deadly, just like you said. I think it takes some kind of a chemical process to make it," Jude countered, "or else Lucien could've made it himself. Don't forget, he's a real smart man, too."

"No, he couldn't make it," Mickey said through a mouthful. "His brother owns the medical equipment company. Mr. A's the one with all the right stuff. All Cain's got is a farm with a bunch of suckers dumb enough to hand over their money and work their guts out. Shit, people are stupid."

"Yeah," Clyde grunted, his mouth dripping with the grease from his triple cheese pizza, "like living in poverty's some kind a blessing. Let me tell ya. Before I met the prophet, I spent most of my life dumpster diving. Poverty ain't no fun."

Jude swallowed the last of his drink, willing to walk away at the latest news about Cain's brother and his company. Surely Floyd had enough to close them down. But nothing happened. Jude tapped his earpiece again.

"I hear you," Floyd said. "I'm checking on the whereabouts of one Aloysius Cain. Hang on. I'll get back to you."

"Hey," Alan leaned in conspiratorially to Jude. "Instead of me calling Mr. A, why don't you come with us? He'll be glad to make your acquaintance, knowing you and the prophet are so close and all. His place ain't too far from here."

Jude shrugged. "Whatever."

"Yeah," Mickey chimed in. "Then you can tell him exactly what the prophet told you about the second coming and phase two and all."

"Sounds like a good idea," Floyd added quickly. "Go with them. Don't worry. We'll track you. I'm still digging up the dirt on this guy. Once we have Cain's brother, locating the ricin ought to be easy."

But I don't know anything about phase two, damn it. Jude grunted in response to all the idiots he was listening to, not willing to put his life in danger for one more stupid idea. Improv was not his forte, either. What was Floyd trying to do? Get him killed? He had to set this straight once and for all. "We might have a problem, guys. The prophet never told me what phase two entailed. Don't you know?"

"Uh huh." Alan grunted. "All we knew was where and when we were supposed to place the first five canisters."

Jude gritted his teeth, wishing the subterfuge ended right then and there. He gulped past the growing knot in his larynx. "Don't look at me. Guess I'm not in that real inner circle, either."

"Humph." Mickey slammed his empty schooner down a little too hard. "Maybe Mr. A knows. Come on, guys. Let's hit it."

Once the Brothers Grimm got it into their heads to visit Mr. A, that was all there was to it. They went through two more pitchers of beer. Alan talked the waitress into letting him use her phone, and before Jude knew it, they'd driven to an out-of-the-way strip mall beneath a dark freeway overpass. The fourth neon sign on the row of deserted shops proudly declared *Palma Christi Medical Supplies*. A real no-kidding, *oh shit* tremor hit Jude. He tapped his earpiece to get Floyd's attention.

"I'm here. What's up?"

"Palma Christi Medical Supplies, huh?" Jude stretched when he got out of the rental car. "Mr. A works here? Feels like we're home."

Mickey shot Jude a drunken leer. "Kinda does, huh?"

"Didn't see that one coming," Floyd muttered.

Another tremor hit seconds later. Mr. A was the spitting image of Lucien Cain. Could've passed for his twin, and he was suspicious the moment he spotted Jude with the Brothers Grimm. One brow spiked while the other lowered. *Aw shit.*

"Who's *he*?" Aloysius asked sharply as he closed his front door behind Jude and flipped the switch to extinguish the outside signs.

Night had fallen fast. Jude flinched. He sensed a different kind of darkness in this place.

"This here's Brother Jude Cannon," Alan introduced him with a friendly slap to the middle of his back. "The prophet sent him to help us get the second coming done. Phase one's complete. We're ready for phase two. What is it?"

"My brother? Lucien changed the plan without discussing it with me first?" Mr. A's brows lifted. "I don't think so."

"Uh-huh. He did, too." Clyde nibbled his take-out order of garlic bread sticks. "Jude's a real good guy. He's smart, and he's been helping us all week. We call him Cannonball, only we're gonna change his name on account of he's got balls of steel. We was thinking Steelballs."

"Yeah, he's the main man, ain't you, Balls-o-Steel, my buddy and friend?" Mickey'd had a few too many beers, but all his jocularity was lost on Mr. A.

"Lucien never said anything about sending you three more help," he hissed. "You were the only ones appointed to this task. No one else."

That statement worried Jude. If Cain had kept in touch with his brother, did Mr. A also know his brother was dead? Jude knew for sure that Alan, Mickey, and Clyde didn't. The

FBI had done a good job suppressing the news, but the cult wasn't far from San Francisco. Mr. A could've made the drive in a couple of hours. Could that be what made Boggs Mountain perfect? Location. Location. Location?

Jude wished Floyd would double-check that little detail and do it in a hurry.

"But he did." Alan pulled Cain's ring out of his pants pocket. "See here? The prophet sent his ring just to make sure we'd know Jude was on the level."

Mr. A took the ring, his brows furrowed as he glared from Jude to the ring in his fingers. "Lucien would never part with this. Who are you?"

Jude shrugged. "Brother Jude Cannon, just like Alan said, and the prophet did send his ring with me. He knew no one would believe me without some kind of proof."

"I still don't believe you." Mr. A scowled.

"Guess that's your right," Jude said calmly. "All I know is what the prophet told me to do. He wants to ramp up the schedule, and to do that we need more canisters. That's the only reason we're here, isn't it guys?"

Mr. A stared at him. It would've been easier staring back if Jude hadn't heard a bunch of racket in his earpiece just then. He winced, and instantly coughed to disguise his reaction. Wherever Floyd was, it had gotten way too busy.

"You gots to believe us." Mickey was past sounding intelligent. "He's our helper and our buddy and my friend and—"

"Shut up," Alan barked. "Listen, Mr. A. I'm sorry if we disturbed you, but we just came from Balboa station. You had your guys deliver the last canister to our motel room this morning. Now we need to set up a new schedule. That's all. Are you gonna help us do what the prophet wants or not?"

"You already used one more canister in New York than you were supposed to." Mr. A's eyes shifted from Alan and back to Jude. "You want to explain why?"

"That was Jude's idea," Alan said. "He and Lucien changed up the plan, and it made a lot of sense. We got Grand Central Station covered, plus the subway stop at the World Trade Center. Thought we'd get some extra bang for our buck."

"Actually," Jude intervened, "we chose to target the Times Square and Chambers Street Subway transfer stations, but that extra canister will impact the World Trade Center traffic as well. The prophet was adamant that we create another 9-11 scenario."

"Yeah," Alan nodded profusely. "What he said."

Mr. A's sharp eyes didn't miss a thing. Jude had the feeling he was coming around. He searched his brain for something else that would pass for evidence, anything to convince this unfriendly man that he was who he claimed to be. But heck, he'd already handed over his ace in the hole—Cain's ring. All he had left was the clothes on his back and... *Oh, hell.* With a heavy sigh he did the only thing he could. He lied. Again.

"Mr. A, I'll be honest. I didn't used to believe in your brother." Guiltily, he offered the evidence burned onto the palm of his hand. "I was a lost soul until I turned my life over. Here. You can see how evil I used to be. I deserved this."

Even Alan looked surprised when he saw the brand. Jude gathered a bit more courage and told another lie. He tried to sound humble. "It's okay if you don't believe me. I can respect that. There were a few times I didn't know if I believed myself, either."

Mr. A's sneer did nothing to alleviate Jude's creeping panic, but he'd done all he could. It would've helped if Floyd had spoken up, but for some reason, his FBI buddy had gone silent.

A final creepy premonition whispered into Jude's ear. *You. Are. Alone.*

Alan lost patience. You gonna help us or not? We ain't got all—"

The front door burst open with the arrival of four young men with guns and a very bedraggled FBI Agent hanging limp between them. One of the men shoved Floyd to the floor at Mr. A's feet. "We found us a Fed snooping around your place. He's wearing a wire. Looks like your place might be bugged."

Mr. A's eyes stabbed Jude's. "Well, isn't this interesting? The same day you guys show up with a change of plans that I know nothing about, my boys find a federal agent. Hmmm."

Jude kept his eyes off Floyd, but he felt the instant shift of allegiance in the room. Like a cool wind had just parted the haves from the have-nots, and he and Floyd were definitely the have-nots. The young guys clustered near Mr. A.

Alan stared at him accusingly. "Who the hell are you?"

Jude rolled his eyes. "Holy cow, Alan. After all we've been through, you're still asking me that?"

"Knock it off, Jude Cannon, or whoever you are." It seemed Alan had suddenly forgotten everything he'd said at the pizza place. "I never wanted your help in the first place. It was all Mickey's idea."

"Was not." Mickey took a staggering step toward Alan. "It's Clyde's fault."

"Is not!" Clyde stopped eating breadsticks long enough to wave the last one in Alan's face. "I told you guys there was something wrong the minute this jerk showed up with the prophet's ring. Cannonball's a liar. His plan stinks."

"And you three are fools, now shut up!" Mr. A roared. "You led a traitor and a spy straight to me." He growled at his four-man bodyguard. "Deal with this mess. I don't want to know how." Storming out of his establishment, Lucien's brother slammed the door behind him. Car tires screeched as he peeled out of the parking lot. And left. Damn. Just like that, he'd run. What the hell did he know that Jude did not?

Panic tap-danced up the back of Jude's neck. Could things get any worse? First, the Brothers Grimm? Now four gangsters with knives on their hips and short stock rifles slung over their shoulders? Tattoos and weird, spiked hair? A bright yellow Mohawk? An unsheathed machete?

These four guys didn't look old enough to drive, but danger surely emanated from the guy playing with his handgun, a tiny thing that looked like Tucker's toy gun.

Shit. Shit. Shit!

Jude offered one final argument before things got uglier. "Listen, guys. I've been square with you from the minute I showed up. I've done everything you asked all week long. I carried the ricin into five different mass-transit stations, right under all those security guard's noses. What's the problem?"

"The problem is, *Mr. Cannon*, I don't like the way you look." Alan pulled a switchblade from his pants pocket and flicked it open. "I never did. So now it's time to put your money where your mouth is. I'll make you a deal. You kill this Fed right here and now, and maybe I'll believe you are who you say."

Jude rolled his eyes, still trying to act like it was no big deal. "Can do. Toss it here."

Alan tossed the open blade to Jude. He caught it, but it nicked his finger. "Geez thanks. You could've at least closed the darn thing."

A glimmer of amusement passed over Alan's face. For one brief second, Jude thought he had an opportunity left. He took it. With a sudden kick to his right, he knocked Mickey down while he hurled the blade back at Alan, hoping against hope he could actually hit him. After that, Jude had no plan at all except to run for his life.

Although Mickey did crumble to a drunken heap, Alan dodged the blade. Jude's heart sank. One of Mr. A's thugs knocked him down. He hit the floor, but not before he caught Floyd's disgusted look. Jude had to admit, the knife looked more lethal now that it was back in Alan's hand. Yeah. No heroes in the house tonight.

"Get on your feet," Alan ordered, then turned to Clyde and Mickey. "Tie these guys up and stick 'em somewhere outta sight. After Mr. A gets back, we'll dump 'em in the Bay."

Jude endured being tied up, shoved, and kicked into the backroom. It took a minute for his eyes to become accustomed to the dark, but when they did...

Oh, shit.

"Umm, Floyd? I think I found your ricin."

Chapter Twenty-Nine

"But how are you?" Tucker asked the minute Judith fell asleep next to him in the corner of Jude's white leather couch. He motioned toward the baby grand, the centerpiece of the spacious room. "This place looks like you've got a handle on what went down in Cali, but do you?"

"I'm fine," Cassidy answered. "Judith needed someone, and I needed some time away. Don't read anything into it."

"You're quite a gal, Dancer," he said smoothly.

She held up an open palm to stop the bullshit. "Don't, Tucker. Okay? Just stop. I'm not fourteen, and I'm not interested."

"And you're not my type." His lips twisted into a sarcastic smirk. "Besides, I've got a new lady in my life."

"And who would that be?"

"Melissa McCormack," he replied quietly, his voice suddenly deep and low.

Cassidy had to really look at him when he said that. The guy was all male, with a cleft chin and a square jaw, and stoked with too much testosterone. Melissa was such a classy woman, and Tucker was such a... a man.

"Yeah. I'm headed to Virginia next. Thought I'd see how she's doing now that she's home again and getting her life back together. Poor thing sure got a raw deal the last time she married. Figured I could show her how good things could be, you know, maybe show her a better time than living at hospitals and waiting on doctors."

"I'll bet she doesn't think she got a raw deal."

Tucker blew out a breath. "That's not what I meant. Marriage should be a helluva lot more fun than emptying bedpans and waiting for your man to die."

"She's a good lady," Cassidy offered softly. Tucker got her dander up, and she didn't know why. "You be good to her. She doesn't need more trouble."

He sighed, his gaze distant and his arm relaxed on the back of the sofa as if his mind was already in Virginia. "Not sure what she sees in me, but it'd be damned nice having a good woman in my life, for a change."

Damn, he had a lot of nerve. "Have you two already dated?"

"No. Hell, no. I just called her a couple days ago, you know, I touched base with her once she got home. Wanted to make sure she was doing okay. Damned if we didn't talk for an hour. She likes to cook."

"Is that all you're looking for in a good woman? One who'll take care of you?"

He didn't rise to the bait, just kept looking down on Judith through those thick, dark lashes of his. "My ex never wanted kids," he said, his voice soft and low. "But she got custody of our boy. Court says he needs his mother. Assholes. They don't think he needs his ol' man, too?"

"Life's not fair," she offered quietly.

"No, it isn't, but... " He paused, his palm flat on the leather, still contemplating the sleeping strawberry blonde at his side. "This little gal's just like her father. Too damned noble for her own good."

Cassidy flat-out couldn't speak, not with the gentle light in Tucker's eye. Damn it. The man was not who he seemed to be. "You're okay, Tucker, you know that? Thanks for talking with Judith. Today's the first time she's really smiled since we came home."

"She's a sweet kid." He arched his back and stretched both hands over his head. Damned if his shirt didn't lift up to reveal a smattering of dark hair on his athletically toned belly. "I'll be glad when this whole business is done."

"Is there anything else going on that I should know about?" She couldn't shake that nagging feeling, not after his *when this whole business is done* comment.

"Not that I know of," he answered, with a shake of his head. "Why? Are you having any problems? Have you seen anyone hanging around?"

"Should I be?" She studied him, still not able to put her finger on what he wasn't telling her. Maybe she'd gotten paranoid. Maybe she was over-reacting. Heck, maybe she just didn't need one damned more problem to deal with.

Again, he shook his head. "Of course not. Hey. Do me a favor, would you?" He reached in to his pocket and drew out a black leather case for glasses. "Give this to Judith for me. Tell her to hang onto it for her dad. I kind of broke his glasses back at the compound. Figured I owed him that much. He'd better appreciate these. They're expensive."

Cassidy took the peace offering. "You'd tell me if we were in any kind of danger, wouldn't you?"

His brows furrowed. "Sure. I've got your number. Listen, I need to get to the airport. Lock your doors when I leave."

Was that supposed to make her feel better? She didn't have a choice. Cassidy settled for that smug send-off as if recovering from tragedy was as easy as he'd made it sound. At least the view of him walking away was worth watching. Tucker Chase made for a damned fine physical specimen. Broad-shoulders with rippling muscles. Trim waist. Strong, bulging calves beneath a deep bronze tan. Cassidy had no doubt that a taut ass was stowed beneath those boxy shorts. Damn… Melissa might be smart to grab him up after all.

Tucker turned at the open door of his rental car and waved before he drove off. Judith stirred on the couch, and that was all it took for Miss Fluffy to resume her place of ownership near her mistress. Even she knew where she belonged.

The only one out of place was Cassidy.

With Tucker gone and Jude's house once again too quiet, she stepped onto the wide wooden deck that spanned the rear of the house. Darkness was falling. The quiet night noises of the riverbank fell like music on her ears at the end of a better day, and all because of a brash Navy SEAL.

She leaned against the railing, wondering where Jude was at that very minute, if he was safe, and when the FBI would send him home. Then she retraced her steps. Locked the front and back doors. Closed all the windows. Cassidy moved her pistol to her nightstand where she could easily reach it. Tucker wasn't kidding anyone. He hadn't come all the way to Florida just to say *how ya doing?* Something was up.

"So call someone," Jude demanded from his prone and bound position alongside Floyd. "Do your thing. Call for backup."

The look Floyd shot him could've withered an onion.

"You do have backup, don't you?"

Floyd didn't have to answer before Jude came unglued. "No one's coming?"

"I'm your backup. Now shut up, and let me think."

"You're it? Just you?"

Again with the smart-assed, withering look, and Jude wanted to beat the crap out of Floyd. "Holy hell, Stuckey! No one else is coming?"

"The Bureau has taken a series of deep fiscal cuts, and—"

"Fiscal cuts! I'm risking my life, and you're crying about your bullshit budget problems?"

"You're not helping the situation. Now calm down. Let's be reasonable and figure a—"

Fuck! Jude banged his head against the nearest ricin canister, sure he'd just developed a hysterical case of Tourette syndrome, he was so damned mad. He'd depended on this lone wolf from the FBI. But now? He was locked in a room with at least a dozen more canisters of ricin standing nearby and enough frustration to light the fuse—if they'd had one. "I put my whole life on hold for you guys. You wouldn't even let me speak to Judith before we left, and you don't have any son-of-a-bitchin' backup?!"

Floyd stopped talking to him. Just as well. Jude had nothing nice to say. He could barely rein his rage in enough to think logically. Their situation was hopeless.

"If I'd known you guys were so underfunded, I'd have told you to take a flying leap back at the compound, and I'd be home with my little girl right now instead of stuck here with you."

Instantly, he regretted his words. He hated everything he'd become. A liar and a thief, and now a bully. Badgering Floyd wouldn't help. Cursing, neither. Plus, he'd lost his glasses when that kid had knocked him to the floor. Once again, he was blind and pissed off. The damned day would be complete if the Brothers Grimm came in and beat the hell out of him.

Floyd still wasn't talking, but one of the young in the other room certainly was. "It's like this. We get to do Mr. A's dirty work for him. It's kinda who we are."

Mr. A's dirty work? Who's he talking to?

Mickey's drunken words were barely discernable, but the young man's were loud and clear. He must've been standing just outside the supply room door. "Yeah. We like, call ourselves the prophet's hit squad 'cause we're so good at it. Which reminds me—"

Blam! Blam! Blam!

Holy mother of shit! Jude damned near climbed out of his skin. It sounded like that punk had just murdered Alan, Mickey, and Clyde. The kid snickered. "That's why you're all dead, fat man."

The time for whining was done. Jude jumped to his knees, his hands bound behind his back. "We've got to work together."

The teenaged thugs laughed. More gunshots sounded. "Ha! Good job. We got 'em all."

"Turn around," Floyd ordered back at him. "Hurry. Stop. That's far enough. Hold still."

Jude did as he was told, but seriously? Floyd had his nose and mouth at Jude's wrists? "You're kidding me, right?

You're going to make like a beaver and chew the rope off my hands? God, we don't have time for this."

"Then think of something else," Floyd mumbled as his prehensile lips pulled the rope away from Jude's wrists and he started chewing again.

Something heavy scraped across the floor in the outer room. One of the young men laughed. Another complained about being slugged too hard. Three more loud pops sounded and Jude could *not* lay still.

"They're making sure your friends are dead," Floyd mumbled around the rope. "We're probably next."

"You think?"

"Come on," one of the boys muttered. "We gotta clean this mess before Mr. A gets back or he ain't gonna pay us."

"Told you to use a tarp."

"A tarp always gives it away. I like surprises."

"Chew faster," Jude whispered urgently. "Come on. Hurry it up!"

"I'm kinda busy here," Floyd growled. "Flex your hands. See if these ropes will give yet."

Jude strained frantically. Nothing.

Floyd went back to gnawing. But damn it! This was the stupidest predicament!

A door slammed once from the outer room, and everything went deadly quiet. Either the four guys had left the building, or they were on their way back in. Or Mr. A had returned. Panic jerked the logic card right out of Jude's brain. There was no time left. Floyd had to chew faster or—

The supply doorknob wiggled. Jude rolled his shoulders, needing to see which one of those punks meant to murder him. That wasn't how he wanted to die, not after all he'd done to save his daughter and his country. Floyd's useless gnawing wasn't working. Something had to happen. Jude lurched it to his feet, still bound, but he could hop. He made it to the door.

"Get back down here," Floyd ordered.

No way in hell. Jude was fed up being bullied and ordered around. Whoever was on the other side of the door seemed inclined to proceed cautiously. He took long enough opening it.

"Wait a sec," one of the young men finally spoke. *Crap. They're all still out there. We're dead.* "Load that fat guy up while I take care of these last two."

"Holler when you're done," one of the others declared. "You want a tarp?"

"Got one."

Shit! He's coming in.

Again the outside door to Mr. A's store banged open and slammed shut. Fat guy. Clyde? Jude couldn't think. The last remaining kid must've figured he was invincible. He wasn't careful entering the supply room. Didn't lead with his gun, just pushed the door open and swaggered in with a folded tarp under his arm, the cocky shit.

Jude lunged. He knocked the delinquent to his knees the minute he cleared the doorway. The punk fell and the door slammed shut. Not good enough! Jude dropped his full weight on the kid's gut. Using the back of his head as a battering ram, he silenced the surprised killer and knocked him out, hoping by some incredible miracle he hadn't made too much noise.

Jude couldn't wait to find out. He rolled over to his back, searching the kid's pockets. It was desperately difficult work with his hands bound, but Jude didn't slow down. Not for a second. This was about living long enough to see Judith and Cassidy again, and he meant to do it.

A knife. Finally! In the kid's front pocket. Jude pushed and pulled until he worked that weapon free of the denim. It literally took the art of rolling around on a supply room floor to new heights, but at last, he had it. He opened the knife and handed it off to Floyd.

"Cut my ropes," he ordered, as he backed into Floyd again. That gave him time to think. All the kid had on him was a knife? No gun? He'd intended on cutting Jude's and Floyd's throats? These punks were total psychos. This was all fun and games to them. Jude refused to consider how much he might have suffered at that degenerate's hand. How much he still might…

"Hold still." Floyd fumbled to maneuver the blade between Jude's wrists before he began a steady sawing motion. At last, both men were freed and on their feet.

"Good thinking," Floyd muttered, but Jude was already rifling through the kid's pockets looking for the one thing every teenager in America never left home without—a cell phone.

Found it! Jude stabbed nine-one-one and demanded police assistance and an ambulance. Hurry, damn it! The operator wanted him to stay on the line. No way in hell. Jude handed the cell off to Floyd. "Call your FBI friends. Step on it. When you're done, I'm calling my daughter."

An outside door banged open before Floyd could make the call.

Shit. The rest of the gang was back. Noises Jude couldn't identify pushed him and Floyd behind the door, listening and waiting. Terror tingled its icy fingertips across Jude's shoulders. He grabbed the knife out of Floyd's hand.

"Give it back. That's all we've got," Floyd growled.

Jude had no response. It seemed all he'd ever had were bad odds, starting with his marriage, the cult, and now this hopeless situation in a damned supply room. Were there any other kind of odds? The outside door slammed again. The saliva in Jude's mouth evaporated. God, what were those punks doing?

"We could barricade the door," Floyd suggested.

"With what? Cans of ricin? No thanks. I'd like to live long enough to see my daughter."

The doorknob began to turn.

Tension spiked Jude's heart rate through the roof. Judith's sweet smile flashed to his mind, the one she'd given him when she'd mouthed her last *I love you* at Jerusha's front steps. God, what he wouldn't give to hold her one last time. And Cassidy. If there were ever a woman he wanted to spend the rest of his life with, it was her.

The door cracked open.

He'd come this far to die in a broom closet? Like hell. Jude poised for one last assault on whoever the asshole coming into the supply room turned out to be. He didn't regret his choice of words. Didn't care anymore. He was done being Mr. Nice Guy. If he had to die, he meant to take as many assholes with him as he could.

The freaking door opened farther.

Jude rammed his shoulder against it. There was no lock. Only raw willpower, anger and the thought of Judith crying over his dead body to spur him on. It all came down to this one moment. Here. Now. Damn it! He groaned, every ounce of all he had left to give, given. He forced the door nearly closed when—

Whoosh! It flew open with an almighty shove, knocking both Jude and Floyd backward to their butts on the floor. A massive shadow filled the doorway. "Son-of-a-bitch! Back off and do it now!"

This guy wasn't one of those skinny kids, though, not the way he blocked the fluorescent lighting from the other room. Even a nerdy accountant could tell this stranger wore plenty of tactical gear and body armor, all except for that baseball cap on his head. The hefty weapon in his hand belied his total domination of the scene—maybe the world. Fierceness radiated off him in waves. Jude's jaw dropped in utter stupidity. "Alex?"

"You really think that little thing's going to stop me?" Alex growled.

Jude handed over the knife. "Umm, no."

"Damned straight." Alex folded the blade before he stuffed it into his pocket. He offered a hand up. "Figured you'd need real help since you were working with the Bureau."

Floyd muttered, "Shut up, Stewart."

Sirens outside announced the arrival of the SFPD, the San Francisco Police Department. Alex knelt beside the kid Jude had rendered unconscious and expertly bound his hands behind his back. Standing, he clapped Jude on the shoulder. "You tired of being a secret agent yet?"

"Hell yeah." Jude breathed a shaky sigh of relief. "Do you have a cell phone on you? I really need to phone home."

"You bet. Soon as we clear the building." He nodded toward the rear exit. "Everyone's out back."

Jude stuck with Alex. Mr. A's hit squad had turned his orderly medical supply store into a slaughterhouse. Blood splatter dripped down the walls and off the shelves. Jude sidestepped the bloody smears on the floor where the Brothers Grimm had been dragged out the back door.

"Are any of Lucien's men still alive?" Jude asked, oddly hopeful despite how much he disliked Alan, Mickey, or Clyde.

"I'm afraid not. Your Brothers Grimm are in the dumpster," Alex said quietly as he pushed the exit open with his palm. "Doesn't look like they suffered. Keep moving."

Jude obeyed, his stomach on the verge of proving how much he wasn't cut out for this business. Alex seemed to take the carnage in his stride. Not Jude. The blast of fresh air was a welcome relief. He inhaled, then quickly did it again before he embarrassed himself by puking his guts up.

But then he had to deal with the young murderers on the curb, their hands zip-tied behind their backs. Three insolent faces glared up at him. None looked older than fifteen. "My God. They're just kids."

"Kids with illegal guns." Alex turned to another armed man in identical protective gear. "That's all for tonight, Murph. You got an ETA on Homeland Defense?"

"They're in transit, along with Hazmat. Give them five more minutes."

"That's why Aloysius Cain took off, wasn't it?" Jude asked. It certainly made sense. "Once he saw Agent Stuckey, he knew he'd been made, didn't he? That all hell was coming for him? That he'd go down for making ricin and everything else?"

"He certainly didn't waste any time leaving, did he?" Alex answered.

"Wait a minute." Floyd seemed perturbed instead of grateful. "You've been tailing me this whole time? You knew we were here?"

Alex shrugged one shoulder at that stupid question. "Would you rather go back inside and wait for the Bureau to show? I've got who I came for. Saving a piece of FBI ass was just icing on the cake."

If sarcasm could kill...

Jude grinned. He really liked this Alex guy.

But wait. His momentary sense of satisfaction was quickly destroyed. Someone was missing. "Where's Cain's brother, Aloysius? Didn't you apprehend him?"

Alex grunted his answer. "Damned good question. Bastard never came back."

Jude's heart stalled. Just when he thought the operation was over, it wasn't. "But he's more dangerous than Lucien. He just grew the beans. Mr. A's the one who knows how to make the ricin. He's the one who aerosolized it. He may have started phase two."

Alex nodded. "From what my team is telling me, he drove straight to the airport. We'll be hard-pressed to locate him now."

Although on the opposite side of the country, Jude's heart had arrowed straight to his little home in Florida. "Mr. Stewart, I've got to get home."

"Good. You're booked on the next flight." Alex clapped him on the shoulder. "Take a deep breath. Your daughter's still in good hands. Cassidy's been with her since day one.

She wouldn't have had it any other way. You ready to make that call now?"

"Hell yeah."

Alex turned to Floyd and the man he'd called Murph. "I trust you two can handle this mess while I run Mr. Cannon home?"

Murph gave him a malicious grin and a quick thumbs-up.

Floyd flipped an ungracious finger. "Shut the hell up, Stewart."

Chapter Thirty

Fireflies and frogs. Crickets and dragonflies. *Florida.*

Cassidy sat in the early morning darkness, watching and listening to the overabundance of nature just off Jude's back deck. If she looked to her left, moonlight glimmered on the rippling surface of the Saint John's River. To her right brought the gray-black shadows of the towering loblolly pine and its hair-like moss, billowing softly in the earliest of the morning hours.

The sudden rainstorm overnight had added to the ethereal setting of Jude's home. Mist clung to the water's edge. The chorus of frogs lessened only to be replaced by a veritable cacophony of bird songs, twitters, and chirps from every tree, bush, and reed along the riverbank.

Morning came gently to Florida, not at all like the stark desert sun of Utah where Cassidy had grown up. Heat and humidity would stifle the pleasant day before long, but sitting in the dark of predawn, a sense of peace settled over her.

Tucker's visit had gone a long way toward smoothing the wrinkles left by the hard hand of grief. When Judith had gone sleepily off to her own bed, she'd wrapped her arms around Cassidy in an unexpected hug and left a kiss on her cheek. "I'm sure glad you're here. G'night, Cassidy."

"Me too. See you in the morning."

With that, Judith and Miss Fluffy had shuffled off to bed. But sleep eluded Cassidy, and there she was, wide awake on the chaise lounge on Jude's back deck, ready to open the package Murphy had given her. A current of cool air circulated through the home. The sheer panels at the sliding glass deck door drifted in and out on the light breeze.

Never a prissy miss, she preferred any time spent outdoors to in. She did housekeeping back in Puyallup sparingly and cooked even less, ever anxious to be off hiking, skiing when possible, or swimming. Indoors meant boredom and chores. Outdoors meant adventure and freedom. At least, it had until now.

Her pistol lay on the table at her side while her fingers fluttered nervously over the plain brown wrapping. What could Rourke have possibly left that she might want? She debated tossing it back in her suitcase, but it couldn't make her feel any worse, could it? Nervously, she broke the tape and unwrapped it, needing to put this last chore behind her.

Wow. Another punch in the gut she hadn't seen coming. Rourke had left a picture. Framed in a rustic frame, it had been taken at the shooting range during one of many TEAM recertifications.

She remembered the moment. All weapons were down. Rankings were stacked. Camaraderie was high. When the results were tallied, she'd outshot everyone. Even Rourke. Eric had said something about her being everyone's boss one day when Rourke grabbed her by the back of her neck and given her a monkey rub, his knuckles to the top of her head. He wasn't prone to tease back then, but whoever'd caught the scene had caught a rare moment, indeed. Might have been

Murphy behind the camera. He was always taking pictures when guys and gals from The TEAM got together.

The happy camaraderie from that long ago moment struck her heart hard. Her eyes had been squeezed tight and both hands latched onto his muscular forearm. She'd been laughing. He had one of those fierce looks on his face, as if he tried to look angry, but wasn't. He'd almost given her a hug that day. Almost. The caption scrawled in his handwriting at the bottom corner of the picture was her undoing. *My girl.*

"Damn you, Rourke." She set the picture on her lap and dashed the tear away. "Why are you doing this to me? Why now when it's too late? What do you want?"

Staring out at the river didn't bring answers. Her thoughts spun back to better days when she was just a newly hired junior agent learning the tough protocol and high expectations of The TEAM. Rourke had been unbearably hard on her, but she was a perfect fit for The TEAM, and he knew it, too. She just had to practice long and hard to become a respectable sharpshooter to finally win him over.

So many good times. Happy times. Exhaustion and tears won. Between the gentle sounds of nature all around her, she drifted off to sleep.

"Well, Butch? Are you coming or not?" In her dream, Rourke stepped from behind the billowing sheers, his long rifle slung over his shoulder and that expectant look in his eye.

She gasped to see him, but hesitated to leave. This couldn't be real, could it?

He held out his hand and snapped his fingers. "Get moving. We've got work to do."

"We do?" She gripped his hand, and felt herself lift. In a twinkling, she was over the river with the shimmering water below and a universe of stars overhead. She looked down to her feet, expecting some kind of support at the height she seemed to be travelling. Not so much. Even the loblolly pine that stood guard over Judith seemed small. Distant.

Cassidy rose with Rourke until nothing but stars swirled around him and her. The thought came to her that she really should leave a note, so Judith wouldn't be scared when she woke and found herself alone. "Where are we going?"

"Don't worry about it." Rourke glanced over his shoulder as he led her away.

"But I have to know," she insisted.

His words came back to her on the wind. "No. You don't. One of these days, your bullheaded way is going to get you in trouble, Butch." Then he turned and really looked at her. "What the heck are you wearing?"

The heat of embarrassment spread up from her toes to the crown of her head. Somehow, she was now clothed in nothing but a slip and those same white bloomers Jude had given her the day he'd helped her escape. No boots protected her slender feet. No tough-chick body armor sheltered her heart.

Rourke stood perplexed in the swirling dark. His eyes scanned her up and down, and she was mortified. He wore his usual warrior's garb: black ops gear, boots and cammies, his pockets bulging with extra weapons, magazines, everything a competent agent carried. The TEAM's cap sat backwards on his dark brown head of hair, while her attire made her feel—naked.

His hazel eyes sparkled. "Where's your gear? Your weapon? Shit, you didn't lose it, did you?"

"I... I don't know," she whispered, not sure where her pistol was, but sure she hadn't lost it. Losing your piece was the most grievous sin an agent could commit. She'd never. "I don't know what I was thinking. I... I'll go change. I'll only be—"

His stern face turned gentle. He brushed her face with two fingers that felt like velvet. "My mistake. You're off the hook. I'm going alone this time."

"But I've always gone with you." She hated the longing in her voice. He was leaving. Again.

"Not this time, Butch." His smile dimmed the light from the stars, drawing her into the vortex of wherever he was going. He caught her up in the hug he'd never given her in life. She held him tight, absorbing the warmth of his strength. His love.

He sighed, and she sighed with him. And then she knew she'd be okay. With gentleness she hadn't expected from her drill sergeant–like senior agent, he kissed the middle of her forehead and settled her bare feet softly to earth. Senior Agent Rourke O'Neill turned, his back to the stars. He still had work to do. A smirk tugged at the corners of his handsome mouth, and he—*mewed?*

Cassidy's eyes sprang open, the sensation of the dream still very real in her head, but Miss Fluffy tight in a stranglehold in her arms. The cat meowed again, as if asking, 'What the heck are you doing to me?'

Oh, hell. She set Judith's cat carefully to the deck and looked around, embarrassed she'd just hugged the stuffing out of the poor thing. Not like there was anyone there to see what she'd done, but still—it was obviously past time to go to bed.

Cassidy eased out of the lounge chair, intending to get a couple hours of sleep before the day began. Just as she brushed the deck curtains aside, Judith stepped out of her bedroom rubbing her eyes. The front screen door opened. She turned and cried, "Dad!"

Jude stepped into his home for the first time in months, his arms opened wide as he caught his daughter and pressed her under his chin. He groaned, his eyes squeezed tight in a father's torment. "God, Judith. I missed you so damned hard."

She all but climbed into his arms, sobbing. "You're here! Oh, Daddy, you're... you're finally here."

Cassidy stayed behind the sheers, her heart stuck in her throat. He looked so good, so much in love with his daughter. As much as Cassidy wanted to run to him, she couldn't. She turned away, wiping her eyes at the all-too-tender scene.

Jude had his daughter in his hands, and the look on his handsome face was akin to torture. He'd suffered greatly to get to this point, and Cassidy knew she shouldn't be there. Not now. This was a private time between him and his daughter. They had a lot to talk about and a lot of catching up to do.

With the dream of Rourke still fresh in her mind, this was the happiest, hardest thing Cassidy had ever seen. Jude didn't need her, and she surely didn't need to be standing there watching him and his only child like an—outsider.

She slipped into her sandals and tucked her pistol into her waistband. Blousing her shirt to conceal her weapon, she made her getaway down the deck steps and beneath the guardian pine. Barely a hint of sunrise glimmered on the eastern horizon. Palming her cell phone, she called a cab and scheduled a pickup in front of the grocery store, just a few blocks away. It was within walking distance. Her mission was done. She could be gone in no time.

Pushing her conflicted emotions away, she focused on the fact that Jude and his daughter were finally together and safe. That was all that mattered. Yeah, she'd promised herself that she'd tell him how she felt, but this wasn't the right time. He needed alone time with Judith and the privacy to get their lives back together. Cassidy Dancer was just in the wrong place at the wrong time, and—

The tears hit like a torrential hurricane. Rourke was gone, damn it! Jude and Judith were behind her. They had each other. A dark street lined with palm trees and pines lay ahead, and she was alone once more. The odd duck. The odd man out. Fifth wheel. It didn't matter. Not really. *Judith isn't my daughter. Miss Fluffy isn't my cat. I don't play piano, and I have a life at the other end of the world, and... and...*

A vine came out of nowhere, and she tripped and fell.

It *did* matter. And she knew it.

"Cassidy!" Jude called in the dark behind her, but crouched on her hands and knees like she was, it was easy to stay out of sight.

"Cassidy!" he called again, but he couldn't see her. She was the best ghost on The TEAM, next to Alex. She knew how to stay low, how to be invisible. How to run away.

"Cassidy! I'm home! Where are you?" The anguish in his voice made her wonder if she'd acted hastily. But it was too late. She'd made her decision. She couldn't go back, and she didn't belong. Not really. It was better this way. Her romantic feelings were based on nothing but the adrenaline rush of a damned hard op. She had to get away to get her head straight.

He must've gone inside. She hurried to her rendezvous with the cab. With knees scraped and bloody, she arrived at the grocery store and the adjoining self-service gas station. A single car sat next to the pump, its owner's back to her as he watched the ticker mark off gallons and dollars.

She looked around for a bench or somewhere she could sit to take better stock of her minor injuries. Of course, there was nothing nearby. The cab hadn't showed yet. The tourist was nearly done pumping gas, and all the freaking birds in paradise were chirping their heads off. She made do with the only seat available and had barely lowered herself to the concrete curb when the car behind her started up. Good. Now she'd have complete privacy to inspect her damaged kneecaps.

Wiping her face with the back of her hand, she pushed both legs straight in front of her. Her knees weren't too badly scraped, but they stung, and they were bloodied. A Band-Aid would help cover them up. She didn't need to attract more attention.

"Cassidy? What the hell are you doing out here?"

She looked up and straight into her boss's concerned face. *Alex?* Before she knew it, he'd parked and sat beside her. All her sins had come back to visit.

"Didn't you see Jude?" he asked, placing a firm hand on her shoulder. "I just dropped him off. We've been flying all night."

She couldn't think fast enough. The early sun streaming over the beautiful Florida horizon made her blink. A lot. She couldn't stop the knot in her throat that had turned into a golf-ball-sized lump of liquid emotion, either.

"He wanted to call, but decided to surprise you and his daughter by just showing up." Alex couldn't have looked more kind, and that was Cassidy's undoing. Jude had flown all night, and she'd run out on him. Why? She honestly didn't know anymore. It had seemed like her only choice when she'd made it, but now?

Her non-existent relationship with Rourke tugged her in one direction. She owed him something, didn't she? Time, maybe? Respect for what they never really had? But her feelings for Jude tugged her in the opposite direction. They'd been through so much together. She was that kite again, flying too high and battling too many opposing winds to ever be grounded to the earth.

Alex wrapped one arm around her shoulders, bringing her into his side. "It's okay," he said quietly, as the first sob hiccupped out of her. "It's okay. We'll figure this out together." And there they sat like a couple of bumps on the log while she fell apart.

At last he pulled her up off the curb and seated her in the passenger seat of his rental, her legs dangling out the side. Dampening a couple of wet paper towels intended to clean car windows, he dabbed at her scraped knees while she dried her tears with another towel. She hadn't said a word, and didn't know if she could. She should've been happy seeing Jude, and she was, but it only made her more aware how much he had that she didn't. He finally had Judith. She was what he really needed. The heartbreak of not having him or that pretty girl in her life anymore just plain sucked.

Alex looked up from his crouching position at her knees. "Are you going to be okay?"

She nodded without speaking, unsure why she'd turned into such an emotional mess. Of course it all had to do with Rourke and the way he'd died. One minute he was there. The next, gone. Just like Jude. A sob hiccupped out of her before she could catch it.

Alex's cell phone vibrated on his belt holster. Glancing at the caller ID, he handed it to her, but Cassidy waved it off. No sense taking a phone call when she couldn't speak.

He answered it. "Stewart." Pursing his lips and nodding, he said, "Yes. She's with me." His gentle blue eyes only made her cry worse. "We're at your local IGA." He stilled as he listened. "You bet. We'll be here."

Cassidy shook her head the second he holstered his phone. "I can't," she said hoarsely. "I want to go. Please. Let's just go."

Alex took a less than comfortable position at her feet, sitting on the asphalt parking lot with his arms on his knees as he faced her. "Do you know the only thing in my life I truly regret?" he asked quietly.

His question caught her by surprise. She didn't really need a thought-provoking question. Cassidy glanced fearfully down the road she'd just come from. Jude was on his way with Judith in tow, and she didn't want to deal with the confrontation of another kind man. All she wanted to do was run away.

Alex didn't wait for an answer. "You'd think it might be one of the targets I've eliminated over the years, but it's not. Not even my first wife's or my oldest daughter's deaths. Those were accidents. They were damned tough, but I've come to grips with them. No. The thing I still regret is the time I told Kelsey to get the hell away from me."

Cassidy stopped her frantic thoughts. Kelsey? Alex's wife was without a doubt the sweetest woman Cassidy had ever met. How could he have said such a mean thing to her?

"I hurt her, and I did it intentionally." His piercing gaze shot a laser straight to Cassidy's soul. "Do you want to know why?"

She shook her head and gulped, but he told her anyway. "Because I was scared, Cassidy, just like you are right now."

Alex? Scared? No way. Me, yes. Him, no.

"Yes. I was scared that a woman as sweet and perfect as my Kelsey could really love a man like me. I'd just suffered my first heart attack. I was half beat to death, and I pretty much hated how bleak my future looked. I didn't deserve her then, and I don't deserve her now." He interlocked his fingers between his knees. "You're a lot like me, Cassidy."

Okay, that didn't help. There was no way she was as tough as this ex-Marine, successful businessman, and probably the hardest man she'd ever met. He'd praised her once for being as good a ghost as him, but to be *a lot like him* was more than she could handle. Cassidy buried her face in her hands, worn out from grief and hope and the world. There weren't enough paper towels on the planet to stop the deluge.

"You're scared of getting too close to someone and getting hurt. It's okay to be scared, honey," he reassured her again.

"That's what Tucker said, but I don't know what to do." There. She'd said it. "God, Alex, Rourke waited until the last damned minute to tell me he loved me, and now he's gone, and I... and I... What if something happens to Jude? Huh? I can't do this again. I just can't lose someone else who I... who I..."

"Who you care about." He finished for her, but he'd used the wrong word.

Love. This was about love, and that unfamiliar depth of that emotion scared the hell out of her. Covet ops she could handle. Training and taking orders she understood. Hell, she excelled at kicking ass, but something as fragile and heartrending as love? Something as tender as sharing her body and soul with a man? With Jude? Relying on him to actually want to spend time with her?

Yeah, no. She'd learned long ago how to use her tough girl persona to scare boys and men away. She just hadn't expected to be ambushed by some nerdy-looking guy in Coke-bottle glasses who made her feel like a woman instead of one of the guys.

The cab rolled into the parking lot, and Cassidy stood to leave. She pulled her pistol out of her waistband. "Keep this for me? I can't fly with it."

"Where's your ID? Your gear bag? Your permit to carry? How will you pay for the cab?"

She tapped her forehead. "Don't worry about me. I keep my credit card number in my head for times like this one. I'll be okay."

Alex stood with her and accepted her weapon, but his eyes were filled with worry and something else. Fear? Sadness? She couldn't pin it down. Deciphering men never was her strong point, not unless they were on the soccer field or in the boxing ring. "Are you sure this is what you want to do?"

"Yes." She'd started down this road, and now she was going to finish it. Vacation was over. It was past time to get back to work.

Alex tried one last time. "Just because the only tool in your tool box is a hammer doesn't make everything a nail."

She honestly didn't understand what that meant. She had no hammer, just her hard head and sheer stubborn determination. Cassidy turned away, her mind made up.

The cab driver scurried around the car and opened the door for her. "Any bags, ma'am?"

"No," she whispered past the lump in her throat. Turning to Alex, she gave him a small wave, and took her place in the back seat.

He pulled out his wallet and shoved a few bills into the cabbie's hand. "Please give her the change."

"Will do," the driver said before he shut the door and turned to Cassidy. "Where to?"

"Jacksonville airport," she said softly. "Please hurry."

"Yes, ma'am."

She waved one more time while the cab pulled away, but Alex didn't acknowledge her goodbye. The pain of leaving him standing there alone, his arms crossed over his chest, jolted her, hard. Fighting more tears, she steeled her emotions and faced forward. The airport lay ahead. Beyond that, Seattle, and another assignment that would make this one a thing of the past.

Just another sad memory.

Chapter Thirty-One

"You're out here quite a lot lately, young lady."

Cassidy looked up from her custom made, bolt-action sniper rifle into the inquisitive face of Range Safety Officer Nathan Dunn. An older man with a neatly trimmed and graying moustache, he rarely came out to chat with the gun owners who utilized his shooting range east of Seattle. Today must have been an exception.

His gentle tap on her shoulder had surprised her. With her safety protection earphones on, she'd been in her own sad little world. Other agents opted for the kind of earmuffs they could hook up to their iPhones and music. She chose silence. It couldn't remind her of anyone.

"Just practicing," she answered, readjusted her earphones and aimed another shot. Sharpening long-range skills meant a deadeye and a steady hand, neither of which she'd had since she'd returned home from Florida.

This place smacked of Rourke, the reason she was there. Her plan for recovery was simple. One by one, she was cleaning house, replacing old memories with new. The quicker she got him out of her head, the better. Then she could work on forgetting Florida.

Aim. Steady now. Short, shallow breaths. Three of them. Wait. Hold.

She held her breath longer this time, hoping to finally kill the target she'd meant to destroy all morning. Somehow her shot groupings all went to the left. She didn't know why. Her nitron sights were dead on. Not wanting to switch to her scope yet, she'd adjusted for windage and elevation. Then readjusted. The groupings still sucked. Persevering meant she needed another cardboard target.

She turned to Nathan, hoping he had nothing more to say. But he did. His lips were moving. She removed her ear protection again.

"I notice you're not hitting your usual marks lately. Do you need some help zeroing your rifle?" His earphones rested at his neck.

"No," she answered quickly, but then decided maybe it was time for someone else to have a go at her weapon. "On second thought..." She handed it over. "Go for it. Maybe there is something wrong that I'm not seeing."

He took it without a word, replaced his earphones while she did the same, braced the butt stock to his shoulder, took careful aim, and—*blam*. Right on. Dead center. Like the expert he was, he emptied the magazine where he meant it to go. The center circle filled with holes placed perfectly next to Cassidy's too-far-to-the-left grouping. Handing her rifle back, Nathan had that same quizzical look on his face.

Great. It's not the gun. It really is me.

"Fires real smooth," he said, peeling his earphones off. "It's a good day for practice, too. No wind."

She nodded. His message was clear. If the weather and weapon were perfect, she must be the problem. Well, duh. She huffed in aggravation, not needing it spelled out like he'd just done in his very circumspect way.

"You need more ammo?" he asked, and she wondered what he was really asking. *Why can't you hit the broad side of a barn, girl? What's the matter with you? How much ammo's it going to take?*

"No, Nathan," she answered patiently. Once her earphones were back in place, Cassidy raised the rifle to her shoulder. If he could do it, so could she. Blowing out a deep breath with measured slowness, she steadied her heartbeat.

The crosshairs connected in her scope, dead center just like before. *I've done this a million times. No sweat.*

Rourke's patient words came back to her. *Find your happy place, Butch. Plant your mind. Block the world. It's all about focus. You can do it. Practice. Practice. Practice!*

And that was the problem. No matter how she tried, she couldn't get him out of her head. He'd always believed in her, but all the practice in the world wouldn't help her now. She had no happy place, either, not with her mind planted a couple thousand miles away in a state with palm trees instead of pines, alligators instead of harbor seals. As far as blocking out the world? God. She'd tried.

Instead of firing and missing yet one more time, Cassidy laid the rifle on the counter. She sent her bangs flying with a deep huff. That custom made weapon was the best on the market. It wasn't the problem.

"You've been out here every day for the last week. Maybe you need a vacation," Nathan offered.

"No," she stated adamantly. "I don't. Thanks anyway."

"Just saying. Sometimes it helps to stop trying so hard." He turned toward his guns and ammo shop. "You're a good customer, Cassidy. If there's anything I can do for you, let me know."

"Thanks. I will."

"I'm sure you're just having a bad day. It happens." He waved a hand over his head and left her alone.

She zipped her rifle into its carrying case and collected her gear. Yeah, like seven bad days in a row. That was all this mental block was. One damned bad day after another, and they weren't about to get any better.

Cassidy loaded her rifle and gear bag into her trusty Subaru and headed back to work. What she really needed was a remote operation to another country, maybe South America. Agent Freeman always seemed to be coming from or leaving for Columbia or Brazil. She decided to check with Murphy to see what international ops were available. Anywhere else had to be better than stateside.

As the lush, evergreen Washington landscape flew by, her thoughts naturally turned to Rourke. This was his country, where he'd been born, and where she'd first met him. They'd spent a lot of time working together, either at the range or running endurance laps at a local community college track.

Rourke was a collegiate track and field runner who'd bulked up in the Army. He knew the ranger creed by heart, and repeated it so often that Cassidy knew it by heart, too. Somehow she'd incorporated the *'move faster and fight harder, though I be the lone survivor'* ideal as her own. Only her plan to replace old memories wasn't working. Rourke was still there. And she that lone survivor.

His last words still ate at her. All of her if-onlys chanted in continual rounds that wouldn't cease. *If only I'd kissed him. If only he'd told me that he loved me sooner. If only I'd been there when he'd first taken that hit. If only I'd listened better. Maybe he'd tried to tell me how he felt sooner.*

If only.

If only.

If goddamned only...

Hooking onto the I-90, she headed west to Mercer Island. Big-city traffic was hectic as usual, but she'd gotten used to it once she'd moved from Utah. Even driving the steep hills of Seattle didn't bother her anymore. For once, the weather was perfect, just as Nathan had said. She couldn't ask for a prettier day. Or a more depressing one.

I'll bet even Mount Rainier is out. Like I care.

The only saving grace to her routine was The TEAM's upcoming survival training, scheduled to begin bright and early Saturday morning, and conducted by a couple of heavyweight super-agents from the East Coast office. Mark Houston and Zack Lennox. They'd designed the rugged course. All selected TEAM members were to be dumped in the middle of the Hoh Rainforest on the western side of the Olympic peninsula. Without gear, food, or water, they were expected not only to survive for one entire seven-day week, but to navigate to a designated pick-up spot for retrieval, and do it in record time. Each TEAM member was given a different pick-up spot. No teamwork was allowed. She couldn't wait.

Known for its extreme rainfall and lush, jungle-like terrain, the Hoh was laced with wilderness trails, plenty of animal life, and salmon in the icy-cold streams, but only if a person knew how and where to find them. The mighty Hoh also brimmed full of trees, every branch, twig, and tree trunk thick with velvety, suffocating moss and vines. That would be the real challenge—to not get lost in the dense green beneath an equally dense canopy. Some hiker had just found a light aircraft that had crashed more than a year ago within the Hoh. She needed to be that kind of lost.

The challenge sounded wonderful to Cassidy, the perfect remedy for her present state of mind. She had no doubt she'd excel. That was what she did. She'd hunted mule deer in the backwoods of Utah, fished monster halibut and salmon in Alaska, and bested the most dangerous ski runs on the planet. This was her kind of exercise, to be so isolated no one could find her, and left to fend for herself. Besides, this was the time to prove to Alex and Murphy she was back on her game. Maybe to herself as well.

Jude.

Of all the dirty tricks...

A man with glasses and dark hair caught her eye from the crosswalk while she idled at a red light in the middle of a hectic Seattle intersection. Her heart skipped a whole lot more than a single beat. The damned thing nearly leapt out of her throat.

Same build. Broad shoulders. Jeans. Simple button-up gray shirt. It had to be him. Her palm hit the horn without thinking twice before he got away. *Jude! Wait! Turn around! I'm right here!*

The guy kept walking. He never even tossed a glance her way. She looked twice, but he was lost in the busy crowd. Disappointment filled her like a cup of bitter day-old brew. It couldn't have been him. She was seeing things. Damn.

For some stupid reason, her traitorous eyes brimmed with tears. The light changed to green. Traffic resumed, and she hurt all over again.

For the last week she'd been fighting a battle she wasn't strong enough to win. Tender memories lurked too close to the surface. Gray eyes smiled out of her dreams with worried kindness. Her fingertips hungered for the angles and scruff of Jude's too-serious chin and jaw; that tingle of warmth when she'd kissed his lips the first time. The smell of him. Part smoke. All man.

It was the intangible things that struck the hardest. A whiff of the breeze off Puget Sound zapped her back to the edge of the Saint John. Walking past Farmer's Market on Pike Place with its colorful array of fresh fruit wasn't much help, either. Her tongue craved a slice of the dragon fruit. Hell, her tongue craved Jude's lips. His mouth. All the rest of him.

But the dark of nighttime was the worst. Cassidy could still hear his heartbeat beneath her ear. Strong. Steady. The heart of a warrior on the noblest mission a man could assume, that of a father on the hunt for his missing child. Cassidy couldn't imagine a finer mission. Or a finer man.

She longed for the steel bands of his arms and the indescribable sense of safety he'd given her. Of all people. Her. An undercover operator who was tough enough to fight the world. Her. An over-confident woman who'd gotten herself into a bit of a pickle. Okay, make that a damned tight spot, but no one, as in *no man on earth* had ever gotten to her like Jude had.

She slapped her steering wheel. Even her sweet Magic reminded her of another cat at the opposite end of the country. Miss Fluffy. And that cat's sweet owner. Judith. And damn it, every thought and every memory led her in the same circle. Always back to Jude.

That was why she needed to get lost in the mighty Hoh for a week. She needed space and time to sort out Rourke and Jude. There had to be a way to get these guys out of her heart, mind, and soul. Jude had been right all along. Romantic responses between people during extreme circumstances couldn't be trusted. Her conflicted feelings proved it. Seven days of rugged hiking and struggling to survive ought to erase both of those men from her life forever.

After maneuvering her vehicle into its assigned parking stall in The TEAM's underground garage, Cassidy opted for the stairs instead of the elevator. The three flights to her office guaranteed she'd be sweaty when she arrived, but the burn in her calves and thighs ought to replace the gnawing pain in her chest. She hoped.

She ran faster, pushed harder at every step. With sheer stubborn determination, she forced her thoughts and energy to the upcoming survival test. She was ready. She could do it. Once again, she'd be the toughest gal on The TEAM, the gal no man could best, not even on his finest day. The notion brought peace of mind. Competition never failed her.

Pushing the fire doors open, Cassidy took a deep breath and calmed. Hers was an office awhirl with male conversation, male ego, and plenty of testosterone. Familiar territory. One she used to rule and would again. She rolled the knot out of her neck and made another attempt to zero her soul. It didn't work.

"Cassidy." Murphy waved her over to the customer service desk. Her two favorite agents from the Alexandria, Virginia, office had arrived.

"There's my girl!" Zack Lennox beamed when he saw her. "How's Miss Cassidy?"

"Hey, Zack." She leveled a fist at the tough guy's massive upper arm. "Doing good. How about you?"

He was eye candy to the entire female population. East Coast. West Coast. And all those states in between. Still shaving his head, he cut an impressive profile in that TEAM shirt stretched across his muscular chest. Thick arms. Thick neck. A heart as big as the Pacific.

She'd never failed to get a kick out of going anywhere with him, even just to get coffee or sandwiches for the office. Female heads swiveled in his direction. Women flirted. Some gave him that silly call-me hand signal of thumb to ear and pinkie to lips. How stupid. Like he was that shallow of a guy? Not Zack.

He handled them like a pro. When they got too pushy, he'd reveal the tribal sleeve on his right shoulder, the one with the names of his wife, Mei, and their three daughters, LiLi, Song, and Miki. He had no problem telling those silly women he was a married man. Yeah. Zack was one of the good guys. Honest. Hard-working. And head-over-heels in love with his wife. Like Jude had been...

Shit. Focus! Everything is not about Jude.

Yes, it is, her heart whispered. *Yes. It. Is.*

Cassidy turned from Zack and ran straight into Mark Houston, who'd come up behind her. It was good seeing him again, too. Mark was Senior Agent-in-charge when she'd joined forces with The TEAM in her home state of Utah a couple of years back. The same time she'd quit the DEA. He'd gotten seriously hurt, and took several rounds. Almost died. Two other agents had been critically injured, two others kidnapped, and two more killed during that single operation. Mark was the reason she'd dumped her DEA career in the toilet and never looked back. Well, one of them. He'd had a tough job, but he'd tackled it head-on while her DEA buddies played politics and stayed safe.

Her friendship with him had been solid since day one. He'd given her a sterling recommendation, and Alex had hired her on the spot. Mark had a light touch when it came to leading, training, and mentoring the new recruits. Alex was the hard ass, Murphy the grandfatherly type, but Mark was big brother, always in your corner even when you screwed up. It didn't hurt that he was as big as a bear, either. Like Zack. All muscle.

"Cassidy!" He grabbed her up into a hug, which was pretty much any hug from the guy. Mark and Zack were both big bruisers—both could block a doorway just by showing up in the morning. Mark had daughters, just like Zack.

Just like Jude.

Damn. That man just would not leave her be!

"How's Connor?" she asked when Mark placed her feet back on the floor.

Might as well get that little piece of gossip out of the way and in the open. She'd gotten a little too close to Connor Maher, another TEAM agent, on that failed Utah operation. Mark was there. He knew about it—not that there was much to tell. Connor had ended the op with Junior Agent Izza Ramos in his bed, not Cassidy Dancer. End of story.

"He's good. They've got a baby boy now, too. Braxton. Little guy looks just like Jamie and Izza."

Jamie. The baby Connor didn't know Izza was pregnant with until they'd squared off in Utah and resolved their disconnects. His baby. Yeah. Good times. *Not.*

"How's Libby?" Cassidy changed the subject to Mark's wife. Connor was another one of *those guys*. She'd gotten too close to him. She got burned. Like she had with Rourke. *Like Jude.*

Focus, damn it, Dancer.

A flash of heat swarmed over her cheeks. Maybe Mark noticed it, too. He seemed to have an extra tender light in his eyes today. Maybe he'd been talking to Murphy or Alex. They knew what a mess she was.

"Libby's good, but Murphy tells me you're at the range most days. Still ol' dead-eye, huh?"

"There's no such thing as a good enough shot, is there?"

"We'll see after this survival exercise." He winked conspiratorially, glancing around the office at her teammates. Ben Ritchie, Roosevelt Jenner and Eric Reynolds surrounded Zack while Teague Daniels and Aaron Proctor were engrossed in conversation with Murphy. Rich Cleary and a couple of the others were at their desks on phone calls. Everyone seemed to be talking about some aspect of the upcoming training, and like her, they were raring to go.

"Hey, Cassidy," Rich called from his desk, his hand over the receiver of his phone. "We've got a pool going. Eric says he'll be first out of the Hoh. You in?"

"No way," she shot back. "Why would I bet on him? If anyone's going to be first, it'll be me. Eric couldn't find his backside with both hands and a spotlight. You all know that."

A black pen sailed end over end through the air from several work cubicles away. "I heard that, Dancer." Eric stabbed a finger in her direction, his eyebrow lifted in challenge. "You're going down."

She caught the pen easily, and sent it sailing right back at him. "Bring it, Reynolds."

Eric was ex-USMC medic, an odd fit for a team of snipers, but a damned good man. He wasn't usually this animated. The upcoming survival test must have everyone excited.

"I'm glad it's you guys instead of me," Paige Royal joined in. Murphy's admin gal, she was a pretty redhead with dazzling blue eyes, and she was also one of Cassidy's few actual girlfriends. "I'd be lost in no time. Murphy'd have to send the whole TEAM to find me."

"Not if you'd been trained properly." Mark winked again at Cassidy. "Did you know a person could survive for weeks on nothing but rainwater and banana slugs?"

Cassidy caught his drift. Paige was squeamish, and Mark was all tease.

"Ewww. Not me." Paige's upturned nose and eyes squeezed tight revealed her disgust. She gave Mark a friendly smack on his muscular upper arm. "Are you taking salt and pepper with you for those slugs you plan on eating to survive, smart ass?"

Mark took the hit with a big grin. God, he was handsome. "I prefer Tabasco. They're best roasted over glowing embers. That's when they sizzle. Like popcorn."

"That's it," Paige declared with another smack. "Enough of the slimy slug talk. Beat it, Houston."

"Aw, come one. It's easy. If you peel the bark off a skinny willow branch and stick it straight up their mucous-covered little—"

"No! Stop!" She all but squealed. "I don't want to know! You guys just go and... just go. Take your tasty slugs with you. Tabasco on chunks of icky slime nuggets? Yuck!"

Mark chuckled, his arms crossed over his chest. "What about you, Cassidy? You ready for a tough challenge?"

"You know I'm ready," she answered confidently. "The sooner the better."

"Good. We leave at zero four hundred Saturday. Wear enough clothing to keep you warm and bring a decent rain jacket. No weapons allowed except your knife. Be ready to go by—"

"She's not going anywhere."

Cassidy whirled around at those very defiantly spoken words from—*Jude?*

He stood at Paige's customer service counter looking very tired, bedraggled, and a little green around the edges. He was there? Dressed in jeans and a simple button-up gray shirt, his glasses were crooked on his nose as usual and his hair needed combing.

God, he looks good.

Concern flashed across his face as he sized Mark up with one quick head-to-toe glare. Jude gulped, but he also shifted his weight like a man ready to fight. Cassidy couldn't help but smile. He thought he had to fight Mark over her? Craziest guy ever.

Damn, he looks really, really good.

"What are you doing here?" She took a step toward him, her foolish heart already kicked into that free-falling, skydiving feeling. She didn't like it. She hadn't lost her nerve, not once in her whole career until the night she'd lost Rourke and Jude. To be honest, she hadn't been herself since. Didn't know how to get back to the smart-ass she used to be.

It needed to stop. She needed to be able to breathe again without her heart sticking in her throat.

He took a step toward her, his hands clenched at his side and shaking. His chest heaved, his breath coming in the short, hard bursts of someone who'd just run up the same flight of stairs she had. "I think the better question is, what are you doing here, Cassidy? Do you have any idea how long a flight it is from San Francisco to Jacksonville? Why the hell did you run?"

Her nose twitched. He'd gotten close enough she could smell him. Clean sweat. Body wash. Some flavor of musk and spice and him all rolled into one tempting treat. Every nerve ending prickled at the memory of being wrapped up in his arms, being squashed against that firm wall of his chest. Desire rippled up her spine and morphed into a buzzing bumblebee inside her head. It obliterated every last excuse as to why a long-distance relationship with him wouldn't work.

The silence in the office didn't escape her notice.

"Answer me," Jude demanded. "I think I deserve an answer after everything I've been through."

The very authoritarian snap to his voice startled her. Where was her mild-mannered savior who didn't believe he was a hero? Cassidy swallowed hard. "I work here," she explained in her most patient and controlled manner. "This is where I—"

"That's not what I meant, and you know it." He rolled one shoulder, as if the weight of the world rested there. "You didn't just come back to work. You ran away from me, damn it. I called your boss. I asked Alex to tell you to wait, that I'd be right there, but you left anyway."

God, he was making this hard. "I needed to get back home, Jude. I have a job, you know."

He stabbed his finger at the floor between them. "You. Walked. Out. On. Me."

She winced. *Not here. I don't want to fight in front of my boss and teammates.*

He never gave her a chance to say it. In two steps he was right in front of her, but still not touching her. She saw it clearly. The hurt in his eyes. The anger in his clenched jaw. And she'd put it there.

"If you've come all this way just to chew me out—"

"Knock it off," he growled. "You know why I'm here."

Her temper flared. He'd embarrassed her, and she wasn't going to put up with it, and to be honest, she really didn't know why he was there. He could've called, damn it. This could have been resolved with one simple cell phone conversation. *Not here. Not in public.*

"Listen," she started again, deliberately infusing her words with a calm, professional tone. "Extreme circumstances create unreal expectations. People caught up in the middle of intense emotions—"

"Is that all I was to you? An unreal expectation? An intense emotion?" He inched closer. "Is that all Judith was? Just some kid to desert the first chance you got? Like her mother did to me?"

Ouch. Damn. Low blow. Cassidy gulped. She hadn't thought how her leaving would affect Judith. She had nothing to say. No placating comment. No cocky comeback. Jude was right to be angry. She had run, and she wasn't proud of it. Those two remaining steps between them felt like a solid wall.

"I made you a promise, and I intend to keep it." His voice softened, the tension still tight. He stood so close she couldn't miss the anguish in his eyes. Or that other emotion. The one that scared the hell out of her. The one that might send her flying off the edge of the world for good.

"You were going to get to know me better. I know, but I don't belong there," she whispered. "You have Judith, and she needs you, and—"

"But I love you, goddamnit."

You do?

All at once, his big, warm hands cupped her jaw, his thumbs wiped away the tears. The tender light in his gray eyes melted the last of her resistance. She saw him then. Truly saw him. Jude was her safe landing zone. The familiar magnetic pull tugged her every bone and muscle toward him. All of her heart. God, she wanted to fling herself into his arms and beg forgiveness.

"I rescued Judith, and now I'm here for you. What are you afraid of?"

Bull's eye and so, so not fair. Out of her peripheral, she sensed Mark on her left, Zack at her right. Eric was out there and nearby. Murphy, too. Watching.

"But he died, and you... you left me." The gut-wrenching words came of their own volition, betraying her to all. She blinked fast but not fast enough to stop the torrent of tears or her big mouth. "He said he loved me, and then he left, Jude. Just like you did. Like you're going to do again. So I had to leave you... first."

His hands moved easily to the back of her head and neck, his fingers laced through her hair. Tilting her forehead to his, he murmured, "You ran so you wouldn't get hurt again. I understand. It hurts when the people you love die, but I'm not going anywhere. This time I came for you."

Her hands reached for those strong wrists. "But... but what if something happens to you?"

A twinkle danced at the corner of his eyes. "I think the two people who brought down Lucien Cain can survive anything if they stand together."

Even a rugged, outdoorsy kind of woman who always had to win couldn't argue with that. He *was* there. He *did* want her.

"Did I ever tell you that you're my very own warrior princess?" he asked. "I know I'm just a nerdy accountant. You're bigger than life, and you do important work. But Cassidy. Sweetheart. I don't want to live another day without you. I honestly don't think I can. Take a chance on me. Take a chance on us. What do you think? Come home with me?"

The truth was she couldn't think, not with those sexy lips of his so close to hers. Not with his breath in her face, and the feel of his skin once again beneath her fingertips. She closed her eyes and breathed him in. No, she absorbed him. She wanted inside of his arms again, inside that strong, honorable heart that had fought all odds and won.

No sooner did she open her mouth to tell him yes than his lips met hers with the softest kiss. Her knees turned to jelly. The puzzle piece that was her crazy life clicked loud enough into place that everyone in the office should have heard it. If they were still out there. She didn't know anymore.

With the man she loved in her face exactly how she'd wanted him for so long, the world fell away and The TEAM went with it. Her hands filled with the scratchy feel of the stubble on his chin and cheeks, the softness of his hair slipping through her fingers. She pulled herself into him, needing to be closer than just a kiss. Her body melded into the one place she belonged.

He picked her up off the floor and gathered her into his arms. She had no choice but to hold on. Tight. So she did. And she breathed. For the first time in days, she could breathe.

But gradually, her ears picked up the faint sound of clapping. It grew closer. Louder. Damn. They were still out there, and she was indeed in the middle of her office, making a spectacle of herself.

"Way to go, girl!" Zack exclaimed proudly.

Eric whooped like a teenage boy at a Friday night football game. "Right on!"

"Woot hoot!" Teague bellowed.

Even traitorous Paige had something to say. "Kiss her again."

Cassidy blushed ten shades of scarlet when Jude finally balanced her to the balls of her boots. She shot a shy glance at Mark.

"I guess this means you're going to miss the fun times in the Hoh?" he teased.

"Yes, she is," Jude answered for her, his arm extended to Mark. "I'm Jude Cannon, and if you don't mind, sir, Cassidy is coming home with me for a while."

Mark accepted his handshake with a boyish grin. "I can see that. Damned good to finally meet you, Jude. Call me Mark."

"I really can speak for myself," Cassidy told Jude, but when she turned to Mark, the sap had a glow on his handsome face. He winked, the brat. She could only scrunch her shoulders and repeat what Jude had just said. "I, umm, need some time off. I'm going to Florida."

Mark called over his shoulder. "Hey, Murph? Are you willing to approve time-off for this junior agent of yours?"

"Of course." Murphy chuckled. "If she promises to come back in a better frame of mind."

"Yes, sir. She will." Jude spoke for her again, and looking up at him from the shelter of his very secure grip, Cassidy smiled. She had her mojo back.

His name was Jude.

Chapter Thirty-Two

They didn't make it out of The TEAM elevator. They barely made it in.

Jude slapped the stop button the minute the doors closed. He pinned Cassidy to the wall, his hands in her hair, and his mouth planted on hers. The last two weeks without her had been hell. She needed to know how he felt, and he needed to know how she tasted. He'd nearly forgotten.

"I've missed you," he said between mouthfuls of the sweetest woman. It all came back—the flavor he'd craved those nights on the road with the Brothers Grimm.

The simple act of his mouth on hers erased the angst of the day. He'd flown all night after making sure Judith was in good hands, and damned near ran all the way from his hotel to The TEAM office. But now, with Cassidy's slender body folded in his arms, the horrors of it all fell away. Her gentle kisses were a sweet oasis in a blistering desert, and he the parched wanderer who had no need to travel farther. He'd found what he needed to live, and he wouldn't fail her again.

Her lips, her tongue, her scent rolled over him as if a soothing gift. One taste wasn't enough. His mind worked the problem of the day even as he sought after more and more of Cassidy. Was it too soon to ask her to marry him, and how on earth did a man know when a woman was ready for the next step?

She answered with a hiccup through her own searching kiss, her tongue making love with his, her fingers pulling him into her body with every clutching handful. He smoothed his way down her ribcage and over her hips until his palms came to rest on her delightful ass. Lifting her off her feet, he wrapped her legs around his waist, needing to feel her heat against his belly.

This woman was no soft and cuddly handful. Her butt hadn't an extra pinch to it. Everywhere his fingers and palms roamed met strong muscle and firm tendons. She was lean, but hotter than hell, and the feminine center of her body commanded every last inch of his.

She had no problem maintaining her grip with her legs while she traded molesting his tongue for molesting his neck. Jude cocked his head, craving the touch of her tongue. Everything between them was hot and heavy. Bump and grind. Give and take. They were out of control with no way to slow each other down. It had to stop. They were in an elevator, for God's sake.

"Not here," he mumbled even though his body screamed, *'Yes, here! Clothes off! Now!'*

She'd unbuttoned his shirt, her slender fingers on his bare chest. Groaning, Cassidy sniffed a deep breath, then moaned. He grinned, his eyes closed with pure unadulterated pleasure at the sound of her enjoying his body.

His fingernails strummed the seam of her camouflaged work pants, the seam between those two athletically toned butt cheeks. The seam that had to get the hell out of his way. If this fire kept burning, her pants would soon be ash.

Jude released her and flattened his palms to the elevator wall behind her, his heart an industrial-strength jackhammer.

This wasn't the time or place to prove his love. "How about we continue this conversation in my room?"

"You have a room?" she asked, her tongue still licking a trail of liquid inferno up his neck, and her legs still hooked to his waist like the belt of a hot-damned sexy backpack.

"I do. It's got a king-sized bed." He didn't want her to stop. Or drop.

She clenched her knees, giving him less reason to leave, but a helluva good reason to stay.

"We need to talk," he murmured against her temple, drawing in the flowery scent of her shampoo mingled with a hint of sulphur. "You've been at the range."

She nodded, her breath hot against his cheek. "I can't hit anything for shit right now, and it's all your fault."

Jude bowed his forehead to hers, grinning at the whining, petulant woman wrapped around his waist. This was what he'd travelled all night for—this woman. The one with the heart of a little girl and a blonde lioness combined into one.

Holding and kissing her had a powerful effect on his body, but the logic he'd built his life around hadn't failed him now when he most wished it would. Oh, to be a headstrong teenager, out of control, and ruled by hormones. He'd have her on her back in no time. But responsible men didn't act on their impulses. They didn't allow wild abandonment. They controlled their urges and...

To hell with that. He grabbed her ass again. Sex in the elevator might not be the smartest, but it *was* a damned good idea.

At last he broke the connection, his eyes closed as he stilled the thunder in his heart and head. She must have felt it too, pressed against his chest and panting like she was.

Tracing the edge of his lower lip with her fingertip, she posed the problem in both their minds. "We're moving way too fast."

Maybe. Maybe not fast enough. A shudder raced up his spine. One of those shudders when a man knows exactly whom his body wants, but it has to wait. He hit the call button and sent the elevator on its way before temptation got the best of him.

Cassidy released her grip. Slowly, she slid down his body until her boots hit the floor.

"I want you," he admitted hoarsely, his fingers tucked into the waistband of her pants and itching to slide lower. Maybe into. "I want you in every possible way a man can want a woman."

She blushed and lowered her eyes. "But I think you were right," she said softly, fingering the top buttonhole of his still undone shirt. "We don't really know each other. The only times I've ever talked with you were during the worst possible hours of my life."

He tipped her chin up to read her eyes. "I'm glad I met you when I did, and I'm glad for everything that happened. I am." He meant it with his whole heart. He'd come out of hell with two of the fairest ladies in the land. He'd do it again. Every second of it.

"Maybe we should just talk for now." She leaned against his shoulder, her hand roaming to the buttonhole.

Just talk, hell. Unless she meant to talk in Braille.

He planted a kiss against her forehead. "I agree, but my goal won't change. I want you in my bed and in my life. I love you, Cassidy."

The way she gulped through more tears had him worried for all of one split second. Where had his warrior princess gone? This woman was someone else entirely. Instead of winking in outright sassy defiance, she seemed shy. Hell, she seemed as scared as he'd been when they'd first met.

"I was going to tell you the same thing only... only..." She hesitated.

"Only you got scared. I understand. Believe me, I know. I'm sorry about the way things happened the morning I went home. I should've never let you go like you did." He buttoned his shirt to help her focus.

"It wasn't your fault. I ran. I panicked."

"You wouldn't have if I'd been smarter and included you in that hug I gave Judith."

"No. That was your time. Judith needed you. It's just that..." She looked away, still thinking about something she obviously wasn't ready to share.

He recognized the signs. Sometimes it took Judith a while to verbalize her emotions, too. Women. So complicated. So beautiful. *So, so mine.*

It didn't take long to get to his hotel room. He'd chosen well. The historic Fairmont Hotel ended up being less than five city blocks from The TEAM's Seattle office. Within minutes, he'd ushered Cassidy into his twenty-first-floor room overlooking beautiful Elliot Bay. The sheer drapes on the huge picture windows were drawn, allowing just the right amount of light into the room. His suitcase still sat near the door where he'd left it.

But by then, the fire had cooled. Cassidy stopped just inside his hotel room door, like another piece of luggage. She blinked toward the open bedroom where its king-sized bed beckoning with tasseled throw pillows galore, a gold and black comforter, and crisp white bed pillows.

He motioned her to the sofa in the sitting area, and instantly detected relief washing over Cassidy's face. "Now, where were we?"

She did what she was told, taking her place beside him, but he sensed trepidation. She looked unsure, her bottom lip bitten like a little girl who knew she had a spanking coming. Tears glistened. She looked so adorable, he had to let her off the hook. He lifted her clenched fist to his lips and kissed the back of her hand. "Judith loves you, and I love you. How can you not know that?"

Cassidy shrugged. "All of a sudden you were there, and she'd been so sad, and I... I just, umm, panicked."

"I made you a promise that night in the cellar."

"I know. You promised to get to know me better." Her voice softened. "We both promised, only so much has happened since then."

Jude didn't understand. One minute this woman was on fire, the next damned near cool to the touch. She wasn't the same Cassidy he remembered. Somehow, they'd traded places. He was the confident one in this op and she the timid little mouse.

Smoothing his hand through her curly blonde locks, he brought their foreheads together. Yeah, she'd run away, but he knew what it was like to be the odd man out, and he didn't want her dwelling on it. He changed the subject. "Let's start over then. How about if you tell me what it was like growing up in Utah?"

That seemed to do the trick. She relaxed and told him about her hometown of Ogden, Utah, where Washington Boulevard was the main hangout for teenagers, troublemakers, and a few too many police officers, some of which she knew by name. Her parents still owned a small cattle ranch west of the city. The story of skinny-dipping at Pineview Reservoir made him laugh, but the minute she mentioned skiing, he sensed her excitement. He'd heard about *the greatest snow on earth.* Hadn't everyone?

"I think you're an avid sportswoman," he announced with pride. Everything Cassidy did made him smile.

"I am. Do you ski?"

"I water ski. Never tried snow skiing."

"You'd love it. We should try it. I know a few secret spots where the powder's dry and the moose still roam."

He twirled a strand of her hair over and around his index finger while she rested comfortably against him. By now they were sprawled across the couch, their legs intertwined like lovers.

"How's the snow here in Washington?"

She scrunched her nose. "I'm spoiled. Once you ski the powder at the Alta or Snowbird resorts in Utah, you'll see. Everything else is just slush or ice."

He tapped the end of her upturned nose with the tip of his finger. "I'd love to spoil you rotten."

The hint of a shadow passed over her face. His arms tightened around her in an automatic, protective response. Whatever caused that shadow was his next assignment. Her smiles turned his life into a rainbow, and anything that diminished them diminished the light in his life. "Tell me. What are you thinking about right now?"

Reluctantly, she told him about Rourke, and how he'd died saving Melissa, Tucker, and Judith. Alex had already explained what had happened, but listening to Cassidy's version of the tragic ending to what should have been a successful operation gave Jude a different perspective. She'd really cared for Rourke. It showed.

"The thing is, he always used to tell me I was hardheaded, that I was going to get myself into a lot of trouble some day, and then he's the one who goes and gets shot."

Jude didn't comment.

"And he used to call me Butch. You know, like Butch Cassidy? Like I was an outlaw or something?"

"And you loved him." He saw it in her eyes.

"Yeah." She nodded. "I think I did. I mean, we never dated, and he never even made a move on me. I kind of wish he had, but he was always so proper. But then, when he's dying, he finally says he loved me, and—what the hell, Jude?" She pushed away from him with that question. "I mean, what good is telling a person that you love them when you're dying? What was he thinking?"

Jude let her talk. He felt sorry for her friend. Waiting until he was dying to reveal that kind of a secret must've been hard on the guy. Rourke had to have died with a broken heart—not something Jude intended to do.

"The big jerk. I always figured I'd have to make the first move because he sure never did. And it's not like I've had a lot of boyfriends in my life. It's not like I—"

The way she shut her mouth right then and there drew his attention from her hair to her locked lips. She hadn't just shut her mouth. No, she'd snapped it closed as if she had a secret she wasn't ready to reveal.

And because he was all man, he had to ask. As immature as it was going to make him sound, he needed to know. "How many men have you had?" It wasn't his business and yet, it was. To lessen the pressure of the telling, he offered a few ridiculous numbers. "A dozen? Twenty? Hundreds?"

"Ha!" She looked away, biting her lip in that little-girl way that was fast becoming his favorite habit. "I wish."

He felt the truth in the way she'd just spoken. Cassidy was a virgin. He was pretty sure. That also explained why she'd run out on him. She'd been scared, but not of him. The reality of love and the consummation of that love was what frightened her, even now. That's why the hesitation at his hotel room door, too.

She might be the leader of the pack when it came to running a covert operation or acing survival tests in some far-off rainforest, but Miss Dancer had no intimate experience with men. The fact that she was pure and clean resonated to the very core of his masculine soul. Tucker was so, so wrong about her and Rourke horsing around on remote ops together.

"Men don't like me." The petulant tone in her voice betrayed her. "I'm not one of those fluffy little cheerleaders with big pompoms and a back flip." Cassidy turned in his arms to meet him head-on. She eased one fist between them. "Most guys won't date a woman who can run faster, ski better, and kick their ass when they're done showing off. I may not look like it, but I can beat you at arm wrestling right here and now. You want to try me?"

Wrestling had definitely come to his mind, just not arm wrestling.

Jude pulled her determined face against his shoulder so she couldn't see the smile on his lips. Despite the all-out challenge, now wasn't the time to make her feel as if he took her lightly. He ran a soothing hand down her back and up again, ending at the base of her skull.

"So I take it no knight in shining armor has thrown you over his shoulder to have his way with you yet?" Jude used his best teasing tone.

"No. Damn it." She blew out a big sigh that made him want to laugh. There was a definite camaraderie between them right now, almost like two guys sitting together after a football game discussing how the quarterback fumbled.

Still, her revelation had to be handled gently. Cassidy Dancer was all woman beneath that rough-and-tumble tomboy exterior, and he wouldn't trample that little girl quality she had going for her. If anything, what she'd just told Jude made him more aware of his own shortfalls.

"What on earth is my favorite warrior princess doing with a nerdy guy like me?"

"What nerdy guy?"

He raised a brow at that silly question, but by then she had both hands on him, her fingers pushed into his hair while she studied his face. The light in her eyes was back. She removed his glasses and set them on the side table. "Remember the cellar?"

He let her take the lead. "How could I forget?"

"Well, when I told you I wanted to feel your face..." She paused as her fingers and palms moved gently over his facial features again. Gentle fingertips traced his brows. He closed his eyes and let her map the line of his nose and smooth over his cheekbones. Her touch was light and firm at the same time, but how she could ignite so much need in another part of his body by touching his face took his breath. His body coiled with need.

She'd done the same thing in the cellar that first night. She'd started a fire that had only grown stronger, and the beauty of it was that she didn't know.

"I never saw a nerd," Cassidy whispered, her voice full of awe. "I saw a man who rescued me when no one else could. I saw a father who ran into hell to save his daughter." She leaned in to his lips, her next words a blessing he didn't see coming. "I just saw you. My hero."

Chapter Thirty-Three

The fire roared back to life. Jude wanted this woman. They needed to move from the couch. Skimming his hands down her back, he cupped the back of her thighs and leaned forward, his hands under her bottom. Without breaking their connection, he was off the couch and striding toward destiny.

She didn't stop him when he nudged the bedroom door shut with his foot, still very much in possession of the beautiful lady in his arms.

She didn't stop him when he sat on the edge of his bed and stripped off his shirt.

She didn't stop him when his hands maneuvered her body to straddle his, but she paused when he leaned back against the mattress and took her with him. Her clenched hands on his chest felt more like stop signs than a come-on. "But..."

By then, he couldn't stop. Didn't want to. She needed to understand he wasn't going to hurt her, but he had to have her. His blood boiled. It didn't just run hot—it ran molten. Sizzling. Got-to-have-her-now hot.

This fear of hers was momentary. If she truly loved him, her apprehension would cease the moment he had her clothes off, and they coupled. He knew it. His body screamed he was right. When he was done, he'd hold her and comfort her, and she'd truly understand how deeply a man could love a woman.

He pulled her face down to meet his lips and kissed her fiercely. Rolling her he pinned her. "I'm not going to wait until it's too late to show you how much I love you."

"Yes, but..."

So much concern flashed across her face that he faltered. Jude jolted back to his senses. He'd seen that scared look before. *What the hell am I doing?*

His overwhelming needs deflated. His selfishness cut and ran. His ego evaporated. Jude remembered who he really was—not some mighty, all-knowing prophet. Not some rutting pig, like Greg or Hank or the Brothers Grimm. He, the man who proclaimed he loved Cassidy more than himself, was going about this all damned wrong.

Taking a deep breath, he swallowed hard, and gathered his wild desires into a manageable tension. He stilled. Lucien was no more. And he, Jude Cannon, wasn't living at the edge of insanity. He had time to live again. To make soft, sweet love.

He rolled off Cassidy, and settled at her side. Repentance hit him hard. *Damn. I'm such an ass.* "I'm sorry. I almost forgot who I was," he admitted calmly. "You tell me, sweetheart. If you're not ready—"

"It's just that... I've never done this before," she whispered guiltily, like she'd just confessed to shoplifting or something criminal. "I ski. Powder. You name it, I can ski it. Corbet's Couloir in Jackson Hole. Delirium Dive in Canada. Hell, Jude. I've been down Christmas Chute in Alaska, but..." She bit her bottom lip, trapping it, blinking like she'd rather be anywhere else but in his bedroom.

"What are you afraid of?" he asked.

"I don't do guys," she said very adamantly. "I mean, umm, I don't do girls, either. I mean... Oh, hell, I don't know what I mean." She rolled her eyes, digging herself in deep, and so damned adorable while she did it. "Most guys don't get me, and I don't know. This thing between us feels bigger than all of those wickedly steep ski runs put together."

He blew out a deep breath. Those words made him smile as much as he wanted to cry. She didn't need to tell him anything more. He was moving way too fast, and she was right. This wasn't her playing field, and it was a damned important first step they were taking. He needed to back his boat up and let out some line.

"I love you, Cassidy. It's difficult to wait, but I will. For you, I'll do anything."

She didn't respond in kind, just nestled under his chin, and that was okay. She'd just lost an important man in her life. She needed to want to take this next step as much as Jude did.

He took a deep breath. Cassidy was worth waiting for.

Cassidy couldn't sleep. Not now. Not with Jude under the sheets with her, his leg alongside hers. He'd taken his pants off and come back to bed in his jockey shorts, but his skin wasn't like hers. Firm, yes. Muscled, yes. But different.

She couldn't keep her fingers to herself. Didn't want to. They kept touching him. Feeling. Gathering information she very much wanted to know.

Jude should've gone into high fashion instead of high finance. He was heart-stoppingly beautiful. Damned near glorious. All the manual labor he'd done while searching for Judith in the cult had created one ripped masterpiece. His belly lay relaxed, yet solid. Soft but firm. A smatter of chest hairs dusted his pecs, but *those pecs*. Well-toned and nicely defined. Irresistibly touchable. She let her fingertips do the walking along the sharp valley cut between them. Damned nice.

She wished she'd taken her clothes off, too. He lay still, his chin tilted upward, his neck exposed and one arm thrown over his eyes. Her fingers thrilled at the well-manicured beard he maintained instead of simply scruff. She indulged, her fingertips strolling over his private property, and she a welcomed trespasser.

A gentle hint of a smile tweaked Jude's lips. And that was another thing. The man had lips she couldn't get enough of. How could two moist pieces of human flesh taste so, so good? The crazy guy had her sounding like Judith.

And his eyelashes. Every time those amazingly deep grays scanned over her, she felt like a piece of dragon fruit on the vine, ready for picking, peeling, and tasting. The idea of being a piece of fruit with Jude doing the peeling and tasting made her wiggle.

Blinking only made him a hundred times sexier. Somehow, those dark lashes turned into the paddles safety officers used to guide Navy Hornet and Super Hornet fighter jets onto aircraft carriers. Each blink seemed to whisper, *Come closer. Closer. You're doing fine. You're right on target. Al... most... there...*

All Cassidy knew was that she was coming in for a landing, and she was coming in hard. She had another challenge to conquer. Him. And she couldn't resist. Not anymore. Not as willing as Jude had become. He wasn't kidding anyone. A man couldn't feign sexual disinterest beneath a single white sheet. She had his complete attention.

She dropped out of altitude. Jumped out of bed. Stripped out of her clothes and touched down. On Jude.

He turned his body into hers, his eyes bright with lust and his hand extended. "Come to me, Cassidy."

"I love you, Jude Cannon," she whispered on her way to his lips. *I am so coming to you.* She took him hard, her fingers in his hair and her tongue in his mouth.

A groan lifted up from his chest as his hands smoothed down her biceps to her ribs to her bare ass. "My God, you're beautiful. Let me see. Let me touch."

There wasn't time to show him, not with the fire he'd ignited. She wanted him deep inside of her body before she exploded. The hunger that began with a wiggle turned into a voracious appetite that Cassidy honestly didn't know how to control. She lifted, needing to impale herself on Jude, arching her back to settle onto him.

"Oh, no," he muttered, clutching the cheeks of her ass before she could sink farther down. "Not for your first time. I won't hurt you. Not like this." He rolled her off his thighs and onto her back. "Let's play with that fire a little first, shall we?"

She nodded. Yes to play. Yes to fire. "But I thought—"

"You thought right, but you're not ready for rough sex, and this first time is all about you." Dark gray eyes scrolled over her naked body. "It may hurt. Let's take it slow. Let's make love, not just have sex. When you're ready, we'll play as rough as you want, but for now..."

She trembled, her knees knocking with excitement and maybe a little fear.

He knelt between her legs, his palms on her quaking knees, holding her still. Warm gray eyes melted over her bare body. He licked his lips, and she wanted those lips on her. All of her.

"Jude?" she asked, her voice all breathy and girly-sounding, damn it. "Is this always about play for you?"

He kissed her kneecap—or rather, he lit another fire, one that travelled at lightning speed to her core, unleashing a wellspring of moisture. And heat. He blessed the other kneecap with more soft, moist nibbling kisses. She groaned as the same jolt of lust ripped through her, straight up the middle of her tightly strung body. If he kept playing, it wouldn't take long. She'd detonate in his hands.

"Play is how I want to make love with you, Cassidy. Like we have all the time in the world to get to know each other."

She reached for his neck, needing more than the sheet to hold onto. "But I'm not a piece of china. I won't break."

He took his time, kissing a trail down her thigh to her belly. He lingered at her navel, licking a pool of thrilling sensation, filling her flesh with a ferocious need. "You're right, but you are the heart and soul of my world. You are my reason for living. I intend to worship you every day for the rest of my life. This is no one-night stand, Cassidy. This is forever. Are you in it with me?"

"Yes," she whispered, in awe of this man's concept of love.

Bowing his head, he cupped her breast and scraped a thumbnail over its tender peak. Another spark lit. His lips closed over the hardened nipple, a bundle of nerves alive with anticipation. He sucked it into his mouth, and another quivering bolt of lust shot straight to her core. She bucked against him, so damned needy.

Dipping low, he bumped his nose to hers, his palms at each side of her head. He closed the distance and took her slowly, slipping the steel of his love into her heart as he slipped the steel of his loins into her core. Gently. Coaxing her clenched muscles to accept him.

It hurt. It pinched. But Cassidy was no stranger to the pain in contact sports, and now she was no stranger to the melding pain of making love. With her body alight with the sweet agony of his gentle lovemaking, she pushed into him and gave him everything. Every. Last. Inch.

The climax struck like the thrill of a zip-line to the stars. She soared, detonating into a brilliant white light at Jude's skilled fingers. He swallowed her cry while he held her shuddering body, and holy hell. She'd never known so many intense sensations at the same time. This was no game. No contest. She, Cassidy Dancer, was—truly, purely loved.

Jude sunk his face into the crook of her neck, a rumbling growl caressing her ear while she fell apart. "You're my warrior princess. Only mine."

Too emotional to speak, her tears spilled over. She'd found where she belonged. Right there. Tucked safe and sound—in his heart.

Chapter Thirty-Four

"Are you okay?"

"I'm good," he said quickly, but Cassidy knew better. Something was wrong. The closer they got to SEA-TAC, the less talkative Jude became. He'd driven her to her apartment so she could pack and make boarding accommodations for Magic. But now that her cat had been dropped off at Jungle Play for kittens, and they were at the airport, he seemed reluctant to leave. Nervous. Or something.

It was late evening. They'd checked in at the airline ticket kiosk, dropped their bags, and made it through security without any problems. Still, he fidgeted. He'd excused himself twice to use the restroom. The poor guy's forehead shone softly with a thin layer of sweat. He paced.

The flight assistant at the check-in desk called their flight. He raked his fingers through his hair, then fumbled and fidgeted when he couldn't locate his boarding pass. First class boarded before he dug it out of his back pocket. It didn't dawn on her until their carry-ons were stowed and he kept double-checking his seatbelt. Jude was afraid to fly.

She really looked at this guy sitting next to her on the aisle seat. Everything he'd done during the past month had been out of his comfort zone. He'd endured torture at the hands of the cult, gone undercover for the FBI, and successfully ended a damned tough mission with his daughter safe and Cain six-feet under. Then, he'd flown across the country to rescue her from herself, not to mention all the flights he'd taken with the Brothers Grimm. But through it all, he'd been scared to fly?

That explained Judith, too. She was her father in miniature—frightened maybe, but courageous in the face of all sorts of bullies.

Cassidy placed her palm on Jude's warm wrist. "I'd like a Bloody Mary. How about you?"

He grunted, anxiety bright in his dark eyes. "I was thinking more like a keg, but no. It's too early."

She shrugged, willing to let him lead but needing to ease his discomfort. "It's a long flight with no layovers. A drink relaxes me. Besides, it's five o'clock somewhere."

"It's way past five in Florida." Again with the quick rake through his hair.

"Long flights like this are boring."

He rolled his eyes. "Boring, huh? Guess I haven't flown as much as you then."

"So tell me about working with the FBI. What was it like?"

He rolled his eyes again, and that was all it took. He had a lot to tell between the Brothers Grimm, his FBI guardian angel who'd ended up being one-of-one instead of one-of-many, and, of course, the Cain brothers and their devious plan for the ricin.

"Aloysius really looks like Lucien?" she asked. By then they were over Kansas, and Jude's anxiety had diminished without the Bloody Mary's. His fingers rested comfortably around hers, and she couldn't remember a more delightful flight. He hadn't gotten out of his aisle seat once.

"Lucien was a little taller, but Aloysius seemed to be the smarter of the two." He corrected himself. "Maybe smarter isn't the best word. Mr. A seemed darker. Kind of like the Emperor in *Star Wars* compared to Darth Vader. They were both evil, just different."

"It's hard to imagine anyone more evil than Lucien Cain."

"Trust me. His brother's worse."

"Did the FBI ever find him?"

Jude shook his head. "Not yet. They've got the ricin, though. He kept a supply in two separate locations, one on the East Coast, one on the West. That was how he delivered it as quickly as he did."

"No doubt Alex is still looking for him." She changed the subject. "Will Judith be angry with me for leaving the way I did?"

"Only if I don't bring you back home with me." His spiked brow set her at ease. "It's too late, Agent Dancer. Don't even think about leaving me now. You're in over your head, woman."

She couldn't suppress a smile. "I wouldn't dare."

A smart woman didn't leave a guy like Jude. They'd spent most of their first day together in bed, the hotel shower, or out on Jude's semi-private balcony, wrapped up in each other's arms and falling more in love. Who knew a tough gal could only be loved by a tougher guy? A man who saw through her bravado and wasn't afraid to call her on it? Someone who conquered his fears just to be with her?

Like he was doing now. The jet touched down at Jacksonville airport, as smooth as glass. Jude didn't seem to notice. They were still talking when the Jetway bumped into the side hatch.

"You think you're pretty clever, don't you?" he asked, while he unfastened his seatbelt. "Was that the plan? Keep me talking all the way home?"

"It worked, didn't it? We're here, and I think you might have enjoyed the flight, too."

He shrugged. "Actually, I did."

Before she knew it, they were rolling their suitcases into Jude's front entry where Judith barreled into Cassidy's arms. "I'm so, so glad to see you!"

Miss Fluffy wound herself around Cassidy's legs. Two dragon fruits were peeled and waiting on the kitchen counter for her. This place felt a lot like home.

"Guess what?" Judith stepped back from Cassidy's embrace, jumping up and down like a little girl. The dark circles under Judith's eyes were gone, and she looked genuinely happy. "I have a surprise for you. Come see."

Cassidy ended up not having to go very far.

Oh, damn. Alex stepped around the corner of the living room. "It's about time."

Cassidy cringed, not quite as excited as Judith might have expected her to be. If that wasn't bad enough, Kelsey peeked around the corner, too. "Hi, Cassidy. Hi, Jude. Bet you didn't expect to see us, huh?"

What an understatement. No, Cassidy absolutely hadn't expected to find her boss and his wife waiting for her in Florida. That put a crimp in her homecoming. "What's up?" she asked suspiciously.

"Just taking a small vacation." Alex rolled his shoulders like he was actually relaxed, rare for a man with mega OCD. "I see you two made up. About damned time."

Judith giggled. "Dad says you left because you had a real important mission to finish."

"She was on a mission, all right," Alex quipped.

Cassidy caught the sarcastic barb. Leave it to Alex to poke at her. She blew out a big breath and prepared to face the music. "Actually..." she paused, not sure how much she wanted to say.

"She's the hardest headed of all my agents," Alex interrupted. "I don't know what I'd do without her. How was the flight?"

Wow. She looked twice, not sure she'd heard right. Alex shot her a real, no-kidding smile.

"Real good," Jude answered, his hand on Cassidy's waist. "Best I've ever been on, and I've been on a few lately."

She leaned into him. "I can't believe you're here, Boss." *So why are you? What's wrong? Is it Cain's brother?*

Alex looked away, but Kelsey spoke up. "We needed a break. When Alex suggested here, I thought, why not? I've always wanted to see Florida. Besides, Jude needed someone to stay with Judith. It's a win-win."

Judith sidled up to Kelsey and linked arms, as if they were old friends. That was the thing about Kelsey. She never intended to make an entrance, but she always did. Dainty, with long brown hair tied back in an easy style, the woman was gracious and sweetly feminine. She had an almost motherly way about her that put people at ease.

"I've heard a lot about you while you've been gone, Jude." Kelsey beamed. "Your daughter is such a clever girl."

Judith grinned mischievously.

"And what story has my clever child regaled you with in my absence?"

"Well, now we know how she came to like sushi."

"Yes. That was one dare that backfired."

"But I also know how to make *maki zushi*. So do you, Dad."

"I do." He murmured to Cassidy, still in his arms. "Judith dared me to stop at Benny Kim's one afternoon. It's a sushi hut in town. By the time we left, we were both hooked. We're certifiable sushi addicts."

"Not me. Fish should be fried or grilled." Cassidy figured he might as well know that about her right now.

"Is that a challenge I hear? Did that sound like a challenge to you, Judith?"

"Or a dare," she giggled.

"No," Cassidy said firmly. "I don't eat raw fish and I'm not going to start now."

Jude kissed the side of her head. "Oh, oh. It sounds like we'll be visiting Benny Kim's real soon, won't we, Judith?"

"Oh, tomorrow? Can we go tomorrow?"

Cassidy had to smile. This father and daughter team was going to be fun. She changed the subject. "So where's Lexie?"

"This week she's playing with Chai Yenn." Kelsey still had her arm around Judith.

David Tao, another agent out of the Alexandria office, had four boys of his own, then adopted a little girl after busting up the notorious Black Dragon child-smuggling ring. That was one really good thing about the men and women on The TEAM—they were all suckers for lost children.

Interestingly, Zack had also been involved in the same sting. He'd adopted one of those lost little girls, sweet Song, the most beautiful baby girl ever.

Cassidy glanced at Judith, wondering how long it would take to adopt her. She wasn't lost, but she was definitely going to get a mother, or at least an older friend.

"It's gotten so Lexie thinks she needs a play date every other day," Kelsey groused. "If not with Mark's girls, then with Zack's or David's. I'm raising a diva."

That made Cassidy smile. She knew better. Lexie was the love child of two of the most romantic people she'd ever known. Just the sight of her handsome boss standing next to his lady warmed Cassidy's heart. Kelsey was so feminine and Alex the ultimate badass. What woman's heart wouldn't flutter at the sight of two such sexy people together.

Cassidy turned to find Jude looking straight at her, a funny smile on his face. The heat of a blush covered her cheeks. *How'd he just do that?*

Jude winked, but pulled Judith away from Kelsey and into a big hug. The happy girl closed her eyes in the comfort of her father's arms. "I'm so, so glad you're here, Dad. What'd you guys do in Seattle?"

That innocent question sent another handsome smile from Jude to Cassidy's direction, which she quickly deflected. "Your dad and I have been talking, Judith. How would you like to come to Washington for a while?"

"Really? Like I could bring Miss Fluffy, too?"

"Of course. You've been to my place. You know I've got room for all of you."

"Oh, can we, Dad?" Judith poured it on. "Cassidy has the coolest cat, and she's got lots of room, and could we? Please? It would be so, so fun."

Jude tipped his head back and laughed. Damn, he became hands-off handsome in that instant. With his broad shoulders shaking and his Adam's apple exposed, the man looked damned masculine and genuinely happy. Cassidy stifled an urge to kiss that neck again. Everything about this guy drew her in, the way he loved his daughter most of all.

"Yes. We can go. I get it. I'm outnumbered." He shot Cassidy a teasing look.

Judith threw her arms around her father. "I love you so, so much, Dad."

Jude gathered his only child up, the tender glow on his handsome face almost reverent. He closed his eyes and kissed her strawberry blonde head. "Now get to bed," he whispered before turning to Alex. "I assume you'll be staying?"

Alex put a quick stop to that. "No, thanks. We've got a room in town. We'll be back first thing in the morning."

"And I'll make breakfast," Kelsey said. "Don't go anywhere."

"Come on. Let's go. I'm tired," Alex grumbled. "See you folks tomorrow."

"Good night," Cassidy called out as he closed the front door behind him.

And good riddance.

Chapter Thirty-Five

Jude had gone down the hall to Judith's room, so Cassidy seized the moment to pull her handgun out of her suitcase. She meant to secure it in the guest bedroom like she had before, but why should she sleep there?

Jude's bedroom lay at the other end of the hall. She hadn't been in there yet, hadn't even peeked inside the last time she stayed in his home. Didn't know what kind of bed he slept on, if it was brass or wood. Didn't know the color of his sheets and comforter. Yet.

A thrill of anticipation skittered up her spine. Soon, she'd know every last thing—and more.

Tingling with expectation, Cassidy stepped out on Jude's back deck to wait for him. It seemed as if she'd never left. Long-legged cranes, tinted silver in starlight, flew in a long line along the bank before she lost sight of them among the shadowy reeds.

She set her pistol on the table between the two chaise lounges, glad to be back. Inhaling deeply of the warm, moist Florida air, she let it out slowly. The sound of Jude padding across the carpet behind her made her smile. In seconds his arms snaked around her ribs, and his heated breath spiked her desires all over again. He growled in the crook of her neck, trailing a moist path of nibbled kisses.

Delightful sensations stirred in her belly. "Someone's watching," she cautioned huskily when she noticed the glint of an aluminum motorboat along the shoreline.

"I doubt that," he muttered, not bothering to look. "Private property. No trespassers."

Cassidy giggled, scrunching her shoulders at the sensual touch of his insistent lips and tongue. Heat coursed up her body. "You're tickling me." *And I like it.*

He sent another wave of shivers over her shoulder before he lifted his mouth to her ear. "You've got goosebumps," he breathed.

"That's not all I've got." She wiggled against him, and gently, he cupped a breast in each of his large warm palms. Cassidy melted. His thumbs seemed to have reached through her shirt to the tender nipples beneath, the ones peaked and hardening at his touch. With her back to his chest, she circled her arms around his neck, willingly exposing herself for the taking.

"You need to know something about my home," he muttered. "I built this place after the divorce and I don't sleep around. You're the only woman I've invited into my bedroom since Rachel."

Cassidy twisted her neck to peer at him. "You're my first man ever."

He gazed down at her, his eyes dark and hooded. "You have no idea what that means to me."

"How did you afford this place?" she asked, lost in the love aglow on his face and thinking more about that bedroom she hadn't seen yet. It had to be as sumptuous as the rest of his home.

He lowered his mouth to her neck, answering against her bare skin with a panty-melting rumble. "I worked for the construction company that built it. I was their CPA. Saved them a ton of money. Invested what I could. The owner was grateful. He made me a deal I couldn't refuse."

"Hmmm." That mouth of his had struck a nerve that ran straight to her gut. And lower. One more nibble and she would never make it to his bedroom.

Suddenly he stilled, the warmth of his hands gone from her breasts to her ribcage. He had her right where he wanted her, and he stopped? She glanced up at his jaw, now tight and hard, his gaze cast somewhere out in the river. Still breathing hard, he growled. "You were right. We're not alone. Get down. Look there."

She crouched with him, following the direction he pointed. The boat she'd seen earlier still bobbed placidly along as waves lapped its hull. Nothing looked out of place. Even the cylindrical diving tank resting in the hull wouldn't have caught her attention if it hadn't been so large. How could a diver possibly handle that thing?

"Cain's brother is here," Jude hissed. "Aloysius. He's got ricin in that boat."

"How do you know?"

"Because I placed six canisters just like it."

Icy fingers of dread crept down her neck, sending a very different kind of shiver to her toes. Automatically, her hand went automatically to her holster, but it wasn't there. "Jude, I need my gun. It's on the tab—"

"You need nothing," a voice snarled from behind them.

Cassidy jumped to her feet and whirled. The man standing in the doorway could've passed for Lucien Cain.

Tall. Angular build. Thinning gray hair. He had to have come through the house. The revolver in his hand, a .38 special, caught Cassidy's eye. That meant he had five rounds. Maybe six. *If* he was any good with that gun. Dead was still dead, but his outstretched hand trembled. He wasn't half the expert she was.

"What do you want, Cain?" Jude asked, shielding Cassidy behind him.

"I want what you took from me. I want my brother," the man hissed, "but because I can't have Lucien back, I'm going to take your whole family, Mr. Cannonball. Or was it Ball-o-Steel?"

Jude growled, backing away from Aloysius, pushing Cassidy along behind him. But this was her game, and she knew precisely how this op had to go down. Draw Cain out of Jude's home. Get the fight away from Judith. Then kill the bastard.

She pinched Jude below his ribcage to signal her intent, then darted down the deck stairs. A man with a pistol had better be a damned good shot to hit a moving target. She was ready to gamble this guy wasn't.

"Stop!" Mr. A bellowed.

No way in hell. Cassidy hit the ground running. Moving targets were hard to hit.

"Keep going," Jude ordered as he veered to the front of his house while she ran away from it. Now Cassidy became the only target, just as she preferred. Jude had Judith to live for. She intended he do just that.

"You want me? Come and get me!" she yelled over her shoulder.

Cain took the steps one at a time. She turned to face him, sucking up enough air to keep going, but making certain she had his full attention. Dancing back and forth like a prizefighter, she looked to see if Jude was out of sight, hopefully inside and calling the police.

Blam! Bark splattered to her left. Just as she thought, Cain couldn't hit shit. A few small splinters ricocheted into her bicep, though. She ignored the pain. She had a predator hunting her, and she meant to lure him to his death.

"Missed," she taunted, sure she could keep this lunatic occupied for however long it took for the police to get there. Ducking through riverside bushes and reeds, she led her adversary to the river's edge.

"Stop right there!" he yelled.

Instead, she ran. A glance over her shoulder caught the glint off barrel of his gun. He fired, but missed again when she ducked, hands to her knees. Two rounds down. Maybe three or four to go. She had him right where she wanted him, out of breath and taking chances he shouldn't. Firing before he'd settled into a proper stance. *Dumbass. This won't take long.*

But he didn't follow. Afraid she'd lost him, she edged back through the shadows, needing him to pursue her, not Jude. And there he stood. His pistol trained on her. Shaking maybe, but damn. He'd gotten closer than she'd thought, less than twenty feet away.

"Put your hands where I can see them," he ordered, still breathing hard.

She lifted her hands but offered insolence. "Happy now?"

He bared his teeth, like she should've been scared of him. Get real.

Cassidy upped the ante. Her heart pounded, but she didn't think twice. Pushing off the balls of her feet, she screamed like the warriors of old and ran straight into the old guy. Sometimes shock and awe worked.

His brows lifted in shock all right, but not enough awe. With a backwards swing, he caught the side of her head with the butt of his gun. It didn't stop her momentum though. She latched onto his bony arms and took him into the slippery mud at the riverbank with her.

"You're going down," she groaned, fighting to get that damned gun away from him.

"Bitch," he hissed as he grabbed a fistful of her hair and wrenched her head back. But Cassidy hadn't trained in covert ops for nothing. Cain meant to unbalance her and shove her face into the mud before he either killed or raped her. Not going to happen. Rourke's continual challenge on the wrestling mat rang out loud and strong. *Make 'em pay for every inch, Butch. Give 'em all you've got, and then give 'em hell, damn it!*

She reached her muddy fingers to Cain's face, tore at his lips, and scratched his nostrils on her way to dig out his eyeballs. Close quarters brawling gave her more personal targets, and all within reach. Yeah, he might have a hold of her hair, but so what? Hair she could live without. How would he feel about losing his balls?

Bringing her knee up fast and sharp, she caught Cain straight in the groin. He rolled to his side, growling in obvious pain, but his gun still in her face. The demented bastard was too close. She didn't dare move.

"Disrespecter of men! Bitch!"

Name calling? Seriously?

Chapter Thirty-Six

"Yeah, yeah, yeah. That all you got? Bitch-slapping a girl and calling names?"

That damned shaky gun in her face stopped further heroics, but Cassidy still meant to make Cain mad enough to take chances. Lifting her butt out of the mud, she assumed her best tackle football stance, one hand to the ground and the balls of both feet poised for launch.

With three, maybe four rounds left in that gun of his, another surprise charge might prevent an accurate shot if she were brave enough to try. Or dumb enough. Cain appeared older than his brother and in some pain, but his chances of hitting her this time were good.

"Back off, you filthy..." He seemed at a loss for nasty words, but spat, "woman!"

"Is that the best you can do?" she taunted. *Disrespecter of men? What was that about?* "You got a mommy complex?"

She and Cain were eye to eye on a slippery playing field, him still on his back, and she on her cocky three-point take-off position. Her confidence never wavered. She summoned her inner Ranger, and her personal mantra: '*...move faster and fight harder, though I be the lone survivor...*'

Without taking his eyes off her, he rolled to his knees, then to his feet. He staggered, but kept that weapon trained on her.

Cassidy spat the mud out of her mouth, tasting blood along with grit, watching for an opening to knock this sucker back to hell where he belonged. She glanced over her shoulder at the ricin tank in the bobbing boat, wondering how long before Jude and help showed up. Her time was drawing short. If this conversation didn't pan out, her last move might just be—her last move.

"That your idea of world domination? Ricin?"

"It'll serve its purpose, bitch. Where is he?" Cain stood erect and still aiming.

"Who?"

"Your man whore."

"Don't matter. You won't like it when he gets here."

Cain snorted. "Then hurry. You're the one I wanted anyway. Now strip."

"Excuse me?" This old guy thought she'd drop her clothes just because he'd said to? "I'm not one of your stupid followers, Mr. A. Drop dead."

He took a step toward her, his eyes narrowed with rage. "But you will obey. Take your clothes off and throw them in the river. You get to be the final sacrifice, and I need you naked when I open that can."

The business end of his gun bore down on her. Less than six feet lay between them. Not enough for a good, hard tackle. He *could* kill her. She had to accept that very real truth. With deliberate slowness, she walked to the edge of the river and crouched, swishing her hands in the water and stalling. Soulless eyes followed her every move.

Slowly, Cassidy unbuttoned her shirt. She wasn't getting into any damned boat, and she sure as hell wasn't going to be this guy's naked sacrifice. "Ricin," she scoffed. "So you're just going to kill me then, huh? You're not much for mass destruction, are you?"

"Shut up. There's still a chance—"

"Not from what I hear, dumbass." She shrugged one arm out of its sleeve. "The Department of Defense quit playing with ricin a long time ago. Trust me. I checked. It wasn't worth the bother. Everyone must know that but you."

"It would've worked," he roared. "It still might. Armageddon always brings repentance."

She blinked at his vehemence. Was this guy for real? Armageddon? Repentance? What did they have to do with a ricin attack and her naked in a boat? This conversation was just too bizarre to be real. Intent on keeping Cain's attention, she let the other sleeve slide down her arm. "What the shit are you talking about?"

His entire forehead furrowed. "This—THIS!—is why men must dominate women. Your gender is too weak and too stupid to understand. Only with true repentance do all the conniving, guilty people turn to the Lord and think they can buy their way into heaven."

She cocked her head. "Excuse me? Is that what this is all about? Money?"

"No," he hissed, his teeth bared and clenched tight. "It's about you dying. I mean for everyone to believe they can save the poor, naked woman floating down the river. The Coast Guard. The police. I want every lying reporter within distance to capture your story before they die, too."

Cassidy glimpsed Jude creeping through the brush, her pistol in his hand. She ran her index finger under her left bra strap to hold Cain's attention. It worked. Mr. A's tongue flicked over his bottom lip, the slimy snake.

Jude gave her a quick nod, his lips pressed tight, his jaw set at a hard angle.

She raised her shoulder just enough that her strap slid to the crook of her arm, baring the top of one breast.

Cain jerked his gun at her. "Drop 'em both. Let's see what you got, whore."

She feigned compliance, both hands behind her back, as if undoing the eyelets and hooks. If he was expecting big boobs to flop out of these tiny B cups, he was in for some serious disappointment. But if the sight of a naked, albeit *inferior* female body got Cain off and gave Jude time to move in, she was all for it. She lowered her bra and exposed herself.

He sneered, not taking his eyes off her chest. "You women think you're so much better than men. You steal our jobs. You sleep your way into promotions you don't deserve. You lord your sex over us, and you lie. You bitches always lie. The only place you belonged was under the yoke of the prophet or beneath him in his bed, but you killed him!"

"I did not. Not technically. I mean, I wanted to, but my boss beat me to it." She jiggled her firm but itty-bitty boobs. Cain had to be out of his mind to be distracted by what little she had to offer. Still, if it worked...

He cocked his head. She changed tactics, thinking he might have heard Jude in the bushes behind him. With one quick move, she unsnapped her bra and let it drop. His eyes lit with the glittering black light of a truly twisted mind. "That's what I wanted. Now for everything—"

"Don't touch her!" Jude stepped out of the shadows, his weapon trained on Cain's back. "On your knees. Now!"

Cassidy took a deep breath. Jude was there. She was safe. But Cain whirled on Jude and—

BLAM!

Oh, my hell. Jude shot him. He really shot him. "I said don't touch her!"

Cain tilted to his left before one knee buckled, and down he went, stone, cold dead.

The love of her life stood there with his glasses askew on his nose, looking as crazy-shocked as she was. *Who is this guy?* Cassidy couldn't believe what she'd seen. Her timid accountant had changed into a man the likes of Alex. Fierce. Unforgiving. And a damned good shot.

Genuine pride tugged at the corners of his mouth. "Where's your shirt?"

She didn't get the chance to answer. Her world dropped out from beneath her when he fell to his knees, his hand to his chest. Only then did she see the crimson blossoming through his shirt. She ran to him, cradled him in her arms.

The son-of-a-bitch shot Jude!

She'd no more than lifted him against her bare breasts when Tucker Chase ran out of the bushes, his pistol lifted to the sky. "Goddamn you, Cannon, I was going to do that. Do you always have to get in my way?" He holstered his weapon and slouched out of his long-sleeved shirt. Tossing it at Cassidy, he growled, "Cover those tits, Dancer. He didn't hurt you, too, did he?"

"Help Jude!" she ordered while she angled into the proffered shirt, her heart in her throat. "Don't you have a cell phone on you? Use it. Call for help."

"Keep your panties on. Police and ambulance are on their way." Tucker dropped bare-chested beside her. He'd already stripped his T-shirt off and torn a piece of it for Cassidy.

"Take the arm wound, Dancer. Press as hard as you can. Slow the damned bleeding."

Arm wound? She hadn't detected another wound. But Tucker was right. Frantically, she ripped Jude's sleeve up from the cuff for better access to the wound on his forearm. Not a bullet hole, though. More of a slice on his forearm. A two-inch slice pouring Jude's life force into the muddy Saint John's riverbank. She folded that scrap of shirt into a tight wad, intending to stick it inside the slice to stop the bleeding if she had to.

"Where's your blow-out kit?" she snapped. Rourke always carried one. She did, too. Usually. Not tonight though. Damn it.

"Believe it or not, I don't keep it on me twenty-four-seven," Tucker muttered sarcastically. He leaned over Jude and applied his portion of the shirt to the bloody hole in Jude's Chest. "This is gonna hurt, buddy."

Jude arched off the ground despite Tucker's attempt to hold him down. "You're killing me, Chase. Damn you. I'm not your buddy. Get off me."

"Stop whining. You're not dying on my watch, so man up. Grit your teeth, asshole, and bear it." He muttered at Cassidy. "Stewart said you were a spitfire, Dancer. That was a damned dangerous stunt you just pulled, leading Cain on."

"I thought I could take him," she grunted, pressing as hard as Tucker. Maybe harder. "You've been waiting for Mr. A, haven't you? That's why you showed up. You've been here all along."

"Stewart and me been taking turns, yeah. Twelve on. Twelve off. Cain must've thought he had a green light when your boss left for the night. Guess you showed him."

"God, I never should've left."

"Shut up, Dancer. Me and Stewart had your back. You made a dumb decision. You were hurting too, now move on. Stop whining." *That's what Rourke would have said. Exactly what...*

Cassidy nodded even as the terrible scene shimmered and turned surreal. She wasn't cradling Jude. It was Rourke in her arms. On the ground. In the stars. She couldn't catch a breath. The metallic smell of fresh blood sent her reeling back into a warp. She was that kite in the sky again, torn loose and lost. The helicopter would come soon and—

"No! Not again. No!"

"Settle down," Tucker growled, annoyed. "What the hell's the matter with you?"

"I can't lose him," she cried. "God, I can't—"

"You're not going to lose him. I promise, baby. I promise."

She had to look twice at that unexpected endearment from a crass man, but had no time to care when Jude groaned. She forgot about Tucker and Cain and—and Rourke. "Stay with me," she ordered. "Don't you dare die."

A quiet moan lifted up from his throat. He closed his eyes. Cassidy glanced toward the house, afraid Judith might come running to her father. Afraid this was her last few seconds with the man she loved. The despair she thought she'd conquered through his gentle love returned with a roar. She had to infuse him with the will to live. To fight!

"You can't leave. Judith loves you," she cried, her tears dripping into his face. "And I love you. I can't go on without you."

But nothing she said seemed to matter. Jude went limp, and it was happening all over again. Rourke, one of the toughest men she'd known, had died. Now Jude lay dying. Lightning did strike twice.

But if this was it, if this truly was his last breath, Cassidy wanted it to be hers. Trembling, she covered his mouth with hers. Breathing all her heart and soul into that last kiss, she gave everything.

"Cass—"

"No," she sobbed, elbowing Tucker away. "Let me be. I won't leave him."

"Cass—"

What? Who? It wasn't Tucker calling her name. It was— *Jude?*

His hand snaked around her wrist. One moment he was dying, the next he had a firm grip on her. "Need to tell you..."

She tipped her head to his lips. "What?" she asked fearfully. *Anything, but goodbye.*

"I'm not Rourke, damn it. My name's Jude Cannon, you feel me, Dancer? I'm not leaving. Not now. Not ever. Now button your damned shirt before I bend you over and take you right here and now." He tugged her into his face, and Cassidy got lost in the lips of the bravest man she'd ever known.

At last, the medics took over and she saw with better eyes. The gunshot was high in his chest. Still frightening, but not fatal. Alex winked at her from where he stood talking with Tucker. No wonder Tucker didn't have his blowout kit on him. He was wearing shorts. The big dummy. Kelsey was there with Judith. Best of all, the EMTs weren't afraid to look her in the eye.

"Is he going to be okay?" she asked.

The EMT working on Jude's shoulder muttered, "I'm not supposed to say, but, yeah. This guy'll be up and dancing before long."

She exhaled a no-kidding sigh of relief, striving for calm. "I didn't know you danced."

He winked. "Doesn't everyone?"

"Not me." He'd better get that idea out of his head.

"You'll learn," he teased.

She would have argued, but her heart wasn't in it.

Jude wasn't done with her. "You really love me, huh?" he asked, a salacious glint in his weary eyes. "It's not just the extreme circumstance or the—"

He never got another word out.

She dove past the medics and kissed the ever-loving hell out of her man.

Epilogue

Life was full of paradoxes. Choices you should've made. Chances you should've taken. Some you shouldn't have.

Sometimes, it was hard to admit you'd made mistakes, that your innate way of handling life's challenges might not have been the best. That someone else *might* have been right. Maybe smarter. That you *might* have caused more trouble than it was worth at the end of a long, hard operation. That you could have obeyed your superiors *if* you'd wanted to. That they actually might know more than you. It could happen.

Back that boat up.

Cassidy Dancer wasn't ready to admit anything. Ahem. Make that Cassidy Cannon, as in Mrs. Jude Cannon, the new wife of the up-and-coming and very handsome manager at the Seattle/Tacoma accounting branch of the best construction company in the Pacific Northwest. The stepmother of one darling daughter, Judith, who would *so, so* live at the Seattle Opera if she thought she could get away with it.

Yeah. That wasn't going to happen, either.

That girl had a definite athletic deficiency Cassidy intended to remedy. As soon as Judith got home from the latest showing of something called *The Marriage of Figaro*, whatever that was. Who was that guy Mozart anyway? Sheesh.

Judith needed to join the local soccer club or learn to mountain climb. Baseball. Football. Something.

Standing on her deck overlooking the lazy Puyallup River, Cassidy had a few minutes to herself. Who would have thought that rascal Tucker Chase had an inside track with a classy lady like Melissa McCormack? But he did.

It was harder yet to believe that Alex and Tucker had worked together that last hectic night in Florida, but they had. That was the real reason Tucker had come to Florida. Despite his own wounds, he'd taken it upon himself to look out for Cassidy and Judith. He'd been there in the shadows the whole time, the sneaky—friend.

And that tender light in Mark Houston's eyes when he'd shown up at the Seattle office? Another surprise. He'd known precisely what Cassidy was going through, because he'd been there in the shadows with Tucker from the day Cassidy left for Florida to the morning she'd turned tail and ran out on Jude.

It seemed Mark couldn't hang around after that. Guess he had an important survival test to conduct somewhere in the mighty Hoh Rainforest of the Olympic Peninsula. He couldn't miss it, so guess what? The man himself stepped in to babysit. Yes, Alex. Along with Kelsey, he watched over Judith while her frantic father went after the foolish, hardheaded woman of his dreams.

The screwed up Church of the Palma Christi cult was no more. The FBI had dismantled the nefarious charitable corporation, returned what funds they could to its *investors*, a kinder description than most of them deserved. The rest was history.

It seemed Aloysius, Lucien's older brother, was the real mastermind behind the cult. He supplied the illegal weapons cache. The C4 came form a notorious local source, but the guns and ammo came from a certain South American cartel, which cannot be named. Classified intel, you understand.

Aloysius employed more of those teenage thugs for other things than brutally murdering his opponents. While he wheeled and dealed with gun runners, a couple of his smarter punks trolled online social networks, obituaries, and social pages for vulnerable targets to *convert*. Once they zeroed in on a wealthy prospect, Aloysius sent Greg and Hank to wrap it up.

Odd though. Aloysius might have set up his baby brother to be lord and master inside the walls of the cult, yet he never allowed Lucien access to the real world. Alex took that puzzle on as a personal challenge. Come to find out, Lucien Cain had been convicted of murdering a nine-year-old girl when he was sixteen. The prosecutor claimed depraved indifference, but the juvenile system sheltered Lucien until his big brother took over. We all know how *that* turned out…

There was no second coming, not in the subways, the, metro, or the BART. That future event was still undetermined. One of those divine mysteries. Like a second coming should be.

Cassidy had stopped being so damned willful. Most of the time. She took more time off to spend with her family and resisted volunteering for out-of-the-country ops. She didn't feel like she had to prove something to her fellow guy agents, either. She actually let the guys win once in a while. She also learned to bake peanut butter cookies with chocolate kisses melted on top. Jude's favorite. Why not? It wasn't like it was hard or anything.

She'd let her feelings for Rourke go, but retained his excellent mentoring. He'd come into her life at the right time, and for that, she was grateful. He'd honed her natural talents the same way he'd tempered her rowdy side. He was responsible for the savvy TEAM agent she became.

It was a good thing she and he had never hooked up. He wasn't *the one*. Wasn't even close to being *the right one*. How did she know? Because he was born tough. He knew it all along. He ate tough for breakfast, lived it, breathed it, and expected nothing less from others.

But tougher than any black operator was the simple, ordinary man defending his family. The accountant who'd taken on the scariest mission of a lifetime without a minute of black-ops training. The man who had nothing more than heart to go on when he'd entered the cult's walls. The guy who did what he had to do simply because it was his job. Jude hadn't even owned a gun when he'd first sought out Lucien Cain. Just a hell-bent determination to rescue what mattered most to him. His child.

Just thinking about her man sent a tropical heat wave straight to her core. He was definitely *the one*. The man who still didn't see himself as a hero. The guy who preferred snuggling with his new wife and delightful daughter at the end of a long, hard day instead of upping his weapons proficiency at Nathan Dunn's gun range. The guy who didn't mind a strand or two of Miss Fluffy's long, gray hair on his lapel when he left for work in the morning.

Yeah. Him.

Cassidy took in a deep breath of the amazing Pacific Northwest. Autumn rains were in the forecast. Nine months of mostly drizzle, low laying blankets of bone-chilling fog, and more drizzle were sure to follow. Why *do* you think the trees grow so tall there? It truly is the water and… All. That. Rain.

Tonight Jude wanted to explore the available real estate on Gig Harbor when he got home from work, but for a moment, it was just Cassidy and her thoughts. The mistakes she'd thought she'd made no longer haunted her. She wasn't that kite lost in the wind anymore, caught between decisions—one lost to her, one she'd been afraid to face.

She didn't have to take on the world alone, either. Jude had her six. Every day. Every night. Every second in between.

Cassidy glanced at the sound of the front door opening behind her, and there he was, the doorknob in his hand, a crooked smile on his ruggedly handsome face. The guy with his sunglasses low on his nose, and the best words in the world on his lips.

"Hi, beautiful. I'm home."

THE END

Sneak Preview of ADAM

Book 11
In the Company of Snipers

There comes a time when a man has to do what a man has to do.

Now was that moment.

"Sir, we are currently at thirty-five thousand feet and holding."

Junior Agent Adam Torrey nodded one curt acknowledgment, stepped to the loading ramp of the lumbering C-130, and with a backward step and a cocky wave, he pitched his body into the midnight sky. The flight chief's admonition, "Jumper away," faded in his earpiece.

Frigid air whipped around him, making him instantly thankful for the polypropylene thermal undergarments beneath his flight suit. He leveled his six-foot, three-inch frame into a belly dive, his arms and legs extended like a giant bug descending to the planet below.

Man, I love my job.

High altitude low openings were common in his line of work, at least for him. Nicknamed *the flying squirrel* by his fellow agents on The TEAM, the ex-Navy SEAL thrived between earth and sky. All agents working had to be capable, physically fit, and qualified to HALO jump. The day a man could not perform was the day he was put to pasture, or worse, turned into something dead called a senior agent. Adam never intended to graze clover. He loved the sensation of flight too much, the freedom of falling, the heady rush of air over, around, and seemingly through his entire body.

Only specialized equipment allowed this miracle, from the Special Forces HALO helmet with its oxygen mask strapped snuggly to his face, the goggles that allowed peripheral vision and much needed facial protection, to the backlit altimeter on his wrist that registered nothing at the moment, its altitude range less than his current position at the edge of the earth's atmosphere.

The experimental GPS wrapped around his wrist matched its digital partner's lack of information. No matter. They would both flash to life soon enough, within seconds if the new technology behind them was accurate. The GPS was part of the reason for this HALO. This was its maiden flight. Its beta-test, and he was just the man for the job.

Until it kicked in, supposedly at a higher altitude than all others, he gloried in the few seconds of an adrenaline rush, free-falling to what very well could be his death if things went wrong. Therein lay the magic of skydiving, all the risk of dying only to cheat the Grim Reaper at the last possible second, to pull up and spit in the stone cold eye of Death.

Yeah. Nothing like it in the world.

The fact that another brave soul had recently made a twenty-four miles jump from the stratosphere only proved Adam's point. Some men were made to fly, and he was one of them. This ordinary jump of nearly seven miles straight down was adrenaline enough. For now. Maybe someday he'd match that other man's record. Maybe not. He truly didn't care about setting records. Just the fall. Just the flight.

He liked that initial *'what the hell have I done?'* sensation moreso because he understood the physics, the very real concept of terminal velocity when the downward force of gravity equaled the restraining force of drag. Yep. Science. Laws of gravity. Risk of splat. Gotta love it.

Every HALO jump involved unique dangers—the frigid cold, decompression sickness, or hypoxia. Death was never more than a heartbeat away. But the thrill. The view. Nothing like it.

He could've gone faster, could've pulled his body into a compact, cylindrical projectile, secured his arms to his side and his legs together instead of splayed like they were. Skydivers called it free flying, when a man's body became more bullet than human. But as much as Adam loved the speed, he loved the journey more. Only HALO jumps brought him out of the world and this close to heaven.

In the sky he was free, not so much bird as shooting star. Plummeting.

On land he became a bulky beast of burden bound to earth's core. A turtle.

Why hurry a three-minute ride?

He glanced up. No moon tonight, just the constellations and Ursa Major glittering in the sub-polar altitude, crisp and clear. Adam's favorite star, Polaris, shone exactly where the pointer stars in the bowl of the Big Dipper indicated. The North Star beckoned like the true friend it was, as constant and a thousand times squared more reliable than any woman Adam had ever known. Always beckoning him home. Always faithful. The ultimate *'semper fi.'*

His last and final relationship encounter flashed through his mind. Like it or not, in a nanosecond he relived Shirley. His ex-girlfriend. Ex-lover. Ex-nightmare.

He forced his very disciplined mind to shove the biggest mistake of his life out of his head. Shirley was old news, the poison of her manipulative grasp at last diluted with enough good times mingled with plenty of scotch.

The digital readouts strapped to his wrist and arm flashed to life right on schedule, reminding him that he had better things to think about. Like living.

Impact in less than two.

South Dakota lay below, now the site of a lost proto-type, the multi-million dollar HH UAV, the Hummingbird Hawk Unmanned Aerial Vehicle. Named for its compact but predatory stealth design, it went down during its initial test flight out of Ellsworth Air Force Base, just miles away. Its advanced technology and extremely small size made it immeasurably valuable in the world of covert ops. All DoD held its breath when they'd heard it went missing. The CIA too. This was their baby. Their future. And now their worst nightmare. Too many others wanted it. Russia. China. Terrorists. Allies.

Checking altimeter and GPS coordinates, he allowed a small smile of success. No meteorological events interfered with his flight tonight. Smooth descent. Right on target.

Earth approached fast.

Fifteen thousand.

His latest favorite song popped into his head, its heavy bass a heartbeat that matched his philosophy. Yeah, he agreed with country singer. What was the use of life? And man, this was living at its most extreme. Adam's hint of a smile easily slid into a grin as he belted out a few more lines at his buddy, Polaris. Live damn it. That's why we're here, to live.

Eight thousand.

His GPS flashed once. Then twice. His target might as well be already acquired and the mission over as far as he was concerned. Smoothest drop ever.

Six thousand.

Thicker atmosphere at the earth's surface brought warmer temperatures. Almost time to deploy.

Four thousand.

Two.

Adam tugged the handle that triggered his chute. *Whoosh.* Instantly, the flat-black, eight-celled nylon fabric of his ram-air canopy released, stopping death in its tracks, and giving Adam a few seconds to view the LZ before his boots hit the dirt. Drifting toward touchdown, the sight below was all he expected. Grasslands. Prairie. Flat. Dark.

He activated another specialized tracking device set to pick up the HH locator signal only. Just in time. The earth rushed up to meet him. To be safe, he removed the night vision goggles from the rucksack and strapped them around his neck. No matter the ease of the landing, it never hurt to be prepared. Freedom lived in the heavens. Not on the earth.

He braced for impact, his knees bent and his senses sharp, primed for all possibilities.

Oomph. Touchdown.

Adam rolled as he landed, expelling nothing more than a soft grunt that none heard, unless the few curious prairie dogs scampering out of his path mattered. Gathering the black nylon chute into big handfuls, he stuffed it into the empty nylon bag he'd stored in another pocket, using those same few minutes to survey the wide-open space around him. The pure silence of the dark Dakota night met his ears. Soft sounds of nature. Nothing man-made.

Smoothest op ever.

Once the parachute was stowed, he let the rucksack drop from his back. It carried what-if supplies like water, MREs, medical supplies, and his all-important EPIRB, his emergency position-indicating radio beacon. Anything could happen, especially on a peculiar mission like this.

The feeling that this was bizarre game persisted, mostly because a HALO drop into harmless South Dakota made no sense in the wary world of a black operator. Why old man Reagan, the billionaire eccentric behind Reagan Industries, demanded such a high security measure in the middle of grassland seemed irrational and foolish.

Adam fought the sensation that he was not alone. He had yet to glimpse any reason for it. Even if he were being watched, this night was still a lot of fun.

He held the HH tracking device up to his face. The soft green glow from the screen lit its map of his immediate area, a red dot pinging a heartbeat less than three klicks to the northeast and the exact position of the missing drone. Good enough. Setting a steady pace, he jogged toward it, watching where he stepped as much as he could. Landing in a prairie dog hole could snap a man's leg. He had no intention of being airlifted, not after the exhilaration of this perfect drop.

The sweet Dakota air smelled good at 0245 hours. Cool. Pleasant. And a good run relaxed a man. It allowed the adrenaline overload from the jump to burn away. He checked the tracker again. Less than a thousand meters straight ahead. Instantly, his mind provided equivalents. Three thousand, two hundred, and eighty-one feet. One thousand, ninety-four yards.

Man, I love my job.

A prairie dog barked off to his left. Adam grinned. He wasn't even breaking a sweat. What's more, this very expensive, very top-secret UAV would be home before the world knew it had gone missing.

The tracking device alarm that indicated he was nearly on target sounded steady beeps. Slowing his gait, he glanced to his right and then left. Only grass and more grass. All good. How hard could it be to find a two-foot long baby bird, attach it to a miniature aerostat, punch the can of helium to inflate, and let it fly away home? Not hard at all in his book. Once the thing was airborne, a larger UAV would snag the line between baby bird and the aerostat with a specially designed pincer attached to its nose. By the time Adam's boss inhaled his first cup of coffee in far off Virginia, baby bird would be back in its hanger at Reagan Research, and all would be well.

As big a fiasco as this loss might have been were the HH not recovered, the mechanics of baby-bird's rescue would once again prove the undeniable need for drones in defense and industrial missions. Technology upon technology. The world was an amazing place, and Adam reveled in it. It helped him fly. Yeah. Technology was great.

Brushing his palms over the knee-high grass, Adam let it tickle between his splayed fingers. Buffalo used to roam here. The Lakota and Sioux Indian tribes too. The place was just plain magic. Ellsworth Air Force Base had been alerted. They'd known he was dropping in tonight, but were advised not to engage. No one else knew. For now it was just him, a missing baby bird, a few barking rodents, and the romance of days gone by.

The foolishness of his mission still nagged. Nearby Ellsworth Air Force Base would've been happy to retrieve the UAV. They could've, and they should've. The request for a HALO was one hundred percent unnecessary, but the CIA said, *'Hell, no,'* to the offer. Hands off. Like the control freaks they were, they demanded that someone non defense-related do the retrieval.

To make matters worse, the man responsible for developing the HH, Mr. Paul Reagan, had gone straight to Alex Stewart, the owner of best covert surveillance company of the East Coast, The TEAM, and the deal was struck before the Air Force could shoot off their well-prepared rebuttal. One agent and one only would handle retrieval. Adam smiled again. Given his aptitude for HALO drops, it was a no-brainer. He was in transit before his boss's signature was dry on the dotted line.

The GPS pinged louder, leading him straight to his prize. A dark shadow in the grass turned into the smooth body of the tiny predator. He knelt on knee to the ground in awe, pulling the HH gently out of the shallow depression of its crash-landing. The weight of it surprised him. He'd expected more, but this little darling felt less than twenty pounds. Coated in flat black, radar absorbent material, the overall smooth design contributed to its invisibility. Wings swept back and tailless, it was the perfect predator. Small. Invisible. Deadly.

He cradled it tenderly, proud of his skill and his aptitude. *Best day ever.*

"Come on, little guy," he said fondly. "Let's get you home."

He stood, turning back to his initial touchdown, and breathed a sigh of relief. The tiny drone did not appear damaged, other that a few scrapes along its metallic skin, nothing a good buffing couldn't handle.

A soft whirring sound overhead interrupted his self-congratulations; the telltale ruffling of silky nylon ballooned tight with air. Adam jerked his gaze heavenward. Another jumper? Here? Nothing revealed itself, but his ears hadn't lied. He crouched one knee in the tall grass, the infant UAV tucked tightly to his chest, letting nature provided the camouflage. No other sound rent the silence. No boots on the ground. No un-oiled squeak of a control lever to bring a chute to pinpoint landing. Nothing.

He held his breath, trusting his gut more than sight. His sixth sense screamed, "You're not alone."

A rippling breeze parted the way ahead of him for mere seconds. Sliding his night vision goggles up over his face, the world turned lime green. But he'd switched to NV too late. Somebody dropkicked the side of his head, hard, but not disorienting him enough to release the baby in his arms.

Adam hunkered into the natural cover of the land until he could make out the man in black beneath a triangular-shaped paraglide flying low and as silent as the night itself. An engine noise would have confirmed the visual, but there was none. Whoever this guy was, he'd banked and was coming around again, no doubt thinking he'd rendered his target unconscious.

Guess again. Adam growled low in his throat. The predator in him sprang to life. Two can play that game.

Rolling to his back with the baby still in his arms, he waited until his assailant was nearly overhead again. And firing. Automatic rounds strafed the ground alongside Adam. Enough was enough! He rolled to his stomach, set the drone on the ground, and pushed off the prairie, charging the would-be assassin.

Surprised, the man banked sharply. Too sharp. With a running leap, Adam grabbed the guy's ankle and jerked him off his seat. Either the idiot hadn't buckled up or the harness broke. Uumph. Down he came, hitting the dirt hard. Adam followed through with a mean kick to the guy's midsection. His boot connected with body armor. The guy had anticipated trouble.

Good to know. Me too.

Reaching to his ankle holster, Adam pulled his knife up, and...

"Got it!" A woman shrieked behind him. He whirled as another black silhouette materialized against the midnight sky, drifting in a similar paraglide and too high to reach. Whoever she was, she now had the HH.

He cocked his arm back and propelled the knife forward, hurtling it at the thief. Bulls-eye! She grunted, sagged, and collapsed limp in her harness. The paraglide continued overhead and away with the tiny drone tucked into the silvery netting beneath the woman's seat.

No way! Adam ran with long-legged strides, his lungs bursting and every muscle on fire to get that damned HH! Fortunately, the paraglide descended as it slowed.

It's not lost yet!

The nearly silent engine offered the barest hum as he closed the distance, his heart pounding with adrenaline and rage. No one—and I mean NO ONE—messed with Adam Torrey.

Six more yards. Maybe less. His lungs burned with the taste of sulphur and blood. Almost there. Almost got it. Almost.

He forced his last reserves into a final burst of speed, stretching with all he had to secure that baby bird again when—

BLAM!

A burning blast of fire and pain caught his shoulder. The blast spun him around and turned him into a ragdoll tumbling end over end over the grassland. Forward momentum finally ceased when he came to a breathless stop, landing face up, blood streaming in a hot, pain-filled spurt out of the hole in his chest.

Blinking up at the dark sky, Adam gasped. Polaris and Ursa Major swirled overhead. He had no way to reach his gear bag or his locator. Thunder rumbled too close. Not thunder. Maybe boots on the ground. Running fast. Coming straight toward him.

A black shadow descended, cruel and cold.

The butt of a rifle.

The last thing he saw.

Thank you for reading Cassidy!

Be sure to check out the rest of the guys and gals of Irish Winters' series: *In the Company of Snipers*

Other Irish Winters' books:

King of Hearts, Deuces Wild Series, *#1*

Joker Joker, Deuces Wild Series, *#2*

Smoke, Hearts and Ashes Series, *#1*

Ash, Hearts and Ashes Series, *#2*

Coming soon!

Seth, In the Company of Snipers, *#17*

One-Eyed Jack, Deuces Wild Series, *#3*

YOU are the key to this book's success!

Please tell other readers why you liked Cassidy and Jude's story by leaving an honest review at the retail site where you purchased it. Recommend it to your friends. Lend it. Most of all, enjoy it!

The best way to keep up with my new releases, giveaways, and actionable intel is to sign up for my spam-free newsletter at IrishWinters.com.

About the Author

Irish Winters is an award winning, Amazon best-selling author who, when she isn't writing, dabbles in poetry, grandchildren, and rarely (as in extremely rarely) the kitchen. More prone to be outdoors than in, she grew up the quintessential tomboy on a dairy farm in rural Wisconsin, spent her teenage years in the Pacific Northwest, but calls the Wasatch Mountains of Northern Utah home. For now.

She believes in making every day count for something, and follows the wise admonition of her mother to, "Look out the window and see something!"

Connect with Irish!
On Facebook: https://www.facebook.com/author.irishwinters
On Twitter: https://twitter.com/irishwinters1
Or at www. IrishWinters.com